For Jo.

HIT AND DONE

A STELLA COLE THRILLER

ANDY MASLEN

TYTON PRESS

"They are not dead who live in the hearts they leave behind."
Native American proverb

1

DEEP CLEAN

Ealing, London, 20th June 2011

A human head weighed more than Detective Chief Inspector Calpurnia "Callie" McDonald had expected.

Five minutes earlier, she had pulled on a pair of medium rubber gloves in a searingly bright yellow and started lifting body parts out of the dead lawyer's freezer. That they were wrapped in black bin liners in no way diminished the grisliness of the task. They were solid and clacked together as she stacked them. When she had finished, seventeen roughly equal-sized parcels formed an untidy pyramid on the floor of the utility room. She closed the freezer door, shutting off the irritating beeping from the temperature alarm.

The packages of – *What, Callie?* she thought. *Human? Meat?* They were heavy, anyway. Surprisingly so. Hadn't she read that somewhere, in a medical journal outside a pathologist's office? A human head weighed around eleven pounds.

Dreading the next part of the operation, she pulled a box

cutter from her jeans pocket and ran it down the freezing plastic shroud of the topmost package.

She pulled the sliced plastic open and gasped.

"Oh, Jesus!"

Looking out at her from eyes like those of a poached fish was the face of Crown Prosecution Service lawyer, Debra Fieldsend. Above the glassy, white eyes, the forehead was cracked open. The massive wound was crusted with blood, which was frozen into obscene red crystals. She pulled the black plastic together again, hiding a view she knew would come back to haunt her.

Reluctantly, she repeated the process with the other sixteen packages, identifying in their turn, the feet, lower legs, thighs, hands, forearms, upper arms, and four grotesquely butchered sections of the torso, the purplish-grey viscera frozen into immobility. Satisfied that she had accounted for Fieldsend's complete mortal remains, she heaved a sigh and left the room.

In the tiled hallway – oxblood, sky-blue and cream – flat-packed cardboard movers' cartons leant against a wall. Above them, a coat rack groaned under the weight of Burberry, Armani and other expensive brands Callie would never be able to afford. She took a roll of parcel tape from the bag lying beside them and began to assemble the first carton.

In went one of the larger, cylindrical pieces, followed by what she already knew was the head. She taped the carton shut and began putting the next carton together.

It took her half an hour to assemble, pack and seal the cartons. She'd used nine. When she finished, she pulled out her phone and tried to wake it up with her thumb.

"Shit!" she said to the empty hallway.

She removed the rubber glove and tried again.

"I'm ready," she said, when her call was answered.

Thirty seconds later, she heard a loud knock at the door. She opened it to a burly man dressed in faded jeans and a dark-grey sweatshirt, a couple of days' black stubble on his cheeks. He towered above her.

"That her, is it?" he said, jerking his chin in the direction of the cartons, which Callie had lined up in the hallway.

"Yup."

"Anything missing?"

"Nope."

"You OK, boss?"

"Mm-hmm."

"Going to hurl?"

"Nuh-uh."

"OK, good to know."

He bent to the first carton and lifted it as if it contained nothing more sinister than a table lamp. Ten minutes later, he was slamming the rear doors closed on a white Ford Transit van.

Callie opened a packet of cigarettes as they pulled away from the curb.

"Thought you said you'd quit," he said, glancing briefly in her direction.

"So did I."

"Do you mind winding the window down, then?"

Callie put the cigarette between her lips and used her free hand to crank down the window.

"Don't they have electric windows on these, yet?"

He shrugged.

"Manual gearbox, manual windows. You're lucky we don't have to pedal."

His wisecrack broke the tension and Callie laughed.

"I hope we don't get stopped by Traffic. Not sure how we'd explain away a dismembered body in the back."

"Teaching aid?"

More laughter.

With the black humour threatening to engulf them, Callie took another long drag on the cigarette, hoping it would kill off the weird smell of butchers' shops that lingered in her nostrils. As they turned left out of Corfton Road, a second van was pulling in, metallic grey this time. The driver nodded as they passed.

The traffic between Ealing and the crematorium in Kensal

Green was heavy, and it took them just over forty minutes to make the seven-mile journey. The male officer, whose nickname was Titch, passed the front of the building and pulled in at the rear. Here, the ornate brickwork and manicured gardens at the front gave way to a more utilitarian style. Concrete, steel, and barred windows were the order of the day.

Callie pointed at the black-painted window bars.

"What d'ye reckon they're for? It's not as if any of the inmates'll be trying to escape, eh?"

"I think it's the other way round, boss. Stops the freaks getting in."

Wondering what kind of person could possibly want to break into a crematorium, and then wishing she hadn't, Callie climbed out of the Transit's smoke-fragranced interior.

She rang a bell beside the blue-painted door. Titch was opening the rear doors of the Transit. She heard footsteps. So, a hard floor on the other side. No carpet for the dead and their handlers.

The door opened. She raised her eyebrows. The man facing her was dressed in jeans and a forest-green sweatshirt. Heavy work boots in tan leather emerged from the rolled-up cuffs of the jeans.

"Sorry, this was all a bit short notice," he said with a small, apologetic smile. "My frock coat and top hat are at the cleaner's."

She held out her hand.

"DCI Callie McDonald."

"Hi. Jack Wilton."

She turned to Titch.

"This is T—"

She stopped. She realised she still didn't know the name of the detective sergeant who'd been assigned to help with the cleanup. He stepped forward and held out his own huge hand, saving her embarrassment, though she could feel the heat of a blush on her cheeks.

"Detective Sergeant Tom Collins."

"Don't forget the cherry."

"Yes. Never heard that before. Shall we get going?"

Callie opened the first carton, and the three of them took a plastic-wrapped parcel each. Then Wilton led them into the business end of the crematorium. He put down his package, a thigh, Callie guessed from the heft of it. He opened a metal door to the rear of the furnace, a solid, cuboid construction of sheet steel and cast-iron, and then put the package inside. She noticed with disgust that it had left a dark, damp mark on the concrete floor, and she wrinkled her nose.

Until recently, Debra Fieldsend had been a high-flying lawyer with the Crown Prosecution Service and senior member of a legal conspiracy named *Pro Patria Mori*. After they'd killed the husband and baby daughter of a Metropolitan Police Service detective inspector, Fieldsend had become first a target and then a victim of DI Stella Cole's relentless campaign of bloody vengeance.

When all the packages were loaded, Wilton slammed the furnace door shut with a clang that echoed off the room's hard surfaces. He thumbed a green button set into the wall. The flames, which had been lying dormant below the grille inside the furnace, roared into life, tinting the thick glass viewing window orange.

"How long will it take?" Callie asked Wilton.

"Judging by the amount of, well, you know, the combined weight of the packages, I'd say two hours, but I'm going to allow three."

"And after that?"

"And after that you'll have about two and a half kilos of whitish-grey ash. I assume you don't want it back?"

She shook her head.

"What will you do with it instead?"

He pointed over her shoulder at the open door.

"You see the rose beds?" She nodded. "Nobody round here has better blooms than us."

An hour later, back in her hotel room, Callie called her boss, Assistant Chief Constable Gordon Wade of Lothian and Borders Police.

"Ah, Callie. How are you?"

"Fine, thanks, Boss."

"How did it go today? Any problems?"

"No. She's gone. Apparently onto a rose bed."

"Aye, well, that'll be the phosphates in the bones. And the house?"

"The cleaning crew were just arriving as we left. Should be there for another hour or two, then you could eat your dinner off the floor."

Wade grunted.

"You know, Callie, I never thought when I joined back in the seventies that this was how I'd end up, arranging to cover up a murder."

"Me neither, Boss. But like you said, what's done is done. And keeping it quiet is the least worst option."

"You mean compared to waking up to a headline in the Times that says, 'Death Squad Conspirator Butchered by Crazed Vigilante Widowed Cop'? Aye, you could have a point. What about the others?"

"A lot easier, thank heavens. Howarth—"

"The barrister?"

"Yes. She appears to have thrown him out of an upper storey window at his chambers. The pathologist's report indicated his system was flooded with flunitrazepam and alcohol."

"Sorry, Callie, back up a little. Fluni—?"

"—trazepam. It's a powerful sedative. Like Rohypnol, the date rape drug?"

"Oh, aye. Carry on."

"Well, Howarth died instantly. Catastrophic head injuries. It went down as a death by misadventure."

"And the Indian woman?"

"Hester Ragib was found dead in the bath at a hotel near Paddington Green nick. Six inches of water."

"Drowned?

"Electrocuted. She was sharing it with a hairdryer. The coroner recorded it as a suicide."

"So with De Bree dead of a heart attack and Ramage's death hushed up as a house fire that means there's only our friend Detective Chief Superintendent Collier left."

"Him and a few foot soldiers, but with Collier out of the way, they'll be easy enough to deal with one way or another."

Callie listened to her boss's breathing. He had a way of inhaling and exhaling through his nose when he was deep in thought that she and his other subordinates had learned to read. Interrupt his cogitations at your peril.

"Are we doing the right thing, d'ye think, Callie?"

Now it was her turn to pause. Wade had taught her years back that there was nothing wrong with thinking before speaking, even when asked a question by a superior officer. She took advantage of the lesson now. When she eventually did answer, it sounded hesitant to her ears.

"Going public would be a disaster. The media would have a field day. This is the rule of law we're talking about. If the public learned that judges, lawyers and cops were conspiring to kill people they thought should have been found guilty by juries, well, it would be open season on sex offenders just for starters."

"I know, I know," he sighed. "But are we any better? Collier ought to be arrested and charged with conspiracy to murder. Instead we're using a detective who is plainly mentally unstable as our own one-woman death squad."

Callie blew out her cheeks and shrugged, even though she knew he couldn't see her.

"Look, Boss. This wasn't your decision. It was a political call. This came from the Ministry of Justice."

Wade snorted. "Aye, and what a very Orwellian name *that* is, don't you think?"

"Agreed."

What neither Wade nor McDonald knew was that as they were speaking, Detective Inspector Stella Cole had just been detained after failing to kill Collier in his own office.

2

YOU DON'T HAVE TO BE MAD TO WORK HERE ...

"HONESTLY! One minute you're a serving DI – a high-flying DI at that – and the next, they're taking your shoelaces and your belt off you so you can't hang yourself."

DI Stella Cole turned to the split-off part of herself that had recently assumed almost permanent presence as a hallucination – "Other Stella," she called her – and scowled.

"It's all right for you. You can just fuck off whenever you feel like it. And anyway, I didn't have any shoelaces. Or a belt."

Other Stella pouted and folded her arms across her chest. She sat down on the narrow cot along the cell's longer wall.

"No need to be like that, Stel. After all, it wasn't my sergeant hiding behind those ridiculous pot plants with a Taser, now was it?"

Stella had to admit, it was not the way she'd imagined her final confrontation with Adam Collier would go. She'd recently discovered that her boss was the new leader of Pro Patria Mori.

"Fine," Stella said. "But you were the one giving the orders when we went charging into his office like the fucking Light Brigade."

"Don't blame me, sweetie. I'm not even real, am I? Laters!"

Other Stella winked, then vanished.

"Great," Stella said to the battleship-grey brick wall of the holding cell beneath Paddington Green police station. "I've been sectioned and even my hallucination's buggered off and left me."

She sat heavily on the taut grey blanket and cupped her chin in her hands. Waiting.

She didn't have to wait long.

A key scraped in the lock and the door swung inwards.

Standing in the brightly lit rectangle of the doorframe was the latest person to interrupt her quest for vengeance, Dr Anthony Akuminde. The station's pathologist had appeared in Collier's office while Stella was still twitching from the aftereffects of the Taser's charge. Together with Collier, he'd escorted Stella – frogmarched was the reality – through the CID office and down to the custody sergeant's desk where he'd instructed the veteran copper to put Stella in a cell, "for her own protection, and that of others." Perhaps because in his decades of service, the grey-haired sergeant really had seen everything, he merely nodded, got Akuminde to sign a form, and then led Stella, unprotesting, to cell number four.

"Stella," Akuminde said in a deep voice she would once have regarded as kindly, "may I come in?"

"Knock yourself out," she said.

He entered the cell. And sat beside her on the hard mattress.

"No," she said. "I meant it. Why don't you knock yourself out?"

He smiled.

"In my judgement as a doctor, you present a threat to yourself and others. That being the case, I have no option but to inform you that you are being detained under the provisions of Section Two of the Mental Health Act 1983. We're going to get you to a hospital where they can have a good poke around in that noggin of yours and see what all this trouble is about."

"You can't do that. It has to be the FMO."

He smiled that infuriating smile again.

"Normally, yes, but the Force Medical Officer is indisposed. I understand she broke her ankle playing soccer at the weekend. Modern times, eh?" He shook his head. "Anyway, as her deputy in this station, I am authorised to section you."

Other Stella had reappeared and was making bunny ears behind the Nigerian's close-cropped head. Stella smirked involuntarily.

"Something funny, Stella?" he asked.

She shook her head, at once tiring of Akuminde's false compassion.

Other Stella said, "He's in it up to his ears with Collier, you do know that, right?"

Biting back her response, which would only help him, Stella glared at Akuminde.

"It was a joke."

"I beg your pardon?"

"All that nonsense about murdering, what did he say I said, Pro Patrick something? It was a joke."

"My dear Detective Inspector Cole, you pulled a gun on your superior officer. A loaded gun. Not that that makes a great deal of difference. Just how was that a joke?"

Other Stella was miming putting a pistol to Akuminde's head and pulling the trigger, puffing out her cheeks and expelling air in a silent rush through pouting lips.

"What can I say, Doc? It was high spirits between fellow officers. Just a bit of cop humour."

"Adam – I mean Detective Chief Superintendent Collier – didn't find it very funny. I have already suggested he report to Occupational Health to see a psychologist. He is completely traumatised. Now, I've arranged transport for you to the hospital. Are we going to come quietly or are we going to make it necessary for Dr Akuminde to sedate us?"

Stella briefly considered putting Akuminde's eyes out with her thumbs. But she dismissed the idea. Sweet though the moment might be, it would probably reduce her chances of getting to Collier to zero. Instead, she shook her head, lowered her gaze and stood, slowly, so as not to startle him.

"Let's go," was all she said.

He smiled and reached for something behind his back.

"Just one more thing before we go, Stella. For your own safety."

He produced a pair of handcuffs and before Stella could register what was happening, he'd closed them round her wrists.

The walk through the basement corridors to the underground car park felt like the longest of Stella's life. Rightly suspecting that she might try to escape, Akuminde had rounded up not one but two burly police constables to escort him and Stella to the car park. They walked, one before, one behind, in stone-faced silence, no doubt inwardly relishing the chance to regale their mates with the story in the pub later.

Stella looked around for an ambulance. Then she saw a white prisoner transport van with its engine idling parked near to the entrance. She turned to Akuminde.

"Really? You're going to stick me in a Black Maria?"

"Regulations demand it, I'm afraid. Though don't you find it odd that we still refer to them as *black* when they're now white?"

The leading PC opened the rear door of the van and stood to one side for Stella to climb in and take her seat on one of the metal benches bolted to the floor. As she placed her right foot on the step, Akuminde closed the distance between them to a few inches and took hold of her elbow in a claw-like grip. He put his lips close to her ear.

"Enjoy your stay in the loony bin," he murmured so that only she could hear his words.

She whipped her face round so that they were nose to nose.

"Watch your back, Doc," she hissed. "When I'm out, I'm going to come and find you."

He stepped back and laughed, a theatrically loud sound in the low-roofed carpark.

"When you're out? Very good, Stella. When you're out. Oh my!"

He turned away from her and she resumed her clamber into the van's dark interior. The last thing she heard before they slammed the door on her was Akuminde's jovial cry to the driver.

"St Mary's, please, and don't spare the horses!"

3

BUT IT HELPS

EVEN though the van's high windows were opaque, Stella had no trouble visualising the route they took from Paddington Green to St Mary's Hospital. She'd made it often enough with crazed smack heads, hallucinating outpatients, or the walking wounded after one particularly horrific spree killing. The knife-wielding psychopath had eventually been put down by a marksman from the Metropolitan Police Service's firearms command. Its official name was SC&O19 but serving officers thought the ampersand was a faff and called it SCO19. At the time, Stella and her fellow officers had been of one mind: "good riddance to bad rubbish." Now she wasn't so sure. The van rumbled out of the station and turned left onto the Harrow Road. She pictured the turns, reciting them in her head like a litany. *Left again onto Harbet Road. Left onto Praed Street. Across the Edgware Road into Chapel Street. Right into Transept Street. Right onto Old Marylebone Road till it changes into Sussex Street. Right into Norfolk Place then straight ahead, through the brick archway and into St Mary's.*

The trip was over in less than ten minutes. The van's noisy diesel engine coughed and clattered to a standstill before dying altogether, and a few moments after that, the rear door swung back. Stella blinked in the bright light that flooded the passenger compartment. Akuminde stood there, smiling. Behind him Stella could see the double doors of the hospital's main reception area. He held his arm wide.

"Shall we go?"

She climbed down to see that he was flanked by the driver and a hospital orderly, a tall black man with a mass of dreadlocks held back with a leather thong.

At the reception desk, Akuminde leaned forwards to speak to an overweight woman in a maroon tunic who was juggling phones, clipboards and a seemingly uninterrupted flow of patients' relatives, minicab drivers and clinical staff, all without breaking sweat or even letting her toothy grin fade.

"My name is Dr Akuminde. I'm the Pathologist at Paddington Green police station. I rang earlier about an urgent, emergency psychiatric assessment. This young lady is under a Section Two."

The receptionist looked up at Stella, not unkindly, but with an open, curious expression as if she were a new species of animal. Though round here, being sectioned would hardly make you exotic, Stella thought.

"Having a bad day, dear?" she asked Stella. "Well, don't worry. We'll get a nice doctor to come and have a chat to you." She turned back to Akuminde. "Hold on please, Doctor. I'll page someone for you."

A few minutes later, a man in his midthirties wearing jeans and a dark-grey jacket over a white shirt strode across the reception area in an odd, half-limping walk towards the ragtag group of uniformed PC, orderly, pathologist and female prisoner. He had an NHS identity badge clipped to his jacket lapel and was carrying a blue clipboard with a sheaf of papers attached. Lengthening her stride to keep up with him was a younger woman, maybe late twenties, in a dark-blue cardigan and black corduroy skirt over thick, black tights. She also had the familiar blue-and-white NHS badge.

The pair stopped in front of the desk, and the receptionist pointed at Akuminde.

"This is the pathologist who called from Paddington Green, Dr Akuminde. This is Mr Hockley."

Akuminde shook hands with the newcomer, introduced his charge, and then spoke in a low voice though Stella caught every word.

"She tried to kill her superior officer with a firearm. Boasted of having murdered several other people, too, though we've not heard a word of any of the people she's talking about having so much as a cold, let alone a one-way ticket to the other side. Clearly insane."

"Yes, well, I'll be the judge of that," Hockley said, briskly. He pointed at the handcuffs. "Please remove those."

The PC released Stella from the cuffs, and she massaged her wrists to get some feeling back into them, grateful for the young doctor's ability to take charge.

"Is that better?" the young woman asked while Hockley completed some paperwork and Akuminde and the uniform disappeared back towards the main entrance. "I'm Becky. I'm a psychiatric nurse. I'll be helping Mr Hockley look after you today."

Something in her tone made Stella want to cry. She cleared her throat instead.

"Mister? Bit young for a consultant isn't he?"

Becky's cheeks dimpled as she smiled conspiratorially.

"He has got a bit of a baby face, hasn't he? But he's very good."

"Yes, I am," Hockley said, as he handed back the clipboard to the receptionist. "So let's get you to our little den and we can find out a bit more about you, OK?"

Stella let herself be escorted out of the reception area and down a long corridor, marked with the usual strips of coloured tape and multi-layered signposts for hospital departments ranging from genitourinary medicine to women's cancer, paediatric renal, and general surgical. Hockley stopped outside a door bearing a simple nameplate of aluminium in a slider at head height. Neat black capitals picked out the words 136 SUITE. He unlocked the door with a key on a ring he pulled from his pocket and pushed the door open.

A sofa and two armchairs in matching royal-blue material awaited them. Marking the geometric centre of the seating group, a circular coffee table supported a box of tissues. Stella took it all in. The peaceful watercolour landscapes to calm the agitated, the lack of hard corners to disarm the violent, the absence of windows to protect the suicidal.

"Let's get comfortable, shall we?" Hockley said. "Stella, where would you like to sit?"

She took one of the armchairs. Hockley took the other and pulled it around until he was facing Stella. Becky, the nurse, sat on the sofa. Other Stella sat next to her, throwing an arm nonchalantly around the young woman's shoulders. She winked at Stella.

"This should be fun," she mouthed.

Hockley cleared his throat. It was about to begin.

Stella realised that her answers here were crucial to her being able to go after Collier. But what was the right course of action? Collier thought he'd been clever by getting her sectioned. But he hadn't known the truth. Stella met *all* the conditions for her incarceration. She was a danger to herself and to others. She was suffering from a full-blown personality disorder. And she had murderous intentions towards Collier and now, Akuminde.

"Better play it careful then, Stel," Other Stella said from her place beside Becky. "Or you'll end up in a padded guest room."

Hockley smiled and spoke. He had a pleasant voice with a hint of a Yorkshire accent.

"First of all, please call me Dan. Only people who work at the hospital have to call me 'Mr Hockley.' So, Stella, isn't it?"

"Mm-hmm."

"Let's start with a simple question. Do you know why you're here?"

"Because I've been sectioned."

"Well, yes. But do you know *why* you've been sectioned?"

"I pointed a gun at my boss." *Who richly deserved it by the way.*

"According to Dr Akuminde, you also boasted of having murdered several people. Is that true?"

"That I boasted or that I murdered people?"

He smiled and made a note on his clipboard. "That you boasted."

"Yes. I can't deny that when there were two witnesses."

"And how about the murders?"

Debra Fieldsend lying in a stinking pool of her own blood in her kitchen. Charlie Howarth's skull smashing open on the York stone slabs at his chambers' party with a crack like a snapping plank. Hester Ragib electrocuted in a shallow bath, her eyes and tongue popping out of her face.

Other Stella was sitting up straight, her right arm held aloft like an eager schoolgirl.

"Miss! Miss! Ask me. How come there's been no press coverage? You don't suppose PPM have been clearing up after you, do you? After all, they've got as much to lose as you if the murders come out."

She has a point, Stella thought.

"Black humour. Cop humour. You medics are just as bad. If I'd really murdered people, don't you think there'd have been a bit of media coverage? You know, a smidge?"

Another note on the clipboard.

She watched Dan's face. Searching for a sign that he believed her story. *Nice eyes,* she thought. *Same colour as Richard's.* He looked up when he'd finished writing.

"I'm not a policeman. I'll leave the detection of murders to those who are paid to do it. But I am a consultant psychiatrist. Detecting mental health problems *is* my job. Tell me, is it also cop humour to threaten to kill a superior officer with a loaded handgun?"

His voice wasn't sharp, but the question had a wicked edge to it. She glanced at Other Stella, who was admiring her fingernails.

"Don't ask me, babe. That's a pretty good question."

Stella frowned.

"I've been having grief issues. Maybe I misjudged how the joke would be received."

Instead of making another note, Dan leaned forward and looked into Stella's eyes.

"Tell me something. Who is it you keep looking at?"

4

SECTIONED

STELLA'S pulse spiked and she felt a hot flush of sweat break out inside her blouse. She could almost smell it. The fear.

"What do you mean? Becky?"

He shook his head.

"No, not Becky. You keep looking to her left. Is there somebody else here with us?"

"No!" Even to Stella, her response came off too urgent, too quick, too desperate. Yet she felt compelled to glance once more in Other Stella's direction.

"Oh, well that's charming!" Other Stella said, crossing her legs at the knee. "You're quite happy to acknowledge me when I'm helping you put shotgun rounds into Albanian gangsters, or dismember the odd dead lawyer, but now, when all I'm doing is sitting sweetly next to nurse Becky here," she poked Becky in the left breast, "you're denying I even exist."

Dan was speaking again.

"Stella, I'm going to get Becky to run what we call an SBAR." He pronounced it *Ess-Bar*. "It stands for situation, background, assessment and recommendation. Please answer all her questions truthfully. I'll just have a think while you two are talking, OK?"

Becky produced a clipboard of her own. Stella hadn't noticed her carrying it. She smiled.

"Let's start with your situation now. How old are you, Stella?"

Stella trotted out short, simple answers to the first batch of questions. They established that she was a thirty-three-year-old police officer, living in London. Had she been able to see Becky's notes, Stella would have learned that she was presenting as calm, rational and with no outward signs of mania, anxiety or depression, although she did appear distracted.

Nodding to Dan and then looking down at her notes to write something, Becky looked up at Stella.

"Now. Let's get some background. Married?"

"Widowed."

"I'm sorry."

"It's fine. You weren't to know."

"Any children?"

"One. She's dead, too." *Though I believed she was living with me for over a year after she was burnt to death in her daddy's car.* "I have to warn you, it would probably be a mistake to ask me how I'm feeling about that."

Becky gave another of what Stella had quickly decided were her *professional* smiles. Everything happening at the mouth, nothing around the eyes.

"Of course. Have you ever had any mental health issues in the past?"

"No. Like I said, I had some severe grief reactions after my family died, but I worked through them with a therapist. I'm back on the job, on light duties admittedly, so basically signed fit to resume work."

"How about when you were younger? At school. Any anorexia, bulimia, self-harming, substance abuse?"

"Christ! You don't mince your words, do you? No, to answer your questions, I was a healthy, sporty, well-balanced girl. Parents separated, and I lived with my mum. And to save you the trouble, I had my first boyfriend at fifteen. He was a lovely Jewish boy called Ira. I lost my virginity at seventeen, not to Ira, sadly for him, as he was madly in love with me although his mother wanted him to find a nice Jewish girl. I did super-well in my GCSE and Λ levels – all A-stars. Then off to university, hate the way they call it *uni* now, don't you? Did psychology at Bath and took a first. Oh, yes, by the way? I did have a try at being a lesbian while I was at Bath, but it wasn't a massive success, to be honest. Taught straight after graduating, then joined the Met. I was on the graduate fast-track and got promoted to detective inspector in 2009."

Suddenly aware she was gabbling, Stella clamped her lips together. Her pulse was racing and she took a few deep breaths through her nose as she tried to slow her racing thoughts down.

"Wow, that was quite a speech!" Becky said. "Very comprehensive. You said you studied psychology at university?"

"Yes."

"Me, too. What was your dissertation on?"

"Abnormal psychology."

Becky made a note.

"Let's move on, shall we? As Dan said, we need to conduct an assessment of your mental state. Now I don't really need to ask you any questions because this is based on observation, but shall I tell you what I'm thinking?"

"Yes, please." *Keep it together, Stel,* she told herself. *I sense we're getting down to the wire on this one. They could let you go or lock you in a buckle-sleeved Versace nightie somewhere nice and soft.*

"You're presenting, sorry, I mean you *appear to be* calm, but it looks forced to me. I think you are under a lot of stress. You're keeping your voice level but every now and again it sounds as though you're about to explode. And, like Dan said, you do seem distracted. I noticed the sidelong glances, too. Are you willing to speak with me about how you're really feeling, Stella?"

Stella locked her gaze onto Becky's round, pale-blue eyes. Willed herself not to flick a look at Other Stella.

"Sure. Why not?"

Becky smiled.

"Good." She put her clipboard beside her. "So how are you feeling? Really?"

Stella drew in a deep breath and sighed it out.

"Honestly? Not so good. Not mad like Dr Akuminde seems to think, but just, I don't know, very tired. Maybe I came back to work too soon."

She hoped it would be enough to convince Becky and Dan to rescind the section and let her out. The room smelled unpleasantly of air freshener and Stella was feeling nauseous.

"Of course, that could explain your behaviour. But you said you worked through your grief with a counsellor."

"I know. I did. Maybe I was wrong." She felt her pulse racing and her anger mounting and couldn't stop it. "He did kill them, you know," she snapped.

Becky picked up her clipboard and made a note.

"Who killed them, Stella? Your boss?" She consulted her notes. "Detective Chief Superintendent Collier? Is that why you took a gun to his office?"

Stella realised she'd made a mistake. A huge mistake. What now? Explain how she'd discovered it was Leonard Ramage who'd murdered Richard and Lola and not a low-life petty criminal named Edwin Deacon, who'd been paid to take the fall? Where would that lead? Agree it was Collier? Might as well try on a few straitjackets now.

"No. They were run down by a man called Edwin Deacon. He killed them. Like I just said."

Becky nodded. Made another note. Each hidden scribble felt like a needle under a fingernail to Stella.

"I understand," Becky said with a smile. "But you see, Stella, what I am hearing, what I am *seeing*, is a woman who is being really brave about a terrible, awful, *traumatic* life event. But that woman is teetering on the edge. Probably feeling very panicky a lot of the time. Maybe not thinking straight. Does that sound about right?"

Stella shook her head.

"Nope. I'm feeling outraged that a prank landed me in this room with you and Dan here."

Becky shook her head.

"The problem is, if you can look at this situation from my perspective, Stella, is that what you call a prank would get a member of the public arrested for attempted murder."

"No it wouldn't. It would be carrying a firearm in a public place. Maybe assault."

Another note on Becky's clipboard. Another needle under the nail.

Dan spoke for the first time since Becky had begun the SBAR.

"Rather than getting bogged down in the legal angles, let's bring this back to the question of what we're going to do next. Would that be OK, Stella?"

He waited and Stella realised it wasn't a rhetorical question.

"Fine by me, Dan." She tried for a relaxed smile but she could feel her cheeks almost splitting from the effort. Her palms were sweaty but she daren't rub them on her jeans.

"I don't think it matters whether it was a joke, a prank, an assault or an attempted murder. What does matter, to me and to Becky, is that your colleague Dr Akuminde had enough concerns about your mental health to section you. No doctor takes that action without a great deal of thought, and I need to respect his decision by considering your case very seriously. Now, here's where we are. A little over a year ago, your husband and baby daughter were killed by a hit and run driver. I'll be requesting your medical notes from your GP, but I am already fairly sure what I'll learn from them. As you say, you were understandably grief-stricken. Perhaps you did come back to work too early. But I don't buy your story about this business with the gun being a joke. I don't know what it really was, and like I said before, that's not my job. I also don't know, yet," he smiled, "what exactly is going on in your head. I need to find out though. And that's going to take a little time. So, we get to the R in SBAR. I'm going to recommend that you stay with us for twenty-eight days. That will allow me to get to know you a little better and hopefully arrive at both a diagnosis and a plan to manage or cure your condition."

He stood, and Stella realised the interview was over. She thought, briefly, of her options. Trying to overturn a section was fraught with difficulties, and she was scared that Other Stella might take over and reveal the true extent of her mental problem. She decided to do nothing. For now. *Meek and mild, Stel,* she cautioned herself. *Meek and mild.*

"OK, Dan. If you think that's for the best."

He paused before opening the door and looked back at her.

"I do. I have to see other patients now. Becky will find you a room and she'll arrange to have some clothes and toiletries brought in for you. We'll speak again in the morning."

"One last question, Dan."

"Yes?"

"What happened to your leg?"

He looked down and rubbed at the front of his thigh.

"Motorbike accident. I've always been a bit of a speed-freak. Fast bikes were my thing. Now it's fast cars."

Then he was gone.

Stella looked at the smiling woman who'd just become her jailer.

Just you and me, then, Becky, she thought.

"Why don't you wait here, Stella? Just while I sort out a little bit of paperwork. Then I'll come and collect you and we can find you a space in the communal area."

Then she was gone and Stella was alone.

Almost.

"Well this is fucked up, isn't it, Stel?" Other Stella said from the chair recently occupied by Dan. "What are you going to tell the gorgeous Dr Dan in the morning? Because quite honestly, I'm not sure that the whole 'prank' angle is really going to work. And let's face it, you *are* mad. You know," she held her thumb and index finger a few millimetres apart, "just a teeny-weeny little bit."

"I don't know. If I stick to the prank story, I'm screwed. He'll say I've lost touch with reality, or I'm majorly stressed out and a danger to the public. If I tell him about you, then I'm *really* screwed. Might as well lie back and wait for them to stick the electrodes on."

"You could tell them about Pro Patria Mori."

"Oh, right, because *that* won't have Dan reaching for his prescription pad." She adopted a singsong voice. "You *see*, Dan, there's a legal *conspiracy* running *murder squads* in London. Judges, CPS lawyers, barristers – they're *all* in on it. And *I'm* the woman to take them all on. Yeah, right. Collier already told him about my boasts of murdering them. Even if Dan did believe the conspiracy story, I'd end up out of here and straight on a multiple murder charge."

Other Stella held her hands up in surrender.

"Only trying to be helpful, sweetie. Only, you're going to have to do something, aren't you? I don't think Dan's just a pretty face. I saw the way he was looking at you. He knows something's up. If he finds out about me, you can kiss your dreams of killing Collier goodbye."

5

SINGLE ROOM, DOUBLE OCCUPANCY

STELLA couldn't remember the last time she'd been locked in a bedroom. Maybe never. She'd gone through a stroppy phase in her teens when her slammed bedroom door was a regular punctuation mark in the shouted conversations with her mother. But even then, there hadn't been a means of securing it.

It was eight o'clock in the evening. Becky had appeared in the communal room at six with some clothes and toiletries after Stella had given her the keys to her house in West Hampstead. After a ridiculously early, and virtually inedible hospital meal, Stella had been led to a small room containing a single bed, a desk, a wardrobe and a chair.

"This will be your home for the next twenty-eight days," Becky said. "The bathroom's down the corridor. You can use it before bedtime and in the morning. If you need the loo in the night, just ring the bell, and whoever's on duty will come and take you."

So it was that, after brushing her teeth, Stella had found herself locked in with only a paperback book for company. Someone knocked at the door, then Stella heard a key in the lock.

Stella straightened her back and waited. Her heart was bumping uncomfortably in her chest.

Becky entered. She was carrying a small white plastic tray. On it were balanced a clear plastic cup of water and two pills. One white, one pale blue.

"Only me," she said. "I've brought you something to help you sleep. It can be very disorientating, spending your first night here. These will relax you."

"What are they?"

Becky smiled.

"Like I said, they'll just relax you and help you sleep."

Stella hardened her tone.

"Please don't patronise me. I'm a police officer, in case you'd forgotten. I've nicked enough drug dealers to know my way round a pharmacy cabinet. What are they? Diazepam? Temazepam? What?"

"Sorry. OK, since you ask, this one," she tapped the pale blue pill, "is Diazepam. Five milligrams. This one," she tapped the white pill, "is Zopiclone. It's a sleeping tablet. It's 7.5 milligrams. Very mild."

"I'm not feeling anxious. I don't need medication."

Becky came further into the room and sat on the edge of the bed. She leant towards Stella before speaking again. Her voice was low and measured, but there was no mistaking the steel core.

"I'm afraid that, certainly for your first few nights with us, we won't be taking your feelings into account when deciding on your medication. Being sectioned is unpleasant for you, I know that. But it's also a very serious step for any doctor to take, and if Dr Akuminde took it then he must have had real concerns about the danger you present to yourself and others. Here," she pushed the tray towards Stella. "Just take them. You can discuss further treatment with Dan in the morning."

"And if I refuse?"

"And if you refuse, I will leave and return with another nurse and we will administer the medication via intramuscular injection." She smiled. But it wasn't a humorous expression. "Under restraint, if necessary."

Realising she was beaten, Stella took the two tablets from the tray and washed them down with the water.

"Thanks," Becky said, getting up to leave. "I'm going off duty now, but there'll be another nurse here all night. His name is Namesh. Try to get some sleep. The pills will help."

She closed the door softly behind her.

"You could appeal, you know," Other Stella said, from the bed.

"Yes, I do know. Or I could ask for a family member to have the section overturned. None of which gets round the two central problems. One, you're here, so technically I belong in here. Two, I have, in fact, murdered a High Court judge and three lawyers. Not to mention," she had to count on her fingers, "five, or possibly six, Albanian gangsters. Which means my other option is a smaller and less comfortable room in a custody suite."

She lay back on the bed, forcing Other Stella to slide sideways. She closed her eyes, feeling the Diazepam beginning to blur the edges of her consciousness as her muscles relaxed. She needed a plan. But thinking was becoming difficult. In the end, she gave up and let her thoughts drift where they may. Amid a swirl of images of bloody corpses and mangled motorcycles, she fell asleep.

The noise of the key in the lock woke her. She checked her watch. Eight a.m. She'd slept for eleven hours straight. Readying herself for her first full day incarcerated in a secure psychiatric ward, she climbed out of bed and stretched.

"Bring it on," she said, as the door opened.

6

A LITTLE CHAT

DAN'S office seemed to Stella more like that of a woman than a man. Soft, muted colours, watercolour landscapes on the walls, cushions for the armchairs, well-tended indoor plants on a bookshelf, and framed photographs of children on his desk. Presumably it was carefully designed to keep his patients calm. In her case, it wasn't working. Her heart was racing. She was trying to figure out how she could persuade him she presented no danger to herself or others. Especially given that it wasn't true.

They were facing each other across a low table. He'd offered her a coffee then fussed around with a dinky little chrome machine on the windowsill that produced a very acceptable latte for her and a cappuccino for him.

Today he was wearing faded jeans and a soft, white shirt beneath a navy cardigan. He took a sip of his coffee before replacing it on the table.

"So, Stella. How are you feeling this morning?"

"I feel fine, Dan. Given I was sectioned yesterday when there's absolutely nothing the matter with me."

"I'm glad you feel fine. It's very disorientating, I know. One minute you're on the outside doing your job, living at home, and the next, you're locked in a room in a psychiatric ward. As to whether there's something the matter, that's what we're here to find out."

"Like I told you and Becky yesterday, it was a joke. Clearly a very poor one, and for whatever reason, Adam," God how she hated even saying his Christian name, the murdering bastard, "couldn't see the funny side. But give me any test you like, ink blots, values profile, the Hare Psychopathy Checklist, and I'll come up as normal as you are."

She watched him frown as she spoke and felt a queasy sensation in the pit of her stomach.

"You seem to know a lot about psychological testing. Is that a hobby of yours?"

She shook her head.

"Studied it at university. I told Becky yesterday. Isn't it in my notes?"

Dan smiled.

"Forgive me, it was a long day yesterday. Summer brings out the crazies."

Stella raised her eyebrows.

"Is that a technical term?"

"You're a cop. I'm a shrink. We can call a spade a spade. I won't tell anyone if you won't."

Stella was beginning to like this relaxed psychiatrist with his lopsided grin and laconic manner. She returned his smile.

"My lips are sealed."

"Hopefully not, as we do need to have a little chat about a few aspects of your behaviour over the last twenty-four hours."

"Fine." She spread her arms wide. "Ask away, doc."

"I've seen your Metropolitan Police personnel file. Your ID photo shows you with long, brown hair. In a ponytail. When did you get the new do? It's very Annie Lennox."

Stella reached up and ran her fingertips through her cropped blonde hair. One of the stratagems she'd employed as she hunted down the remaining members of Pro Patria Mori. She realised she'd forgotten she'd done it.

"Couple of weeks ago? Why?"

"It's quite a change. Women in their thirties tend to find a style that suits them and stick with it."

"That's a bit sexist, isn't it?"

"Just an observation. Of course, there are times when it makes sense."

"Such as?"

"Traumatic life events. Divorce. Redundancy. Bereavement. Even menopause. Sometimes people like to reinvent themselves. For women, their hair is one of the easiest things to change."

"You know about my background. You know I lost my husband and baby daughter. So it was a delayed reaction to that."

"OK. You're probably right. And believe me, in no way do I want to diminish the effects of your grief. Or its cause. Perhaps we could talk about the gun."

"What do you want to know?"

"You said it was all a joke?"

"That's right."

"Was the safety catch on or off?"

"It's a Glock. It doesn't have an external safety. There are three internal mechanisms to prevent accidental discharge."

Dan smiled.

"I stand corrected. Have you had much firearms training?"

"I did a standard rotation with SCO19 – that's the firearms division – as part of my fast track. And I keep up my certification with regular reviews. You don't have to, but I like to keep my options open." *Like shooting the fucker who's still walking around free as a bird while my family lie beneath the ground.*

"Where did it come from?"

"Pardon?"

"The gun." He consulted his notes. "The Glock. Where did you get it?"

"From the Armoury." *Illegally, and with a considerable amount of effort.*

"Are you sure?"

Shit! What does he know?

35

"Why?"

"Because according to the Armourer at Paddington Green, no Glocks were issued yesterday. 'All present and correct,' was what he said."

Stella could feel pressure building inside her head. It was interrogation 101 – lies are harder to tell than the truth. *The higher you build your house of cards, the harder it gets to stop the whole FUCKING thing from collapsing under its own weight. One slip, one breath of wind, and there're Jacks and Kings and Queens and little baby princesses every-fucking-where.*

"He must have made a mistake."

"Maybe. So you *collected,*" unmistakable emphasis, "a Glock from the Armoury and took it to Adam's office to play your prank."

"Yes. As I think I told you before."

"And you're perfectly sane. Nothing the matter. Just a joke that got out of hand. Adam and Dr Akuminde overreacted and here we all are. All I need to do is reverse your section and you walk out here to resume the fight against crime, yes?"

What was wrong with Dan? The smile looked lopsided. Quizzical, as if waiting for her to make a mistake.

"Is that so hard to see?"

"Tell me something, Stella?"

"Anything."

"Who were you talking to in your room last night?"

7

THE HEAVY SQUAD

A week after he'd had Stella sectioned, Collier stood outside the door of the fifth-floor flat in Achilles House, his finger jammed on the brass-effect doorbell. The block of flats had been built in the sixties. It was located in a rundown part of East London now populated almost exclusively by migrants, refugees, asylum-seekers and the remains of the poor white underclass without the wit, contacts or sheer bloody-mindedness to get out. Below the walkway, a posse of youths in hoodies and low-slung, baggy jeans sat astride BMX bikes looking up at him and then exchanging glances. He half wished they'd come and confront him. Having abandoned any shred of professional respect for the law, he was carrying a Glock 17 pistol in a shoulder holster beneath his immaculately tailored suit jacket. But brandishing the gun, while satisfying, would draw attention he would prefer to avoid.

"Come on, Monica," he muttered. "Open the door, for Christ's sake."

He raised his fist, intending to add knocking to the incessant ringing of the bell. Then the door opened a couple of inches before the security chain chinked taut against the stop.

"Who the fuck are you?"

The speaker's face, glimpsed through the narrow gap between door and frame, was tanned, lined from smoking and thin-lipped with hostility.

"Don't be like that, Monica," Collier said.

"Oh, it's you."

The door closed. Collier waited while the chain scraped. Then the door was opened just enough to admit his wide-shouldered frame. He slipped inside.

Monica Zerafa was Maltese by birth. She had come to England in the nineties. Since then, she'd earned her living as a drug dealer. But that wasn't why Collier had come to see her. In her business dealings, and many arrests, she had responded with violence whenever she felt she had been badly treated, which was essentially all the time. More than a handful of small-time dealers and at least three police officers bore scars she'd given them. With her fingernails. With improvised weapons. And with knives, of which she always carried at least two about her person. Collier himself had arrested her on one occasion, stepping back from an incoming carving knife that ended up embedded in his sergeant's left bicep. There had been rumours she'd put at least one business rival permanently out of competition, but there hadn't been enough evidence to take to the Crown Prosecution Service.

She led him into an over-furnished sitting room. Leather armchairs in varying shades of turquoise and orange vied for space with nested coffee tables and pot plants on ornate carved wooden stands. Dominating an entire corner, a vast, flat-screen TV surmounted a black-and-chrome shelving unit containing DVD recorder, VCR, Sky box, PlayStation, sub-woofer and sound bar.

She was solidly built. Not fat. Muscular, with large breasts and a barrel-shaped body. She crammed herself into one of the armchairs and motioned for Collier to sit.

"What the fuck do you want now?" was her opening sally.

"It's nice to see you, too, Monica."

"Ha. Funny man. How are you Mr Collier? Keeping well? Mrs Collier doing all right, is she? That better for you?"

He nodded.

"Much. And how are you? Keeping out of trouble?"

She winked.

"I'm just a housewife now. Looking after my son, Nathan. Since his dad buggered off with that Scotch tart, it's just the two of us."

"And Nathan. He's a good boy? Got himself a nice steady job, has he?"

She shrugged.

"Austerity, Mr Collier. No jobs for boys like Nathan."

"Not even in your old line of work?"

He suspected that her old line of work was her current line, too, but he didn't need to share that feeling. Not yet.

Her gaze flicked to a cupboard in a corner then back to him.

"He does a bit of courier work. You know, parcels and that. Zero-hours. What is this country of ours coming to, Mr Collier, eh? No work for honest folk like Nathan and me."

He spread his hands wide as if to say, What's to be done? Thinking what it was coming to was him having to treat with monsters like the woman opposite him instead of ordering their execution.

"Funnily enough, that's why I'm here. I have some work for you."

"What kind of work?"

"I need you to kill somebody for me."

8

NAMING NAMES

THE pressure inside Stella's head threatened to burst its banks. A flush of terror coursed through her bloodstream. She could feel her breath coming in short, quick gasps. *Slow down, Stel. Hold it together.*

"Nobody."

"Really?"

Dan stood up, slowly, she noticed – no sudden movements around the crazies – and went over to his desk, where he picked up a slim, black laptop with a blue-and-white NHS sticker on the lid. He brought it back and set it on the coffee table. He opened the lid and pressed a few keys before swivelling the machine round to face her. The screen showed, in full colour, a woman sitting on a single bed in a small bedroom furnished, apart from the bed, with a desk, a wardrobe and a hard chair. The woman, whose hair was blonde, and cropped short, was facing the chair, which was empty. At the foot of the screen was a set of video playback controls.

"You filmed me! Isn't that in breach of about a million ethics codes?"

"Actually, for the first twelve hours we are legally allowed to observe patients without their knowledge or consent. It's part of a new Department of Health protocol for the diagnosis and treatment of mental health disorders. Play it," he said.

Trapped. Nowhere to go. Nowhere to run. There she sat on the single bed. The moment she started moving, Stella knew the jig was up. But what else could she do? She hit the green triangle to play the video.

Dan had used her hesitation to come and kneel beside her. They watched together as Stella engaged in an animated conversation with the chair. What was more disturbing to Stella than the absence of any physical interlocutor were the two voices coming from her mouth. Even issuing from the laptop's tinny little inboard speakers, her own pleading tones contrasted sharply with Other Stella's sarcastic, mocking and occasionally threatening voice. When she raised her right hand and slapped herself hard across the cheek, Dan reached across and stopped the playback. He resumed his seat facing her.

In a quiet, soft voice that made her want to cry, he asked her, "Who were you talking to, Stella? Why did you slap yourself?"

She shuddered. Felt herself sliding sideways. Tried to answer before it was too late.

"I—I—" She jumped to her feet, and carried on travelling upward until she, Stella, bobbed against the ceiling, leaving Other Stella in charge. "I'll tell you why, you self-righteous little prick. Because she's not strong enough to finish what we started. Now and again she needs to be reminded what this is all about. What it's always been about." She adopted a sassy American accent and began singing. "R-E-V-E-N-G-E." As she continued vamping on the Aretha Franklin classic, Stella watched Dan. He didn't seem scared. He maintained the same relaxed posture as before, looking up as Other Stella pointed her finger at him, wailing that he'd find out what it meant to her.

The impromptu karaoke session over, Other Stella slumped back into her armchair.

"That was quite a performance," Dan said. "And you are?"

"*She* calls me Other Stella. But you can call me anytime." She winked lasciviously.

"Pleased to meet you, Other Stella. Do you mind if I ask you a few questions?"

"Ask away, doc. My calendar is unexpectedly empty. My time is yours."

Stella looked down in horror at Other Stella, who returned her gaze with a steely glare that said, *Too late, babe. You fucked up. Now it's my turn.*

"When were you born?"

"Clever. I can see why you made consultant so young. I was born, hmm," she looked upward for a second or two, "about ten months ago."

"When Stella lost her family?"

"Not quite. They were killed nearly two years ago. Poor girl could handle her husband's death, but not the baby's. Thought Lola was still alive. In the end, I had to come and straighten her out. She'd been paying an imaginary nanny to look after a fucking teddy bear. I mean, it's sad and everything, but there was work to be done and she wasn't what you'd call firing on all cylinders."

"And when you say work?"

"This is all covered under doctor-patient privilege, right?"

"If it relates to events in the past, yes."

"In that case, when I say 'work,' I mean killing members of a conspiracy who were running a little death squad in London. Her husband got too close to the truth so they wiped him out. Lola was what they'd no doubt call *collateral damage.*"

Dan rubbed his chin.

"Does Adam Collier belong to this conspiracy?"

"Give the man a round of applause, folks," Other Stella said, looking around her and flapping her hands palms uppermost, as if inviting an audience to show their appreciation.

"So when you went to his office ..."

"It was to kill him. Yes."

"Tell me, is Stella still here. Is she in there with you?"

"Don't be daft. She can't handle it when I kick off nowadays. She's up there in the gods." Other Stella pointed straight at Stella.

"Could I speak to her, please?"

"Why?"

"Indulge me."

"Oh, fine," she said with a sigh. Then she looked up again. "Babe, you're wanted."

With a nauseating feeling as if she'd just stepped off a whirling fairground ride, Stella found herself facing Dan across the coffee table. Tears were running freely down her cheeks. Dan spoke. The compassion in his voice was almost unbearable.

"Leaving aside the question of what Other Stella may or may not have done, it's clear to me, Stella, that you have developed what we now call a dissociative personality disorder. Normally, these types of disorders arise as a result of childhood trauma. But while Other Stella was speaking, she said she'd been 'born' less than a year ago. After your husband and baby daughter were killed. That suggests to me that this is a temporary condition, brought on by the intense grief you suffered. And that, although it may not feel like it to you right now, is actually good news. There are a number of treatments that have proved to be very successful, combining drugs and psychotherapy."

She sniffed.

"Am I mad, Dan?" she said, in a voice clotted with despair.

He smiled and shook his head.

"No. You're not mad. I know I talked about crazies a little while ago, which was my somewhat unprofessional attempt to lighten the mood. But we don't really use the term 'mad' anymore. If it means anything at all, it refers to only a couple of psychotic illnesses including schizophrenia and severe forms of bipolar disorder."

"I'm guessing this means you're not going to overturn my section."

He shook his head.

"Nope. I think what will be best for you is to begin a treatment regime here and take the full twenty-eight days to rest and see how the treatment works. Then we have to review your case anyway, and it may be you can move to seeing us on an outpatient basis. Of course, there is the question of this conspiracy fantasy. We need to explore that in a little more depth together. I don't think it's very helpful. I suspect you – or rather, Other Stella – are using it as a way to make sense out of the deaths of your husband and daughter. But that's for another day. I am going to prescribe more Zopiclone to ensure you are getting enough sleep, and an anti-anxiety medication called Lorazepam. Don't worry, it won't turn you into a zombie. But it will help you to relax while we use psychotherapy to get to the heart of your problem."

Sitting in the communal recreation room twenty minutes later, a book open on her lap, Stella looked around her. Apart from the poor souls staring off into space or repeatedly scratching at imaginary bugs under their skin or talking to themselves, it was hard to tell who was a patient and who was a psychiatric nurse. The latter wore their own clothes, and unless their badge was visible on its blue lanyard, they could be John with fears of open spaces or Marie who thought aliens were telling her what to have for tea every day. She turned back to the book and tried to concentrate on the story, but one of the bug-scratchers had started keening to herself and eventually the noise became too much and Stella wandered off to watch TV.

9

DOWN PAYMENT

IF Monica was surprised by Collier's statement, she masked it well. He observed her as his words sank in. Her face was impassive, though her deep-brown eyes flicked left and right. Finally, she uttered a single word.

"Who?"

"Not why?"

She shrugged.

"None of my business, is it?"

"No, you're right. Her name is Stella Cole."

"Friend of yours, is she?"

Collier permitted himself a small, tight smile.

"Not exactly. A former colleague, as a matter of fact."

Monica reached for a packet of cigarettes balanced on the arm of the chair. After she'd lit one, taken a lungful of smoke and hacked it out again, she fixed Collier with a stare.

"You want me to kill a cop?"

"Do you have a problem with that? I seem to remember you weren't averse to trying now and again."

Another shrug. Another drag on the cigarette. He watched her considering her options. He knew the way her mind worked. Fear of justice was a part of the equation. But for Monica Zerafa, money always came first.

"Why me?" she asked, finally. "Plenty of blokes out there," she jerked her chin at the window, "who'd do her for a couple of grand."

"You'd think that, wouldn't you? But the boys are too cocky. We've tried twice, with … disappointing results. I need someone who can actually get the job done. Someone who can try a different approach."

"You got deep pockets, have you, Mr Collier? You're going to need them. I mean, look around you. This shithole the council give me and Nathan, well, it ain't exactly Buckingham Palace, is it? Maybe me and him'd like to move out. Find ourselves a nice little house over Essex way. By the seaside."

Collier was just about to speak, calculating how far he could beat the wary woman down when she spoke again.

"And who's this 'we'? I thought this was something personal."

"As you said, it's none of your business. But we have funds available. Did you have a figure in mind?"

She drew deeply on the cigarette and Collier watched as the red tip glowed brightly and advanced towards her puckered lips. Before she could answer, she was seized by a coughing fit, doubling over and almost retching. Eyes watering, she returned to an upright position, reached into the front of her V-necked jumper and retrieved a tissue from her cleavage. Having wiped her streaming eyes and replaced the tissue, she stubbed the cigarette out. Her face was scarlet with the effort of drawing oxygen into her lungs, and for a moment he wondered whether he'd chosen badly. An assassin crippled by what had to be galloping lung cancer was hardly a safe bet. But then, he thought, neither of his two previous picks – a borderline psychopathic rape-murderer and a ferocious Albanian gangster nicknamed 'The Shark' – had proved up to the task of eliminating Stella Cole.

"A million," she wheezed.

Collier laughed. Genuinely, this time. You had to give the

woman credit. With the rest of the Pro Patria Mori committee dead, control of its private bank account had passed to him and he knew what he could afford.

"Who are you, Monica, the woman with the golden gun? We could probably go to thirty thousand. That would make a nice deposit on a house somewhere better than this." He waved his arm round at the cramped living room.

She lit another cigarette, held it between thumb and forefinger and jabbed it towards him as if about to throw a dart.

"Listen. You already admitted you failed twice. I'm strong, Mr Collier, and you know I don't mind getting my hands dirty. I put more than one cocky little runt in the hospital for disrespecting me. But I'm not a professional hitter. Yet here you sit, in my second-best armchair, asking me to off a cop. That makes me think you're running out of options. Two hundred thousand."

Collier pictured the last statement he'd looked at online for the PPM account at Greville & Thackeray, a private bank so discreet they made Coutts look like a market trader with a wheelbarrow full of cash. The sum she'd come down to would barely make a dent. He held his hands wide in surrender.

"I can see why you did so well in your former profession, Monica. OK, cards on the table. I can go to fifty K and a Get Out of Jail Free card for young Nathan if his *courier* job lands him in trouble."

She smiled and held out a hand decorated with several heavy gold rings.

He took it. Then winced as she exerted more pressure, grinding the undersides of the rings against his unprotected knuckles.

"Sixty. A favour for Nathan. Plus one for me. Deal?"

Wondering whether he could extricate his hand without losing a finger, he pushed a smile onto his face.

"Deal."

Then Monica raised a palm to her mouth and widened her eyes theatrically.

"What am I thinking of? I haven't offered you anything to

drink. My mum, God rest her soul, would have killed me. Hospitality is very important to us Maltese. You want a cup of tea, Mr Collier? A little something to eat?"

Resting his right hand lightly on his knee and wishing he could rub it, he nodded.

"Lovely. Thank you."

She levered herself out of the armchair and took her cigarette with her into the tiny kitchen off the living room. While she busied herself making tea, he massaged his right hand, examining the deep, red depressions where Monica's gold rings had ground against the skin. *Bitch!* Maybe once she'd dealt with Stella he'd come back and repay the favour. With interest.

"Here we are!" Monica announced, returning with a large, bamboo-edged tray bearing a teapot, milk jug, sugar bowl and two cups and saucers in matching, rose-patterned bone china. Beside the teapot, a side plate was loaded with small, pale-brown biscuits decorated with halved glacé cherries. "Pull out one of those tables, would you?" she said, speaking past the cigarette, which dangled from her lips, trailing smoke upwards into her eyes.

Collier did as he was asked, placing the smallest of the three nested tables into a free couple of square feet of carpet.

Monica put the tray down.

"Milk? Sugar?"

"Milk, please."

She handed him a cup and pointed at the plate of biscuits.

"I made those yesterday. Nathan's favourite. *Biskuttini tal-lewz*, we call them. Know what that means?"

Collier shook his head.

"Try one"

Collier selected one and took a bite. It was sweet, with an intense hit of almond.

"Almond biscuits?"

She smiled, revealing a gold tooth at the back of her mouth.

"Very good. So, about this Stella woman. Where is she?"

Collier took a sip of the tea, which was so hot it burnt his lower lip.

"St Mary's, Paddington."

"What's that, a church?"

"Hospital. She's in the psychiatric ward."

"Mad, is she?"

"Very."

"You put her there, did you?"

"Yes. I needed to contain her."

"So how am I supposed to get to her, then? You can't just walk in and book a room?"

"Actually, that's where you're wrong. You just turn up at the front desk and tell them you're hearing voices telling you to kill yourself. Or you think you're married to Jesus. Say you want to voluntarily admit yourself to the psychiatric ward. You don't need to be sectioned and because it's voluntary, you can leave whenever you like. Once you're inside, you do what you have to do then leave. Make it look like an accident, or suicide. After all, unlike you, she *was* sectioned. It happens all the time. There'll be an internal enquiry, but that's not going to affect you. And if there's any suggestion of a police investigation, I'll either squash it or misdirect it. You'll be free and clear and looking at houses in Clacton-on-Sea with Nathan."

She sipped her tea and bit one of the biscuits in half. Once she'd finished chewing, she spoke.

"Lot of powerful drugs in hospitals."

"Blades, too. Not to mention stairwells. All kinds of hazards for someone who's not feeling themselves."

Perhaps picturing herself taking strolls on the sand with Nathan, Monica grinned at Collier.

"Have another biskuttini."

They spent another ten minutes discussing the timings. Today. Right now. And the financial details, which amounted to a thirty-thousand-pound down payment in cash from Collier, the rest to be paid on completion. Then, after imparting a few pieces of what he called "intelligence," he left.

* * *

At ground level, the youths on the BMX bikes were still there. He moved to skirt the tight little group, but one pushed himself backwards so he blocked Collier's path.

The youth – black, muscular, hair razored tight to his skull at the sides and carved into a sharp geometric quiff – looked Collier up and down.

"Sharp suit, mate. Must have cost a fortune."

Collier shrugged.

"You're a fan of men's tailoring, then?"

He sensed the youths priming themselves. He caught movement out of the corner of his eye as two others detached themselves from the group and wheeled their bikes behind him.

The youth facing him smiled.

"Would be if I had the money, know what I mean, bruv? Maybe you can help me out. You know, a donation for my first suit?"

Cackles from the group at this.

"Sure, why not?" Collier said. He reached into his jacket, watching the youth's eyes tracking his hand.

When it emerged curled round the grip of the Glock, the boy's expression snapped from greedy expectation to naked terror. Eyes wide, hands held out palms outward, he reared back, almost falling off the bike.

"Whoa, man! Don't shoot! No need for the gat. I was joking, yeah!"

Collier sensed the other boys pulling back. Enjoying the moment, he turned a slow circle, making eye contact with each of them in turn.

"Wallets," he said.

Hurriedly they produced a variety of leather and nylon wallets.

"Throw them over there." He pointed the Glock at a couple of industrial-sized rubbish bins in a glass-strewn square of concrete.

They complied at once.

"You know who I am?" he asked.

Much shaking of heads, eyes downcast, owners afraid to make contact.

"I'm the man your mothers warned you about. Now fuck off before I decide to use this."

They pedalled away towards the rubbish bins, not looking back, as Collier strolled away, back to his car, holstering his pistol and wishing it was standard equipment. When he reached the safety of the Audi's leather-scented interior, he thumbed the "lock all doors" button and drove away. Once out of the wannabe thugs' fiefdom, he pulled over and made a call.

10

NEW ADMISSION

MONICA Zerafa stood at the main reception desk, five hundred yards away from the psychiatric ward, and her target. Grey-faced people dragging oxygen bottles or saline drips on precarious wheeled stands shuffled past her. She leaned over the counter and pinned the young, tired-looking receptionist with an intense stare.

"I want to be admitted to the psychiatric ward," she said in a low voice so that the woman had to lean forward to catch her words.

"Can you tell me why you want that, please?"

To Monica's way of thinking, the woman with dark circles under her eyes wasn't displaying the correct amount of concern. Maybe her next line, worked out with Collier, would do it.

"He is inside my head," she said, tapping her left temple for emphasis and then crossing herself. "He told me to kill myself. He said his father," another crossing, forehead to belly, breast to breast, "would welcome me in Heaven personally."

The receptionist sighed. Maybe she was used to mad people turning up in front of her, demanding sanctuary.

"Name?"

"His name is Jesus."

"*Your* name, madam."

"Gloria Danktesh. Mrs."

The receptionist made a note on a pad in front of her.

"Can you wait over there, please, Mrs Danktesh?" she asked, pointing at a row of seats beneath a notice board advertising free chlamydia testing kits. "I need to call a doctor."

"Hurry, please," Monica hissed. "He's getting impatient."

She wandered over to the seats and lowered her bulky frame into the endmost chair, next to a bright orange dump-bin full of cardboard cartons marked, "1 in 12 of your friends probably has it."

She passed the ten-minute wait observing the comings and goings through the sliding doors. She amused herself by trying to guess the ailments that had brought so many people to the hospital. She considered herself a student of human nature. It was helpful in her line of work. Figuring out what people needed was one step away from meeting that need. For a profit, naturally. Her philosophising was interrupted by the arrival of a man in his midthirties wearing a dark blue cardigan over a white shirt. *Handsome*, Monica thought. *Lovely eyes.*

"Mrs Danktesh? Gloria?" he asked. His accent was one of those northern ones. Monica herself had never travelled further north than Camden.

"Yes, Doctor."

He took the next seat to her. He smelled of soap.

"My name is Dan. Can you tell me why you're here today? Laura over there," he pointed at the reception desk, "told me you want to voluntarily admit yourself to the psychiatric ward. I am in charge there and before we take that step, I need to understand your reasons for coming here today."

Monica looked up at the ceiling before returning her gaze to those wide, trusting, brown eyes.

"Jesus tells me to kill myself so I can be with God. I'm a good Catholic. From Malta. Valetta. I don't want to disobey him, but I'm frightened. What if he's Lucifer in disguise?"

Dan smiled and laid a hand on her right forearm, covering a tattoo of a rose.

"Don't worry. We'll keep you safe. At least for a few days while we work out what's going on. Why don't you stand up and come with me? We can fill out a couple of forms and then find you somewhere to stay." He looked down at her rings. "Strictly speaking, we should take those away from you, but I think you can be trusted to be a good girl, can't you?"

She looked down at her hands and flexed her thick fingers.

"Completely, Dan," she said, then winked.

* * *

Back in his office, Dan closed the door and sat at his desk. Resting dead centre on the closed lid of his laptop was a small, padded envelope. In neat black capitals across the front, someone had written DAN HOCKLEY. He picked it up and squeezed it experimentally. Whatever it contained was hard and irregularly shaped. It moved under his fingers as if jointed somehow.

He pulled the red tab at the side of the sealed flap to open the envelope. He upended it and smiled when he saw what slid out onto his palm. A black leather key fob bearing a metal shield, quartered with red and black stripes and deer antlers, with a black prancing horse in the centre. Across the top, in the unmistakeable font of the German car maker, was the word, PORSCHE. A cardboard label was attached to the split-ring by a piece of white cotton. On it, in more black capitals, someone had printed:

FOR SERVICES RENDERED.

He picked up the internal phone to speak to his secretary.

"Fran, who put this Jiffy Bag on my desk?"

"I did, Dan. A motorbike courier dropped it off ten minutes ago. Is there a problem? Do you want me to call security?"

"No, no, it's fine. Just curious, that's all. It's probably a medical sample. One of those creative pharmaceutical PR companies having a bit of fun, I expect. Listen, can you reschedule the rest of my appointments for this afternoon? I have to go out."

The call ended, he slid the key fob into his pocket, grabbed his jacket from the hook on the back of his door and headed for the lift. His normal walk to the car park took five minutes. This one took four.

As a consultant, Hockley had his own space, with his surname painted in tall white letters at the front edge. Usually, his two-year-old VW Golf GTI would have occupied the space, but today it was being serviced and the space should have been empty. Instead, facing out and broadening his smile to a full grin, sat a scarlet 1980s Porsche 911 Cabriolet. As bright and shiny as the day it had rolled off the production line. It was a sunny day and the roof was down.

He settled himself into the caramel-coloured leather seat and twisted the key in the ignition. The roar from the engine set his pulse racing and he pulled away making a mental note to write a proper thank-you letter.

11

GLORIA. FROM MALTA

"WELL?"

Other Stella was sitting in an armchair in the corner of the communal area, glaring at Stella. Stella glared back.

"Well, what?" she whispered.

"Well, how are you going to get out of this loony bin, dummy? Or did you plan to spend the rest of your days doing fucking jigsaws and popping Prozac?"

"I'm going to demonstrate to Dan that contrary to what that bastard Akuminde said about me, I am perfectly sane."

"Good luck with that. You don't think the whole '*I'm gonna moiderize ya*' business with the Glock will be a problem, then?"

"I've thought about that. We've been looking at it the wrong way. Treating it as part of this situation instead of something separate."

"Explain?"

"It's simple. I don't know why it's taken me so long to figure it out. Look. The first problem is getting out of here. That requires them to agree I have capacity. That I'm mentally stable, in other words."

"Yep, got that. I know exactly the same amount of law as you do, remember?"

"Fine. So they do that and they can't hold me under the section any more. It might take twenty-eight days but I can wait that long."

"And then what? You're out and facing firearms charges at best and attempted murder at worst."

"No! That's just it, don't you see? How can Collier possibly charge me? He'd end up having to expose PPM. He'd be putting himself at the centre of the investigation. That's why he put me in here. Out of the way."

Other Stella shifted her weight in her chair.

"Just for a moment, let's say you're right. And I agree, what you're saying does have merit. They won't be able to hold you here for ever. So my question to you is, why?"

"Why, what?"

"Why did he stick you in here, dipshit? What's the plan?"

"I don't know. Maybe he's going to try to have me moved to a high-security psychiatric hospital. But I won't let that happen. Despite everything he and his little gang of murderers have got up to, this is still England. We don't stuff people away in psych hospitals just to make them disappear."

Stella suddenly tired of being interrogated by her inner demon. She rose from the chair and walked to the far end of the room, relieved to see that Other Stella had vanished once more. She found a free armchair by one of the tall windows that overlooked an inner courtyard. She'd just picked up a celebrity magazine when a heavyset woman with dyed blonde hair and a smoker's lined face slumped into the chair opposite her. Her nicotine-stained fingers were adorned with chunky gold rings.

Stella stared down at the pages before her. They depicted a young couple smiling vapidly at the camera, both dressed in white, with identical orange tans and over-styled hair. The woman, "model and aspiring actress, Tia," had thick brown eyebrows and about fifty thousand quid's worth of plastic surgery between her hairline and the "stunning diamond necklace" that descended into a cleavage as deep as the Grand Canyon. Her "ecstatic husband-to-be, Caspian" had skin that appeared to have been polished using an industrial buffer. His designer stubble couldn't mask a weak chin that seemed to recede into his open-necked silk shirt.

"All the same, aren't they?"

Stella looked up.

The woman opposite her was pointing a brown-tipped index finger at the photograph.

"Who are?"

"Them celebrities! They never done a proper day's work in their life, have they? Just famous for being famous. I mean, look at her. If those boobs are real then I'm Margaret Thatcher."

Stella laughed. It was the first time she'd been able to since she'd seen her niece, Polly. When was that? Jesus! It seemed such a long time ago.

"I was never a fan, to be honest."

"What?" The woman's eyes widened. "She put this country back on its feet, she did. Plus, she was a woman. You should be a fan."

"Just because she had tits and a handbag doesn't make her a role model for women. I never saw the benefits."

"She wasn't afraid of hard work. And she liked people who were the same. Take the Jews, for example. She liked them because they worked hard. Pulled themselves up by their bootstraps. Like us."

"Us?"

"Sorry, darling. Where are my manners? I'm Gloria. I'm Maltese. Came here in the nineties. So I'm an immigrant. But she didn't mind where you came from as long as you worked hard and didn't sponge off the state."

Stella leaned across the table and shook hands.

"Stella. Maybe we should just agree to differ about Thatcher."

"Fair enough. Sorry. I get a bit over-excited sometimes, that's all."

"Is that why you're in here?"

"Oh, no. I'm here to get you out."

12

A FRIEND OF VICKY'S

WHATEVER Stella had been expecting the woman to say, it wasn't this.

"I beg your pardon?"

The woman smiled. She looked behind her. The duty nurse, a slender blonde about Stella's age, was sitting with a young woman with straggly black hair and a ladder of scars up the inside of her left arm.

"I'm a friend of a friend of yours. Vicky Riley."

Stella sat back in her chair. She hadn't spoken to the freelance journalist since the day she'd thrown Charlie Howarth out of his own office window. Now, a middle-aged Maltese woman built like a professional wrestler had appeared in a psychiatric ward claiming to know her.

"How do you know Vicky?"

"I'm what she likes to call one of her sources. I'll be honest with you, Stella. I don't know what line of work you're in on the outside. But me, I'm afraid I haven't always managed to keep my nose clean. Nothing too bad, but I know a few people in the drugs trade. Now and again I let Vicky know little titbits about what's happening. She thinks she's found a way to get you out of here. Something about a faulty sectioning process."

"But how? I mean, it all happened so quickly. How did she know I was in here?"

"She didn't say. Must have a contact at the hospital. Look. Let's not talk here. One of these nutcases will probably think we're plotting to take over his brain and tell one of the doctors. You know the chapel?"

It was one of the few places the residents of the psychiatric ward were allowed to venture unaccompanied. No sharp edges. Nothing they could use to harm themselves. Unless you counted staring at bland art prints of a vaguely spiritual, non-denominational character until they wanted to scream.

Stella nodded.

"Meet me there at lunchtime. I overheard one of the nurses saying it's always empty."

With that, the woman rose from the chair with a wheeze of breath and walked off towards the nurses' station.

Unable to remain in the large, bright room with the mumblers and the shakers, the screamers and the twitchers, the catatonic and the manic, Stella retreated to the sanctuary of her own room. She lay back on the bed, free, for once, of her alter ego's mocking presence, and closed her eyes. Then she opened them again. They'd allowed her a digital clock-radio. She set it to come on at 12.30 p.m., then lay back and stared at the ceiling. At some point she fell asleep. She dreamed of Lola. A laughing, smiling girl of five who looked a lot like Polly. As she swung her daughter round in a sunlit park fringed with deep-red copper beeches, Lola started crying. Then screaming. Stella watched in horror as her daughter's face blackened and peeled away before her whole body smouldered for a second then burst into flame. With a scream, she let go of Lola's crackling hands.

She sat straight up, soaked in sweat.

"Jesus fucking Christ!" she said. "When I get out of here, Adam, I'm going to make you suffer an eternity for every second my little baby was in pain."

She checked the time. 12:25. She turned off the alarm and got to her feet. On the way to the chapel, she went into the shared bathroom and splashed cold water over her face. Peering at herself in the mirror she saw a red-eyed woman with a haunted expression beneath the pixie cut of bleached-blonde spikes. The light above the mirror was bright, and she held her hands out in front of her, palms up, under the blue-white glare. She'd paid a heroin-addicted Greek plastic surgeon to remove her fingerprints the last time she'd been in Marbella, returning Ronnie Wilks's holdall of cash. Not being able to spare the enormous sum Yiannis Terzi had asked for, Stella had gone after two Albanians who had blinded his medical student daughter in one eye to encourage him to pay protection. After kneecapping both men, she'd shot one through his own eye, while the other had tumbled, she hoped to his death, over the edge of a ravine.

Without prints, she was freer than the average murderer to go about her business undiscovered. Though as her end-game involved suicide, she wondered why she'd bothered in the first place.

"You never know, Stel," said the identical woman standing beside her at the sink. "You might find you can make a career out of this. Then being dab-free would be a distinct competitive advantage."

"Fuck off!" Stella said without looking round.

She left the bathroom, shoving the door hard behind her, though its damped closer rendered the gesture little more than an excuse to jar her shoulder.

The hospital authorities had located the chapel at the very end of the corridor that ran beside the psychiatric ward. Perhaps they were afraid that with so many of their patients suffering from religious delusions, the presence of even a non-denominational place of worship might provide fuel for the fire. In fact, the room beyond the pale pine door wasn't even labelled as a chapel. The sign on the door read, "Mindfulness Space."

Stella rolled her eyes as she pulled the door towards her and entered.

The room beyond the door was unoccupied. Maybe fifteen feet to a side, it held half a dozen of the ubiquitous armchairs upholstered in royal blue fabric. A window looked out onto a car park. The walls held yet more of the bright, colourful paintings that someone in facilities had clearly bought in a job lot. Stella suspected the artist probably specialised in "uplifting art for troubled minds" or some such rubbish. They made her want to throw them spinning to the ground, three storeys down, had she only been able to open the window beyond the white-painted concertina shutters.

She sat in the chair nearest the window and crossed her legs at the ankle. She folded her arms. Then unfolded them. She stood and paced over to the far wall to inspect the signature at the bottom of a print depicting horses running along a beach, the sun setting in a blaze of orange and red behind them. The door opened, startling her. Turning she saw Gloria enter the room and pull the door closed behind her.

Stella realised her pulse was racing. The woman knew Vicky. Was one of her sources. Maybe she could get her out of here.

"You said you knew Vicky," she said. "Where is she? Tell me."

Gloria shook her head.

"Not here. I found somewhere better."

"Where? There's only the communal room and our bedrooms. And I think they're all covered by CCTV."

By way of answer Gloria held up a small brass key.

"Look what I got."

"What's it for?"

"The stairwell."

"How did you get that?"

"You know I said I was in the drugs trade?" Stella nodded. "Only in a small way, mind. Well, before that I used to help my old man work the crowds up West. Leicester Square, Oxford Street, Piccadilly Circus, you know. He was a dip. Taught me all his tricks before he passed over."

"You took it off one of the nurses?"

"That blonde one who looks a bit like you. Same short hair. Come on."

She flashed Stella a conspiratorial wink-and-grin then turned and pushed through the door.

The ward was deserted. Everyone had moved, or *been* moved, to the canteen to collect their tray of institutional food. Like a couple of children slipping out of school, the two women hurried to the far end of the corridor. Gloria unlocked the door and they were through and onto a landing. The floor was concrete, painted grey. White railings surmounted by a black plastic handrail spiralled down the staircase to the ground floor and basement beyond.

Stella turned to Gloria and opened her mouth to speak.

"Did Vicky—"

Her question was cut off by an incoming right hand, which smashed into the side of her face, knocking her round in a half-circle. She staggered back and fell to her knees, tasting blood in her mouth. Gloria Danktesh had reverted to Monica Zerafa.

13

ALL THAT GLISTENS

MONICA kicked her in the ribs and delivered another blow to the back of her head. The gold rings opened a long cut on Stella's scalp and she reached round to feel the damage. Her palm came away wet with blood.

"Now for the final jump, dearie," Monica said. "Poor little suicidal Stella just couldn't cope with the voices in her head."

Stella felt the older woman's hard hands grab her beneath her armpits. She was dragging her towards the handrail.

Instead of trying to pull free, Stella back-pedalled her heels against the smooth flooring, pushing back into her attacker's body. The added impetus made the woman stagger, and in that moment, Stella straightened. Without thinking of her scalp wound, she dropped her head forward for a second then jerked backwards. She began the movement with her hips and used every muscle in her back and neck to accelerate her skull into the woman's face.

The women shrieked in unison. Stella as the cut on the back of her head took another impact, Monica as her nose broke with a sound like a stick snapping. Their screams echoed and bounced off the hard surfaces of the stairwell.

In that moment, Stella twisted halfway round and wrenched herself free of the older woman's wrestler-like grip. She was panting, dragging oxygen into her lungs.

With a grunt of effort, Monica lunged forwards, hands extended, fingernails aimed at Stella's eyes. Adrenaline numbing her pain, Stella found herself with enough time to see the incoming attack. Almost as if Monica were moving in slow motion.

"Her knee, Stel," Other Stella shouted. But this time from directly between Stella's ears.

Stella ducked under the approaching arms and kicked hard on top of Monica's right knee. The whole leg folded back on itself as if the joint had been put on the wrong way round. The ligaments, and the patellar tendon holding the kneecap in place, sheared in a volley of dull pops.

Monica's face seemed to split in half as her mouth opened wide in a silent scream of agony. She staggered back towards the handrail.

Stella leapt forward and shoved her clawed fingers at Monica's crêpey breastbone and pushed hard, accelerating Monica's progress towards the bannister. As the small of Monica's back met the handrail, Stella hooked her foot around her right calf and levered her up, pushing harder on her chest until her centre of gravity was up and over the edge.

Finding her voice again, Monica screamed. But it was too late. Arms windmilling, she rotated over the handrail.

She stretched out her right hand towards Stella as she fell. The grabbing fingers missed Stella's face by half an inch and smacked down onto the handrail. Stella watched, horrified, as they closed reflexively on the plastic grip of the upper surface. Monica had saved herself.

Then Monica's weight made its presence felt. Her body descended past the level of the handrail and, as it dropped towards the abyss, her hand slipped round to the underside of the rail and slid sideways between two of the square-section metal balusters.

With a sound like a butcher's knife being sharpened on a steel, her gold rings whistled down the metal rods as her hand turned through ninety degrees. When it hit the bottom of the bannister's steel frame, Monica's body was completely below the level of the floor and picking up speed.

The thick gold rings on her index and little fingers jammed against the rods, turning her hand into a stopper knot on a cable of flesh and bone. With two loud cracks, Monica's shoulder dislocated and her wrist snapped. She screamed.

"Yell all you like, darling," Other Stella said. "They'll just think it's one of the loonies in here having a moment."

White faced and swinging gently back and forth from her broken wrist, Monica looked up at the woman she'd been sent to kill.

"Help me, please. Mother of God, help me!"

Other Stella looked back. But not into her pleading eyes. At the hand, trapped against the steel rods by the thick gold rings.

"Never went in for much in the way of rings," she said, squatting and reaching for the woman's hand. "Just these two."

She held out her left hand and straightened the fingers into a fan.

"Wedding and engagement. Oh, and this one."

She held out her right, presenting the eternity ring.

"The diamond's for her little girl. Lola. Did you know they burnt her to death? I wonder what the Mother of God would make of that, eh? Because here's the thing, Gloria. Or whatever your name is."

She reached for the woman's hand and tugged hard on the ring on her middle finger. It came free, bringing a shred of skin with it.

Monica's breath was coming in fast, shallow wheezes.

"No! Please!"

The ring on her fourth finger followed.

"It's all too fucking late," Other Stella said with a smile.

Monica's hand started sliding between the steel rods. With the two rings gone, the fingers were able to squash together by a few fractions of an inch. Just enough. But the harsh steel edges of the rods didn't want to give up their catch. With a wet, ripping sound, her hand – in the medical parlance common in the hospital – degloved. The stark red flesh and white bones emerged from the glove of skin like a baby from a caul. Monica Zerafa's screams continued all the way to the ground.

Other Stella leant over the handrail and watched her fall, blood spraying from the damaged blood vessels in her hand in scarlet arcs that spattered the stairwell on her short journey to the bottom.

With a lurch, Stella found herself leaning over the handrail. Other Stella whispered in her ear before vanishing.

"Oops."

The crunch as Monica Zerafa's head met the concrete floor made Stella want to vomit, but she swallowed hard and turned away. She looked down at the bloody glove of skin, lying between the two steel rods as if left there by a careless cleaner. Looked away.

Holding a hand to the back of her head, which was now hurting like a bastard and dripping blood into her collar, she pushed through the door and back into the corridor.

14

STOPPING ELSIE

BECKY was back on duty. As Stella emerged into the communal room with a crash from the door into the corridor, the nurse looked up.

"Oh, my God, Stella! What happened!" she shouted.

The patients who had returned from lunch swivelled their heads in unison at Becky's cry. Their expressions were a mixture of horror, fear and curiosity. Eyes dulled by drugs, or wide and staring. Hands fluttering over mouths. Smiles flitting inappropriately across faces normally slack from inattention.

Stella had been intending to put on an act and stage a graceful collapse into the nearest armchair. Instead, her body made up its own mind to do it for real. Vision blurring, she fell sideways until her shoulder banged into the wall. Then she slid down until her bottom hit the floor. Legs straight out in front of her, she watched Becky rushing towards her before the curtains closed and everything turned black.

"That was an absolute quality move, Stel."

Stella opened her eyes. She found herself sitting on a white-painted bench

73

looking across a body of water to a white stone city on a hill. Crowning its summit was the hemispherical dome of a cathedral. It reminded of her of St Paul's. But the temperature was in the nineties. The sky was a pure, cobalt blue. And the people around her were speaking no language she recognised.

She turned to her right. Richard was looking at her. His skin was tanned beneath his white linen shirt. The honey-brown colour contrasted with his cropped blond hair. Lola sat gurgling on his lap.

"You sound like her," Stella said.

"Who, darling?"

"You know, Other Stella."

He smiled indulgently and bounced Lola on his lap until she let out a squeak of pleasure.

"The way you butted that Maltese bitch with the back of your head. She never saw it coming. Hurt like fuck though, didn't it?"

"Where are we?"

"Don't you recognise it? You should."

Stella looked at the cathedral across the water. Listened to the voices swirling around her – the sounds were almost Arabic.

"Malta?"

"We spent our honeymoon in Valetta."

"Did we? I must have forgotten. I thought it was Sicily."

"No. It was Malta. You remember. You remember everything. You remember what you were like when we first met. Ambitious. Funny. Embarrassingly honest. Passionate about the law. Oh, and not a serial killer."

Stella frowned and tried to stand. But something was preventing her from rising. She looked down. Lola had climbed onto her lap. She weighed a ton. An iron child. She looked up into her mother's eyes.

"It's true, Mummy," she said, in the same mocking tone that came from Richard's smirking lips. "By my reckoning, you've killed, ooh, let me think," she held up a pudgy hand, dimpled over the knuckles, and counted on her fingers, "Moxey, Ramage, Fieldsend, Howarth, Ragib ... Oops! Ran out of fingers. Start again. That fat bloke with the shotgun in Freddie McTiernan's lockup, the guy in the Beemer who tried to kill you ... um, ooh, yes, the two Albanians shaking down nice Dr Terzi. Oh, and Tamit Ferenczy and, she winked twice, his two bodyguards. There! Twelve. I'm all out of fingers. And eyes."

74

"But they killed you and Daddy. I had to."

"Yes. You did. And don't forget that bad man, Collier. I burnt to a crisp because of him. And Daddy didn't come off much better."

Stella looked over at Richard. He smiled apologetically. The top half of his head was smashed like an eggshell and he was wearing the top of a red cast-iron pillar box like a hat.

Stella screamed.

People were pulling her to her feet. People with strong arms and gentle grips. Becky and a brown-skinned nurse she'd spoken to once or twice. What was his name? Hamish? That was it.

Hamesh was clamping a wad of something soft to the back of Stella's head.

"Come on," he said. "Come and sit down, Stella."

They led her to the nearest royal-blue armchair. She slumped down immediately, groaning from the throbbing pain at the back of her head.

Becky knelt in front of her while Hamesh maintained pressure on the makeshift dressing. Becky's face was crimped with concern, her eyebrows drawn together and her mouth turned down.

"I've called for a wheelchair. We'll get you over to A&E. They'll stitch up that gash and then we can talk properly. But what happened? Where were you? And how did you get out of the ward?"

"It was Gloria. She said she had something she needed to tell me about Adam Collier. My boss?"

"Yes, I know who he is."

"She stole a key from one of the nurses. She took me into the stairwell. Then she went crazy. Sorry. I mean she, well, she did. She attacked me. Hit me from behind with those gold knuckledusters she wears. She tried to kill me, Becky. She tried to throw me over the bannister."

"Where is she now?"

"I fought back. I had to. I thought she was going to kill me."

"Yes, I'm sure you did. But where is she, Stella? Where's Gloria?"

"Where she tried to put me. She overbalanced and went over the bannister. Her hand got trapped between the uprights."

Becky's eyes widened.

"You left her swinging there?"

Stella shook her head, then grimaced as the sudden movement set off a blast of pain at the back of her skull.

"Go and see."

Leaving Hamesh to wait with Stella, Becky stood up and ran down to the end of the corridor and unlocked the security door.

She reappeared moments later, white-faced. Back with Stella and Hamesh, she knelt in front of Stella again.

"We have to call the police."

"I know. Do it. But please can you hurry up with that wheelchair? I think I'm going to faint again."

While Becky was talking to the police, Hamesh wheeled Stella out of the psychiatric ward, along a series of corridors, down in a lift and along a grey vinyl-floored corridor to A&E.

Stella had spent her fair share of time hanging around in accident and emergency departments waiting for suspects, or occasionally witnesses, to be stitched, stomach-pumped or sedated. Mercifully, she'd largely avoided the places as a patient or … What did they call it these days? Service user? The NHS was as full of pointless jargon as the police.

"What do we have here, then?" a triage nurse said, approaching Stella but speaking over her head to Hamesh.

"She was attacked by another patient," Hamesh said. "Nasty laceration to the back of the head."

The triage nurse went round to the back of the wheelchair, and Stella felt firm but gentle pressure pushing her head forward. She let her chin drop towards her chest and gasped as a sudden wave of nausea flooded her.

"You all right, pet?" the nurse said. "Not going to faint on me, are you?"

"I'm fine. How bad is it?"

"You're going to need a few stitches and I daresay the doctor will want to give you a tetanus shot while she's about it. That's a nasty gash. Any idea what they used?"

"A fourteen-karat knuckleduster."

The nurse laughed.

"If I didn't know better, I'd say you were a cop with that kind of humour."

"I *am* a cop."

"Oh." The nurse re-entered Stella's field of vision and squatted down in front of her. "Sorry you ended up in the psych ward. Job got on top of you, did it?"

Stella shrugged.

"Something like that."

"Well, let's get you patched up physically first, then Hamesh and his colleagues can sort you out on the inside, eh? I'll get you the next free slot for surgery, OK?"

"Thanks," Stella said. "I appreciate it."

Ten minutes later, Stella was sitting on a bed in a screened-off cubicle in the middle of the ward, while a nurse shaved the back of her head.

"I like your hair," she said. "Very punky."

"You don't look old enough to remember punk," Stella said, wincing as the razor clipped the edge of the wound.

"My mum and dad were punks. Sometimes I used to get their records out and have a listen. The Sex Pistols, The Stranglers, Polly Styrene and X-Ray Spex."

"Your mum and dad? Jesus, do you have any idea how old that makes me feel?"

"Sorry. There, smooth as a baby's bum. Now, you just hang on here and I'll tell Miss Petersen you're ready when she is."

Miss Petersen turned out to be a frighteningly efficient and very well-spoken A&E consultant with long red hair tied back with a black velvet scrunchie.

She had just "popped" the anaesthetic in on each side of the gash when a high-pitched scream shattered the relative calm of the room. Moments later, an elderly lady, dressed in a backless hospital gown that revealed a scrawny behind and spindly, blue-veined legs, staggered into the centre of the room, grabbed a metal bowl full of surgical instruments and hurled it at the wall before tugging frantically at the gown until it came free of her wrinkled frame.

"They took my Bobby!" she screamed. "He was going to play for Chelsea, he was. Then they took him from me!"

She ran off, crashing into trolleys and tearing down cubicle curtains as she went.

A pair of nurses in green scrubs arrived in A&E, red-faced and panting. One shouted at the old woman.

"Elsie, come here, please. You're frightening the other patients."

They advanced on Elsie, who bent to pick up a yellow plastic waste bin marked "SHARPS."

The consultant, Miss Petersen, put her newly-threaded needle down.

"Oh, for God's sake!" she muttered.

Turning to a nurse trying to protect a trolley from any further attack by Elsie, she barked out an order.

"Haloperidol. Now!"

The nurse rootled among the glass phials on his trolley, selected one, added a syringe and handed both to the consultant.

"Need a hand?" he asked.

"Yes, please. You grab her while I stick her full of this."

Together they began approaching the old woman who was keening in distress as she tried to raise the waste bin over her head.

Stella looked around. All eyes – of patients and medics – were on the trio. She slid down off the edge of the bed and took a few quick steps over to the abandoned drugs trolley. Looked down. Picked up a glass vial and a syringe package and pocketed them. She returned to her cubicle just in time to watch as Miss Petersen jabbed her loaded hypodermic into the old woman's almost fleshless right buttock. With a sigh, Elsie collapsed into the waiting arms of the nurse who had helped corner her. Her watery blue eyes rolled up in their sockets.

"Wow! Proper knockout drops. What did that posh bitch call them?"

Stella didn't even turn to greet Other Stella. She had a knack of appearing at moments of heightened stress or excitement.

"Haloperidol. I was actually going to see if I could find any ketamine."

"Yeah, that would have done it, too, I guess. We've seen enough junkies do the floppy dance after a bit too much Special K, haven't we?"

"Piss off! She's coming back."

Brushing her hands together as if she'd just finished a particularly gruelling *Times* crossword, Miss Petersen arrived back at Stella's cubicle.

"Sorry about the delay. Silly old dear does that about once a week. Never had to give her the old chemical cosh before though."

"Who's Bobby?"

"Her baby."

"Bit old to have a baby, isn't she?"

"She had him in 1950. At fifteen. He was taken away immediately for adoption. Poor old Elsie lost the plot. She's been in and out of institutions ever since. She shouldn't really be here but they can't find a bed for her in a nursing home so here she stays, grieving for Bobby and occasionally finding new and ingenious ways to test the resources of the NHS. Now, let's get this rather *flamboyant* laceration closed up and those scratches tended to, and you can be on your way."

15

ACCIDENT & EMERGENCY

AS the stitches went in, Stella surveyed the comings and goings of one of London's busiest A&E departments. Young guys with hands wrapped in towels, still cocky enough to flirt with the nurses despite the blood dripping onto the vinyl flooring. White-faced mums and dads accompanying stunned-looking kids with cut hands or amateurishly bandaged wrists. Drunks with smashed faces – what happens when the pavement or the boot of someone more sober than you comes up to greet you at high speed – railing against the bastards who'd kicked them into this state and relieved them of their wallets.

And the oddities. The rarities. The freaks who would fuel after-hours unwinding sessions in the pub. Police, nurses, paramedics, doctors, firefighters: they shared a macabre sense of humour that was never so acute as when they were "rescuing," treating or just generally dealing with members of the public who'd decided on the spur of the moment to do something fucking stupid. All were processed at the entrance to the machine that sucked them in broken and spat them out whole again.

Highlight of her afternoon was a portly middle-aged man wearing a mustard-coloured waistcoat over a Tattersall shirt and a pair of rose-pink trousers that he clutched to his legs at mid-thigh. He'd a pale-pink bath towel wrapped round his middle. Without even needing to overhear the consultation occurring in the cubicle next to hers, Stella knew already what he'd done. Not the details. But the general proposition. His furiously blushing cheeks said it all.

The doctor treating him was in her midthirties. An Indian woman with high cheekbones, kohl-rimmed eyes of the deepest brown and a thick mane of jet-black hair.

"You had an accident, is that right?" she asked in an educated voice Stella decided was clearly calibrated to carry to all four corners of the room.

"Yes," the man mumbled.

"What kind of an accident?"

"Well, you see, doctor, I had just got out of the shower in the en suite when the lightbulb in the bedroom ceiling went, so I had to change it, you see."

He cleared his throat, presumably hoping the doctor would take pity on him and not force the rest of the confession from his reluctant lips. No such luck.

"And—?"

"And I'd got the light bulb out of the box when I slipped off the chair I was standing on. My feet were wet from the shower, you see. And then, well, and then—"

"—and then you fell on your bottom and the lightbulb was accidentally inserted into your rectum?"

His reply was all but inaudible. Stella smiled despite the grimness of her own situation.

"Well, we'd better get it out then, hadn't we?"

The curtain was whisked aside so that the metal rings whistled along the thin pole suspended from the ceiling.

"Nurse!"

"Yes, Doctor?"

"I need a speculum, a pair of artery forceps and some KY Jelly, please."

"Yes, Doctor." Stella watched the two exchange complicit glances. Not smiles, but not far off, either.

The nurse reappeared a few moments later clutching a couple of stainless steel implements, fresh from the autoclave, which sat in a corner, like an oversized microwave oven, emitting clouds of steam each time the door was opened.

"Now then," the Indian doctor said. "Let's just insert this," a sharp indrawing of breath from the man, "into there," a gasp, "and open it up like this," a groan, "Aha! A sixty-watt energy saver. Shame you haven't power up there or we could do a routine colonoscopy at the same time."

Behind Stella's head Miss Petersen paused from stitching to emit a stifled laugh.

"Now, I'll just grip that— damn! Missed it – there we go, with these, and then we just pull gently, but steadily—"

"Oh, Jesus, that really hurts, Doctor."

"Yes, it will. Your anus is not designed to expel lightbulbs. Or to receive them, come to that. Now for the tricky bit. Can you take a breath and let it out slowly, please?

Stella heard the man inhale dutifully, noted a shudder in his breath. Waited.

He yelped in pain.

"Bingo!" the doctor said, the note of triumph detectable.

A couple of the patched-up drunks gave a slurred cheer.

"Well done, Doc!" one called out.

"Bet that's taken a weight off your mind, mate," another called.

Over the good-natured banter, Miss Petersen finished her final suture.

"There we are," she said, in a voice that, unlike her colleague's, was clearly only intended for her patient's ears. "They'll dissolve on their own in a couple of weeks. When your hair grows back, nobody will ever know. Can you find your way out? I think Hamesh is waiting for you in A&E reception."

"Yes, and thanks."

Stella stood, turned and shook hands.

Miss Petersen nodded her head sideways at the neighbouring cubicle.

"Sometimes I think they should call these places Accident & Stupidity."

Stella smiled. And for a moment, their statuses were equal, consultant and cop, not doctor and patient.

As predicted, Hamesh was sitting at the end of a row of blue-upholstered chairs, the wheelchair by his left hip.

"Ah, there you are!" he said, beaming. "All done?"

"Good as new." Stella plonked herself down into the wheelchair. "Home, James, etc."

"You not feeling strong enough to walk, then?"

"It's not that. I just fancy being pushed."

She leaned back to look up at Hamesh, whose face bore an expression part indignation and part tolerant good humour.

"Cheeky mare!" he said, seizing the handles and waltzing her off down the corridor.

As they entered the psych ward, Stella and Hamesh were greeted by Dan Hockley. He limped towards them, brow furrowed.

"Stella! I am so sorry. Are you OK?"

"I'm fine, Dan. Really. Nothing I haven't had worse on a rough Saturday night. On duty," she hurriedly added as Dan's eyebrows shot up.

"Can you come to my office please? There's someone here to see you. To ask you some questions about the attack."

Stella followed Dan through the communal area, avoiding a drooling young man whose antipsychotic medication clearly needed a dose adjustment, and towards his office.

Reaching the door, Dan held it open and motioned for Stella to precede him.

"Thanks," she said, turning her head to him as she stepped over the threshold.

The gesture meant she heard the visitor's voice before she saw his face. Or his crisp, black uniform, adorned with silver.

"Hello, Stella."

Stella whirled round at the first syllable, trying to control her emotions.

16

VICTIM IMPACT STATEMENT

ADAM Collier rose to greet her. Through a determined effort of will, Stella stopped herself from attempting to break his neck with her bare hands.

"I'll be here to look after Stella's interests Detective Chief Superintendent," Dan said with a solicitous smile, "but the interview's your remit. I shan't interfere unless Stella becomes distressed."

Stella noticed that Collier had installed himself behind the desk. Ever ready to assume the power seat in any room. Dan took a seat in one of the armchairs.

She sat facing Collier across the desk. Behind her eyes, she could feel a wild fury spreading like a forest fire. Not just a rage, but a person that embodied it. She knew she had to retain control. If Other Stella pushed her way through the psychic membrane that separated them, she'd try to decorate Dan's office with Collier's entrails. Then Dan would intervene, sedate her, and that would be that. They'd transfer her to a high-security psychiatric hospital and she'd never see the light of day again.

"I'm so sorry you ended up in A&E, Stella," Adam opened.

"Thank you, sir." *Because you wanted me to end up in the morgue, didn't you?*

"I hear you sustained a nasty head wound."

"I'm just grateful it was only a gash. If Gloria had got her way, it'd be me with my head smashed in at the bottom of the stairwell instead of her."

"Can you tell me what happened?"

"She said she was going to help me get out of here. Said she'd stolen a key from one of the nurses. She took me out into the stairwell, then attacked me. She got a couple of kicks in, then she tried to heave me over the bannister. I fought back using what I considered reasonable force to defend myself. I think if you get a CSI to take scrapings from under my fingernails you'll find Gloria's blood and skin. As we struggled, she lost her footing and fell over the railing. I tried to save her, but she was much too heavy. You saw what happened, what got left behind. I was in shock." *You hear that? 'Reasonable force.' That's the law on my side for one. Two, a fucking great gash in the back of my skull. Three, my attacker's tissue under my nails: classic evidence of self-defence. Four, no witnesses. So it's my word or nothing.*

Collier shook his head and then leaned forward, steepling his thick fingers under his chin.

"There's no need for CSIs, Stella. It's pretty clear what happened. I just wanted to let you know you are in my thoughts. Even in here. I won't forget you."

His dark eyes were boring into hers.

She stared back.

Heard a distant scream of rage deep in her mind.

Felt red-painted fingernails scratching at the backs of her eyeballs.

Tried to ignore the shouted threats to Collier issuing from somewhere not so far from the surface of her consciousness.

Collier blinked first. At once, the murderous pressure building inside her evaporated.

You're scared, she thought. *You sent some Maltese Ma Barker in here after me, and all you have to show for it is the world's grottiest rubber glove. With Moxey and Ferenczy pushing up daisies, I make that nought for three.*

"Thank you. Sir. And I won't forget you either. Not while I have breath in my body. And if … when … Dan is able to satisfy himself I'm no danger to myself or anyone else and lets me out of here, believe me, you will be the first person I come to see."

Collier stood.

"I look forward to it, Stella. Really, I do. I'm afraid I have to go. Meeting at Scotland Yard. Take care of yourself, OK? Maybe avoid any more clandestine meetings in stairwells for a while."

Stella ignored his outstretched hand, not caring whether Dan made a little note on his ever-present clipboard about "diminished social skills." She stared straight ahead until she heard the door close behind Collier. Turning, she met Dan's gaze.

"What?"

He smiled.

"Nothing. But I think after today's little adventure, I tend to agree with your boss. Let's stay within the ward, OK?"

"Fine by me."

* * *

Dan was sliding into the Porsche's driving seat at 6.30 p.m., inhaling a wonderful aroma of leather, wax polish and petrol. The car was twenty-five years old but it made him feel like a small boy. His phone rang.

"If you want to hold onto that little Dinky toy I bought you, there's something you need to do for me."

"Look, I did what I could to give that Zerafa woman a clear field. I even saw to it she kept those ridiculous gold rings. And she fucked up. Christ! She must have weighed at least twice what Stella does. I don't know how she ended up on the losing side but—"

"It doesn't matter! Listen, you've got all kinds of powerful psychoactive drugs in there, haven't you?"

"I have, but—"

"So you could put her under permanently."

"— I'm also a doctor. The principle of *primum non nocere* is sacred. First, do no harm."

"Oh, come on, Dan. I think we're way past the Hippocratic Oath, don't you? Just because you don't have blood on your hands doesn't mean you get to walk away with a clean conscience. Or did you think I gave you a Porsche because you made an honest woman out of my sister? And let's not even get started on the drugs charge that I and my friends made vanish. You'd have been lucky to get a job as a cleaner, never mind a promotion to consultant. We own you, lock, stock and barrel."

Hockley looked down at the key he'd just inserted in the ignition.

"Fine. What do you want me to do?"

"Patients must have psychotic breaks all the time in there, yes?"

"Yes. Goes with the territory."

"So, here's the story. She freaks out in the middle of the night. When do they all top themselves? Three a.m., is it? You're forced to administer a powerful sedative. You call me first thing in the morning because she's one of my officers and you think I ought to know. I come to check on her and you leave me unattended in her room for a few minutes. Tragically, her heart gives out later that day. Death by misadventure. I give a statement to the press. Internal investigation clears you of any suspicion of wrongdoing. Life goes on."

"And when does all this happen?"

"No time like the present. Do it tonight."

17

MIDNIGHT TILL DAWN

SANITY. Stella had never given much thought to it. She'd mostly been too busy studying or pursuing her career to worry about her mental health. Of course, every copper knew of colleagues who'd hit the bottle or resigned on grounds of ill health, which as often as not meant stress. Then that day when Collier had called her into his office and told her Richard and Lola had been killed in a hit and run. A hit and run he'd conspired to make happen. Well, she sure found out about mental health after that. Even when she'd reset her relationship with booze and flushed her remaining antidepressants and tranquilisers down the toilet, she'd spent a good few months living in a partial fantasy world where two-and-a-half-month-old Lola had miraculously escaped a burning car and returned to live with her.

And now? She wasn't sure. She didn't *feel* crazy. Not *crazy*-crazy, anyway. Not talking-to-aliens-through-the-telly-crazy. Not wandering-down-Oxford-Street-naked-crazy. But then again, there remained the small matter of the woman sitting beside her on the bed. The woman with Stella's looks and murder in her eyes.

"Why haven't you got the same hair as me?" she asked Other Stella.

"What?"

"How come I've got the whole Annie Lennox blonde crop thing going on and you kept the brown ponytail?"

"Er, hello? I'm not a real person. I don't go to the hairdresser."

"I know that. But shouldn't you be, I don't know, keeping up with me or something?"

Other Stella tilted her head on one side and put a finger to the point of her chin.

"I've got bigger fish to fry, babe. Like getting us out of the booby hatch before Collier sends anyone else after you."

"So you reckon Gloria was on the PPM payroll?"

"I'm not so sure PPM is in a position to manage anything as complicated as a payroll, Stel. I mean, who's left? You did Ramage. Fairly comprehensively, if I may say so. Shot through both arms, kneecapped with a cleaver, a bit of self-inflicted dentistry then burnt half to death and shot in the head. Then we finished off Fieldsend, Howarth and Ragib together. That upper-class idiot De Bree popped his clogs before we could reach him. So we're left with Collier and a ragtag bunch of foot soldiers. But do I think she was doing Collier's bidding. No question in my mind. I mean, you know, yours."

She winked.

"I'm getting out of here tonight," Stella said.

"Oh, yes? How?"

"Stick around and you'll see. Now fuck off. I need a few hours' sleep."

Stella lay down on the bed, fully clothed, and closed her eyes. She felt a subtle shift in the air around her. Risked opening one eye. Other Stella had gone.

She checked the time: 8.57 p.m. Her head was throbbing beneath the analgesic blanket of ibuprofen and paracetamol Becky had delivered from the pharmacy. Her ribs weren't too happy either. Gloria, or whoever she was, hadn't cracked any, but her kick had turned Stella's left side a fetching shade of purple. To avoid concentrating on the pain, she tried to anticipate Collier's next move. At some point he'd try another attack. Surely now he'd give up sending hired muscle after her? Each of the three hitters so far was dead. But if not a psychopathic gangster – of either gender – then who, or how?

* * *

SITTING in his home office and circling his fingertips over his temples, Collier was struggling to answer exactly the same question. He was running out of ideas. The bloody woman was invincible. Where she'd learned to fight well enough to defeat people like Peter Moxey, Tamit Ferenczy and Monica Zerafa, he had no idea. He suspected it wasn't the unarmed defence tactics instructors at Hendon Police College. A few weeks earlier, he'd made a call to Special Agent Eddie Baxter at the FBI's Chicago field office, who'd confirmed that the offer of a sabbatical was still open. Collier had said to put the wheels in motion. Maybe it was time to put some distance between himself and Stella Cole. A tentative knocking at the door derailed his train of thought, which was barely out of the engine shed.

"Adam, are you coming to watch the film? It starts in a few minutes," Lynne Collier asked through the narrow gap she'd created.

He sighed. He needed her. But he couldn't confide in her. A teaching assistant in a local primary school? Christ! She'd have a fucking breakdown.

"Coming, darling," he said, levering himself up from the chair. "Why don't you fix us both a drink?"

"Already have. Come on, I don't want to miss the beginning."

Later, in bed, he freed his right arm, which she was using as a comforter, propped himself on one elbow and shook her awake.

"Huh? What is it, darling? Was I snoring?"

"No. You were fine. It's just, there's something I need to discuss with you. Something important."

"Can't it wait? I was having such a lovely dream."

"No. Come on, wake up properly. I'll go and make us a cup of tea."

He could feel his wife's baffled gaze on his back as he got out of bed, put on a dressing gown and left for the kitchen.

Returning with two mugs of tea, he sat on the edge of the bed and handed one over. Lynne was sitting up in bed, the duvet pulled up over her chest.

"Adam, what is it? What's up? You normally like to fall asleep cuddled up after we've done it."

He sipped his tea, which was too hot, and scowled as he burned his lip for the second time in three days.

"Do you remember that FBI guy we met that time we all went to Chicago for a holiday?"

"Yes. Why?"

"The thing is, he's invited me, well, to be honest he's pretty well begged me to go over there."

"What do you mean. To give a talk or something?"

"No. For a sabbatical. They have a programme for international law enforcement officers."

Lynne was wide awake now. She placed a hand on his free wrist.

"A sabbatical? For how long?"

He shrugged.

"The standard period is six months but off the record Eddie told me they'd be well disposed to recruiting a senior detective from the Met on a permanent basis and of course, we'd have to get citizenship, but apparently the Bureau really get behind you and as you can imagine that counts for a lot when you're talking to —"

"Hold on, darling. You're going way too fast. You're gabbling. Tell me again, slowly this time."

Collier realised he was nervous. His heart was racing, and he could feel the tightness in his chest that normally only appeared when he was meeting very senior law officers or politicians. He took another sip of tea. Inhaled.

"Six months to begin with. But if it works out, they could make it permanent. If," he reached for her hand, "we both felt it was for the best."

Lynne Collier sighed.

"Well, it's not as if my career's holding us back, is it? A teaching assistant in an inner city primary school where half the children are destined for the dole queue and the other half for encounters with the police."

"That's funny. I thought you'd be dead set against it. That I'd have to do some serious heavy lifting to persuade you. So you'd be OK with it? Leaving London. Moving to the States?"

She shrugged.

"Why not? If it'll help your career and get me out of this country, I'm all for it."

Collier smiled.

"Then I'll call Eddie tomorrow. I'll need to speak to Rachel Fairhill, too. But she's already given her blessing in principle, so with the Deputy Assistant Commissioner behind me, the rest will just be a formality." He paused. He knew why Lynne hadn't offered so much as a single word of opposition. Tonight was going to be one of those nights. He rolled his head on his neck and heard the joints in his spine crackle.

"You're thinking about Theo, aren't you?" he asked her.

"Why? Aren't you?"

"Not all the time. But yes, of course I think about him."

"I carried him, Adam. Nine months inside my belly. Then in a sling, or on my hip while you went straight back to work. I carried him in my arms when he was poorly and couldn't sleep. And since that bastard stabbed him after that concert, I've carried him in my heart. He was nineteen, Adam. My baby boy was only nineteen. He had his whole life before him. An engineering student. The brightest in his year, that's what he said his tutor told him. He was going to design spaceships, or solve global warming or invent cheap computers for poor kids in Africa. And what did that little thug do? Stuck a knife in his chest because he wouldn't give him his wallet."

Collier felt the old familiar lump in his chest. Like a cold block of stone. Hated how it made him feel. Powerless. Weak. Useless.

"Lynne, please don't let's do this again. You know—"

"I'll tell you what I know, Adam," she interrupted, eyes flashing now. She pointed her right index finger at him and for a moment his gaze dropped to her breasts where the duvet had fallen away. "I know that our son died because some junkie mugged him for twenty pounds. I know that even when the police finally arrested the little shit, his rich, privileged, entitled parents hired the best lawyers in London and saw to it that he received a ridiculous sentence. What did that defence barrister say? Oh, yes, I remember, 'A long spell in prison would ruin every chance of redemption this troubled young man has. He has admitted he cannot remember the circumstances of that fateful night. He has agreed to enter a drug rehabilitation programme …' Shall I go on? I can recite his whole closing speech from memory."

Collier realised he'd been holding his breath. He exhaled slowly.

"No. Please stop. I was in court, too, Lynne. Remember? I was the one who held your hand, who got you home without having to face that pack of jackals on the court steps. I was the one who got you into therapy at that private place. I was the one who paid for the psychiatrists, the drugs, everything!" He heard how his voice had increased in volume, and roughened in tone, but he couldn't stop himself. "Do you think it's been easy for me? Having to pretend to colleagues everything at home was just fine when all I had to come home to was a zombie for a wife so off her head on antidepressants and tranquilisers she hardly recognised me? Having to sit in meetings where some well-meaning bleeding-heart liberal or other from the Prison Reform Society lectured us about prisoners' rights and police brutality? I miss him, too. God, how I miss that boy."

Lynne was crying now and he leaned over to wipe the tears from her cheeks with the back of his finger.

"He's in Leeds now," she said, sniffing.

For a moment, Collier imagined his wife was taking about their son.

"Who is?"

Then reality reasserted itself. The other boy.

"Crispin Radstock. He's changed his name, by the way. Calls himself Simon Halpern. Doing very well for himself. He's an *entrepreneur*." She pronounced the word syllable by syllable, curling her lip and wrinkling her nose, as if she'd said "sewage worker" or "abattoir cleaner." "Rather a successful one. Pots of money. More even than his parents, apparently. Engaged, too. She's ever so pretty. Blonde, naturally. Thin. Good skin, no, *great* skin."

"Lynne, have you been following him on Facebook?"

"Facebook? No, darling. In Leeds. I take the day off now and again and get the train. It's only two hours and ten minutes from King's Cross. He doesn't know. I'm very careful. Very discreet."

Collier was struggling to make sense of what she was telling him. He'd imagined that since her mental state had settled down she'd got back into her job and that was that. Now he'd found out she was stalking their son's killer. Although the name change and move north would explain why he'd had no success tracking him in his early days as a member of PPM.

"He could lodge a complaint. The police could get involved. Stalking's a crime now. You need to stop doing that."

She shook her head.

"No, what I *need* is to see him in a hospital bed hooked up to those bloody machines, pipes and tubes going in and out of him, a ventilator pumping air into his poor lungs until those bloody doctors tell his parents that he's brain dead on account of all the blood that poured out of him through the hole in his chest and it would be kindest to turn off his life support. *That's* what I need!"

Collier gathered her into his arms and slid down until they were lying horizontally. How he wanted to tell her about the dinner he'd had with Leonard Ramage a few weeks after they'd buried Theo. And the one after that where Ramage had introduced him to "a few friends." The proposition that he join

Pro Patria Mori. The initial horror. Then the dawning realisation that this would be his way of getting justice for Theo and all the other victims failed by the legal system. Finally, the full-throated acceptance. But then, that would mean telling her how he and the other members had conspired to silence Richard Drinkwater, Stella Cole's nosy human-rights-lawyer husband. How Ramage had messed up the hit and run, killing the baby as well as the husband. And how, in an increasingly bloody fight, Stella had fought off and killed everyone he'd sent against her and was systematically wiping out PPM, one member at a time. No. Maybe there'd be a time one day. But this wasn't that day.

He glanced over at the digital clock: 2.43 a.m. – Stella should be on the receiving end of a serious dose of sedative any time now. And now he knew Radstock's new identity, he wondered whether he could finally draw a line under Theo's murder.

18

UNDER SEDATION

DAN Hockley put down the psychiatric journal he'd been reading in the harsh light of his desk lamp. The clock said 2.45 a.m. – the perfect time for catching someone unawares. The screamers had shut up for the night, and the drugs dispensed in miniature paper cups from the steel trolley were doing their jobs. Inducing or maintaining sleep. Reducing the symptoms of anxiety to the point those experiencing them could relax enough for their sleeping medication to work. Supressing the hallucinations that could have patients hammering at their doors begging to be freed from the ghosts of their dead mothers and fathers, werewolves and vampires. Or just the unnamed horrors that festered inside the mind in the daylight hours and then clamoured, clawed and scratched their way free during the hours of darkness. He pulled open his desk drawer and looked down at the white cardboard carton lying on top of the notebooks he stored there.

The lid bore a few lines of plain black text in unadorned typography. On the top line it read:

.   .   .

ANDY MASLEN

Suxamethonium – 1 mg/kg solution

Suxamethonium, or Sux for short, was a drug used in anaesthesia. As such, it was not a substance Dan Hockley ever employed himself. There were other, easier ways to knock out patients on the psychiatric ward. Ketamine and haloperidol being just two. They were just as effective at inducing unconsciousness as Sux and didn't carry the additional risk that the patient would stop breathing. Not a problem in an operating theatre with an intubated patient on a ventilator, and anaesthesiologists ready to tweak dosages and blend in other drugs to maintain life signs, but definitely a problem in a thinly staffed psych unit.

He unwrapped a syringe and picked up the vial of Sux. Strange how little of the drug you needed to knock a fully grown woman unconscious. The glass phial was so small. Less than half the size of his little finger. A sleek, glass cylinder topped with a circle of foil-backed plastic film. Printed on its side, the long, scientific name of the drug within. The drug that would sedate instantly when injected into the muscle, dropping the recipient like poor old Elsie in A&E earlier that day.

In went the slant-tipped needle, penetrating the foil-backed film with a tiny squeak. A bubble of air wobbled from one end of the vial to the other as it was upended and its contents drawn down into the barrel of the syringe.

Wanting to avoid the psych ward's communal area, Hockley turned right out of his office, and took a long, tortuous route through a couple of the general wards and back corridors, using staff-only doors and disused staircases, before arriving at the landing from which Monica Zerafa had taken her one-handed dive into the unknown. In front of him was the locked door to the corridor of bedrooms.

Arriving at Stella's room, Hockley slid his master key into the lock. Earlier that day, he'd taken the precaution of squirting a little WD-40 into the barrel, and the tumblers lined up silently. He took a breath, leaned down on the handle and was inside with the door shut behind him seconds later, heart pounding.

She was lying face down on the bed, fully clothed. Good. He didn't think he could bear to inject her while looking at her face. Something about her posture scratched against the surface of his brain like a burr. But he couldn't place it and instead, moved closer. Close enough that he could stretch out an arm and touch her. The nurses were supposed to administer sleeping pills or mild tranquilisers at bedtime. Nothing serious, just a little something to take the edge off being locked up in a ward full of crazy people and help the patients get some sleep. He paused and listened to her breathing. Steady. Slow and steady. Actually, very slow and steady. Her short blonde hair looked ash grey in the faint bluish light from the illuminated plug pushed into a wall socket by the bed.

He held the syringe up to the plug-light and checked there were no air bubbles in the barrel, flicking it with a fingernail and ejecting a thin stream of the clear liquid into the air. A few drops landed on her cheek and he tensed, ready to jam the hypo home if she woke. Nothing happened. Not even a snort of disturbed sleep from the cold drips on her cheek. He reversed his grip on the syringe and placed his thumb over the plunger. Leaned over her. Breathed in. Another catch in his mind. He ignored whatever signal his olfactory nerves were sending him.

He extended his right hand toward her buttocks – a physician's favoured spot for an intramuscular injection. Even a first-year medical student with Coke-bottle glasses and a severe case of the shakes couldn't miss the *gluteus maximus*. He placed the needle tip against the curve of her bottom. He was just increasing the pressure on the plunger when he stopped.

The posture. Who slept in the classic recovery position? And the smell? It was perfume. Not just any perfume, either. He recognised it. *La Vie Est Belle* by Lancôme. As worn by Lisa, the agency nurse he'd passed the time of day with after he'd finished his evening rounds. Lisa, the slender, short-haired blonde, about the same height and build as Stella Cole. Lisa, who liked working nights because, as she'd explained to Hockley, she could pursue her studies. "I want to train as a clinical psychologist," she'd told him, smiling shyly from under her fringe.

He shook the uppermost shoulder of the woman lying before him on the bed. No response, although her head did loll back on her neck, giving him a good view of Lisa's face.

"Shit!" Then again, with more venom. "Shit! What the fuck have you got me into, Adam?"

Back in his office and sweating profusely, he dragged out his phone and with shaking fingers tried to compose a text that would be informative and deniable all at the same time. In his haste, he hit send earlier than he meant to and had to start a new message.

* * *

While Hockley had been making his way to the staircase behind the psych ward, Stella was stalking her own victim. Keeping to the edge of the communal area, she slid through the darkness towards the nurses' station.

There she was. What was her name? Lina? Lisa? Bent over a book. Or was it a Sudoku? Illumination coming from a swan-necked lamp catching her short blonde hair and making it shimmer like silver. *Stay like that, with your back to me. Don't turn round. It's a book, OK, good. Hope it's a real page-turner. One that sucks you in until you forget you live in that fucked-up place called the real world.*

Stella inched closer. She held the syringe like a dagger, thumb over the plunger, ready to depress it the moment the needle was embedded in a muscle.

Four paces …

Three …

Two …

Ah! You've got your earbuds in, too! Good girl.

OK, I'm sorry it had to end like this.

Stella brought her fist up like an assassin's. Light from the desk lamp glinted off the tip of the needle, from which a drop of the sedative hung, suspended, like rain on a blade of grass. She closed with the nurse, silently, swiftly, and jabbed the syringe down.

In we go! Fast and true. Not too hard. Don't want to break the needle, after all. Now thumb that plunger in nice and smooth, all the way to the end.

The nurse jerked backward, but Stella's hand over her mouth and a restraining arm across her chest gave her no chance to raise the alarm before the drug kicked in.

There, there. Sleep now.

The nurse's eyelids fluttered, then closed. Stella held her, feeling the muscles soften, then relax completely.

Aaaand she's out. Thank you, Big Pharma!

Dragging Lisa's dead weight back from the communal area to Stella's room was hard, but not impossible. Thankfully, the nurse was on the slim side. Stella took a firm grip under her armpits, fingers interlaced over her sternum, then leaned back and pulled.

Stella laid the nurse on the bed, placing her face down, one arm down by her side, the other curled above her head. Right knee lifted, left leg straight. She retrieved her boots from the wardrobe and pulled them on. Then she lifted the NHS ID badge and lanyard free of the nurse's neck, taking care not to pull her hair or snag a rough edge on her nose. She slipped it over her own head, took the keyring off the nurse's belt and locked the door behind her as she left.

The walk through the communal area to the reception office at the far end was no more than thirty yards. As Stella walked between the armchairs, abandoned board games and card tables, it felt more like thirty miles. A large, white-faced station clock seemed to watch her progress down the room, and she could feel her pulse accelerating way past one beat per dryly-ticked second. A scream from one of the private rooms brought her to a panicked stop. Then she remembered. The only person who might come running was currently enjoying what she hoped were pleasant, haloperidol-induced hallucinations.

"And when you say 'pleasant,' I'm assuming you're making some kind of a point about me, are you?"

Stella turned. Other Stella was standing facing her, hands on hips, eyes gleaming in the low-wattage light from the night security lamps.

"Look, can we focus on getting out of here, please? We can discuss your low self-esteem when I've found somewhere to lie low."

Other Stella held her hands up in mock surrender. Stella noticed a large-bladed scalpel gripped in her right hand.

"Where the fuck did you get that?" she hissed, walking again.

Other Stella fell into step beside her.

"A&E. The Haloperidol was a masterstroke, but I saw this in a tray and, well, a blade's a blade, isn't it? I know you like your broken bottles, but me, I'm all for a bit of surgical steel."

Other Stella was referring to the weapon Stella had used to mortally wound Peter "Foxy" Moxey, the psychopath Collier had sent to kill her. Two grinding stabs to the eye sockets in a canal-side fight had caused catastrophic damage that had led to his bleeding out before the following morning.

"Fine. Just keep it hidden, OK? I'm just a nurse from the psych ward, not a surgeon."

"Fine by me, Stel," Other Stella whispered, winking broadly and slipping the slim instrument inside her jacket.

The reception office was locked. No need for lock picks when you had a bunch of keys. Stella was inside and looking for the locker marked with her name. She found it in the centre of the topmost row. The first key she tried, a small chromed number, almost jammed in the lock. Swearing under her breath, she wiggled it free without snapping it off in the barrel. The second key, brass, with a neat, raised ABS logo, wouldn't even go in.

"Come on, come on," Stella murmured. "Third time ..." She pushed the stainless steel key all the way into the keyhole and turned it clockwise. With a smooth click, the lock opened and she pulled the door wide. "Lucky!"

She grabbed her wallet, house keys, a heavy, four-inch long leather tube fastened with a press stud, and phone, and dropped them into the daysack she'd arrived with. Closing the locker and locking it again she turned to see Other Stella at the door, peering through a narrow gap.

"Hurry up, Stel!" she muttered. "I can hear someone coming. Too late! Get down."

19

INGATESTONE

CROUCHING below the level of the window set into the plasterboard wall, Stella reached for her little helper. It had been given to her by Sergeant Doug "Rocky" Stevens, an unarmed defence tactics instructor with the Met. The leather tube contained a stack of thirty one-pound coins. "To help even up the odds," he'd told her as he handed it over all those years earlier. And it had, repeatedly.

Gripping it in her right fist, she crouched low, out of sight, straining her ears to catch the slightest sound. She'd made her mind up. Anyone coming into the reception office was going to be asleep before they sensed the presence of the intruder.

"There!" Other Stella whispered. "Hear him?"

"Hear who?"

Then she did hear. Dan Hockley's unmistakable limping gait. Even though he was obviously trying to move silently, the step-slide beat was audible through the thin partition. Realising she was holding her breath, she made a conscious effort to exhale. The hiss of her outflowing breath drowned out Dan Hockley's steps and when she listened again, they were gone.

"He's finally gone home. Time for us to go, too, Stel," Other Stella said, nodding at the door.

Stella crawled to the door in a half-squat and turned the handle. She poked her head out and looked towards the main doors of the ward. Hockley's back was just disappearing.

"We need to wait till he's gone. Five minutes."

Other Stella nodded in agreement.

"OK. But if we meet him in the car park, I'm going to gut him like a fish," she said with a grin, holding up the broad-bladed scalpel and swishing it vertically through the air.

This time Stella got the key decision right first time. She was through and locking the main door to the ward behind her a few seconds later. Ignoring Other Stella's grinning, swaggering presence just beyond her peripheral vision, she made sure the NHS badge was facing outwards, dropped her gaze to the floor about ten feet ahead and walked away.

"Here, take this," Other Stella said, handing her a clipboard. "I snagged it on the way out. Better than a wig and false glasses."

Hospitals are still busy at night. But apart from A&E and Maternity, most departments settle into a calmer, quieter nocturnal rhythm as darkness falls. Patients, or the lucky ones at any rate, are sleeping. Nurses can drink coffee, eat chocolates left by grateful patients, do crosswords, catch up on paperwork or read, only occasionally troubled by someone needing a bed pan or a dose of pain killers. No visitors clogging up the passageways. Nobody from human resources, finance, or facilities prowling the wards, bugging clinical staff about procurement policy, health and safety or patients' rights. Just the bleeping of heart monitors, the wheeze of ventilators, and, if you work in maternity or neonatal care, the occasional plaintive cry of a newborn.

People are less alert, too. Without alarms, shouts or fire bells, most hospital staff zone out apart from their own immediate area of responsibility. So a nurse heading away from the psychiatric ward wearing the correct badge and lanyard and holding a clipboard drew precisely zero attention.

Scanning ahead the whole time for Hockley, but not seeing him, Stella reached the main reception area of the hospital by 3.15 a.m., and assumed a world-weary expression. The total complement of staff consisted of two bored-looking security guards and a single receptionist behind the desk. She offered the receptionist a small smile and mimed putting a cigarette to her lips. The woman smiled.

And then, just like that, she was free. Outside the main doors, listening to their pneumatic closers pulling them together behind her back. She resisted the urge to run. Instead, she zipped up her jacket, turned right and walked out of the hospital. She passed under the brick archway that marked the edge of the hospital grounds and walked along Norfolk Place until she reached Praed Street. Turning right, she walked southwest for five minutes until she reached the Hilton. The street was silent: no traffic of any kind, and worse for her, no black cabs.

Stella reached the hotel. The pale cream stonework – classical columns and a frieze of Greek figures four floors above the ground – glistened in the moonlight. She trotted up the five red-carpeted steps, into reception, head held high, NHS badge bouncing against her chest. She approached the night porter with a smile, noting his swift glance at the badge.

"Yes, love?" he said.

"I'm a nurse at St Mary's. I don't suppose you could call me a taxi, could you? My boyfriend was supposed to pick me up at the end of my shift but I got stuck with a few hours of overtime and he got called out. He's a fireman. I know it's a cheek but there aren't any cabs about and my phone died and —"

He laid a calming hand on her forearm and smiled.

"It's not a problem, OK? You lot deserve all the help you can get, that's the way I see it. You all right to wait for a few minutes?"

"Yeah, sure. Thanks so much."

He picked up the desk phone beside him and punched a button.

Five minutes later, Stella was climbing gratefully into the back of a black cab and waving to the night porter who'd insisted on accompanying her right to the kerb.

The driver, a burly man with a glistening, shaved skull above a thick, tattooed neck, twisted round in his seat.

"Just come off shift, 'ave you darlin'? Where's home, then?" the driver asked.

Yes, good question. Where to? Somehow I don't think going back to mine would be a smart move. Collier's probably got someone watching it.

The driver's East End accent reminded her of Freddie McTiernan, the gangster who'd helped her fashion the sawn-off shotgun she'd used to kill Tamit Ferenczy and two of his men. Freddie knew all about Collier. He might have retired, but he was still connected and wouldn't ask the wrong kind of questions. Might be willing to help her out again, seeing as he wanted Collier to pay for fitting up his son-in-law.

"It's an address in Ingatestone, in Essex. Mill Green Road, do you know it?"

"Bloody 'ell, love! Ingatestone? I mean, yes, I know it, but that's a two-hundred quid fare this time of night. You can't afford that, not on a nurse's pay. Look, I live in Chelmsford. Ingatestone's on the way. I was thinking of knocking off anyway, business has been terrible tonight. I'll take you, all right? On the 'ouse."

Not needing to feign surprise at the man's generosity, Stella looked at his eyes in the rear-view mirror.

"That is incredibly kind of you. I'm not going to insult you by arguing. Yes, please!" she said, beaming at him.

Traffic was non-existent as the taxi sped eastwards through Central London, then the City with its glass-and-steel towers, each topped with a red light to warn aircraft away. Stella was wide awake, adrenaline doing a fine job of keeping sleepiness at bay. They picked up the A12, and Stella stared out the window as they entered, and left, each new settlement along the way. Gallows

Corner, about halfway, made her smile. An hour and twenty minutes after she had climbed into the taxi's warm, pine-scented interior, she was standing on the pavement on Mill Green Road, a long tree-lined avenue.

"Blimey! The taxi driver said, as he buzzed his window down. "Maybe I should've charged you after all!"

Stella laughed.

"Yeah, right. I wish. Still living with my parents, aren't I?"

"You going to be all right, then?" he asked. "Only I've got a long day tomorrow and as you can see, I need me beauty sleep."

Stella nodded.

"I'm fine. And thanks again. You're a life-saver."

With a wave, the taxi driver performed an effortless U-turn in the wide road and clattered off back the way he'd come.

Like his neighbours' houses, Freddie McTiernan's home was invisible behind a conifer hedge that wouldn't have looked out of place guarding a fairy princess's castle. Entrance to the castle required the visiting knight to pass through a looming gate of solid timber. In the pale light of early dawn, the wood gleamed like metal.

Stella pressed the button on an intercom screwed to the left-hand gatepost. Three short buzzes for attention that she hoped Freddie would hear, and decide to answer.

She looked around, realising as she did that there was every chance Freddie wouldn't be in, let alone awake. He might have decided to visit his favourite daughter, Marilyn, and her husband Ronnie Wilks, in Marbella on the Costa del Sol. Or the "Costa del Crime," as the tabloids had rather unimaginatively christened the stretch of Spanish coastline between the cliffs of Maro-Cerro Gordo in the east to Punta Chullera in the west.

Mill Green Road at 4.30 a.m. made Praed Street at 3.00 a.m. look like Oxford Street on a Saturday lunchtime. To call it deserted was an insult to deserted streets the world over. With so much off-street parking, the road harboured not a single parked car. And as a cul-de-sac, albeit a mile-long cul-de-sac, it welcomed no through traffic, either. Somewhere in the thick woodland behind the houses, an owl hooted. Its "Tu-whit, tu-woo" call was almost comically accurate.

"Come on!" Stella said. "That *has* to be a recording."

The voice that barked at her from the squawk box, making her jump, was definitely not a recording.

"Whoever the fuck you are, you'd better have a fucking good reason for waking me up."

Stella leaned in closer to the grille.

"Freddie, it's me. Stella. Can you let me in, please, because it's bloody freezing out here."

It wasn't cold at all. But as an undergraduate studying psychology, Stella had learned that providing a reason – any reason – why someone should go along with your suggestion made it more likely they'd comply. Even if they were heavily built gangsters with workshops full of firearms and voices like angle grinders chewing through concrete.

"Jesus-fucking-Christ, it's four thirty in the fucking morning."

The intercom bleeped into silence. The latch buzzed and clacked, and the heavy wooden door swung inward on silent hinges.

20

HOUSE GUEST

STELLA breathed a sigh of relief and crunched her way up the gravel drive towards the house. Named for the trees that dominated the huge front garden, and which were now in full bright-green leaf, Five Beeches bore all the hallmarks of what the snobbier architecture critics would call "Stockbroker Tudor." Black beams over white stucco. Climbing roses and wisteria draped over the mullioned windows and pantile-roofed porch, their colours muted in the soft dawn sunshine. A few petals had fallen onto the roof and bonnet of Freddie's gold Rolls Royce Silver Shadow.

"I bet the Commissioner hasn't got a nicer place than this," she said under her breath as she reached the front door. Looking up, she scanned the front of the house, looking for a box supplied by whichever security company protected Five Beeches. Not seeing one, she frowned, then extended her finger towards the black, antique-finish doorbell. No need. The banded and studded oak door swung inwards on silent hinges.

Freddie McTiernan had wrapped his muscular, seventy-year-old frame in a black-and-gold silk dressing gown. Stella looked down and was relieved to see dark pyjamas beneath the hem of the garment. Even having been roused from a presumably peaceful slumber, he looked well groomed. His thick silver hair was swept back from his high, unlined forehead. The crow's-feet and lines etched at the corners of his mouth weren't too deep. And his purple-grey eyes were bright and clear. Clearly "the life" had been good to Freddie.

"Stella Cole. Last I heard, you were sorting buttons in the funny farm," Freddie said. "You'd better come in."

Sitting in a comfortable pine chair at the kitchen table, Stella watched Freddie make tea and toast.

"Tell me something," she said to his broad back. "How come you keep that beautiful car outside? Shouldn't a Roller be in a climate-controlled garage or something?"

Without stopping his practised movements, spooning tea into a pot and filling the kettle, he answered.

"I bought that car new in 1980. Forty grand she cost me. Cash, obviously. Back then you could have got yourself a nice little semi in Ingatestone for less than that. A lot of people who make a bit of money, well, they go off and buy something foreign and flash, you know." He adopted a wildly comical Italian accent. "Ferraaari, Maseraaati, Lamborghiiini. But for someone like me, there was only ever one choice. Gotta be a Roller, hasn't it? It's a big two fingers to all those snotty teachers who told me I'd never amount to nothing. And what did their university education get them, eh? Driving around in some piece of Japanese shit they've bought on the never-never, while I," he turned and jabbed a thick finger into his chest, "cruise past my old school in a car longer than their house is wide. So, to answer your question, I keep it out there because I like looking at it. Every morning, every evening, every time I'm in the garden feeding the fish or off out for a walk, there she is, as bright and shiny as the day I took the keys off this smarmy salesman called Rupert or Julian or some stupid fucking name."

Having delivered himself of this speech, which had left him panting a little, he turned away and assembled the breakfast things onto a tray. Freddie carried it through to a conservatory that looked out onto the immaculate back garden. A pair of blackbirds hopped about, pulling up worms from the lawn. A lawn mown into regimentally-exact pale and dark stripes by a gardener who clearly suffered from OCD.

Accepting a mug of tea and a plate, Stella spoke through a mouthful of buttery toast.

"How did you know I was in the loony bin? I thought there might be a few places where your tentacles didn't stretch."

"After that business with those Albanian fuckers, I thought I might've heard from you. When all I got was, 'Hi, this is Stella, leave a message' I made a couple of calls. Ended up speaking to a DS. Nice bloke. Helpful. Banner? Tannon?"

"Tanner. Jake."

"That's it. Tanner." Freddie winked at her, though to Stella it felt like a wildebeest being winked at by a crocodile. "Anyway, he told me what happened in Collier's office. I've got to give it to you, girl, you've got brass-fucking-balls. Marching into your guvnor's office with a shooter. So you were actually going to do him, right there, were you?"

"That was the plan."

Freddie frowned, though his brow didn't so much as crinkle. *Botox?* Stella wondered for a second.

"And then what, Stella?"

"And then I intended to kill myself, Freddie."

He rubbed a hand over his face, then took a swig of tea. He regarded her over the rim of his mug, blowing on the surface.

"Maybe they did you a favour, sticking you in the hospital, then. Cos you're clearly not thinking straight."

"Maybe. Maybe I haven't been thinking straight since I found out those murderous bastards killed my baby girl as well as her daddy. But that's not really your problem."

"No? Then how come I've got a certifiably bonkers DI from the Met drinking my English Breakfast and eating my sliced white in my conservatory at five thirty in the fucking morning? Do I get an explanation? I think I'm entitled to one, don't you?"

Stella sighed. He was right.

"Collier can't use official channels to get to me. Not without blowing his cover and ruining his chances of getting out of this in one piece. But he's still got contacts. Still got a few foot soldiers willing to follow orders. I can't risk going back to my place, or my family or friends. I just thought, who'd be the last person Collier would think I'd go to for protection?"

"And you thought of me?"

"It was a spur of the moment thing. I'm sorry, I can go if you want?"

She half rose from her chair but Freddie was quicker. He leaned forward and placed a meaty palm on her knee.

"No. You can stay here. You look done in, for a start, and I've got plenty of spare rooms. Plus, like we discussed last time, I've got unfinished business with Collier myself."

"Yeah, I remember. Um, can I ask you a question?"

"Fire away."

"How come you haven't got a burglar alarm? I'd have thought all the houses in this road would've had them as standard."

Freddie smiled.

"Never felt the need. I let it be known in a few select hostelries round here which house was mine. And what line of business I used to be in. I guess the thieving little shits who make a living burgling rich folk decided out of respect to leave me in peace."

Adam Collier woke at 5.30 a.m. while Stella and Freddie were still drinking their tea. He eased his still-sleeping wife off his right arm, from which all sensation had departed sometime in the night. Wincing, as blood and feeling came flooding back into the deadened limb, he climbed out of bed. He donned a dressing gown, grabbed his phone, and padded downstairs to make coffee. He checked his phone, looking for the missed call from Dan and the voicemail telling him Stella Cole had become unruly – violent, even – and had had to be sedated. And could he come in to St Mary's and offer his distressed officer some much-needed support?

He smiled with satisfaction as the phone woke up and displayed a little white "1" inside a red circle over the green-and-white phone icon. The message icon had its top right corner clipped by an identical alert symbol but carrying a "2."

Choosing to read first, then listen, he tapped the message icon. As his eyes skittered over the first, two-word text, he punched the air. Even better than expected. Dan must have overcooked the dosage. Or just decided to man up and do the job himself.

She's gone.

He noticed that the second text was also from Dan and apparently sent a minute after the first.

I think she's escaped. I have to report it.

A cold weight settled in the pit of his stomach. For the first time since the whole wretched business with Richard Drinkwater, Detective Chief Superintendent Adam Collier was frightened.

21
___

ONGOING INVESTIGATION

EVER since Collier had pressured her into using the Taser on Stella, Detective Sergeant Frankie O'Meara had been struggling to stay focused on her current cases. It wasn't as if they were run-of-the-mill. On the whiteboard listing cases by team member, Frankie was down for a double-murder, a suspected child abduction and a serious sexual assault. But what was eating at her conscience, and waking her at three in the morning, was the nagging suspicion that she'd been played.

She hadn't managed to speak to Stella since she'd disappeared up to Scotland on the trail of the man who'd murdered her family. Stella had been cagey about his identity. But Frankie was a detective, and a good one at that. So she'd decided to do some digging in her own time.

Frankie had made a list of a few questions she needed to answer if she was going to discover what was going on with Stella. Not on a computer, nor an official police notebook. She wanted something deniable. So this list was on a sheet of paper in a kitchen drawer in her flat.

. . .

WHO would need a fall guy for the murder of a human rights lawyer and his daughter (husband and daughter of DI S. Cole)?

WHO did Stella go up to Scotland to arrest (kill)?

WHY wouldn't Stella follow official procedure?

WHO did Stella trust (apart from me)?

It had been so long since Frankie had worked with Stella – *properly worked* – that she'd lost her sense of intimacy with her boss. Who she was tight with, who she confided in, who she shared fag breaks with. But she knew a man who might be able to point her in the right direction. Which is why, at 11.00 a.m. on a sunny day when she would rather have been outside soaking up some rays, Frankie found herself in the subterranean, supermarket-sized space that was the Exhibits Room.

Pushing through the swing doors, she sighed as the smell of stale air, stale blood and stale ambitions assailed her nostrils. The space before her was crowded with some of the tattiest, saddest and downright ugliest office furniture in the entire station. IT had once had worse. But the commonly believed rumour was that one of the managers there had wiped porn from a senior officer's computer just hours before an ethics audit and been rewarded with a trolley dash round Staples.

Two civilian staff – both young women – were pecking away on keyboards blackened by years of use. One, a plump blonde with a nose ring. The other, slim, with dark purple lipstick and long black hair. She looked up as Frankie coughed a polite "Ahem." Her face was white. Not with fear, Frankie quickly realised, correcting her initial impression. This was makeup. *Jesus, Mary and sweet Joseph*, she thought, *the Goths have taken over the asylum.*

"Hi there. Can I help?" the young woman asked.

"Is Reg the Veg – I mean, is Reg Willing around?"

Reg Willing, plump, lazy, transferred from active duty years before, the master of the Exhibits Room. And Stella's former colleague during the time she'd worked there on light duties.

The young woman smirked.

"He's through there. Want me to get him for you?"

She nodded towards a door beyond which lay the secured evidence room, packed to the rafters with bagged and tagged exhibits from thousands of current and historical cases. Bloody knives, semen-stained knickers, friction-ridge prints, hair samples, insect larvae, paint chips, plaster casts of footprints – they, and many hundreds of other evidence types, waited for their moment in court on miles of industrial racking.

"No thanks, you're all right," Frankie said. "Is it OK if I go through to speak to him?"

"Of course. You just need to sign in. Here."

She pushed a visitor book towards Frankie, who jotted down her name, rank and warrant card number, along with the time.

The fluorescent lighting of the outer office was depressing. In here it was frustrating. Bluish-white, dim and hardly any use. *A bit like you, Reg,* Frankie thought, stifling a giggle. Peering through the gloom, she saw a rotund figure moving with surprising grace among the shelves.

"Reg?" she called out.

The figure straightened. Turned.

"You called, Milady? Oh, it's DS O'Meara. Top o' the morning to ye. Oi'll be with yez in two shakes of a lamb's tail, so I will."

In terms of accents, Reg's "Guinness-and-Leprechauns" Dublin Irish was out by about a hundred miles. But even a proud Belfast girl like Frankie didn't have time or the energy to correct him. Weaving his way along the racks of wire shelves, Reg kept up what he presumably felt was an amusing murmur of fiddle-de-diddly "Oirish" until he arrived in front of her.

"Hi Reg, how are you?" Frankie asked.

"Couldn't be better, dear lady, couldn't be better. And how may Sir Reginald of Recordsia help you this fine morning?"

Face to face, Reg had dropped the accent in favour of his own unique brand of English. He'd dropped his gaze, too.

"I'm up here, Reg," she answered, talking to his bald patch.

He jerked his head up.

"Sorry, DS O'Meara. Old habits and all that. You won't report me to HR for inappropriate ogling, will you?"

Frankie sighed. At school, her bust had been the envy of her friends, the focus of attention of the boys and a cross she had learned to bear. At the station, it was as if the intervening years hadn't happened. Male officers were simply incapable of maintaining eye contact.

"It depends." She paused, relishing the expression of anxiety that flickered on Reg's reddening face. "I need to ask you something. And I don't want it going any further."

She gave him a hard stare and was gratified to see that this time his eyes were locked on to hers.

"Anything, DS O'Meara. Ask away. You can trust Old Reg."

"When DI Cole was working with you, did anyone come to see her? Was there anyone she seemed friendly with?"

"What, down here, you mean?"

Frankie shrugged.

"Down here, up there. I just need to find out who she was hanging around with."

Reg made a show of thinking, cupping his chin and looking up at the ceiling.

"She introduced Daisy to Barney Riordan. It was all the poor girl could talk about for weeks afterwards. Don't think I ever really saw Stel talking to anyone else. I had a bit of a tummy bug that kept me out of circulation for a while. Stel basically went AWOL shortly after I got back, so …"

"That's OK, Reg. Is Daisy the vampire in your front office?"

Reg laughed.

"No. That's Thea. Jackson. She's actually very nice. You know, when she's not drinking *wirrgins' blaad*." He rolled his eyes and bared his yellow incisors, pushing his hair back into a widow's peak.

Feeling that she really needed to be somewhere else before she rammed a stake through his heart, Frankie thanked Reg, turned on her heel and left him to his comedy accents.

Back in the main office she looked around. The blonde had disappeared. She approached Thea.

"Excuse me. Is Daisy going to be long?"

"Shouldn't be. I think she just went to the loo."

"Thanks."

Frankie asked for directions to the Ladies then left, breathing a sigh of relief as the swing doors closed behind her. She found the plump young woman at the sinks in the Ladies.

"Hi. Are you Daisy?"

"Yes. You're DS O'Meara, aren't you?"

"Well remembered."

"I saw you come in with Stella once, before she was working in Exhibits, I mean. You introduced yourself then."

Frankie felt a momentary flicker of awkwardness that Daisy had remembered their previous meeting when she had not.

"Yeah, I remember now. Stella introduced you to that footballer, didn't she? What was his name?"

Daisy's face broke into a wide and innocent-looking smile. Eyes round, she answered in a rush.

"Oh. My. God. Barney Riordan. Rear of the Year Barney Riordan. He came over at the Café Royal and said hello to me personally. And gave me a kiss. In front of the paparazzi and everything! I was actually in heat, can you believe it?"

Frankie blinked in surprise. For a second she thought Daisy was describing her state of sexual arousal. Then reality kicked in. Not heat. *Heat*! The celebrity gossip magazine.

"Kudos," she said, drily. "So, listen, you spent a bit of time with Stella, right? Did she ever say who she was close to since she came back on light duties?"

Daisy offered up an almost exact copy of Reg's body language. Apparently drawn from a book called *How to Show You're Thinking*. Then she returned her blue eyes to Frankie's.

"I don't exactly know if they were close, but she did go to dinner with this really good looking black guy. He came down looking for her once, but she'd gone by then."

Dinner? That sounded like someone Stella might share a confidence with. But the description was a bit rubbish.

"And when you say, 'good looking black guy'?"

"Oh, right." Daisy frowned. "Tall. About six-one. Midthirties. Slim, athletic build. Not muscly, but you know, fit-looking. Golden-brown eyes. Very short hair, cropped, really. High forehead, no wrinkles. Great smile. Super-good dresser. Not suited and booted like the detectives. More casual. But, like, with amazing taste. Oh, and he talked really posh. Like he went to Cambridge or something."

Frankie mimed applause.

"Wow! OK, that was truly impressive."

Daisy blushed.

"I've trained myself. To be observant, I mean."

"Well it worked. Because I know exactly who you're talking about."

"Really?"

"There are dozens of good-looking black guys at Paddington Green, but only one who's also posh and a clothes horse."

22

AMAZING WHAT YOU CAN FIND ON
THE INTERNET

FRANKIE walked into the forensics office already scanning for Lucian Young. Daisy couldn't have described him more accurately if she'd produced a high-resolution photograph. As the door squeaked to a close over its final couple of inches, three or four heads popped up from behind screens. *Like meerkats*, Frankie thought. She spotted Lucian at the rear of the office, hunched over a microscope.

"Hi," she said, when she reached his desk.

He raised his head from the scope and turned to her.

"Oh, hi. Frankie, isn't it? You work with Stella."

"That's right. Nice of you to say *work*, not *worked*, too. At least you think she's still a copper."

He smiled, and Frankie reflected that he was, actually, very good looking. And the fact he wasn't staring at her tits was a bonus.

"Well, she is, isn't she? Last I heard. Despite everything."

Something in his look, made Frankie feel instinctively she could trust him. She leaned closer and spoke in a low voice.

"Is there somewhere we could go for a chat? About Stella?"

He stood.

"Fancy a coffee?"

Avoiding a cluster of coffee outlets owned by one global chain or another, they settled on a little cafe in a row of tatty shops including a dry cleaner, a betting shop and a convenience store. Frankie ordered the coffees, and a currant bun for herself, and brought everything over to the table Lucian had chosen in a corner by the big plate glass window overlooking Edgware Road.

She took a careful sip of the coffee. Scalding hot, but a genuinely pleasurable hit of caffeine beneath it, not just the usual milky overload. Lucian mirrored her action, eyeing her over the rim of the thick, white, china mug, but clearly waiting for her to make the first move. A young guy in jeans and a scruffy denim jacket came in and called out a cheery hello to the girl behind the counter. Using the distraction, Frankie spoke.

"You heard what happened."

He put his mug down.

"About Stella's being sectioned? Yes. I doubt there's a single person in the nick who isn't aware one of our finest went postal in CID."

"She had dinner with you, didn't she?"

"A couple of times, yes. Why?"

Why are you being so cagey? Frankie wondered. *Press on.*

"I'm worried about her, that's why. I'm trying to find someone, anyone, who she was close to after she came back to work. She told me she'd found out who murdered Richard and Lola. She was going to gather intelligence, she told me. But I think she went to kill him. Look, Lucian, if you know anything, you have to tell me. Please."

Maybe it was the beseeching note in her voice, she didn't know, but something in Lucian seemed to change. His eyes lost the wary look they'd had since they sat down. He leaned closer, across the tabletop.

"Stella told me she'd uncovered evidence that pointed to a high-level conspiracy inside the legal system. She thought they'd murdered Richard because he was getting close to exposing them. Lola got caught up in it, but it was Richard they were after."

Frankie rocked back in her chair. Whatever she'd been expecting – or hoping – to hear, it wasn't this. She took a distracted bite of the currant bun and yelped as her teeth closed on her tongue. A couple of the other customers jerked their heads round at the noise, then turned away again, presumably having reassured themselves it wasn't some nutter about to pull out a carving knife.

"A conspiracy?" she hissed. "Are you serious?"

"I'm serious that's what she told me. She had a letter Richard wrote to her before he died. Whether it's true or not," he shrugged, "you'll have to ask Stella."

"But do *you* think it's true?"

"I'm really not sure. On the one hand, we work for an organisation that feels constantly undermined by the courts, by defence lawyers, by special interest groups. What could be more natural than for a few rogue elements to decide to set things straight by other means? On the other hand, this is still Britain. We don't really go in for death squads, black sites and secret police, do we?"

"Oh, come on Lucian. Stop being such a bloody rational scientist for a second and just give me your gut feel. I need to know. This is Stella we're talking about, not some case study."

He held his hands up in surrender. Or maybe just to ward off Frankie's pointing finger.

"OK, OK, I'll tell you what I feel. Although being a bloody rational scientist is rather what I do, you know. I think she was – is – onto something. There were three pieces of evidence she turned up. She found a paint chip from the hit and run. It had been misfiled. Deliberately, she thought. And Linda Heath from HR. The way she said something about justice being done made Stella think she was quoting a mantra instead of just indulging in wishful thinking. And finally, that guy who was convicted, what was his name?"

"Edwin Deacon."

"She told me he'd been – what do you call it, when you move someone between prisons without notice?"

"Ghosted?"

"That's it. She said he'd been ghosted from HMP Bure to Long Lartin. Where he was beaten to death after being misclassified as a sex offender."

Frankie inhaled deeply and blew out across the surface of her coffee. If she'd gone to Stella with that quality of evidence about a case in the old days, Stella would have kicked her arse and told her to go away and do some proper police work. Now, she wasn't so sure. *Are you really onto something, boss? Or is it all in your head? After all, you were acting like Lola was alive when she'd died in the FATACC.* She made a decision.

"I'm trying to find out what's really going on. I need to do some digging on my own time. But if I need some help—"

"Just ask. It's what I told Stella as well. I won't break the law, but if you need any help with forensics or computing, I'm in. Here, let me give you my number."

* * *

Frankie stayed late that evening. When the last of her colleagues had left for home, or the pub, Frankie logged into HOLMES - the Home Office Large Major Enquiry System. Staring at the top-level search screen, she spoke aloud.

"Now. Just supposing there were a top-level legal conspiracy, who are we talking about? Chief constables? Judges? CPS lawyers? Barristers? Lucian said Deacon had been ghosted, so let's add prison governors into the equation."

Working through the list, she keyed in a series of searches linking various keywords. If Stella had discovered the real murderer, it stood to reason he or she would be a conspiracy member. And after seeing Stella's performance with the Glock, Frankie was convinced whoever they were, they weren't breathing God's good air anymore.

She typed in CHIEF CONSTABLE + MURDERED. No

hits. She wasn't really surprised. She felt sure the office would have been awash with chatter if someone had gunned down a CC.

She tried again. JUDGE + MURDERED. Again, nothing.

And again. LAWYER + MURDERED. Zero.

"Shit!" she murmured, scratching at the back of her scalp.

Then she slapped her forehead.

"Frances Nicola O'Meara! God, you're a stupid girl sometimes. They'd have covered it up."

In which case, she reasoned, HOLMES was as much use as a condom machine in a convent. She launched a web browser and entered a short phrase.

Top judge dead

"Oh, my fucking God!" she said, as the screen refreshed.

The search results all referred one way or another to the death of a High Court judge, Leonard Ramage, in a house fire at his home in Scotland. Of course, houses caught fire all the time, and regrettably their inhabitants perished. Frankie had seen more than enough crispy critters to last her the rest of her career. But the date brought her up short. It was three days after her last meeting with Stella. She searched for the judge by name and nodded with satisfaction as the search engine returned hundreds of hits.

"Popular fellow," she muttered, clicking on a couple of news stories.

Idly, she clicked the IMAGES link at the top of the page. The face looking back at her was of a type that had always raised her hackles. Lustrous silver hair swept back from a high forehead. Healthy tan. Confident gaze. It was a face that spoke of privilege. Establishment privilege. Here was the judge outside the Old Bailey. Here, at a legal reception. Here, at a high society garden party. Posing languidly beside a shiny purple Bentley outside the car company's hospitality tent at Royal Ascot. Receiving his knighthood at Buckingham Palace.

She called Lucian.

"Hi Frankie, what's up?"

"When Stella talked to you about the conspiracy, was it just to use you as a sounding board or did she have some kind of evidence? You said she found a paint chip?"

"That's right. I analysed it for her."

Frankie was staring at the picture of Ramage by the Bentley. Her heart was suddenly beating very fast.

"Was it purple?"

"Yes. A special colour called *Viola Del Diavolo*. It's only used on high-end stuff. Ferraris, Aston Martins—"

"Bentleys?"

"Yes. Was that a guess?"

"No. I think I've found the owner of the car the paint chip came from."

"That's great! You can pull them in for questioning. Maybe finish what Stella started."

"It's too late for that. I think she finished it herself."

"What do you mean?"

"He was a High Court judge. Past tense."

"You think she killed him, is that what you're saying?"

"It says he died in a house fire."

"Well then?"

"I don't know, Lucian. Maybe I'm getting jumpy with all the talk of conspiracies. Listen, don't worry about it, OK? I'm going home now. I'll see you soon."

But Frankie didn't go home. Instead, she repeated the search process on a dozen or so different legal job titles. An hour later, she was sweating, and chewing her bottom lip until it bled and she could taste the coppery tang of blood in her mouth. She'd made notes as she'd searched and consulted the sheet of scrap paper now.

. . .

Leonard Ramage. High Court Judge. Died. House fire.

Charlie Howarth. Barrister. Died. Fall at chambers party. Suspected accident caused by excessive alcohol consumption.

Debra Fieldsend. Crown Prosecution Service lawyer. Missing. Dead?

Hester Ragib. Barrister. Died. Electrocuted in hotel bathroom. Suspected accident.

Sir Christopher De Bree. Barrister. Died. Heart attack at home.

Frankie closed her eyes and pinched the skin at the bridge of her nose. She re-ran the film of the confrontation with Stella in Collier's office. Everything that had happened was a blur, but she tried breathing slowly and using a relaxation technique she'd seen on YouTube. Although her own anxiety as she crouched out of sight holding a Taser had obliterated most of the details, one line of Stella's came back in crystal clear audio now:

"You're forgetting your friends in Pro Patria Mori. Ramage, Fieldsend, Ragib, Howarth."

"Fucking hell, boss," she breathed. "What have you been up to?"

She folded the sheet of paper into four and tucked it into her purse. Thinking about home and a nice big glass of wine, she moved the cursor over to close the browser. Then she stopped the movement and rolled her eyes.

"You're not going to leave your search history there are you, you muppet?" she said to herself. "Some undercover copper you'd make."

She'd just brought up the menu for clearing her search history when a noise behind her made her swing round in her chair. The door to the CID office had just banged shut, and walking towards her was Adam Collier. She stood, hurriedly, catching her hip on the corner of the desk.

"Burning the midnight oil, Frankie?" he said, a smile on his face. But was that a wary look behind the eyes as well?

"Oh, you know how it is, sir. Just a case I can't let go of."

He was standing right in front of her now. She could smell him. No aftershave for once. Instead a faint but unmistakable odour of perspiration. Odd.

"The case will still be there in the morning. And hundreds more like it, sadly. Go on, go home." He smiled again. "That's an order."

23

FOLLOWING IN STELLA'S FOOTSTEPS

AFTER ushering Frankie out of the CID office the previous night, Collier had wasted no time checking the computer she'd been using. As had become his routine, he'd waited until he thought every one of his team had left before checking their computers, both for official logins and any unusual browsing activity. Somehow, he'd missed the fact that Frankie was still in the building. It was lucky he'd forgotten his car keys. Otherwise he wouldn't have been able to review her search history. Five minutes checking on what she'd been researching, and he knew he was in trouble. Correction. More trouble.

So he'd come in early and prepared a new case file. Then left a Post-it on Frankie's desk asking her to come and see him the moment she arrived at her desk.

* * *

Standing outside Adam Collier's office, Frankie could feel a cold worm of anxiety wriggling around in her stomach. She'd got home at after one in the morning following her research and had managed no more than three hours' sleep. The two cups of strong black coffee she'd drunk at breakfast to wake herself up had done their job. But they'd also given her a bad case of the jitters. Being summoned by Collier the moment she arrived at work hadn't helped matters. She hitched up her trousers, straightened her blouse and knocked smartly, three times.

"Come!"

She opened the door and walked in. Tried to avoid glancing at the screen of potted ferns and palms she'd hidden behind before Tasering Stella.

"Ah, Frankie. Take a seat."

She sat in the chair facing Collier across his desk, which was covered in paperwork. He looked stressed, she thought. Eyes tight, tie crooked, and a couple of spots of dried blood on his neck where he'd nicked himself shaving. For someone nicknamed The Model, he was looking decidedly off his game.

"Everything all right, sir?"

Collier grimaced. Frankie watched as he tried to chase the sour expression off his face with a smile, but the effect was forced. It looked as if he were about to vomit.

"Fine, Frankie. Yes, thank you. I have a case for you. Something that's come over from our colleagues in East London. Bow, to be exact. You heard about the shootout at that club in Shoreditch ten days ago?"

"Yes, sir. Three down, all Albanians, including one Tamit Ferenczy. Pretty major league drug dealer. Ran his business from the club."

"Very good. Glad to see you don't just focus on our patch. The initial assumption was a deal gone bad but there's new intelligence pointing to a gang war with the McTiernans."

"I thought Freddie had retired."

"Maybe he has. Some old folk like to get part-time jobs to while away the hours. Old Man McTiernan seems to have gone for something a bit more, shall we say, proactive. Anyway, I want you to take it on. As a priority. I'll get your other cases reassigned. First stop, go down to that neo-Tudor pile of Freddie's in Essex and have a chat. Test the waters. Nothing serious, just putting out a few feelers. You know the drill."

He pushed the manila folder across the desk. Frankie took it, spun it round and opened it. The top sheet was Freddie McTiernan's criminal record. Not a huge document but with enough serious offences to keep anyone with less expensive lawyers than Freddie's in prison for a long time.

"Thank you, sir."

She stood and left. Collier had already returned to his papers and merely grunted as she left. Back at her desk, she spent the next hour reading the file on Freddie McTiernan. Then she picked up her desk phone and called the landline number listed under "PERSONAL INFO."

"Hello?"

"Mr McTiernan?"

"Who wants to know?"

"I'm Detective Sergeant Frances O'Meara. Metropolitan Police. We're looking at the shooting of three Albanian men in Shoreditch ten days ago. Could I come and see you for a chat?"

"I'm retired. Doesn't it say that in your file on me?"

Keep it light, Frankie.

"It does. I'm just collecting background. You're not under suspicion."

"I don't give a flying fuck whether I'm under suspicion or not. You lot fitted up my son-in-law without a shred of evidence, did you know that? Is that in your file as well?"

Frankie paused before answering. Breathed out. *Don't answer questions, ask them.*

"When would it be convenient for me to come and speak with you, Mr McTiernan?"

"It won't ever be *convenient*. But if you want to waste a couple of hours, be my guest. Tomorrow afternoon, say one o'clock. I'm playing golf at two so you've got an hour."

He hung up as Frankie framed the words, "Thank you."

"Fine," she said. "One o'clock tomorrow it is, then, Freddie. And then we'll see who's retired and who's wasting whose time."

Frankie was on her way to the canteen when out of the corner of her eye she saw Collier's office door opening. She threaded her way through the desks in the CID office to catch up with him before he left.

"Sir?"

"Yes, Frankie, what is it? I'm on my way out."

"I spoke to Freddie McTiernan. I'm going down to see him tomorrow. One o'clock."

Collier stopped walking.

"I'll come with you. I could do with a break from this interminable paperwork. I tell you, Frankie, being the Chief Super is far less glamorous than it sounds."

Then he was gone.

Glamorous? Boring, more like, she mused as she waited for the kettle to boil. She took her cup of instant coffee back to her desk and sent a text to Stella. She assumed patients, or inmates, or whatever they called them, had their phones confiscated, but surely she'd get her messages at some point?

24

A DAY OFF

FREDDIE put the phone down. Slowly. Carefully. Puffed out his cheeks then hissed the air out through his teeth. He could feel his old anger banking up. The doctor had warned him about his high blood pressure.

"I don't want to alarm you, Mr McTiernan," she'd said. "But at your age there is a very real risk of a stroke unless you adopt the changes to your lifestyle we talked about."

Hence golf. Hence half a bottle of wine with dinner and only one cognac before bed instead of two or three. Hence visiting the local dog charity to talk about adopting a rescue. Hence resisting the urge to pick up the fake antique handset and hurl the whole fucking thing through the window. *Breathe, Freddie. Don't give them the satisfaction.*

He turned at a sound behind him. Stella was standing there, towelling her spiky blonde hair dry. Wrapped in one of his fluffy white bathrobes, she looked like a little girl wearing her dad's dressing gown.

"You all right?" she asked. "You've gone red."

"Just had a call from one of your lot. Coming down to see me tomorrow afternoon. Something to do with that Albanian fuckwit Ferenczy and his goons. You should probably make yourself scarce."

"Anyone I know?"

"Detective Sergeant Frances O'Meara, she called herself." He observed the way Stella's eyes widened. "Know her, do you?"

"She's my sergeant. Was, I suppose, since I'm not exactly on duty at the moment. What with technically being under a section."

Freddie grunted. He was beginning to like this whack job copper, and that was dangerous in his line of work.

"Even more reason for you to disappear for the afternoon. Don't want any awkward conversations, do you?"

She smiled at him. Something about her reminded him of Marilyn when she'd been younger. He smiled. Marilyn had called from Heathrow earlier. She and Ronnie had got in on time and would be coming to Five Beeches at seven the following evening. Now they had the money Stella had liberated from the lockup, they planned to finish the business with Collier.

"Thanks, Freddie," Stella said. "You know, for everything."

He shrugged his shoulders.

"Gets lonely here sometimes. Rattling about in this place. I don't mind a bit of female company. 'Specially attractive female company." He held up a hand as her mouth dropped open in mock outrage. "You know, attractive for a cop."

"Ooh, you cheeky sod."

Then she must have caught something in his expression, and her face fell. He knew what she'd seen. He could feel it. The tug. The pain in his chest that never really went away. Only faded from time to time. She spoke again, face serious now, eyes looking right into his.

"What happened to your wife, Freddie?"

"Oh, bloody hell. You want me to go back over ancient history?"

"Why not? I'm not exactly over-employed at the moment. Why don't you pour us both a drink? I'm a good listener."

With a generous tumbler-full of cognac for himself and a vodka on the rocks for Stella, Freddie sat back in the buttoned-leather sofa and took a pull on the warming spirit. Stella sat opposite him, legs tucked up beneath her, like women seemed to do by instinct.

"You know that old saying, 'Live by the sword, die by the sword'?"

"Mm-hmm."

"Came true for me, big time. You know my wife's name?"

"Yes. Mary, wasn't it?"

"Mary Catherine Walsh. Till we got married, I mean. She kept her maiden name in the middle after that. Irish Catholic family out of Wexford. Third of eleven kids. Her old man was a big name in horse dealing over there. We met at a horse fair outside Colchester in the seventies. Seventy-five, it was. I tell you, Stella, she was beautiful. Raven-black hair, bright-green eyes, real emerald green, you know? All the blokes had their eye on her. Everywhere she went, three of her brothers used to tag along after her like fucking bodyguards. Not that she needed them, mind. Mary Walsh could take care of herself. There was this one lad, fancied his chances. Big strapping cunt from Dublin, come over for the fair.

"Anyway, he blocked her way between two of the marquees and put his arms round her waist. 'Give us a kiss, you beauty,' he said. 'And tell those three corn-fed fuckers to get lost.' Next thing he knows, he's on the ground with his balls halfway up his throat."

"You saw it, did you?"

"Saw it? I was laughing so hard I nearly pissed myself. I'd been thinking of trying to talk to her, but after what she did to the lad from Dublin, I kind of lost me bottle for a while. But it was a three-day fair, so you know, I thought, bide your time Freddie-Boy. Pick your moment."

"What happened?"

"Oh, well, the last day, I found out where the Walshes' caravan was, and I hung around till I saw her dad and brothers go off to the beer tent. I think they'd won some money on the trotting races, or sold a couple of horses. I just marched up to the front door and knocked. I'd bought a massive bunch of flowers off a stall, so when she opened the door I kind of stuck them right in her face and introduced myself. It worked. She stepped out and asked me who the feck I was and what the feck did I think I was doing giving a girl feckin' hayfever?"

Stella snorted with laughter. Freddie couldn't help smiling at the memory of his first encounter with the woman who would become his wife a year later. The woman who'd leave Ireland to be with him in the East End. Who'd bear him three kids, then move with him out to the moneyed Essex suburbs.

"So then what? After you'd charmed her with your East End blarney?"

"She joined me in the family firm. I said she was tough. We built it up together. She enjoyed the money side. But the thing with my Mary, she couldn't abide being bullied. Round about 2003, we started getting some aggro from this Afghani gang. Bringing in heroin from Pakistan. Violent fuckers, they were. The word going round was they were ex-Mujahideen or however the fuck you say it. They destroyed the Robertson gang. Took Gary Robertson out to Hackney Marshes and cut him up into about a hundred little pieces. They filmed it and sent the video to his wife. Told her the sons would be next unless they gave up the business. So, she did, didn't she? Hadn't got any choice. But those fucking Afghanis did them anyway. Simon and Gary Junior got found in the middle of Lower Clapton Road early one morning. In half a dozen black bin bags. After that, Junie lost the plot. Did herself in with pills and vodka inside six months.

"Anyway, we held our ground. It got pretty brutal for a while. Lot of good people got burned. Those mad bastards didn't care. They had Kalashnikovs, for fuck's sake. Brought them in with them. I mean we had shooters, too, but it was mostly shotguns like that one I gave you to do Ferenczy. In the end, I decided we had to go all out. Me and Mary, we worked out a plan. Massive, end of the world, pre-emptive strike. We had about thirty blokes, all tooled up like something out of a war film. Called in favours from everyone who owed me. We steamed into their HQ at four in the morning with sawn-offs, pumps, Browning Hi-Powers, hunting rifles, everything. It was a bloodbath, basically. We lost five blokes, but every single one of those fuckers was dead by half-past. There was so much blood you could taste it in the back of your throat. I mean, we were literally splashing through it."

Freddie stopped, cleared his throat, took a swig of the cognac. Felt it burning his throat and enjoyed the sensation. He looked at Stella. Her eyes were fixed on his. She took a pull on the vodka, rattling the ice cubes against her front teeth.

"What happened?" she asked.

"One of 'em wasn't dead, was he? Mary was standing in the middle of them. Shotgun over her shoulder. Hair tied back, blood all over her top. My God, I never saw her looking more beautiful. She looked like a pirate queen. This one Afghan, he rolled over and grabbed a Kalashnikov off this dead bloke. Shot her point blank. She never knew what happened. Dead on her feet. That was the only mercy."

"Jesus. What did you do?"

"Me?"

He closed his eyes and rubbed them with his fists until sparks shot in all directions under the lids. Remembered the blind rage that ignited inside him. Saw himself standing there, poleaxed. Then rushing over. Grabbing the Kalashnikov and emptying the mag into the man's face. The dry sound of the gun clicking as the last round left the muzzle. Turning it round and grabbing the barrel, still burning-hot. Battering what was left of the Afghan's torso until all that was left of him was red paste on the floor. Being wrestled away by two McTiernan cousins. Screaming with rage and grief, twisting in their grip to see his beloved Mary being borne aloft by two more and carried away, back to the trucks. Giving the order that would cement his reputation. "Kill them all. Every middleman. Every dealer. Every runner. The accountants. The shippers. The packagers. The mules. Every, single, fucking one of them. And nail one of my business cards to their faces."

· · ·

"Me?" he repeated. "I grieved. That's what I did. Sold my shares in the business and retired."

"I'm sorry."

He grunted and drained his cognac.

"Ancient history, Stella."

"You know you said you went in tooled up?"

"Yes. Why?"

"You still have those long guns in your workshop. Did you keep any of the shorts?"

"Bloody hell, you don't fuck about, do you? We sent you off in a fucking wheelchair with a sawn-off under your blanket, and now you're asking me for a pistol. Well, as it happens, you're out of luck. Those guns in my workshop are for sport only. In case you didn't know, handguns are illegal in this country."

Stella nodded at the irony of being lectured on the Firearms Act by a retired gangster.

"Just asking."

The following morning, Stella got up early and called for a cab. Freddie had told her Frankie was coming down at one and that he was going to play golf afterwards, but she didn't fancy hanging around the house and said she'd make a move straightaway.

"Gate code's twenty-nine, eleven" Freddie said. "Mine and Mary's wedding anniversary. Take the spare key off the rack by the front door. It's the keyring with the little silver shamrock."

While the cab driver took her to a little coastal town called Westcliff-on-Sea, Stella re-read the text Frankie had sent the previous day.

Boss. I think you were right about The Model. Call me.

But she didn't call. It was best if she did what she had to do without involving Frankie. The girl had a great career in front of her, and what Stella was planning as the final act of her revenge against Pro Patria Mori would taint anyone beyond all hope of redemption.

25

A NICE TRIP TO THE COAST

SHADING her eyes against the sun, Stella watched the taxi drive off along the grandly titled Western Esplanade. Despite the good weather and its being the height of summer, Westcliff-on-Sea had apparently failed in the mission of all seaside towns to attract tourists, trippers and holidaymakers. She turned a complete circle, checking out who had ventured to this quiet, quaint corner of the Essex coast. The answer seemed to be a few dozen elderly couples – white haired, matching windcheaters in shades of sage, beige and heather – and, oddly, a group of bikers, cruising westwards on a long convoy of well-maintained Honda Gold Wings, Harley Electra Glides and BMW R 1200s. The bikes were more like small cars than Stella's old Triumph Speedmaster. Hard panniers with matching paintwork, top boxes, and even trailers adorned the heavy bikes. Most were two-up, and Stella was amused to see how many of the pairs wore matching leathers and helmets.

Walking towards the beach, she passed between two palm trees, part of a row that stretched for fifty yards or so along the pavement.

"Like LA from Poundland," a sardonic voice said from beside her.

"Haven't heard from you in a while," she said, not looking round.

"You haven't needed me. Nice job on that fat Maltese cunt at the hospital by the way."

"I half expected you to turn up then, to be honest."

Other Stella shrugged.

"What can I say? I don't like hospitals. Especially psychiatric wards. They're full of mad people!"

"Is that why you only appeared again when I was leaving?"

"Relax! You did OK. Don't worry, I had your back. You do remember the scalpel, don't you? No way would I have let anyone stop you leaving."

"Yeah, that's what worries me."

Stella reached the sand. Here and there, a few old couples, and families with very young children, were sitting on blankets or woven mats. Eating ice creams, drinking coffee from tartan flasks, making sandcastles, checking phones ... being normal.

Not a vigilante or a murderer among you, Stella thought.

"For all you know, they're all at it," Other Stella said. "Look at him." She pointed at a man in late middle age, thinning hair, glasses, trousers rolled up to just below his knees. "He might have taken a butcher knife to a few skateboarders making his life a misery. Chopped them up and buried them in his immaculate rose garden. Or her." A young mother, white cargo shorts and a black bikini top, dandling a toddler on her lap. "Some of the other playgroup mums said unkind things about her baby so she held a coffee morning and laced the carrot cake with strychnine. You're a copper, tell me it isn't possible."

Stella knew it was possible. Of course it was *possible*. Just not *likely*.

"You know as well as I do, nine out of ten murders, it's one spouse doing the other. That or rival drug dealers. Just because the media prefer to report the outliers doesn't mean this lot," she waved her arm in a half circle, "aren't all psychopaths."

"Whatever you say, Stel. You're the expert."

"I'm the real person, that's what I am."

"You think? I'm not so sure. I think I have a far better hold on reality than you do. I'm the one keeping you on track. We're free now. That means Collier's time is up. We're going to get him this time. And then the others."

"What others? He's the last of them."

Other Stella took a step closer until she was standing right in front of Stella. Then she slapped her, hard, across the face.

"I told you! Their wives. Husbands. Lovers. Children. I don't care. I'm going to track them all down and kill them. One by one. And let's not forget the foot soldiers. Linda Heath, that prissy little bitch in HR. She's one. I'm going to enjoy doing her. Maybe I'll choke her with one of her stupid professional aptitude forms. And Pink. That fat, racist lech. He supports them. The SCO19 shooter, too. You blew her foot off, which was actually pretty funny. She had to take a medical discharge. Obvs. But she's still walking around. Well, hopping. She tried to kill you, Stel. So she's going down."

"No. I told you. Collier has to pay. But when he's dead, this is over. I'm over."

"And I told you," Other Stella jabbed a sharp fingernail into Stella's sternum, "that I won't allow it. I'm having too much fun. Remember why you started this."

Stella turned away, towards the sea, looking towards the horizon, a bluish-green fuzz where the sea met the sky. Trying to shut Other Stella out. Willing herself back in control. Forcing her violent, sarcastic alter ego to disappear.

Sunlight bounced off the water in glittering splinters, making her squint. Seized with a sudden urge to paddle, she bent to take off her shoes and socks. She tucked the socks inside and lined the shoes up beside each other facing the water. As she straightened, bright white sparks fizzed and wriggled on the edges of her vision and she staggered a little. She caught the sun full in the face. A bright flash. She squeezed her eyes shut.

She opened them again.

Looked around.

Frowned.

Rubbed her eyes and shook her head.

Everyone had disappeared. The beach was empty. The sun was still high in the sky, but now it was a boiling, angry orange. Sharp-edged streaks of black cloud raced across the sky with a tearing shriek, as if someone were dragging a knife through a cloth revealing a hellish abyss behind the slashes.

Stella's pulse was bumping in her throat, and her skin felt cold and clammy. She felt an overwhelming urge to run, but when she tried to move, her feet wouldn't obey her. Looking down, she wailed with fear. Bony, bloodless hands, one missing its index finger, one naked of skin, had emerged from the rippled sand to grasp her ankles. She strained to pull herself free but the hands just gripped tighter, until the fingernails dug deep into her skin, making her cry out with pain as blood began to flow over her insteps in narrow rivulets.

"Turn around."

Stella felt herself rotating on the spot. To face Other Stella.

Other Stella was stone-faced. She pointed away, down the beach.

"Look who's coming."

Stella screwed her eyes up.

"No. Stop. You can't."

"Yes. I can. Open your eyes."

26

L IS FOR LOLA

IN the distance, a low, rectangular form is emerging from the heat haze rising from the sand. It shimmers. It is dark, and at first, Stella can't discern the colour. Dark brown, maybe, or blue. Deep red? No. It is purple. A deep, glistening purple. Clouds of dry sand boil up to each side of the onrushing shape.

It is a car. Moving fast. The sun bounces off the paintwork, making it sparkle. She hears the roar of the engine. Deep, growling, snarling: a predator racing towards her, intent on a kill.

She looks to her right, away from the sea. From Western Esplanade, a small, silver car emerges between two palm trees. It has turned off the road and is trundling towards the beach. The palms are whipping to and fro, their broad, deep-cut leaves snapping in a sudden, squally wind that has sprung out of nowhere.

Stella knows the car. It's Richard's Fiat Mirafiori.

"No," she moans. "Don't do this to me."

"It's for your own good."

The purple car … the Bentley … Ramage's Bentley … it's speeding closer to Stella. Tearing along the hard-packed sand. The engine bellows. She sees his skull-like face behind the windscreen. It's grinning obscenely and the tooth she forced him to pull out with pliers has grown back.

She can hear Richard singing to Lola inside the Fiat.

"We're all going to the zoo tomorrow, the zoo tomorrow, the zoo tomorrow. We're all going to the zoo tomorrow, we're going to be OK."

"No, Richard!" she screams. "You're not! He's going to kill you! Turn round!"

But of course, he doesn't. He can't hear her. He's halfway across the flat expanse of sand. The sea beckons him. Lola will love it. He can hold her up and dangle her beautiful little feet in the water. Lift her up as she squeals with delight when the waves tickle her toes. They are moving right to left in front of her. Ramage is approaching in a straight line towards her. The two cars are writing a big capital L in the sand. L is for Lola.

She tries to turn away, but Other Stella holds her head in a vice-like grip.

"You have to see this," she hisses, right in Stella's ear. "You have to remember."

Ramage is so close now, Stella can see his eyes. They glitter with murderous intent. He is speaking in a dark, smoke-roughened voice. She can hear him.

"You bitch. You killed me. Me! When all I was doing was preserving justice. He would have exposed us. This was sweet and proper. He had to die for his country."

The little silver Fiat is almost at the water's edge. Stella sees Lola in her baby seat. That soft, pink face. Blue eyes. Wispy blonde hair. She looks happy. She's waving her pudgy hands and smiling at her daddy. She looks to her left and catches sight of her mother. She waves. She speaks.

"Mama—"

The bang is so loud, Stella thinks she has gone deaf.

The Fiat flies towards her, spinning in mid-air.

Who thought it was a good idea to stick a pillar box on the beach? It's far too far for the postman to walk.

The Fiat hits the red iron cylinder with the grinning black mouth.

Richard's head slams sideways under the impact. It meets the scalloped rim of the pillar box, which has punched in the side window.

Stella's hearing returns in time to catch the sickening crunch as Richard's skull shatters against the blood-red iron. He flops back in his seat. Dead.

"Lola!" she screams. "My Lola!"

The flames burst in a bright yellow ball from the engine bay. Lola isn't smiling anymore.

Stella is weeping and moaning as the petrol tank ignites with a *whoomp*. Soon the car is burning, and she can see nothing but flames and black smoke.

Her nostrils fill with the acrid stench of burning rubber, and through her streaming eyes she sees Ramage driving away in the big purple car. Then the scene before her freezes and the colour leaches out of the flames. Stella realises she is staring at a faded photograph held between her shaking fingers.

She sinks to her knees. Pounds her fists against the sand.

"Make it stop," she wails. "Please. I'll do what you want, but please make it stop."

27
RETIRED

JUST before noon on the day of her interview with Freddie McTiernan, Frankie found herself holding open the door of her silver Audi A3 for Collier. She felt like a chauffeur and resisted the urge to salute as he approached. He must have read her mind because as he approached the car he smiled.

"No peaked cap, Frankie?"

When they were both buckled in, she let off the handbrake and drove out of the Paddington Green carpark and onto The Westway. The traffic was heavy all the way through central London, the City, the East End and out into the eastern suburbs.

Frankie and Collier had been caught in an embarrassing clinch at an office party some years before. Frankie tried to avoid thinking about the sweaty, alcohol-fuelled snog as she piloted the car towards the A12 and Essex. She glanced down and saw, with regret, that the seat belt had tightened against her breasts, opening a gap between two of her blouse buttons.

"Is Stella going to be OK, sir?" she blurted, more from a nervous desire to distract herself than anything else.

"For a start, it's Adam, as I think I told you before. And in answer to your question, I really don't know. You saw her point the gun at me, Frankie. You heard her raving about conspiracies and murders. I'm not an expert in mental health disorders, but at the very least I'd say she's suffering from some kind of delusion. I'm guessing some kind of delayed reaction to the deaths of Richard and Lola. What do you think? You've worked with her for the last few years."

Frankie pulled out to overtake a lorry and used the time to frame some kind of response. She'd become convinced that Stella was onto something. Lucian had settled the matter for her. And overnight, replaying that crucial line of Stella's about Collier's "friends in Pro Patria Mori," she'd had the unsettling thought, *What if Collier really* is *involved? What if Stella was right about him?*

"Stel's strong. I think she just needs some help. Maybe some therapy. It's just—"

"What?"

Do I say something or not?

"I'm worried she's just going to give in and leave the job."

Not, apparently. That's interesting.

"I think we need to take things one step at a time. She may decide she's had enough. I wouldn't blame her. Or she may manage to find her way back from all this. The trouble is, there's something of a legal conundrum, isn't there?"

"What's that, sir? Adam, I mean."

"Think about it. She threatened to kill me. You were a witness. Now, at the moment, under a section, she's deemed not responsible for her actions. She doesn't have *capacity*, in the jargon. If the doctors at St Mary's decide she's well, then we have to return to her original actions. At best, she could face a firearms charge, at worst, attempted murder. Either way, I find it hard to see how a continuing career in the Met would be a realistic option. Anyway, this is all hypothetical. At the moment, she's in a secure psychiatric unit and we're on our way to interview one of London's most powerful gangland figures, whether or not he's *retired*. Let's focus on that for now, OK?"

"Yes, sir. Adam."

. . .

Thirty minutes later, at 12.55 p.m., Frankie pulled up at the kerb on a small side road leading off Mill Green Lane in Ingatestone.

"Just in case he's got a security camera," Collier said. "Let's keep him off guard if we can."

With the engine and exhaust ticking behind them, and bright and dark bands of sunlight filtering through the trees lining the pavement, Frankie and Collier walked round the corner to Five Beeches. Collier stood by the gatepost, while Frankie spoke into the intercom.

The latch clacked and the wooden gate swung open.

"How the other half lives, eh?" Frankie said, as they marched side by side along the gravel drive to the front door.

"There's more blood than cement in the foundations of this place, Frankie, don't forget that."

As they reached the front door, Frankie checked the lapels on her suit jacket, making sure they were lying flat. She looked down and plucked at the front of her blouse, straightening it out and wishing, not for the first time, that she'd bought the next size up.

Collier pushed the doorbell. Somewhere inside, the chimes of Big Ben rang out. He turned to her.

"Best foot forward, Frankie." And he gave her an encouraging smile.

The door opened. Freddie McTiernan stood before them. Clearly he had already dressed for his game of golf. His outfit was a tribute to casual men's tailoring: a subtle blend of pale pink, fawn and lemon-yellow, with Argyll checks much in evidence.

He smiled. The expression didn't reach his eyes. Frankie noticed the way his jaw muscles worked as he turned from her to Collier.

"Well, well," he said to her. "Not just the monkey but the organ-grinder, too. You'd better come in."

They followed his broad, cashmere-clad back down a wide hallway and into a formal sitting room, furnished with bottle-green, buttoned-leather sofas. Freddie took an entire sofa to himself, sitting dead-centre and spreading his arms along the curved back. The body language wasn't hard to read. Frankie sat at one end of the facing sofa. Collier remained standing and took up a position behind her. *Classic*, she thought. *We're presenting an even bigger physical threat than the suspect.*

"First of all, thank you for seeing us, Mr McTiernan," she began. *No harm in starting off with a bit of politeness.*

"Always happy to help London's finest. And if they're not available, the Paddington Green fit-up mob." That wolfish smile again. Yellow canines and a look in the eyes that spoke clearly to Frankie: *I'll huff and I'll puff and I'll kneecap you and put you through a wood chipper.*

"No need for that, Freddie," Collier said from his position out of Frankie's field of vision. "Ronnie was as guilty as sin, and you know it."

"Really?" Freddie leaned forward, placing his hands on his knees. "Because the way I heard it, in this country, a man's innocent until proven guilty. The judge declared a mistrial."

"Yes, and as I'm sure you remember, the retrial jury found him guilty."

Freddie barked out a cynical laugh, loud enough to make Frankie flinch.

"Yes. After you planted evidence at his and Marilyn's place."

"Ancient history, Freddie. Ronnie's living high on the hog in Marbella now. Costa royalty. Just like you in your mock-Tudor hideaway down here in Crooksville, Essex."

Freddie leaned back. Smiled. Replaced his arms along the back of the sofa.

"You ever study Buddhism, Detective Chief Superintendent Collier?"

"What do you think?"

"You should. Very interesting religion. Especially the concept of karma. Fate, you might call it. I met this lady at a party last Christmas. Lovely woman. Retired magistrate. She was telling me all about it. You know what she said to me? 'Karma keeps the receipt.' I asked her what it meant. She said, not in these exact words mind, very cultured, she was. Anyway, she said you can shit on people all you want and in the short-term you might get away with it. But in the end your bad deeds catch up with you. Karma keeps the receipt, see?" He leaned forward again, hands on knees. "Fuck up other people and eventually karma fucks you up right back."

Collier's voice hardened.

"Which is all very fascinating, Freddie. But sadly for you, we didn't come all this way for a religious studies lesson. Detective Sergeant O'Meara. You have some questions for *Mister*," heavy sarcasm, "McTiernan."

Frankie cleared her throat. She realised she'd become so engrossed in the aggro flying between the two men that she'd forgotten the original purpose of the visit.

"Yes. What do you know about Albanian drug gang activity in east London?"

"Me? Nothing. Like I said on the phone, I'm retired."

"But your former associates aren't, are they? This morning, I asked a couple of people I know about the McTiernan operation. They seemed to think you're very much still a player."

Freddie shrugged.

"What people?"

Frankie smiled. Counted a three-second pause in her head.

"Tamit Ferenczy. Name mean anything to you?"

She watched his face closely as she pronounced the dead Albanian's name. Not much, but enough. A twitch of the lower lip. Slight dilation of the pupils. Deeper breath before speaking. *Yes, you know him, all right.*

"Never heard of the bloke. Is he one of the people you spoke to this morning?"

She shook her head.

"He's having trouble speaking at the moment on account of having his head splattered all over the roof of his club."

"Yeah, that would make conversation difficult. Like I said, it's not a name I'm familiar with."

She was framing another question when Collier cut in from behind her.

"Stop lying to us, McTiernan. You had Ferenczy and two of his minders killed. They were muscling in on your territory and you didn't like it. Couple of the clubbers reported a young lady leading a gang of female supporters waving a sawn-off around. One of them called her Orla, apparently. You've got a granddaughter with that name, haven't you?"

Freddie was on his feet in a single move. Face flushed, finger jabbing at Collier over Frankie's head.

"Don't you fucking dare come after my family, you cunt! I warned you last time. If you—"

Frankie tried to manoeuvre away from Freddie so she could stand to face him. She slid sideways along the shiny leather upholstery. The metallic double-snap from behind her didn't make sense.

The bang was huge in the confined space. Freddie jumped back. His eyes were wide with shock. Then he looked down at his stomach.

Frankie followed his gaze.

Something had happened to the pink and yellow jumper. The central portion had exploded outwards in a red rose as vivid and bright as the blooms climbing over the front porch.

The rose spread, wet and glistening. Then a flood of red soaked through into the fine woollen weave all the way down Freddie's ruined stomach and onto the front of his fawn golfing trousers. His eyes locked onto Frankie's again. The look was pleading. His mouth, lips bloodless, was working, but no sounds emerged. Clutching the massive wound in his midriff he stumbled backwards.

A second bang.

The sweater over Freddie's heart exploded outward in a mess of red.

She felt red-hot sparks on her cheeks and the backs of her hands. And the air smelled burnt somehow. She screamed as Freddie's lifeless body fell back against the sofa, releasing a fresh gout of blood that pooled on the leather seat. Grabbing the armrest, she wrenched herself round.

She looked up at Collier. He stood, arm out, Glock gripped in his right hand. A wisp of blue smoke curled up from the barrel. She clambered to her feet, using the arm of the sofa for support.

"Wh— what the fuck did you do?" she shouted. Her voice sounded distorted and muffled beneath the ringing in her ears.

28

FAMILY SCRAPBOOK

"DEAR? Are you all right."

Stella opened her eyes, dashed away the tears that were running freely over her cheeks. She looked up, blinking, into a pair of watery blue eyes behind gold-rimmed glasses. Beyond the elderly woman crouching over her, she could see a man she assumed was her husband. His face was creased with concern. A young couple hovered a little further back, their hands gripping a young child between them.

"I'm fine, thank you. Just a touch of the sun. I get migraines," she improvised, getting to her feet. She stumbled and the woman took her firmly by the elbow and turned to her husband.

"Bill. Give us a hand, would you? Don't stand there like a lemon."

He hurried over and took Stella's other arm.

"Let's get you a nice cup of tea. Marge and me have a flask. Look, it's just over there."

He pointed to a stripy rug spread out on the sand about thirty yards away. Two folding chairs stood guard over a small picnic. Mugs and a silver vacuum flask nestled against an array of Tupperware boxes.

ANDY MASLEN

"My shoes," Stella said.

"I've got them," he said. "Come on."

Stella allowed herself to be led by the couple to their spot on the beach. She accepted the offer of one of the chairs and sank, gratefully, into its springy embrace.

"Migraines, eh?" the woman said, unscrewing the top of the flask and pouring Stella a mug of tea. "They can be bastards, can't they?"

"Marge!" her husband exclaimed from his kneeling position on the rug. "Language!"

"Oh, please. I'm sure she's heard worse, haven't you, love? Young people today, they don't mind a bit of bad language. Anyway, that's what they are." She patted Stella's free hand. "My sister, Ange, was a martyr to them. Three days, some of them would last. She told me they got so bad she wanted to die."

"I'm feeling much better, thanks," Stella said. "It must have passed. They do sometimes. I'm Stella, by the way."

"Pleased to meet you, Stella. You already know our names. Marge and Bill. Watson. We've been coming here since the sixties. Haven't we, Bill?"

Bill nodded in agreement. Stella deduced he was the type of man – the type of husband – content to let his wife make the running in social interactions, supplying agreement when called on but otherwise happy to sip his tea, or pint, and watch the world go by.

"Here on business, are you, love?" Marge asked.

"Business?" Stella repeated, still half-stunned by the vision she'd just escaped from. "No. Not really. I'm on sick leave. Thought the sea air would do me good. Shows what a fat lot I know, doesn't it?"

Marge leaned across the short distance between the two chairs and patted Stella's knee.

"Don't be too hard on yourself, lovey. You couldn't have stopped it."

Stella stopped moving, her hand holding the mug halfway to her lips.

162

"What did you say?"

"You couldn't have stopped it. The migraine. They just come on out of nowhere, don't they?"

"Oh. Yes. They do. Just when you're least expecting them."

"'I wish I could put a stop to the bastards.' That's what Ange used to say."

Stella felt a firm pressure on her shoulders. Didn't look up. Just waited for the voice in her ear.

"You should tell her we're going to," Other Stella said. Then the pressure vanished.

Stella finished her tea and stood up, carefully.

"Thanks for the tea. I have to go. Enjoy the rest of your holiday," she said.

Keeping her eyes down, she walked across the sand to the road. In front of her, an ugly, rectangular building announced itself as Genting Casino. Stella wrinkled her nose at the thought of overpriced drinks and the sour smell of last night's beer and roulette losses. She turned to the right. A few hundred yards to the east, she could see what appeared to be a beachfront cafe and set off towards it.

Oliver's On The Beach turned out to be a tiny cuboid block with a few aluminium tables and chairs on the concrete apron at the front. Stella ordered a cappuccino and a cheese and ham toastie and sat at the table furthest from the serving hatch. She was thinking about the hit and run. How it had started her descent into grief, then madness, then the murderous quest for revenge. She still wanted Collier to pay, but Other Stella's insistence on wiping out whole families frightened her. What if she couldn't stop? What if Other Stella stopped being "other" at all?

Her phone rang, startling her. She looked down. And smiled. Thank Christ! Caller ID told her it was Vicky Riley, the freelance journalist who'd been working with Richard on exposing Pro Patria Mori.

"Vicky. How are you doing?"

"Honestly? I'm not sure. After they killed Ralph and Bea, I

just fell apart for a bit. Living in a camper van with Gemini Moon didn't exactly help with my sanity either."

"I can imagine. Did the police give you any more information about the killer?"

"I saw their bodies in the morgue when I did the identification. Ralph had three bullet holes in his chest. They shot Bea right in the middle of her forehead. Like the little girl in the nursery rhyme."

Vicky laughed. A broken, mirthless sound that sent a shiver down Stella's spine. Stella took a sip of the coffee. She had the seating area to herself but a few people were queuing at the serving counter. She turned away and lowered her voice.

"Look, I'm sorry to have to ask this, but we have to be objective. Are you completely sure it was PPM? I mean, and no offence, but farmers do keep guns and I know that a fair few commit suicide that way if, you know, they have debts on the farm or whatever."

"I'm totally sure. The detective who interviewed me said, and I quote, 'There are certain signs that the murders were the work of a professional.' Plus, they weren't shotgun injuries. I know enough about guns to know the difference. These were holes. Big ones, but holes. Like from a rifle or a pistol. I talked to a friend in the US. He covers the crime beat in Baltimore. I asked him what the cop meant about 'certain signs.' He said it was things like grouping. That's when the bullets are close together. Ralph had three over his heart. You could have covered them all with your palm. And headshots. No brass at the scene. You know what that means?"

"They collect the casings so forensics can't trace the weapon."

"Yes. And nothing was taken. So robbery wasn't the motive. They were executed. To threaten me."

"Where are you now? Still with Gemini?"

"No. I had to leave before I throttled her. All her talk of rebirth and reincarnation was making me ill."

"At home?"

"Nope. I don't know if I can ever go back there. I wouldn't feel safe. I'm staying with a friend. A journalist."

Stella felt a momentous decision approaching. *How far do I let Vicky in on this?* A roulette wheel in her brain spun, then slowed, and the little white ball skittered and bounced between the black segments marked "TELL" and the red, marked "DON'T." It came to rest.

29

A PROMISING CAREER

COLLIER looked at Frankie with a dead-eyed stare. He lowered the Glock to his side.

"He was scum, Frankie. They all are. Parasites in pink cashmere, ruining lives, getting fat on the profits of evil. We were doing fine work."

"We?"

"Pro Patria Mori. I'm sure you've figured it out by now."

"The conspiracy that Stella claimed killed Richard and Lola. It's real?"

"Oh, yes. It's real. The trouble is, I'm the only one left. There are a few people out there who are willing to help me out with operational matters, but Stella has been surprisingly effective in reducing the council's numbers."

Frankie's breath was coming in sharp little gasps, and sparks were flickering in her peripheral vision. She lifted her chin. *I'll finish this for you, Stel. I'll bring him in and you can get justice for Richard and Lola.* She held her hand out, noticed it trembling. Stiffened her arm.

"Give me the gun, sir. It's over."

Collier smiled sadly.

"I'm afraid you're right, Frankie. It *is* over."

He held out the gun towards her.

She reached for the muzzle, fingers opening to curl round the squared-off black barrel and began speaking.

"Adam Collier, I am arresting you under—"

Then she saw his index finger curling tighter round the trigger.

No! she said. But the word was only audible in her head.

The hollow point rounds took her full in the chest, over the heart. She died while she was still standing, as the organ ruptured and burst. She fell sideways, blood soaking the front of her blouse around the entry wounds.

* * *

"You were a good cop, Frankie. You had a promising career in front of you. In or out of PPM, you would have made it. Now we have to tell a little story together. You can help me with that, can't you?"

Collier knelt beside Frankie, avoiding the blood pooling beneath her body. He wiped the Glock thoroughly with his handkerchief then placed it in her right hand and curled her fingers tightly around the grip and over the trigger.

He lifted her arm and, holding her right hand in his, fired a round from the Glock into the wall behind Freddie.

He took the gun from her unresisting hand and repeated the process with Freddie, taking care to place the shot near the existing wound in Frankie's chest.

"There. Lots of GSR for forensics to find."

Collier looked down at his clothes. The blood spatter wasn't too obvious on the charcoal-grey suit. And after his experience meting out some summary punishment to one of Ferenczy's low-level dealers, he had also opted for a dark shirt. He left the crime scene and went upstairs in search of a bathroom. As he lathered his hands and face with Freddie McTiernan's sandalwood-scented soap, he pondered his next move. The story he'd arranged at Five Beeches would hold up, no question.

Frankie had removed the Glock from the Exhibits Room without proper authorisation. No doubt from a misplaced sense of loyalty, she had embarked on a quest to avenge what she saw as McTiernan's involvement in the murder of Stella's family. The file Collier had doctored would supply corroboration for that part of the narrative. She travelled down to Ingatestone to murder the former gangster. Dying, McTiernan summoned enough strength to wrestle the gun away from Frankie and kill her. Both their fingerprints were on the gun. Both had gunshot residue on their hands and clothes. Carpet fibres in the floor would match both the CID office and Collier's office. Which was fine, because hadn't he spoken to her that morning about her request to interview McTiernan?

He reckoned it would be a day or two before Frankie's absence started causing consternation at Paddington Green. From then until her body was discovered, along with Freddie's, who knew? If he had a cleaner, it could be tomorrow. Otherwise, when a family member got worried and went round to check on him. Once through the front door, they'd discover the carnage in seconds.

But as Collier dried his hands on one of Freddie McTiernan's soft, fluffy towels, the sound he could hear most clearly above the ringing in his ears was of doors closing, not opening. The FBI transfer was taking too long. He needed to get out while he still could.

30

CONFESSION

THE ball clattered to a stop in a black section.

"I think you're safe to go home," Stella said in a rush.

"How can you say that after what they did to Bea and Ralph? They're probably just waiting till I put the key in the door then they'll shoot me, too."

Stella finished her coffee and walked away from the cafe, still speaking.

"Because there is no 'they' anymore. I've killed them. All but one. And he's going to bolt, I'm sure of it."

While she waited for Vicky to respond, Stella smiled to a woman pushing a buggy along the pavement past the cafe. She was about Stella's age. She smiled back.

"Sorry. Did you just say you killed them?" Vicky asked, her voice transmitting scepticism down the line like a blare of trumpets.

"Yes. I did. Four Pro Patria Members out of six. One had a heart attack before I could get to him and one's still at large. As I'm laying my cards on the table here, I've also killed two psychos they sent after me and seven gangsters, six of them Albanian. I probably got the guy who killed your godparents if it's any consolation."

"You're joking, right?"

"Do I sound like I'm joking?"

"Where are you? I can't get my head around, I mean, I can hear you but I can't process this. Can we meet?"

"I'm in a rather pretty if empty seaside town called Westcliff-on-Sea. Fancy some fish and chips?"

"What train do I need?"

Stella gave Vicky the train times.

"OK. I'll call you from the station when I get there."

Ninety minutes later, Stella stood outside Westcliff-on-Sea station, waiting for the 18.13 train from Fenchurch Street.

In ones and twos, then in larger clumps, the passengers emerged from the grey-and-white sliding doors. The flow of people slowed to a dribble, then petered out altogether. No Vicky. Stella checked her watch, then the arrivals board. No doubt about it: this was the London train. She turned around, worried that maybe she'd missed Vicky. Or that Vicky hadn't recognised her, what with the all-new do.

A tap on the shoulder brought her whirling round. Standing in front of her, blonde hair blowing about in a sudden breeze, was Vicky Riley. Her eyes were hidden by oversized sunglasses. Together with the white cotton jacket and tight jeans over high-heeled, silver-toed boots, they gave her the look of a movie star. The two women embraced. Stella could feel the tension in Vicky's shoulders and back muscles.

"Come on," she said, as she released her. "Let's walk down to the beach. It's a lovely day to be at the seaside."

She crooked her right elbow, and Vicky threaded her left arm through the gap. As they walked, she started asking questions in an urgent whisper. Stella was glad the pavements were largely unpopulated, it having reached that time of the evening when the day trippers had gone home and the holidaymakers were off having a drink or an early dinner.

"Did you mean what you said on the phone?"

"About what I did to the PPM members? Yes. Every word. I shot one, smashed one over the head with a skillet, threw one out of a top storey window and electrocuted the other one in the bath."

"Shit! And you said there were others. Psychos? And Albanians? Jesus, Stella, what's going on?"

"OK, look. After we spoke last time, my investigation turned up trumps. I identified the members of the conspiracy. But they must have found out I was after them. Don't ask me how. Maybe I wasn't as careful as I should have been about covering my tracks. They sent people after me. One of them was the guy who killed your godparents. And I'm so sorry you got dragged into this. They were innocent. It should never have happened."

"Please don't apologise. And remember, I was already digging into PPM myself. That's why they went after Richard."

Stella nodded.

"Anyway, the hitters they sent weren't good enough, apparently. The last one got herself admitted to the psychiatric ward at St Mary's in Paddington. I threw her down a stairwell."

"Wait. What? What were you doing in the loony bin? Sorry, I mean—"

Stella laughed.

"It's fine. Everyone there called it that. Well, everyone who didn't get to choose whether they went home at five-thirty did. My boss and the station pathologist sectioned me. He's the final piece of the jigsaw. My boss, that is. Detective Superintendent Adam Collier."

"Fucking hell, this is crazy! And he's the only one of them left? You're sure?"

"I took their leader's mobile phone off him right before I killed him. He had them all listed. All the members."

They'd reached the beach by this point and Vicky sat on a bench facing the sand.

"I'll sink up to my ankles in these heels," she said, bending to unzip her boots, then taking her socks off. Stella sat beside her and for the second time that day, went barefoot as they walked onto the beach.

"Arresting them was never part of the plan," Stella said. "It wouldn't have worked, anyway. They'd just have got each other off. They killed my family, Vicky. They had to pay. Properly."

Vicky turned her face towards Stella. She pushed the sunglasses onto the top of her head, revealing the amazing blue eyes that Stella had noticed the first time she'd met Vicky.

"Are you OK? I mean, you're really calm, but you've just told me you've killed, like, a dozen people."

"Thirteen, actually, but let's not split hairs."

Vicky stopped walking and faced Stella. She gripped her by the upper arms and stared intently into her eyes. Stella stared back. She could feel it. The moment of truth. How was Vicky going to play it? As far as Stella could see, there were three possibilities. Option one, call the police and report a mass murderer strolling along the soft, golden sand at Westcliff-on-Sea. Option two, keep shtum and write the whole thing up as a "story of the century" exposé of criminality at the highest, and some of the lowest, levels of the British legal system. Option three … well, yes, what exactly *was* option three? She watched Vicky's mouth open as she began to answer.

Other Stella was standing behind Vicky's left shoulder. She'd cocked her head to one side. Waiting. Stella prayed Vicky wouldn't go for option one. Didn't know if she'd be able to control Other Stella. Vicky spoke.

31

HONESTY IS THE BEST POLICY

COLLIER stood in front of the mirror in the hall and checked his appearance. Hair in place. Tie straight and properly knotted. He tweaked it with thumb and forefinger anyway. Leaning closer, he examined his face and neck for blood spatter. Nothing. He looked down. A forensics officer would see the fine droplets of blood dotting the charcoal suit jacket and trousers. But he wasn't planning on subjecting himself to that level of scrutiny. The toecaps of his shoes shone. He rubbed each one up and down on the calf of the opposite leg. And then he left.

Outside, he glanced at the Rolls Royce. A sudden urge to defile the gold bodywork seized him. *No. Don't spoil the story, Adam.* On a whim, he wandered across the striped lawn, past a shed, heading for a stand of black-stemmed bamboo waving in the soft breeze blowing left to right across the garden. As he reached them, he heard the tinkling of an ornamental fountain. Underlying the sound was a coarser burble, as from a pump. Beyond the stand of bamboo, a huge pond had been built, raised up from the ground rather than sunk in. The foot-high brick walls were topped with rough-hewn stone cappings. At one end, a heavy-duty pump had been concealed beneath more stonework, but its outflow pipe was clearly visible and an island of bubbles spread out across the water. He leaned over and peered in.

Gliding just beneath the surface, a huge, white-and-orange fish flicked its tail, rippling the water. Two more giants hove into view, one bluish black, the other a pale lemon yellow.

"So you were into koi carp were you, Freddie?" he said, prodding one of the fish on its back with a finger. "Expensive hobby."

He walked back to the shed and opened the door. Inside the dim, pine-smelling space, he saw a large petrol mower. Above it, on a shelf, stood a green plastic container that sloshed heavily as he took it down. Smiling, he wandered back to the pond. He put the container down beside the brickwork, then leaned down and wrenched the cable from the rear of the pump. With a stuttering burble, the pump died. The last few bubbles dispersed on the surface of the water. Without hesitation, he unscrewed the cap on the container and emptied the petrol into the pond. With the harsh smell irritating the inside of his nose, he walked back to the shed, tossed the empty can inside, shut the door and made his way back to the drive.

He stopped at the Rolls Royce.

"Oh, well. In for a penny," he said.

His front door key had a sharp point. As he drew it down the side of the car facing the garden he grinned at the obscene metallic screech.

"A cop who was trigger-happy *and* a vandal! Just wasn't your day, was it?"

He waited on the pavement for the gate to close. The clack as the latch engaged behind him brought a final smile. "If he was our final target, then I'd say we did a pretty good job," he said to a squirrel clinging to a tree. He looked left as he drew level with the side road. Frankie's compact Audi looked out of place on a street where all the residents seemed to park their cars on private drives or in garages. But it was clean, smart and didn't look like it had been dumped by joyriders. No doubt some suburban busybody would eventually stick a printed note under the wipers asking the owner to "kindly park your car somewhere else," or report it to the local neighbourhood watch, but until then it would remain hidden from the police.

Collier walked from Mill Green Road to Ingatestone station. The journey took him half an hour. While walking he made a call.

"Linda? It's Adam."

The HR manager's voice was breathy.

"Hello Adam. How can I help?"

"What have you been doing this afternoon?"

"Oh, you know, paperwork. Endless appraisals, evaluations, and on top of that, we're trialling a new piece of recruitment software that's supposed to help us make better hiring decisions."

"Anyone with you?"

"Sadly, no. Just little me. I've been all on my own in my office."

"No, you haven't. I've been with you. We were discussing staff budgets all afternoon."

He heard a moment's hesitation. When she spoke again, the girlishness had gone, replaced with something altogether steelier.

"Yes, of course. When did our meeting finish? Six? We went for a drink afterwards?"

He smiled, causing a man trimming a privet hedge with old-fashioned shears to smile back and nod.

"Perfect. Thank you, Linda."

Next, he called one of the detective sergeants under his command.

"Jake, it's Adam. Have you seen Frankie?"

"No, sir. I think she was going to interview a snitch or something. She wasn't specific."

"If you see her, will you ask her to come and find me? I'm in HR with Linda Heath. Been there all afternoon for my sins."

He took the 15.02 train back to Liverpool Street, paying for his ticket with cash. Back in London he took the tube to Kew and was back home at 5.00 p.m.

Closing the front door behind him and dropping his keys into the bowl on the hall table, he called out.

"Hello? Lynne?"

He went through to the kitchen and opened a bottle of red wine, pouring himself a decent-sized glass and downing half of it.

Lynne appeared in the doorway, towelling her hair.

"You're home early. I just had a shower."

He saw her looking at the wine. He picked up the bottle.

"Want one?"

"Adam Collier! It's not even six!" Then she smiled. "Sure, why not?"

He poured her a glass, topped up his own then motioned to the table.

"Sit down, darling. There's something I need to get off my chest."

Her forehead creased and her eyebrows drew together, carving a deep groove above the bridge of her nose. She gulped some wine down then immediately started coughing. Collier waited until the paroxysm had passed, leaning round to pat her on the back. She looked across at him and he could read it in her eyes. The fear. That this would be the moment it all unravelled.

"What is it?" she asked. "Is everything OK? Has something happened at work?"

He laughed, a sardonic sound that sounded harsh even to his own ears.

"You could say that."

"You're not leaving me, are you? Please tell me it's not that."

He reached over and placed his large hand over her smaller one, feeling the wedding and engagement rings under his fingers.

"No. I'm not leaving you. But after I tell you what I need to, I wonder whether you'll want to stay married."

Her face creased still further and for a moment he wondered whether she would start crying.

"Don't keep me in suspense, for God's sake. What is it, darling? Tell me. Whatever it is, I promise I'll help you. We'll get through this like we always do."

He took another mouthful of the wine, swallowed it without tasting. And spoke.

"Do you remember what you said when Theo died?"

Her eyes popped wide.

"What?"

Collier tried again.

"When they turned off the life support and came to tell us when he was gone. Do you remember what you said? The very first thing?"

Lynne gulped some wine. He could tell it wasn't what she'd been expecting. She looked up then returned her gaze to him.

"I said – I think I did, anyway – that I wanted to kill the little bastard who stabbed him."

Now or never, Collier thought. *I need someone I can trust.*

"I felt that way, too. A few weeks after that, I had lunch with a judge. He invited me to join an organisation. An organisation that was providing justice for people who'd been hurt like we were."

Lynne opened her mouth to speak, but he held up a hand. If this was going to go the way he wanted it to, he needed to keep talking.

"We looked at miscarriages of justice. Basically, where the guilty walked free. Like Crispin Radstock. We were putting things right. Then things got messy. A journalist and a lawyer started investigating us. The lawyer died and his wife started coming after us, one by one. The others are dead, all but one by her hand. It's just me now, and I'm frightened she's coming after me to finish the job. That's why I want us to move to the US. We need to get away, Lynne."

He paused, watching, waiting for a response. Trying to figure out his options if she took the high ground. Not wanting to look the obvious answer in the face. She saved him the trouble.

"This organisation that recruited you."

"Yes?"

"They kill people, don't they? Criminals I mean. The bad ones. The rapists, the murderers."

Collier nodded. She stared straight into his eyes and he waited.

"Why didn't you kill Radstock?"

"I wanted to. But he disappeared. I looked for him, Lynne, believe me, I did. But in the end other things just got in the way. But you found him where we couldn't."

"So—?"

"So now I know."

She nodded, her lips set in a grim line.

"Yes, you do. But you said the lawyer's wife is coming for you. Is it Stella Cole?"

He blinked. *How did you get there so fast?* He decided to ask.

"Actually it is, but how—"

"You've been talking in your sleep. Last night you said, 'Not me, Stella. Not guilty.' I met her once. The barbecue you organised just after you moved to Paddington Green. She seemed nice."

"She was. But when," he sighed, "when we killed her husband, her daughter was in the car with him. She died too. It sent Stella over the edge. She basically lost it while she was on sick leave. She came back but she was changed. Basically insane. She's been on a killing spree."

Lynne finished her wine, topped up both their glasses, then reached across to stroke his cheek.

"Darling, why didn't you tell me?"

"About her?"

"About everything. The organisation that recruited you. Her … everything."

This is going better than I hoped.

"Honestly? I thought you'd disapprove at best, and ask for a divorce at worst. Then when she started the killings, I was frightened she'd come after you. I've been trying to sort it out but she's just, I don't know," he rubbed a hand over his face, suddenly aware that he wasn't acting. "She's a bloody monster. I can't stop her."

"Then let's go. Right now. Let's go and pack. We'll live in a hotel or rent somewhere till you get your transfer to the FBI sorted out."

Collier thought back to their early-hours conversation three days earlier. About Crispin Radstock – aka Simon Halpern.

"OK. Book us flights to Chicago. As soon as you can. Tomorrow if possible. Pack for me, too. Just the basics. We can buy new clothes when we get to Chicago." He stood up.

"Why? Where are you going?"

"Leeds."

32

JOURNALISTIC ETHICS

STELLA'S mouth dropped open. She shut it again with an audible clack from her teeth. Glanced over Vicky's shoulder to see Other Stella winking before vanishing.

"Sorry. Did you just say what I think you said?"

Vicky's mouth was drawn into a straight line.

"Let's kill him. PPM murdered my godparents. After my parents died, Bea and Ralph brought me up as their own. They gave me everything. Helped me get my A levels when I could've just gone off the rails. Supported me at university. And those *fuckers*," she hissed out the obscenity, "killed them just to intimidate me. You're right. They've put themselves above the law. Beyond it. What would be the point of calling the police? No offence, but how can we be sure there aren't more bent cops on the PPM payroll?"

"Honestly? We can't. And none taken, by the way. If I am still a police officer it's more by luck than judgement. I think Adam, I mean Collier – shit! How did I ever go around chumming up to him and using his Christian name? Anyway, he can't use official channels to instigate disciplinary proceedings, let alone charge me.

He knows if he did it would blow back in his face like the ultimate shit-fan combo."

"Right, so I say we track Collier down and kill him" Vicky whispered, though they were alone on this stretch of beach, and the waves shushing over the sand and shingle at the water's edge would easily drown out their conversation.

"Whoa, slow down. I'm in this up to my neck. I've pretty much chosen my path. Plus when it's over I'm … I'm going to leave anyway. But you're a journalist. A bloody good one. I'm fairly sure committing murder is against journalistic ethics."

"Yes, and look where they got me. Nobody will touch the story. I can't get my hands on Richard's source material. And the two people I loved the most in all the world are dead. All because I wanted to win a bloody journalism prize."

Vicky bent to pick up a flat stone, then crouched and skimmed it expertly across the flat surface of the water between two incoming waves. The stone skipped half a dozen times before seeming to slide over the surface then sink out of sight. She straightened and brushed her hands off against her bottom.

"Nice," Stella said. "The skimmer, I mean."

"Ralph taught me."

"Vicky, listen. You're a writer. You tap keys for a living. Even before I got myself some additional training I was on the streets, dealing with the scum of the earth, day in, day out. I've got my hands dirty and I know I can do it. You can't. I bet you've never even hit someone, have you?"

Vicky frowned, then her eyes widened.

"Actually I have!"

"When?"

"In Year Ten. Philippa Gray kissed my boyfriend at the school disco right in front of me and I slapped her."

Stella laughed at the absurdity of it, then started choking. Vicky administered a few good, hard slaps between her shoulder blades until Stella flapped her hand to indicate the fit had passed.

"I also just hit a police officer," Vicky finished.

"OK, I'll give you that one. But seriously, you can help me.

That would be great. Fantastic, I mean. But leave the actual deed to me. It isn't as easy as they make it look on the telly."

"Maybe. I'm not promising. If Collier's the only one left then I want to tell him to his face what an evil bastard he is right before he dies. I want him to hear it from me."

"We'll see. There's quite a queue you know. You ever hear of Ronnie Wilks?"

"What, Ronnie "The Razor" Wilks? Doyen of the Costa del Crime who claimed he was fitted up for his last stretch inside?"

"The very same. Well he and Marilyn want revenge on Collier. As does Marilyn's dad."

"And that would be?"

"Freddie McTiernan. I'm staying with him at the moment, actually. He has a lovely house."

Now it was Vicky's turn to splutter.

"Excuse me? You're staying with Freddie McTiernan? He's, like, what, the biggest gang leader in the East End since the Krays?"

Stella smiled, amused at Vicky's wide-eyed look of amazement.

"He's retired. Sold his shares in the business and spends his days playing golf. He's thinking about getting a dog."

Vicky shook her head, then swept her hair back from her face after the wind caught it.

"I'm just trying to recalibrate, you know, literally everything I thought I knew about you, which admittedly isn't much. You're a house guest of Freddie McTiernan. You appear to be on first-name if not intimate terms with Ronnie and Marilyn Wilks. And you've put a dozen, no, thirteen, people under the ground. Stella Cole, should I be frightened of you?"

Stella paused before answering. Because the answer was simple.

Yes. Very.

"Vicky Riley, are you a good person?"

"Yes. I am." She touched the skin at the notch of her throat. "I hope so."

"Then, no. You don't need to be frightened of me. I'll tell you what, though."

"What?"

"I could murder a drink right now."

Over drinks – a glass of pinot grigio for Vicky, a large gin and tonic for Stella – the two women discussed how best to murder a detective chief superintendent serving in the Metropolitan Police Service. The pub was quiet, old couples mainly, enjoying their pints and schooners of medium-sweet sherry. In a corner, a skinny young dude, full sleeves of tattoos on both scrawny arms, was feeding pound coins into a fruit machine.

"Have you got a plan?" Vicky asked, running her index finger down the bowl of her wineglass.

"That's a very good question. I *did* have a plan. I got as far as his office with a loaded Glock, then my sergeant Tasered me and I ended up in the loony bin fighting off the psycho bitch from hell."

"I'd run if I was him."

"Run where? He's not exactly a drifter. He's got the job, the pension, the career, everything."

"Yeah, and he's also got you coming after him. He knows you won't stop. Not after you've killed those people he sent after you."

"Can you look into that end of things for me?"

Vicky nodded vigorously.

"Yes! It's what I do. OK, so I may not be any good with the rough stuff, but I can wheedle information out of people like a toddler getting sweets from their parents – oh, God, I'm sorry."

Her face fell and she looked down in embarrassment. Stella reached across the circular table and closed her hand over Vicky's.

"It's OK. I even smiled at a woman with a buggy today. Look, that would be great. If you can find out what Collier's planning. If he's going to run, I need to know where. And I have another idea."

"What?"

"There are a few people I reckon I can still count on at the station. Well, two really, and one possible."

"Who are they?"

"OK, first, Lucian. Lucian Young. He's a forensics officer. Tall, black, extremely good looking, rich and great with computers. I had to test him out before I told him about PPM. Made out I was trying to recruit him. Jesus! He nearly had a heart attack."

"And number two?"

"That would be Danny Hutchings. He's the armourer. He's—"

"Deep Throat!"

"Pardon?"

"Oh. I shouldn't tell you but … oh fuck, where I'm headed, worrying about protecting my sources is probably going out the window. Your friend Danny is … was … my source on the PPM story. I call him Deep Throat. I spoke to him the last day I saw Bea and Ralph alive."

"Huh." Stella drained her gin and tonic. "Small world. So, Danny's one of the good guys. I may have taken advantage of him, just a teeny-weeny bit. Stole a pistol from his armoury and a box of hollow points too. Probably got him into a shitload of trouble when they did the stocktake."

Vicky sipped her wine.

"You said one possible."

"Frankie O'Meara. My sergeant."

"Wait. What? The one who zapped you with a Taser?"

"It's complicated. I'm sure she thought she was doing the right thing. That's Frankie all over. But I'm convinced Collier got to her. If we can set up a meeting between all five of us, I think I can get her to see what's been happening. Then she'll be onside and we have someone on the inside who works in the same place as Collier. It has to be worth a try, don't you think?"

Vicky shrugged.

"You know her. I don't. But if she's as upstanding as you say she is, then I can't see her volunteering for anything as desperate as killing her boss."

"No. But she might be persuaded to help get us information. I can always tell her we're gathering evidence."

They sat over more rounds of drinks, picking at the scab of how to get to Collier. Then they ordered some food from the bar and a bottle of wine. At ten-thirty, Vicky announced she had to go to get the last train back to London. After Stella had repeated her belief that it was safe to go home, Vicky had agreed to head back to Chiswick and wait for Stella to call her.

"You going back to Freddie's tonight, then?" Vicky asked.

"Nah. I may have had slightly too many G&Ts. It's a long drive and I don't want to throw up in a minicab."

Stella kissed Vicky goodbye outside the pub then headed back inside. A small blackboard in an A-frame stand by the front door announced "Rooms. Sky TV, tea and coffee facilities, en suite." A few minutes' conversation with the landlady and she was heading up the uneven, carpeted stairs holding a blue rubber dog toy shaped like a bone with a brass Yale key dangling from a split ring.

Stella awoke with a ferocious hangover. She countered it with two ibuprofen, two paracetamol, three mugs of excellent tea in the pub's dining room and a full English breakfast.

At one point during the interminable taxi ride from Westcliff-on-Sea back to Ingatestone, as the driver swung the ageing Nissan out of a roundabout, Stella thought she was going to throw up. But by breathing deeply, and staring fixedly out of the window, she managed to keep her breakfast down. The car had not been optioned with air conditioning by its first owner, and the heat inside had been stifling when she'd first climbed in. A strawberry-shaped air freshener swinging gaily from the rear-view mirror only added to the cloying atmosphere, made worse by the driver's aftershave. The rear window motor had apparently failed with the drop-glass halfway down, but even that was better than nothing.

It was with no small measure of relief that Stella paid the fare and exited the sauna-like interior. She punched in the code on the intercom box and stood back while the gates swung open. Above her head, a blackbird trilled and warbled somewhere in the thick, waving branches of a copper beech tree.

Mindful of Freddie's privacy, she waited for the gate to close behind her before making her way up the drive to the front door. The Rolls was parked in its usual spot, a gold-painted behemoth in the centre of a smooth, undisturbed circle of pale gravel. Rose petals still lay across its roof and bonnet.

Stella frowned. Something about the big car bothered her. But whatever it was would have to wait. She needed to pee.

Once inside she called out.

"Freddie? You in?"

No answer. All the doors leading off the hallway were closed. She took the stairs two at a time, heading for the guest bathroom and its gold-plated taps. Once she'd finished and washed her hands she came downstairs at a more leisurely pace and sauntered into the kitchen. Nothing out of place. Not a cup or side plate, apple core or leftover glass of wine.

"Freddie?" she shouted again. Louder this time.

33

CRIME SCENE

RETURNING to the hall, Stella turned right to enter the dining room that Freddie had told her he used as a study from time to time.

"Even a pensioner still has a bit of paperwork to do now and then, Stella," he'd said, winking.

The room was as immaculate as the kitchen. The sitting room, then.

As Stella reached for the polished brass door knob, something caught at her brain. The Roller. Freddie had been to play golf. But there weren't any tyre marks through the gravel. A heavy car like that would leave bloody great trenches, surely? And the rose petals. They looked as if they'd been there since the day she arrived.

She looked down at her hand twisting the door knob. At her wedding ring and the eternity ring next to it.

Something felt off.

The Rolls.

The gravel.

The petals.

The silence.

As the door opened, it sucked a few litres of air out of the room beyond. Air contaminated with the scent of decay. With the gases that form inside corpses and start to issue forth like a ghastly warning of what lies ahead for each and every human being born of woman. Stella inhaled. The smell was familiar from a thousand crime scenes. A fly buzzed out through the gap, almost colliding with Stella's right cheek.

"Oh, fuck," she said, pushing the door wide and stepping into a nightmare.

Stella's first murder case had been "a proper Tarantino" as her then boss, Detective Sergeant Roman Harper, had called it. In the murder squad at the time, a few of the senior detectives, all film buffs, had devised a scale of goriness that they delighted in applying to murder scenes, and then arguing over in the pub after work. Deaths caused by blunt force trauma, poisoning and strangulation were all classified at the lowest level. Hitchcocks. Basically, horrible but anaemic. Conquer your fear of the unknown and they weren't too bad to look at. Common-or-garden stabbings, attacks with edged weapons, shootings with small-calibre firearms: these were Leones. Moderate bloodshed but confined to pools, runs and spatters. Then you moved into altogether bloodier territory. Shotgun wounds. Large-calibre handguns. The more frenzied knife attacks. Peckinpahs. Finally, at the top of the tree, the Tarantinos. Dismemberings. Multiple victims. Body parts. Brain matter. Lakes of sticky red blood. Jackson Pollocks of the stuff all over the place.

The scene confronting her was a Leone. No question. At first, all she saw was the blood. Pools and runs had soaked into the rug and the carpet beneath. And both leather sofas were now more red than green.

Then her training kicked in. Two victims. One male, one female … Oh, no, not "a female." *Frankie! Oh, Jesus, girl, what the fuck happened? You poor, poor thing. He shot you. Freddie shot you!*

Standing back, and breathing deeply, despite the smell of blood and decay, Stella observed the scene. Frankie lay on her back, one leg twisted beneath her. The front of her white shirt was soaked in blood all the way from her collar to the waistband of her black trousers. Blowback had painted the underside of her jaw with a stippling of red.

Freddie lay on his back, too. Sprawled across the leather sofa. Arms outflung as if he was keen to prevent anyone joining him. Not that anyone in their right mind would want to, seeing as half the contents of his abdomen had tumbled from his stomach in a slew of dark blood.

His right hand was clutching the pistol he'd used on Frankie. Skirting her fallen sergeant's body, Stella edged closer to Freddie and bent to sniff the muzzle. No doubt about it. This was the murder weapon. The whiff of burnt cordite said all that needed to be said. No need for ballistics. Except. Except …

"Except the old man told you he didn't have a pistol," Other Stella said, standing behind the sofa and resting her elbows on the blood-spattered backrest. "And, what, he shot Frankie then stuck a couple of rounds into himself to prove a point?"

"You're right. She must have shot him first. But then——"

"How did he get the pistol off her? Good question, because old people with abdominal gunshot wounds are always beating fit young police officers in wrestling matches. Plus, look. The one to the heart would have been fatal on its own. So if she shot him there first, he couldn't have got the gun off her. And——"

"If she didn't shoot him in the heart, then who did?"

Other Stella pushed herself upright and strolled around the end of the sofa. She came to a halt right in front of Stella, her shoes squelching on the blood-soaked carpet. She put the tip of one finger to her chin and looked up at the ceiling.

"Hmm. What did that text she sent say?"

"She said she thought I was right about Collier. That he was dirty. Oh, shit. He found out."

"Must have done. So he brings her down here on some pretence, does Freddie, does Frankie, then stages the whole thing. You have to admit, babe, he *is* a murdering bastard."

"Right, well I'm fucking *un*staging it."

ANDY MASLEN

Stella picked her way over to Freddie's corpse and bent to retrieve the pistol. The fingers were stiff with rigor mortis. Muttering "Sorry, Freddie" under her breath, she pried them open one after another, wincing as the ligaments crackled and snapped. After a few minutes' work, the pistol came free.

"A Glock. There's a surprise," Other Stella said. "Penny to a pound says it came from the Armoury at Paddington Green. Where your *boyfriend* works."

Stella stood, sticking the gun into the back of her waistband.

"Danny's not bent. He's been feeding tips to Vicky Riley. Collier must've lifted it. Or taken one from the Exhibits Room."

"So what now? You might want to think about cleaning this place up. Your fingerprints will be all over it."

Stella frowned.

"No they won't. Don't you remember? Yiannis disappeared them for me."

"Huh. Apparently not." She held her hands out by her sides. "What can I say? Even alter egos make mistakes."

Stella shook her head. Then she walked closer until she was just a few inches from Other Stella.

She poked her in the chest.

"You."

Another poke, harder this time.

"Aren't."

A real stab.

"REAL!"

She shoved her hard with both hands and was gratified to see her vanish in the act of falling backwards onto Freddie's bloodied lap.

Stella turned and left the sitting room, closing the door softly behind her. Without the presence of the murder weapon, the local police would have a big hole in their case. Yes, it looked like a murder-suicide – albeit a murder-suicide of the bloodiest and most unlikely kind – but the question would loom large in their investigation. Where's the gun? *Not my problem*, Stella thought. *Collier's little stage play just got taken off before the first night.*

194

Out of nowhere, her vision darkened and with a swirl of dizziness making her stagger, she sat heavily on the stairs. Head in hands, she waited for the sensation of falling to stop, breathing steadily in through her nose and out through her mouth. Finally she felt OK enough to open her eyes. As she did so, tears rolled free, tickling her cheeks on their way to drip from her jawline onto her jeans.

"Oh, Frankie. I'm sorry I got you caught up in this. You just wanted to chase the bad guys and instead you got caught between me and Pro Patria Mori. You too, Freddie. You did some pretty bad things but you were retired. I believe that. But don't worry. I'll put things right. I'll make Collier remember you before I kill him."

Heaving a great, shuddering sigh, she stood, turned and ascended the staircase. As Freddie's guest, she had kept to the guest bedroom and the downstairs rooms of the house. As his avenger, she had no qualms about having a poke around.

"After all, it's not as if I'm invading your privacy anymore, is it?"

Freddie's bedroom, she knew, was at the end of the hall, overlooking the back garden. The door wasn't locked, though she was half-expecting to twist the knob and find the door immoveable. The room beyond was large, but not breathtakingly so. Maybe twenty feet by fifteen. Super-king but not suite. Thick, white shag pile carpet that gave under her tread; rich, red velvet curtains that puddled on the floor; and, dominating the masculine space, a vast sleigh bed, its deep-brown wooden base curving at the foot and head to suggest to its occupant that he might be speeding across the snows behind a team of huskies. The sage-green bed linen was immaculate, neatly arranged as if by a soldier. *Were you ever in the Army, Freddie?* she thought incongruously.

She crossed the room and sat on the bed. The nightstand was as neat as the rest of the room. A couple of paperback editions of Agatha Christie novels, squared up. *Very old school, very Freddie McTiernan,* she thought. A brass-stemmed reading lamp with a green glass shade. A pair of reading glasses. She began opening the drawers of the night-stand one at a time. The top drawer contained socks, all black, folded. The middle, underpants, all white, rolled into stubby sausages. *Definitely something military about all this.* She pushed it home and pulled out the bottom drawer. And inhaled sharply.

Filling the drawer as if it had been constructed specifically to hold them without any wasted space, were bundles of cash. Twenty-pound notes. Used, not new. But girdled with robins-egg-blue paper bands as if by a banker with an eye for colour. Resting dead-centre on the money was a flick-knife with a red-and-chrome handle.

"Fuck me, Freddie! What's this? Petty cash?"

She stuck the knife in her back pocket then picked up a bundle of twenties, destroying the symmetry of the top layer, and flipped it over the edge of her thumb. No newspaper one layer down. No blanks. She lifted the cash to her nose and sniffed.

"Well, it smells like money."

It did. It had the faintly cheesy whiff of banknotes that have been through many hands.

She placed it on the bed beside her and began emptying the drawer. When she had finished, forty bundles lay beside her in an uneven pyramid. Slitting the paper band of the topmost bundle she counted the notes. One hundred in all. *OK, Stella, time for your best mental maths. Remember Miss Evans always gave you top marks for that at school. So, a hundred times twenty is two thousand. So two grand per bundle. Eighty grand in total.*

She didn't even have to ponder what to do. The money was dirty, no question. But then, she wasn't exactly in the running for whiter-than-white cop of the year, either. A little extra cash might come in handy while she waited for Jason to sell her house in West Hampstead. She'd checked her bank balance in Westcliff-on-Sea while waiting for Vicky's train to arrive and was gratified, if surprised, to see that her salary was still being paid in at the end of the month. But then, as she'd reasoned, she was still on the payroll, even if sectioned.

She returned to the front hallway and retrieved her daysack from the coat rack by the front door. Back in Freddie's room, she took four bundles and stuck them in the bag then cinched the drawstring tight before clipping the straps shut. The rest she replaced in the drawer.

"I know what you should spend some of it on, babe."

Stella didn't bother looking round.

"What? A samurai sword? Knuckledusters? Rat poison"

"Oh, you! No. I think we need to get ourselves to the nearest branch of M&S. Because I don't know about you, but *I* could do with a change of undies."

True enough, Stella reflected. She'd left the rest of her clothes at St Mary's, in the simple chest of drawers in her room.

Ignoring Other Stella, who this time had contented herself with a mere auditory presence between her ears, Stella rose from the bed and started searching the rest of the room. The other furniture consisted of a chest of drawers and a wardrobe, in wood that matched the sleigh bed. The wardrobe revealed nothing out of the ordinary, though Stella was surprised to find not one but two dinner suits, one with a plum velvet jacket, one a more traditional black with watered silk lapels.

She moved across to the chest of drawers: two full-width surmounted by a smaller pair. Braces, belts and varicoloured handkerchiefs occupied the left-hand top drawer. The right held photograph albums. Stella lifted the cover of the topmost album. A grinning Freddie, arm around a stunningly attractive woman who, from his description, had to be Mary. The caption: Camber Sands, July 1975. She took it out and flipped through the rest of the leaves, but it was a simple family album like those she'd seen in dozens of houses and flats she'd searched. The others charted more episodes in the McTiernan family's existence. Nothing more exciting than a blurred polaroid taken at a funfair: two long-haired girls, faces blurry as they shot past the photographer clinging to the safety rail of a rollercoaster car, their mouths open wide in delight, or fear, or, most likely, a potent combination of the two. The middle drawer held a selection of sweaters, for golf, Stella decided, judging from the colours and preponderance of Argyll patterns.

"So far, so boring," she murmured, before pushing the drawer closed and opening its downstairs neighbour. "Bingo!" she exclaimed.

The drawer contained several box files, ring binders and thick notebooks secured with fat, red rubber bands. She picked up the box files and dumped them on the bed, returned for the folders, then the notebooks.

On opening the lid of the first box file, she let out a low whistle. The document directly under the spring clip was a photocopy of an evidence list from *Regina v Wilks* in the matter of an armed robbery of a branch of the National Westminster Bank.

"The case Collier framed Freddie for," she whispered.

The rest of the boxed-up documents also related to the case. Copies of witness depositions, phone records, bank statements, the trial judge's instructions to the juries, transcripts of the defence and prosecution opening and closing statements.

She'd just picked up one of the notebooks when something made her stop. A noise from outside. Crunching. Like – *Oh shit!* – tyres on gravel. She froze. Not a delivery. They'd have had to buzz the intercom. Who then? A cleaner? A gardener? She decided to brazen it out.

She headed for the door across the wide expanse of carpet. So soft, so fluffy, so not soaked in the blood of her dead colleague and the man she'd become fond of despite his violent criminal past. She closed the door behind her and went downstairs. Dumping the daysack out of sight behind an antique writing desk, she approached the front door, ready to turn away whichever of Freddie's domestics had arrived to keep the house and garden looking smart.

She decided not to wait until they put their key in the lock. Take the initiative! Maintain control! Ask questions! Make proposals! The old training mantras jostled in her mind for prominence. They all sounded good.

Taking a deep breath and pasting a smile on her face that she hoped would look genuine, she grasped the inside handle and pulled the heavy, iron-studded wooden door inwards.

To find herself face-to-face with Marilyn Wilks née McTiernan.

34

BEAUTY SPOT

COLLIER drove to Leeds without stopping. Arriving in the city centre at just after 6.00 a.m., he bought a large black coffee and a bacon roll in a cafe and spent thirty minutes with his phone tracing Simon Halpern. He didn't even need to use official databases. Google provided everything he needed.

"Simon Halpern, Leeds entrepreneur" led directly to the website of the man's holding company. Work address, check. He also found the announcement of his marriage. The key phrase leapt out at him as if printed in extra-large red capitals:

… the marriage of Mr Simon Anthony Halpern of 231 Roundhay Park Lane, Leeds to Miss Emily Marie Temple of The Old Rectory, 97 Wakefield Road, Halifax …

And a local press announcement in the *Leeds Evening News* informing all who were interested that the happy couple would be living at Mr Halpern's architect-designed house in Roundhay Park

Lane, one of the most desirable addresses in Leeds, if not the whole of West Yorkshire.

Collier drove to Roundhay Park Lane, arriving at a little after seven. He parked in a side street, climbed out into a warm summer's morning, and walked along until he was opposite 231. The house was white and built in a modernist style: lots of horizontal surfaces, white smooth-rendered walls and brushed steel window frames. Through the steel-barred gates, Collier could see a scarlet Porsche convertible and a metallic grey Ferrari.

Twenty yards to his right stood a bus shelter. Collier ambled along the road and planted himself on one of the hard, red plastic seats and settled in to wait. After five minutes, he was joined by an old man towing a scruffy black-and-white terrier on a bright-green lead.

"Lovely day," the old man said.

"Beautiful."

"Holiday?"

"Business."

"Looking after the pennies, are you lad? I thought you lot all had company cars."

Collier smiled.

"Research. I'm in urban transport planning."

"Oh, aye? Time and motion, is it? Well you could plan a few more buses round here. That wouldn't go amiss."

Collier laughed.

"I'll see what I can do."

At that point, the gates at 231 swung inwards. Collier stood. The Porsche nosed out, a blonde at the wheel. She looked left and right, then eased the low-slung car across the pavement and out into the early morning traffic. Collier stood.

"Time's up, I'm afraid."

He walked towards the white house at an unhurried yet long-paced stride and slipped between the closing gates, listening to them clang shut behind him as he approached the front door. He stretched out an arm, pleased to see that his finger was as steady as a rock, and rang the doorbell.

The man who opened the door was instantly recognisable. He'd lightened his hair and had his teeth capped, or veneered, and he sported a year-round tan, but the face was the same face that had stared across the crowded courtroom at him and Lynne while his QC pleaded and wheedled and hectored until the jury returned a verdict of involuntary manslaughter.

"Can I help you?" he asked. In his right hand he held a half-eaten piece of toast.

"Simon Halpern?"

"Yes."

Collier pushed him hard in the sternum, sticking out a foot and tripping him at the same time. Halpern flew backwards, ending up sprawled on the parquet flooring of the hallway. Collier stepped smartly across the threshold, slamming the door behind him.

"What the fuck!" the man cried out.

"Hello Crispin," Collier said in a low voice.

"Who? My name's Halpern. Simon Halpern."

Collier took a step forward and kicked him hard in the centre of his right thigh, bringing forth a cry of pain.

"No. Your name is Crispin Radstock. On Friday, March 7, 2003, you stabbed my son for his wallet. He died in hospital a week later. You escaped justice then. But now your time's up."

Radstock's eyes were wide. He held his hands out palms towards Collier.

"Wait! Just, wait, OK? Please. I did my time. I paid for what I did. I'm sorry about your son. I was high. I was——"

Collier pulled the knife from his jacket pocket. Nothing from the Exhibits Room this time. He'd brought it from home. A deep-bellied cook's knife with a brass-riveted handle. The sort of weapon used in hundreds of attacks, including murders, every year, up and down the UK. No need for anything flashy like the stupid Samurai swords the gangbangers in London were so fond of.

"Get up."

Radstock pushed himself away on his elbows then scrambled to his feet. His eyes were gratifyingly glued to the blade.

"What are you going to do? I have money now. A shitload of money. I could pay you. Compensation. I mean, you know, name your figure."

Fighting down the urge to stab the arrogant young man in the face, Collier spoke.

"I have a better idea. Let's go for a ride."

Walking stiffly beside Collier, partly because of the bruised thigh and partly because of the knife, which Collier kept tight against his side, Radstock reached the driver's door of the car and unlocked it.

"In," Collier said.

Radstock opened the door.

"Keys."

"What?"

"Give me the keys."

Radstock handed them over. Collier locked the doors then ran round to the passenger side, unlocked them again and climbed in beside Radstock, who had frozen into immobility.

"What are you going to do to me?" Radstock asked, his lower lip trembling.

"I'm going to show you some of the most beautiful countryside in the UK. Head for Nidderdale. A place called Greygarth."

"Why?"

"Because I want you to. Now get this fucking car moving."

Radstock twisted the key and pushed the starter button. The engine started with a raspy bark.

They drove the one-hour journey in silence. Collier warned Radstock right at the start to stick to the speed limit. He could smell the rank tang of fear emanating from Radstock's skin. *Good. I want you to get the full experience.*

The final three miles of the journey took place along a narrow lane that was little more than a track. Eventually, it ended in a small turnaround marked with a brown sign displaying a white fan. A beauty spot.

"End of the road, Crispin," Collier said. He reached across and turned off the engine, keeping hold of the key. "Out."

The temperature outside the air-conditioned interior was comparatively warm, despite the altitude. Before setting out for Leeds, Collier had checked the elevation. Two hundred and fifty-seven metres above sea-level. He gestured with the knife.

"Through the gate. And don't try to run."

Radstock fumbled with the latch for the gate before getting it open.

"Where are you taking me? What are we going to look at? Is it his grave? Is that what this is all about?"

"It's not his grave. And his name was Theo, by the way. But yes, it is what this is all about. Head for that tree."

Collier had identified the tree from a tourist photo he'd clicked on from Google maps. Wind had shaped it into a sideways-leaning smear of dark green against a bright blue sky. Beyond lay the whole of the Yorkshire Dales National Park.

Reaching the tree, Radstock stopped. He walked on a few paces to a bare rock ledge and peered over. Then he turned back to Collier.

"Please," he said, holding his hands out in front of him like a supplicant.

Collier closed the gap between them to a foot or so.

"No. Jump."

He watched as a shudder passed right the way through Radstock's body.

"What?"

"Jump, Crispin. You have a chance this way. You might break a few bones, maybe even your pelvis. But it's a warm day and a popular hiking spot. A walker might hear your cries and call mountain rescue. You could escape from this with just a plaster cast and a few bruises."

Radstock turned away and peered over the edge again.

Collier stepped forward, palms outstretched and shoved him, hard, between his shoulder blades.

Screaming, Radstock fell outwards and down, arms flailing.

Collier watched his progress as he hit an outcropping fifty feet down, then a second, before sailing out from the cliff face. He counted. Five seconds. That was how long it took for his son's killer to reach Mother Earth. The smack of skull on rock reached him a split second after he saw the bloom of red. He turned away and walked back to the car.

Back in Roundhay Park Lane, he blipped the gate opener on the key fob and parked the Ferrari exactly where it had been before, lining it up on the scuff marks in the gravel. He locked it, opened the door with Radstock's key and replaced the car keys on the hook he'd watched Radstock lift them from.

Locking the front door behind him, he pushed the button on the gatepost to manually open the gate, walked out onto the street and waited for the gate to close behind him. He started walking, back to his own car.

* * *

In his office at Lothian and Borders Police HQ in Edinburgh, two hundred miles to the north, Gordon Wade was talking to Callie McDonald.

"You were due for a promotion anyway, but if we're going to send you down south to clean up this unholy mess, I think we'll just bring it forwards a wee bit. So congratulations, Detective Superintendent McDonald."

Callie smiled. Though Wade discerned grim determination as well as her natural pleasure at the promotion."

"Thank you, sir. I won't let you down."

"Aye, well, for all our sakes, Callie, I hope ye don't."

35

A REPUTATION TO MAINTAIN

MARILYN'S face was a mask of surprise. Blue eyes dazzling against the mahogany tan, and enhanced further by the fans of white crows-feet at the outer corners. Frosted-pink lipsticked mouth open wide.

"What the *fuck* are you doing here?" she said, hands on hips. Then she turned and shouted over her shoulder. "Ronnie! Get over here. Now! Your *friend* Stella is in Dad's house."

Without waiting for her husband, Marilyn turned back to Stella and advanced.

"Marilyn, wait, please."

It was a pointless plea. Stella knew it. Marilyn Wilks was not a woman to take orders from anyone. Least of all a copper she considered as bent, whether or not said copper had retrieved a couple of million in illicit cash from a lockup for her and Ronnie.

She took a shove in the chest from Marilyn's expensively manicured right hand and gave way as she marched through the front door. Stella followed her.

"Marilyn. Stop!" she barked.

The shout worked. Or something in its urgent tone. Marilyn stopped dead and spun round.

"What's going on?" Then she walked to the foot of the stairs and called out. "Dad? Dad? It's Min, Dad. We're early."

"He can't hear you," Stella said, dreading the next few minutes.

"What d'you mean, he can't hear me? He's not deaf. He knows we're coming. He said he'd be in."

She turned and marched towards the sitting room door. Stella tried to catch up, to get a hand on the door knob before Marilyn, desperately trying to figure out a line that would save the situation from descending into chaos.

Then she heard Ronnie's voice behind her.

"Min, stop, she's got a shooter!"

Too late, Stella remembered the Glock she'd pried from Freddie's hand and stuck in her waistband.

Marilyn stopped. Turned. Took two paces towards Stella. Eyes blazing.

And Stella's head exploded in pain.

Stella came to, leaned over to her left and vomited. Straightening, and wincing at the flare of agony at the side of her skull, she looked up through teary eyes. Her arms ached. They were sandwiched behind her, between her back and the sofa cushions. She leant forward and tried to pull them free, only to realise her wrists were tied. She groaned.

Facing her, in the smaller sitting room that Freddie called the snug, Ronnie sat in an armchair, leaning forwards. The Glock in his meaty right hand looked like a toy. No beige velour leisure suit today for Ronnie. In Marbella, his preferred choice of outfit had robbed him of his dignity let alone his menace. The Ronnie whose hard eyes were boring into hers now looked every inch the kind of man with whom law-abiding citizens would avoid eye-contact. A black, roll-neck sweater beneath a caramel leather jacket, neither of which did much to disguise his still-impressive musculature. And the mouth set into a grim line across a freshly shaved face as if slit by a knife.

Stella leaned her head back, then jerked it forward again as she made contact with the top of the sofa.

"Shit, Ronnie, what did you hit me with? A length of two-by-four?"

"Shut the fuck up. Why did you shoot Freddie?"

"I didn't do it. It was Collier. You know he's bent. We talked about it."

"How come you had the gun?"

"He left it. He put it in Freddie's hand. He killed them both, him and Frankie. She was my sergeant. To look like they killed each other, you know?"

Ronnie's eyes flashed.

"No. I don't fucking know. What I do know, is we just walked in on a fucking bloodbath and there's a cop, a mad cop, wandering about in Freddie's house with a shooter. A recently fired shooter."

"Please, you have to believe me. It went down the way I said it did."

Ronnie leaned back, though she noticed the grip on the pistol had tightened and it now lay across his right thigh.

"You think I'm a joke, don't you?"

"What? No! Of course I don't. You're—"

"Fannying around on the Costa, running my little pub, getting my marching orders from Marilyn, opening bottles of Bolly for *houseguests*. You know what my nickname is, don't you?"

"The Razor."

"That's right," he said, his voice dropping into a low-toned murmur. "Ronnie 'The Razor' Wilks. Do you know how I got it?"

"Did you start off your career as a barber?"

Ronnie smiled. Lifted the Glock off his thigh and turned it this way and that in the light so Stella saw the barrel's dull gleam.

"Very funny. I saw this documentary once on the telly. About these tribesmen in Africa. Masai, I think they were. Maybe Zulus. Tough little fuckers, anyway. So, if you wanted to become a man, you had to go out on your own, into the savannah, and guess what?"

"What?"

"Kill a lion. A fucking lion! With a spear. Like I said, tough little fuckers. So, anyway, when I was growing up, I got myself into a little firm over in Lewisham. Commercial burglaries mostly, but we weren't averse to a little protection, armed robbery, whatever looked profitable. The boss said anyone who wanted to be counted as a full member had to do him a favour. My favour was to deliver a beating to one of the boss's business rivals who'd got too big for his boots. He told me to make it count but to leave him alive. But it went sideways. The bloke pulled a razor on me. Got in a decent cut to my cheek," Ronnie drew a line down his right cheek with his left index finger, "and I saw the red mist, didn't I? I had brass knuckles on and I knocked his fucking head off. When he went down he smacked his head on the pavement and that was that. KO'ed him. So I took the razor off him and sliced him open. Both cheeks, forehead and chin. Kept it, too. After that, the boss made me his number three. He was the one who called me Razor."

"Why are you telling me this? What do you want from me?"

"I want *you*," he pointed the Glock at Stella's face, "to tell *me*," he waggled it from side to side a little, "the truth."

Stella opened her mouth to answer. To protest that she was telling the truth. But before she could speak, the door to the snug burst open. Marilyn stood there, her eye makeup blotchy, giving her the panda-eyed look of a homeward-bound clubber after one too many margaritas. Her white trouser suit, the jacket buttoned over her luxurious bosom, was smeared and stained with red.

"What the fuck have you done?" she said. Her voice was toneless. And that made it all the more frightening.

"Marilyn, please. It wasn't me. It was Collier. I'm trying to tell you both. He tried to have me killed. He put me in the loony bin. I escaped and came straight to Freddie."

"Don't you —" Marilyn, heaved in a breath and let it out again in a juddering sigh, dashing tears away with the back of her hand and further blotching her makeup. "Don't you *ever* call him Freddie again. He was my Daddy. *I* never called him that."

Before Stella could frame an answer, Marilyn closed the gap between them and slapped Stella hard across the cheek. Then again. And again.

The pain of the impacts wasn't bad. Stella had had worse. It didn't worry her that she was tied up in the presence of the Wilkses, with their suspicions that she'd murdered Freddie. What worried her, what *frightened* her, was the sound she could hear deep inside her head. A deep-throated roar. A big motorbike, all black, throttle wide open gripped by a red-nailed hand, its rider laughing maniacally as she headed for the gates of Stella's conscious mind, ready to burst through and assume control.

"Leave them to me, Stel," the rider shouted over the thrashing engine and screaming exhaust. "Leave them *all* to me!"

Stella shook her head as Marilyn's latest back-handed blow raised sparks in her peripheral vision.

"You have to let me go. Please. Right now!" Stella said.

"What's Collier planning?" Ronnie said from his spot on the sofa, from which he hadn't moved during Marilyn's assault.

"I don't know. I told you. I'm after him, too."

Stella concentrated on trying to erect mental road blocks in front of the onrushing bike and its grinning rider. She thought of Lola, willed herself to picture her baby girl, despite the pain it caused her. The white cot with the mobile clamped to the headboard. Little furry zoo animals that turned slowly as it played "We're all going to the zoo tomorrow."

Marilyn stepped out of Stella's eyeline, behind the sofa to the fireplace. Stella heard a metallic clank. When Marilyn came back into view, she was holding a wrought-iron poker, the business end tipped with a hooked point.

"You heard him," Marilyn said. "Tell us what that scumbag is going to do next."

Other Stella was hunkered down over the Triumph's handlebars and riding straight at the cot and its slowly revolving mobile of gaily coloured fluffy toy animals. The cot splintered under the front wheel. Other Stella threw her head back and opened her mouth wide.

"WE'RE GOING TO STAY ALL DAY!" she shouted.

The point of the poker was icy cold against Stella's chin. Marilyn pushed it up so that Stella felt it underneath her tongue. She felt it as the skin in the soft place between her jaw bones split.

"I'm sorry," she choked out, her tongue working overtime to form the words around the bulge the poker was pushing into her mouth.

"You should be, you cold-hearted bitch," Marilyn said. "He didn't deserve to be killed in his own lounge."

"Not for Freddie. For what's coming next."

Other Stella had arrived. She killed the engine and climbed off the bike.

"Stick around Stel," she said, grinning. "No need to go floating off to the ceiling for a birds-eye view of the action. Let's do these two together."

Stella leaned back into the soft sofa cushions. She looked up at Marilyn and spoke in a low, sardonic growl.

"You're dead."

Behind her back, she pushed her hand down into her jeans pocket and clamped the index and middle fingers round the handle of Freddie's flick-knife.

"Why? What's Collier going to do next?"

"It's too late."

Extracting it was easy, despite losing her grip a couple of times. The polished handle slid free without snagging.

"Hang on, Min," Ronnie said.

He rose from his seat on the sofa opposite Stella. He crossed the rug between them and gently eased Marilyn to one side, mercifully lowering the point of the poker out from under the soft flesh of Stella's jaw. Then he reached into the inside pocket of his jacket. The hand that reappeared held a cutthroat razor. A gleaming, stainless steel implement that, closed, looked exactly like the long, thin clamshells it gave its name to.

"I never go anywhere without one of these," he said with a smile. "I've got a set of seven in a lovely black, leather case. That's what gentlemen used to do in the old days, buy seven. One for each day of the week. Kept them sharper that way. Gave the edges a chance to recover."

Stella shuffled her bottom forward on the sofa cushion to give herself space to work.

"Uncomfortable, are we? Rope a bit tight is it? It's gonna get worse before it gets better, Stella, I can promise you that."

He opened the razor. The fearsome weapon was almost a foot long from the tip of the blade to the end of the handle. The blade shone like silver. He leaned forward and placed the edge on the tip of Stella's nose.

"I took a bloke's face off with one of these. One feature at a time. He told me what I wanted to know. In the end."

36

CLOSE SHAVE

RONNIE flicked his wrist and Stella gasped at the sharp flare of pain. She felt the blood dribbling down across her top lip. Instinctively, she put her tongue out to catch the flow. Salt. Iron. Copper.

And behind her back, the sound masked by her cough, she pressed the button to open her own blade.

"You better tell us what we want to know," Ronnie said. "Compared to Marilyn, I'm the good cop."

Other Stella issued an instruction that only Stella could hear.

Keep him happy, babe. Make something up. Just for a minute or two.

Stella inhaled. Fixed Ronnie, then Marilyn, with a stare that she hoped would look penitent.

"Collier sent me to Marbella. The whole thing was a setup. To get you two back in England. He's assembled a snatch team. He's going to track you down and take you off the street."

"I knew it!" Marilyn cried.

Ronnie's questions came like bullets.

"And the Glock? Your story about your kid? The death squads?"

"Oh, the death squads are real enough. But we cooked up the

other business between us. He thought an old school villain like you would go for it. I'm single, Ronnie. There never was a kid."

Freddie had been as meticulous about keeping his blades sharp as he had about everything else in his house, from the neatly made bed to the squared-up paperbacks on the nightstand. The flick-knife cut through Stella's bindings as if they were ribbons round a child's Christmas present. With a small jerk, the last of the thin ropes parted.

Stella readied herself.

So did Other Stella.

"Changed my mind, Stel. I'll take it from here."

Stella felt the familiar nauseating lurch in the pit of her stomach. It had happened when she'd butchered the CPS lawyer Debra Fieldsend. When she'd thrown Charlie Howarth QC to his death several storeys down onto York stone flagstones. And again when she'd shot Tamit Ferenczy on the roof of his own club. The violence of Other Stella's takeover sent Stella shooting backwards out of her own body into a corner of the snug, where she remained trapped, a passive witness to what came next.

Other Stella lunged forward, her right hand swinging out wide in a semicircle. The flick-knife's wickedly sharp blade punched deep into Ronnie Wilks's abdomen on the left-hand side. By the time he'd thought of lifting the pistol it was too late. As his eyes widened in shock, Other Stella pushed herself off the sofa and dealt him two slashing blows across the face. Left, then right. The knife opened two deep cuts across both cheekbones and the bridge of his nose, and on the return trip sliced clean through his left eye. Over his screams, she yelled defiantly.

"Dead man walking!"

He staggered back, dropping the pistol and the straight razor to clutch abdomen and ruined eye. Other Stella leaned back and kicked him in the stomach with the sole of her right boot. Then she turned her attention to Marilyn, who was standing paralysed, as she tried to assimilate the information her own eyes were sending her brain.

Too much thinking. Not enough acting.

Other Stella slashed down at her right hand, half-severing it as the ultra-sharp blade sliced through the tendons and ligaments of her wrist. Marilyn screamed. As her fingers opened and the poker she'd been holding rolled free of her grasp, Other Stella darted forward and caught it.

"You crazy bitch!"

This was Ronnie, who'd fallen back against the sofa he'd so recently vacated. One hand was clamped over his eye, viscous pink liquid leaking from between his fingers, the other over the spreading patch of blood on his shirt.

"Oh, do shut up, Ronnie," Other Stella replied. "I've had enough of you. I should've cut your cock off when you made a pass at me at your house."

She ducked as Marilyn launched an attack with her remaining good hand, which was holding a Chinese vase. She straightened after the crockery had passed harmlessly over her head and swung up and across with the poker. With a crack, the hook buried itself in Marilyn's temple. A low moan issuing from her frosted lips, Marilyn's eyes rolled upwards in their sockets until only the whites remained visible. Other Stella stepped back as the dead woman toppled backwards, blood jetting from the head wound, and came to rest with a thump on the rug.

She bent to collect the razor then straightened and climbed onto Ronnie's supine form so that her knees came to rest one each side of his chest. Her weight drove his wind out of him in a gasp that sprayed a fine mist of blood into her face.

She leaned down until the tip of her nose, which had stopped bleeding, was just touching his.

"Live by the razor, Ronnie," she murmured.

No practice cut.

No hesitation.

No need for a second attempt.

In a single, powerful move, Other Stella drove the edge of the razor against the freshly shaved skin of Ronnie "The Razor" Wilks's throat and opened him like a fish, right to left. What little breath remained in him escaped the rent in his throat with a bubbling hiss like an uncapped beer bottle.

She moved back fast, but not fast enough.

The first spurt caught her full in the face and she swiped her sleeve across her cheek as she climbed off the dying gangster.

From her vantage point – or prison – in the corner of the room, Stella watched in horror as Ronnie Wilks died, the jets of bright scarlet blood spurting six or seven feet into the air. Other Stella turned and beckoned her, and with a sucking sensation she felt herself streaming across the room.

Stella shook her head. She was standing between the blood-soaked corpses of Ronnie and Marilyn Wilks. She dropped the razor. Looked around. At the walls. The furniture. The antique, gold-framed mirror above the fireplace. The paintings on the wall. The curtains. The ceiling.

"Tarantino," she said.

Then she went upstairs to shower and change. Rubbing the towel over her hair, she discovered that Ronnie's initial blow had popped the stitches in her scalp wound, but the tissue beneath had more or less healed.

She sat on the edge of the bed in the guestroom and called Vicky.

"There've been some developments. I need to leave Freddie's. Can I come and stay with you for a few days?

"Of course. But what developments?"

"I'll tell you when I see you."

Downstairs, she paused to collect the rucksack full of Freddie's illicit cash. She'd decided while showering off the blood that she was going to keep the Glock, but leave the razor. The scene inside Five Beeches would baffle even the most ardent and experienced investigator. Christ alone knew what the media would make of it when the news eventually leaked out. The flick-knife she also kept.

A thought occurred to her. Collier might have cancelled her ID card. She turned towards the sitting room door.

Hand on the knob, she took a deep breath and tried to prepare herself mentally. *She's gone, Stel. Nothing in there but DBs, now. You need it. So, in, get it, out, close the door. Mourn her later.*

She pushed through and let out an involuntary sob as she saw Frankie. Avoiding the blood on the carpet, Stella picked her way over to where Frankie lay. Leaning over her and lifting her head gently, Stella eased the Metropolitan Police Service ID card and its blue lanyard clear of the dead detective sergeant's long brown hair. She laid Frankie's head back down on the carpet and retraced her steps. The white plastic ID card was spotted with blood and the lanyard had turned almost black with it in places. Stella took it to the kitchen, unclipped the badge and washed it under the cold tap before sliding it into her purse. The lanyard went into a zip-lock sandwich bag, which she sealed and pocketed. She ran upstairs and retrieved the cash-stuffed daysack.

In the hall, she pulled up the number of the taxi firm she'd used to take her to Westcliff-on-Sea. Then smacked herself on the forehead.

"Come on, Stel. Use some common sense! Why not just call a press conference in the sitting room while you're about it?"

Instead, she lifted the keys to the Rolls from a hook beside the front door.

She frowned at the long swooping silver scar on the car's golden flank. The interior smelled of leather and cologne. Everywhere she turned she saw richly figured wood, cream leather, chrome, or cream carpet with dark-green piping.

Stella placed her rucksack in the passenger footwell. She twisted the surprisingly delicate key in the ignition. She felt, rather than heard, the engine start.

"Huh," she said. "I've been in hybrids that make more noise than you do."

She moved the slender, column-mounted gear selector lever into Drive and, after a moment of confusion, located, and let off, the floor-mounted parking brake. Keeping her hands at the ten-to-two position on the slim-rimmed steering wheel, she gave the throttle pedal a gentle push.

Freddie had explained how he'd had a mechanic fit a transponder inside the car that opened the gates. Nosing the big car forwards, she held her breath. Then released it as the wide wooden gates swung open. She let the big car ease itself out onto Mill Green Road, content to guide the seventeen-foot-long beast with the steering wheel and let the idling engine do the rest. Freddie hadn't been lying about the car's dimensions. She was sure it was longer than her house in West Hampstead was wide.

She watched over her shoulder as the gates closed behind her. And sighed.

"I'm sorry I brought all this down on you, Freddie. You were kind to me."

Then she pulled away, leaving the slaughterhouse behind the tall wooden gates and refocusing on her need to track down Collier.

From beside her, Other Stella spoke.

"Now this is what I call a classy motor. You can see why he bought it, can't you?"

"Yeah, well, sadly he's not around to enjoy it anymore, is he?"

"Don't look at me, Stel. I didn't do him. That's on Collier. Along with your sergeant."

"No, but you did kill Ronnie and Marilyn."

"Of course I did! They were going to torture us then kill us."

"They just wanted information. I was handling it."

"Oh, right, *handling*. You mean with a fucking great razor in your face and a poker shoved up under your chin. Yeah, I saw how well you were *handling* it."

"I could have talked them down. They were just in shock."

"Well, they're not in shock anymore, are they? Now, let's forget all about the dead gangsters and concentrate on our next move. How are we going to get to Collier? Something tells me a full-frontal attack is out of the question."

"I don't know. I need to think. Talk it over with Vicky."

Other Stella swivelled round in the armchair-like passenger seat.

"How about this? Call it in. The murders back there. The media'll have a field day. I can see the headlines now. 'East End Crime Family, Detective, Slain: Police Seek Deranged Killer.' That'll flush him out."

"Maybe. But he left the gun to tell a story. He'll be expecting press coverage. He's not to know you took it."

"All right then. Call it in and say you know who did it. Hint at a vigilante cop. A senior vigilante cop. Say they should be looking at management at Paddington Green."

Stella shook her head.

"No way. He's too much of a smooth operator to get caught that way. He'd just smile that PR smile of his and say, 'Oh yes, we know all about these allegations. It was this psycho-bitch DI who I sectioned and who just escaped from the loony bin by murdering another patient.' Put out an APB on Stella Cole."

Other Stella's eyes flashed.

"Stop the car!" she shouted.

"Fuck off!"

"I said," she growled, "stop the car."

"And I said, fuck off."

The slap was so hard Stella saw bright white stars dancing in front of her eyes.

Other Stella's hand was around her throat.

"Last chance, Stel. Stop the car."

Choking, Stella stamped on the brake, bringing the Rolls to a halt at the kerb outside a dress shop. She pushed the selector lever into Park and waited for Other Stella to release her.

37

THE DYNAMIC DUO

STANDING on the narrow pavement outside a boutique, fifty-year-old Julie Foster and her husband Mike, two years her senior, were discussing which of Ingatestone's coffee shops they should stop at for a latte when a gold Rolls Royce pulled in sharply and stopped right beside Julie's right hip. She jumped back.

"Jesus! Learn to drive," she yelled in at the driver. Then she pulled back. "Here, Mike. What do you think she's up to?"

Her husband bent down and peered in at the driver. He saw a youngish woman, early thirties, maybe, with a shocking blonde punk haircut he'd last seen in Ingatestone in about 1977. She was gripping herself around the throat and he could see her lips working as if she were talking. He couldn't see a phone, and he was pretty sure Rolls Royces of this vintage didn't come with hands-free or Bluetooth.

He knocked on the window with the back of his knuckles, intending to say something to this unlikely Rolls owner about road manners and watching out for pedestrians. When she turned to face him, the expression on her face, and what was clearly a stream of invective issuing from her taut lips, persuaded him that this would be a bad idea. The slap she delivered to her own right cheek convinced him of it.

"Come on, Julie," he said, straightening, and turning to his wife. "Let's go and get that coffee. Something not quite right in there."

* * *

Other Stella's eyes were blazing and all the colour had left her cheeks, giving her skin a pale, waxen sheen like a mannequin's.

"I *am* trying to help you. Making suggestions. And all you do is throw them back in my face. Now I'm going to tell you what to do. Get Collier's address. We'll go there together. And then we'll show him the true meaning of justice."

Stella thought of Collier's wife, Lynne. She hadn't done anything wrong. She was an innocent party. And she thought of Other Stella's repeated mantra that she would kill them all and then move onto their families. She couldn't risk it.

"Let me talk to Vicky. Then we'll decide. OK?"

"Fine. I'm tired."

With an odd snap inside her head, Stella felt her Other disappear. She groaned. Other Stella was getting stronger, and more malevolent. What would happen if she decided to take over completely and never leave? Would it be Stella who vanished? She shook her head. Not. Going. To. Happen. She pointed the big car towards the A12 and London.

"Bloody hell, where did you get that monster from?" Vicky asked with a smile. She'd just opened her front door to Stella and was looking beyond her to the Rolls, parked among the sleek grey and silver hatchbacks on Vicky's narrow Victorian street like a whale amongst dolphins.

"I'll tell you inside."

Stella dumped her rucksack on the kitchen floor. It now

contained several changes of underwear and a few white T-shirts that she'd bought in the Ilford branch of M&S.

"So?" Vicky asked, pouring boiling water into two mugs.

"It belonged to Freddie McTiernan."

Vicky turned from her place at the kitchen counter.

"And when you say 'belonged'?"

"He's dead. Collier shot him. And my sergeant, Frankie O'Meara. He left them together at Freddie's so it looked like they'd killed each other. But I found them. Then Ronnie and Marilyn Wilks turned up. They were about to torture me to find out what Collier was up to and—"

"And what?" Vicky placed a mug of coffee in front of Stella then joined her at the scrubbed pine table.

And my psychopathic alter ego took over and killed them while I had an out-of-body experience and watched from a corner.

"And now they're dead, too."

Vicky took a cautious sip of her coffee.

"You killed them."

"It was self-defence. Reasonable force. Look."

She placed the tip of her finger to the scabbed-over cut on her nose. Then lifted her chin to show Vicky the dark purplish-black bruise the size of a penny, dead-centre between the wings of her jawbone.

"It's fine, Stella, really. I'm way past caring what happened to a couple of gang—"

"Three—"

"—three gangsters. I daresay they had it coming one way or another. What I really want to do is get Collier."

"OK, look. Here's what I think." She started counting off points on her fingers. "One, he's isolated. All his scumbag PPM friends are dead. He can't rely on the foot soldiers. They've probably already got wind of the deaths so they'll be praying it all goes away. Either that or checking out how many points they could rack up in the Australian immigration system. Two, he's a senior cop. He can't just disappear. He goes to work. He goes home. So we should be able to track him down without too much trouble. Three, he knows I'm coming for him, but he doesn't know you are. So we have the element of surprise plus superior forces. Plus, I took the gun to spoil his little scenario."

"What can I do? I thought about what you said and it's true I'm not much good at the physical stuff. But I have contacts, investigative skills."

"I've been thinking, too. The first thing we need to do is, as my colleagues and I like to say, ascertain his whereabouts." Stella put on a comically precise police-officer-in-court voice for this last phrase and Vicky snorted with laughter.

"I can do that. I'll call the media officer at Paddington Green. Say I want to interview him for a piece."

"OK," Stella said.

Then she leaned back and folded her arms.

"What, now?"

"Why not? Are you working on something more important?"

Vicky rolled her eyes.

"Sorry. I'm just not used to this whole vigilante thing yet.

"Believe me, it gets easier."

* * *

Metropolitan Police press officer Tim Llewellyn was putting the finishing touches to a press release about improved community relations in Paddington when his phone rang.

"Press Office," he said crisply.

"Hi, Violet Rourke here, *Daily Telegraph*."

Tim liked the broadsheets. They generally wanted to run features or general news on ongoing investigations. Not hit him with allegations of racism, police brutality or minor-league corruption like the local rag and the proliferating crowd of bloggers. He stood up. He'd been on a presentation skills course where the trainer had explained how taking or making important calls standing up made your voice sound stronger, more authoritative.

"Hi, Violet, I'm Tim Llewellyn. What can I do for you?"

"I'm writing a piece called 'Fifty Under Fifty: People to Watch in Britain Today.' It's about a generation of people making things happen in British society. Lawyers, engineers, doctors, politicians, entrepreneurs, academics, teachers. I'd like to interview one of your senior officers. Detective Superintendent Adam Collier. Would he be able to make himself available? I'm sure he's very busy but this really would be excellent personal PR. For the service too, I should think."

Tim smiled. Wouldn't it just? Like everyone else in the station, he called Collier The Model behind his back. Actually he suspected that Collier both knew about and enjoyed the nickname.

"Can you hold, Violet? I'll call his office."

He pushed a button on the handset then dialled the internal number for the boss of the Murder Investigation Command. It went straight to voicemail. Tim left a message then retrieved his other call.

"Violet?"

"Yes?"

"I'm really sorry. It went to voicemail. Listen give me your number. I'll make a couple of enquiries. See if I can track him down. I'll call you back, OK?"

"Thanks, Tim."

Tim left his office and made the five-minute journey to the CID office for the MIC. He pushed through into the busy, open-plan space, marvelling once again at the way all police station CID offices had the exact same smell. Dry-wipe markers, stale coffee, BO and the underlying sweet tang of last night's alcohol. Nobody looked up.

He approached the first occupied desk. A male detective with cropped silver hair and an ill-fitting suit looked up from his screen.

"Can I help you, mate?"

"I'm looking for Adam Collier? Is he in today?"

The detective frowned.

"I think he's on leave. Hey Jake!" he shouted across the room.

A second detective wandered over, a sheaf of computer

printouts dangling from his right hand. He was younger than the first, but already sporting a paunch and a receding hairline.

"All right, Tim?" he said, when he arrived at the desk. "Is this about GQ wanting me for a photoshoot. You know, best-dressed DS in London?"

The older officer snorted. "Cockiest, more like."

"Sadly no," Tim said with a smile. "I'm looking for your boss. Adam Collier. Is he on leave?"

"Don't think so. I mean, I haven't seen him for a couple of days but I was filling in my dates on the holiday roster and I didn't see his name on there."

Tim shrugged. "Not to worry. I'll ask HR."

Unlike the CID office, the HR department smelled like a country garden. Hardly surprising, given the vases of flowers placed strategically around the room, on filing cabinets, desks and coffee tables. Whiteboards were much in evidence, but where those in CID were covered in words like "forensics," "murder weapon," "multiple victims" and "sexual assault" these bore business jargon Tim only partially understood: "360-degree evaluation," "balanced scorecard," "onboarding strategy" and, most baffling of all, "coterminous stakeholder engagement."

Shaking his head, Tim repeated his routine, approaching a young woman in a funky black-and-white jacket, jeans and Converse.

Five minutes later, he returned to his own office, puzzled, and disappointed that he wouldn't be able to help the woman he saw as his colleague at the *Daily Telegraph*.

"Hello?" she said when she picked up.

"Violet?"

"Yes."

"It's Tim Llewellyn. Paddington Green."

"Please tell me you have good news for me, Tim. I could really do with it, the day I'm having."

He winced. If there was one thing Tim Llewellyn hated, it was letting down journalists.

"I'm afraid not. I checked with the MIC – sorry, the Murder

Investigation Command, and with HR. Adam didn't turn up for work yesterday or this morning. He's not on leave and nobody seems to know where he is."

"Oh. Well that is a pity. I'll just have to find another dashing fortysomething detective to interview. Thanks for trying, Tim."

She hung up.

Tim looked at his phone in disgust.

"Bollocks!"

* * *

"What?" Stella said, seeing Vicky frown.

"He's gone AWOL. Nobody's seen him since the day before yesterday.

"When he was down killing Frankie and Freddie."

Vicky put her phone down on the table. She looked across at Stella.

"He's running."

"That's what it looks like."

"What do we do?"

"We run faster."

"But we don't know where he's gone."

Stella paused. Leaned her chair back onto two legs and stared at the ceiling. Remembered the look of the ceiling in Freddie's snug. Arcs of blood spatter decorating the expanse of white. She shifted her weight to make the chair right itself with a clunk as the front legs hit the slate floor tiles.

"You're an investigative journalist. I'm a detective. Together we should be able to track him down. Like I said, he can't just go off the radar. He's going to leave a trail. All we have to do is find it, then follow it."

The two women spent the next hour discussing the division of labour and possible approaches. If they'd bothered to set up a whiteboard, this one would feature the phrases:

· · ·

Call wife.

Ask line manager.

Call Met contacts: media/cops

Track down friends/acquaintances: ask on pretext of organising surprise party for 25-years in the service.

Google "Adam Collier + career move"

Ask CIs: anyone heard any whispers?

Over the next few days, they worked all the angles, making dozens of calls, meeting with confidential informants and pushing them for information on anything they might have heard about a senior officer going AWOL, tiptoeing around the upper management echelons at Paddington Green.

And …

Nothing.

In the end, the break in the case came from the same man who felt he had disappointed "Violet Rourke."

38

FLIGHT

COLLIER looked across the aisle at Lynne as the plane landed in Chicago. He reached out and took her hand. Squeezed.

"You all right?" he asked.

She nodded.

"Good."

Checked in at The Marriott on North Michigan Avenue, unpacked and sitting side by side on the king-sized bed, they looked at each other. Lynne Collier broke the silence.

"We're here, then?"

"We are. And it's going to be fine."

"But is it? How can you be so sure? What if she follows you here?"

"She can't. I asked Rachel Fairhill to keep the move quiet, at least until I tell her the sabbatical's going to work. There's no way she can track me."

"And then?"

"Then what?"

"Then when you tell Rachel you're staying? They'll issue a

press release, won't they? They're bound to. And she'll read about it or find out from someone at the station."

Collier scratched the back of his head. His wife had put her finger, unerringly, on the one, small, gigantic, hole in his plan. Yes. How, exactly, *was* he going to outrun Stella Cole and her murderous rampage?

"Look love, you've been amazing so far. To be honest, I wasn't sure how you'd react when I told you about what happened after Theo died. So this is how I see it." *I don't see it this way at all. But I'm putting my faith in it, all the same.* "This is America, OK?"

"OK. And?"

"I'll be with the FBI."

"And?"

"And they'll arm me."

Lynne twisted round so she was facing him directly.

"And if she comes for you, you'll shoot her, is that it?"

"In self-defence, yes. It's the best I can think of."

"Jesus, Adam. You'd better be right." Her eyes flashed. "Tell me what she looks like these days. It's a long time since that barbecue and I had a few too many glasses of wine that night."

Collier grimaced.

"She's hard to miss, I promise you that. She's had all her hair cut off and —"

"What, she's bald?"

"No. Not bald. You know, a crop. Super short. And she's gone blonde."

"So we're looking for Psycho Tinker Bell?"

"Something like that, yes."

"Fine. Shouldn't be too hard to spot. Now. Enough about her. At least for now. Hungry?"

The next morning, Collier called Eddie Baxter. Collier had finished the paperwork before leaving England, and Eddie had fast-tracked the application through the Bureau's admin systems.

"Adam, my man. How are you?"

"I'm good, Eddie. Really good. And I'm here."

"You're here? What, here London, or here Chi-town?"

"Here, here. Chicago."

"Whoa! I thought you were going to take a few more weeks to, what did you say, leave things shipshape for your successor?"

"I know. You're right. I did say that. But I had a lot of leave owing so I took some personal time. Thought Lynne and I might settle in at a more leisurely pace before you start cracking the whip."

"Ha. Very good. It's not a bad idea. Listen, it'll probably take me a week or so to get the final sign-off from our human resources people on the sabbatical. You good till then?"

"Totally, yes. Absolutely. But there is one thing?"

"Name it, buddy."

"We'd really like to find somewhere to live. Do you guys have a relocation person who could help us?"

"Oh, sure. We work with a real estate agent who looks after folks transferring in from out of state. I'll hook you up with her. She's a real nice lady. Her name's Yvonne Wallace. I have your email address. I'll introduce you, then you guys can meet with Yvonne and she can show you around a couple neighbourhoods. You need a car?"

"I guess so."

"Talk to Yvonne. I think her brother, or her brother-in-law, some family member, anyway, well, he owns the Ford dealership out in Lincoln Park. Maybe he can set you guys up with a ride."

"Thanks, Eddie. Let me know when I can come in."

"You bet. Soon as I get a date from human resources, I'll give you chaps a little tinkle."

"You're a star. Oh, and one last thing?"

"Shoot."

"'Little tinkle'? That was literally the worst British accent I have ever heard."

.   .   .

By the time Eddie called two days later to announce that Collier could come in for his formal induction in a week or so, Collier and Lynne had met Yvonne Wallace. They'd spent the time looking round apartments and houses in a couple of different neighbourhoods that offered quick commutes to the FBI office on Roosevelt Road. Two more days later, and they'd signed a lease for a three-bedroom house in Lincoln Park. The drive to work would take Collier just twenty minutes.

The Saturday before Collier's induction, he woke early. The digital clock on his side of the bed read 5:30 a.m. He turned over and curled his arm round Lynne's sleeping form. She mumbled in her sleep, but didn't wake. As he waited for the alarm to go off, he tried to anticipate what Stella would do next.

Be honest. She'll find us, was his first thought. *She's a good detective. No, a great detective. At best, all I've done is to buy time.* He turned onto his back and clasped his hands behind his head. *Well, what would you do if you were her?* Yes. Good question. What *would* he do? The answer was obvious. In Stella's shoes, he'd do what he himself had done to Crispin Radstock.

Track him.

Find him.

Kill him.

But Radstock wasn't expecting me. That's the difference. I know she's coming. I need to set it up. Lay the groundwork. Tell Eddie? Maybe. Or my partner. They'll team me up with an experienced agent. When the time's right, I'll tell him. He'll have my back. Two against one. Provoke her into trying something. Then we bring her down. We—

The alarm buzzed, startling Collier, who'd almost fallen back to sleep as he revolved the problem of Stella Cole in his mind like a particularly lethal Rubik's cube. One where if you failed to get the colours lined up face by face, the whole fucking thing would split apart and a wild-eyed vigilante would burst out and murder you in cold blood.

39

ALL PR IS GOOD PR

VICKY'S sigh as she ended the call was so loud that Stella looked up from the laptop she was working on.

"Another dead end?"

"Yup. Have you got anywhere?"

"Nope. It's tricky. I don't want to alert him, so direct approaches are out. But nobody at Paddington Green has seen hide nor hair of him for a couple of days. Which is not like him."

Vicky took a sip of the coffee by her elbow, then winced.

"Cold. Want another?"

"I'll make them."

Stella got up from the table and arched her back, easing out the kinks in muscles that had been stuck in one position for most of the morning.

"He wouldn't have, oh, I don't know, gone to a conference or something, would he?" Vicky asked.

"Not without telling someone. No, I think he's decided to take this completely underground. Gone off the radar."

"Into the tunnels."

"Down the rabbit hole."

"Into a hidey hole.

"A black hole."

"Up his own arsehole."

Stella snorted, and soon both women were convulsed with laughter. Vicky's phone rang, silencing the rising peals of hilarity as each tried to outdo the other with choked-out ideas about where Collier had disappeared to.

Vicky's eyes widened as she checked out the caller ID and signalled Stella to be quiet with a raised finger.

"Violet Rourke," she said in a clipped, business-like voice.

"Hi, Violet, it's Tim Llewellyn. Paddington Green? We spoke a few days ago."

"Oh, yes. Hi, how are you?"

"I'm fine, thanks. Listen, you were trying to find Detective Chief Superintendent Adam Collier for your piece. 'Fifty Under Fifty,' wasn't it?"

"That's right. Good recall skills."

"Yes, well, I now know why I couldn't track him down when you called."

"Oh, really? Why? Has he been arrested?" Vicky adopted a stagey mock-whisper for this last question.

Vicky looked straight at Stella. Stella raised her eyebrows. Vicky gave her a thumbs up, then waggled her hand, palm downwards. *We might have found him.*

"Ha, very good. No. Um, listen, I shouldn't really be telling you this, so it will have to be off the record, or at least that you got it from me."

"Fine. Absolutely. Now, what is it that you shouldn't be telling me?"

"He's left the country. Apparently he's taking up a six-month sabbatical as a guest of the FBI in Chicago."

Vicky didn't bother trying to hide the surprise in her voice. "Violet Rourke" would have every reason to sound doubtful. She nodded and mouthed "thank you" as Stella put a fresh mug of coffee down in front of her.

"Isn't that rather sudden? And why the secrecy? Surely this is exactly the sort of thing the Met likes to trumpet. Hands across the sea and all that?"

"I agree. And knowing the man a little, I have to say it does seem out of character. Our Detective Chief Superintendent hasn't exactly been media-shy in the past. Apparently he wants to make sure the whole secondment thing works out. So if it doesn't, he can slide back in and put the trip down as an extended leave. I got this from the Deputy Assistant Chief Commissioner. Rachel Fairhill, do you know her?"

"I've heard of her, obviously."

"Well, she asked me to draft a couple of press releases so that if and when the move is confirmed, we can make some noise about it. I thought, if that happens, you might like the exclusive. You could do a profile or work up some sort of feature about inter-agency cooperation. You know, the Met's brightest stars now shining at Quantico."

Vicky nodded at Stella and smiled.

"Tim, I absolutely love it," she gushed. "And of course, an exclusive would be fantastic. Just let me know when and where I can meet your golden boy. I have a travel budget so a trip to the Windy City might well be possible."

"I will. But like I said, for now this is all off the record."

"Of course. I understand. And Tim?"

"Yes?"

"You're a star."

Vicky ended the call and punched the air. "Yes!"

Stella held her hands wide.

"Well?"

"He's in Chicago. With the FBI. Some sort of sabbatical or secondment. They're not making it public in case it doesn't work out."

Stella sat up and slurped some coffee.

"This is it. This is the final act. We follow him to Chicago. The FBI will have a field office there. We find out everything we can about his routine. Then we pick our moment and take him off the street or from his house or something."

Vicky felt a sudden surge of adrenaline that made her skin clammy and her hands shake. Stella's glib confession of having murdered – all right, killed – a dozen or more people came back to her. She put her coffee down.

"I'm not sure I can do this." Relief washed through her, and the feeling convinced her she was making the right decision. "Right up until a second ago this was like a massive adventure. You know, the avenging angels. And now——"

"You're going to kill someone. Like I said, I'm in this too far to back out. But you aren't. Stay here, Vicky. Support me from London. I'll need help, that's for sure. Just, not for the business end of things. You'll know he's gone. You'll know Bea and Ralph's murderer is gone. There's your closure. Hate that word, by the way. Draw a line under it. Move on. You don't want to come with me where I'm going, believe me."

"Why? Where are you going?"

"It doesn't matter. Just, keep all your notes on PPM. All the research you did with Richard. And when this is all over, publish the lot. The whole fucking lot. If you don't get a Pulitzer or whatever they give out over here for journalists then there really is no justice in the world."

Vicky watched Stella stand up and leave the kitchen for the hallway. When she reappeared she was wearing her jacket.

"Fancy a shopping trip? I believe Chicago gets pretty hot in the summer."

* * *

Later that night, when Vicky was asleep, Stella left the house. Dressed all in black, she headed for a minicab firm office and asked the controller there for a car to take her to Paddington.

40

ENTERING, BUT NOT BREAKING

PERHAPS in telly-land, police stations are 24/7 hives of activity. Detectives staring at crime scene photos under the harsh light of halogen desk lamps. Forensics officers scrutinising blood spatter or friction ridge prints under microscopes. Senior officers pacing in front of subordinates exhorting them to greater efforts or yelling at them for incompetence. The reality is different. The front desk will be welcoming a steady stream of drugged, drunk or mugged citizens. Bloody-faced scrappers will be arriving in handcuffs, sandwiched between eye-rolling constables in uniform. Wide-eyed teenagers who've taken their parents' cars without permission will be standing sheepishly next to traffic cops while their situation is explained to them. But elsewhere, the station will be quiet. Yes, detectives work shifts like everyone else, but budget cuts mean CID offices aren't buzzing with activity once the small hours roll around.

Stella arrived on foot at the rear entrance at 3.30 a.m., having told her minicab driver to let her out a hundred yards to the east. She took a quick look around to make sure none of her colleagues were approaching from the car park and swiped Frankie's ID card through the security scanner.

The motion-activated lights flicked on as she closed the door behind her. Opting for the stairs over the lifts, she made her way to the Murder Investigation Command floor. Her feet scraped on the bare concrete steps, making a sound like sandpaper.

Can't be helped, Stel, she thought. *Just pray you don't meet anyone coming down.*

"Be realistic babe," a voice behind her said. "Who takes the stairs at this time of night? Feels like the set of a bloody zombie film."

"Yeah, well you'd better be right. I'm not sure how my 'Oh, I got better' speech will wash if anyone asks me what I'm doing out of the nuthouse."

"We could always do what we did to that Maltese bitch."

"No!"

Stella stopped dead and whirled round.

Other Stella stood waiting for her response. A smile curved her lips upwards but it didn't quite reach her eyes.

"Squeamish?" Other Stella said.

"It's not about squeamishness. Jesus, after the things I've done, I think we can safely say I'm not bothered by the sight of blood. But no cops, OK? I'll talk my way out of trouble – if we meet any."

"Fine. You're the boss."

The corridor leading to the MIC office was empty. Checking the way was clear, Stella hurried along to the door into what she realised she was thinking of as her former workplace. She peered through the small rectangular window. Nobody about. Perfect! She swiped Frankie's card again and was in. Weaving through the desks, she made her way as quickly as she could to Collier's office. The door was locked. She pulled a set of picks from her pocket. Twenty seconds later it was unlocked and she was inside and closing the door softly behind her. She tweaked the blind cords to close the slats. Withdrawing a small black torch from her pocket, she switched it on and sat down at Collier's desk.

"Right, you bastard. Now, let's see what you've been hiding."

She leaned over and pulled on the handle of the deep file drawer to her right. It didn't move. Another five seconds work with the lock picks and it did.

She looked down onto thirty or more hanging dividers, each meticulously labelled in neat blue capitals in Collier's distinctive handwriting.

"Oh, Jesus, senior management," she said. "When did you last do any real police work?"

The labels almost made her laugh as she read them out.

"Quarterly budget forecasts. Staffing and resource allocation. Risk assessment. Project management protocols. Inter-departmental management meetings. Fuck me, Collier, I knew you were corrupt but I had no idea you were so fucking boring."

"What were you expecting?" Other Stella said, from her perch on the corner of the desk. "Death squad rotas? Target lists? Body disposal sites? Get real, babe. And get them all out."

Stella lifted the entire contents out of the drawer and spread the pale blue cardboard folders out on the floor. Was she worried about Collier's coming in? No. In fact, she was half-hoping he'd put in a late-night appearance. She still took her little helper everywhere and had decided if he put his nose round the door she'd first break it and then beat him to death. Perhaps allowing Other Stella to provide some additional rage-fuelled force.

Surveying the morass of paper in front of her, she blew out her cheeks in frustration.

"Shit! This is going to take all night. I'll still be here when everyone rocks up for work."

"Then be a detective. What did they always say. Think."

"Think of what?"

"Broaden it out. You know he's fucked off to Chicago, but what did he leave behind in his hurry? He must have a list of members or supporters or whatever he calls them."

"Right. That's good. So. I'm head of Pro Patria Mori. I want to keep it secret. I'm cunning. So I don't keep anything on my phone. Not like Ramage. Bloody idiot. What if some kid had stolen it out of his car or picked his pocket? I zig when everyone else zags. I hide all my top secret shit in plain sight."

"Exactly. Homes get burgled. Safes get cracked. Where's the best place on Earth to hide something valuable?"

"A police station," they chorused, the sound an odd, echoing double-track in Stella's head.

Stella snatched up the first folder and riffled through its contents. It did, indeed, contain quarterly budget forecasts, to judge from the multiple pages of gridded spreadsheet printouts with red, green and yellow highlighted cells. The second folder, marked "Case Management Reports" yielded nothing unexpected. She shook her head. Impatient. There were still too many documents to work through.

"I'm going to run out of time."

Other Stella pushed a few of the folders to one side. Tapped a blood-red fingernail on one that looked older than the rest.

"Why doesn't this one have a label?"

Stella looked. All the other folders had sticky labels that matched the labels clipped onto the hanging dividers from the file drawer. This one was blank. Her heart rate accelerated. She pulled the folder towards her and opened it on her lap. Then her face fell and she felt her pulse slowing.

"Seriously?"

The top sheet of paper bore the legend:

Human Resources Operational Protocol Embedding Team Meeting Update 19

Below it the entire page was taken up with just two dense paragraphs of text that Stella didn't even bother reading. She put it to one side. Then groaned.

. . .

Resource Management Best Practice Overview, Recommendations for Next Steps

"Who'd be a Chief Super, eh?" Other Stella said. "No wonder he went into the death squad business. Mind you, committee work would have been safer, as it turns out."

Stella placed the second stapled document face down on the first and started riffling through the rest. Halfway down, she came to a document bearing a title of such mind-numbing tedium that she held it up for Other Stella to see.

"Check it out. Third Quarter Operating Budget Initial Projections. And they say the Met has lost its focus on crime."

This document's author had managed to separate the front page of their report into just three, slab-like paragraphs. Only a fool or a madman would venture further. *Or a madwoman, Stel.*

"I thought the quarterly budget projections were in the other folder," Other Stella said.

"They are. Hang on."

She flipped over the page. And gasped.

"Shit! Look."

She held up the document so its second page was facing outward. At the top of the page Vicky Riley's face stared out. She was frowning and not looking straight at the camera. The image was grainy. Taken with a long lens.

Beneath the stealthily captured portrait, a list of bullet points enumerated Vicky's personal details, address and contact numbers, her email addresses, social media accounts. The dossier, for that's what Stella realised it was, went into her upbringing, her political views, her career and, finally, her investigation into PPM with Richard Drinkwater. The final two words were chilling: Termination recommended.

"Yeah, well you fucked that one up, Collier, didn't you? I terminated your hitman instead. And his brother. And I'm going to terminate you."

"You should keep that," Other Stella said. "Now, keep looking. There might be some other stuff we can use against him."

Stella spent the next twenty minutes looking through the rest of the folders, flipping past each top sheet of any stapled documents in the hopes of finding more evidence of PPM. But she came up empty-handed. She gathered up the folders and replaced them, laboriously, back between the hanging dividers. She pulled the dividers at the rear of the drawer forwards so she could slide the folders home. The final divider caught on something and wouldn't move.

"Oh, for fuck's sake, come on," Stella hissed.

She reached into the drawer and felt around under the final hanging file to see what was obstructing it. Her fingertips brushed against a notebook. Its cover was partly open and had caught against the bottom of the file. Up went her pulse again as she withdrew the book.

"Look," she said, holding the A5 notebook out towards Other Stella. "This could be it."

"Well open it, then, dummy, and let's find out."

Stella opened the notebook. Smiled grimly. And nodded.

"Got you," she murmured.

Only someone feeling one hundred percent certain of never being discovered would use the label Collier had. But there it was in black and white.

PPM supporters.

No flim-flam about management meeting minutes or communication strategy. Straight to the point. A list of everyone the conspirators had brought into their vicious little club. Better yet, as Stella flipped over the pages, she saw that Collier had even organised the foot soldiers by role. Pages bore headings of OPERATIONS, TECHNICAL, COVER and RECRUITMENT.

Stella counted ten pages of names, mobile numbers, email addresses and notes. Under operations she noticed the name of the shooter she'd disabled up at Ramage's house in Scotland: Lucy Van Houten.

She snapped the book shut and slid it into an inside pocket in her jacket. Thought for a moment. Other Stella interrupted her thoughts.

"Anything else you need before we go? A blood-soaked shirt? The first draft of *My Death Squad Diary* by Adam Collier? A smoking gun?"

"This'll do. Not that I need it but I've got evidence of a plan to murder Vicky and a list of all remaining active members or supporters. No. This is enough. I'll give it to Vicky. When I'm gone she can have a field day with it."

"Yeah, and like I told you, the whole, 'when I'm gone' business? Not a massive fan, tbh. I think it would be better to hang on to that little black book of Collier's. There are enough names in there to keep me busy for years."

Stella patted the book subconsciously.

"Yes. And like I told *you*, that's not going to happen. And if you *dare* slap me again, I swear I will rip you out of me by your hair and kill you right now."

Other Stella put her hands on her hips.

"Well, well. Been watching female empowerment videos on YouTube have we? Fine. We'll discuss this another time. Laters."

Stella nodded with satisfaction. A small triumph. But a triumph all the same. She closed and locked the desk drawer then got up from the chair, straightened it and crossed the expanse of carpet to the door. She switched off the torch and waited a minute or so for her eyes to adjust. Then she slipped through into a mercifully empty and still dark CID office, locking the door behind her.

A shadow moved towards her from the gloom.

Stella jumped and dropped her torch. Every nerve ending in her body jangled. She tensed, digging her right hand into her pocket to close reflexively on her little helper. The person moving towards her looked relaxed, but she couldn't make out the features. They were dressed all in black and walking on soft-soled shoes that didn't make a sound. But that voice. She recognised it. A soft Scottish accent.

She placed it just as its owner emerged from the shadows to confront her.

41

AN OLD FRIEND

"HELLO, Stella. Or am I still supposed to call you Jennifer?"

"You!" she said.

Standing in front of Stella, and offering what appeared to be a smile of genuine good humour, was a woman. A woman Stella had last seen on a ferry taking her from Portsmouth to Santander, just after she'd killed Leonard Ramage.

"Callie McDonald at your service, ma'am."

The speaker was in her midforties. Short auburn hair and a penetrating gaze that seemed to Stella to be capable of X-raying the person on which it was focused. Stella bent to retrieve the torch and switched it back on, though she resisted the urge to shine it right in Callie's eyes.

"What are you doing here?"

"I could ask you the same thing. And in fact, I'm going to. But not here. I think we should find somewhere a little more comfortable. A little less, well, *policey*, don't you?"

"Where do you suggest?"

"I'm staying at the Mercure Hotel. It's only ten minutes' walk from here. We can walk and talk."

Like New York, Tokyo, Berlin and Singapore, London is a 24-

hour city. But in this particular part of the capital, criss-crossed by flyovers, railway lines and long, curving terraces of Georgian townhouses, the ratio of party people to urban foxes scavenging in bins was heavily in the foxes' favour. The two women, one a newly promoted detective superintendent, the other not sure of her own professional or legal status, talked as they walked back to Callie's hotel.

Stella's initial suspicions evaporated within seconds of their leaving the station building and turning away and onto the public road.

"Before you say anything," Callie said, "we're on your side."

"We?" relaxing her grip on the little helper but leaving her hand in her pocket where its smooth leather sides bumped reassuringly against her knuckles.

"Me, Gordon Wade and one or two other people outside the Met. You met Gordon at a charity ball didn't you? I heard you were, what shall we say, squired by Barney Riordan?"

"Yes we did, and yes I was. He's a decent bloke. You know, for an overgrown kid who gets paid millions to kick a football around."

Callie laughed. "Not a fan, then?"

"Of football? Not really. Of Barney, yes. Totally. He helped me help a friend of mine."

"Vicky Riley."

Stella stopped dead, so that Callie walked ahead a few paces before stopping and turning back to face her.

"My God!" Stella said. "Have I been under surveillance this whole time?"

"Let's get a drink in our hands and then I'll tell you what's going on."

The hotel bar was empty, but open. A bored-looking bartender poured them both a generous measure of brandy and Callie signed for the drinks then led Stella to the lifts. As soon as the steel doors closed Stella turned to Callie.

"Cheers!"

She held out her brandy snifter and clinked rims with Callie before taking a gulp of the fierce spirit. Every moment in the lift felt like an hour as it made its tortoise-like progress to the fifth floor. She was bursting with questions, but she felt that Callie wanted to attain the privacy of her room before opening up.

Once inside, Callie seemed to relax. Stella saw tension, which she had only subliminally noticed, leave Callie's shoulders. Her face, which had looked pale in the street lighting, regained a measure of the colour she remembered from their one and only previous meeting on the ferry.

"Have a seat and ask your questions," Callie said with a smile, before taking a sip of her own brandy.

Stella plonked herself down in an armchair. Callie sat on one of the two beds.

"This 'we' you talked about. What are you doing in London? Why are you tailing me?" Another sip of brandy. "Basically, what the fuck is going on?"

"OK, look. Keep calm, but we know all about Pro Patria Mori. We didn't know how you were involved at first, but we have been tracking you ever since you asked Gordon where Leonard Ramage's Scottish house was."

Stella didn't feel calm. Her pulse was bumping uncomfortably in her throat and she could hear a rushing noise in her ears. Amidst her confusion, and swirling emotions, the only relief was that so far Other Stella was keeping herself to herself.

"Does that mean you know about Five Beeches."

Callie's face fell. No copper liked seeing a colleague killed in the line of duty.

"I'm afraid so. For now it's being kept under wraps. At the right time, Frankie will get a proper funeral with full honours."

It wasn't much, but it would have to do, Stella thought.

"OK, next question. How? I mean, how do you know about PPM?"

"Would you believe it was an intern? Well, not technically an intern. We had a lassie from the University of Glasgow over doing her PhD research. She was looking at miscarriages of justice south of the border. Bright wee thing. She got hold of a huge pile of court reports, probation records, all manner of bumf. Then she set about entering it into a computer program she'd designed. She came to me one day, a Friday, as it happens. I remember because I'd been planning to get away early and have a few drinks with the team. She was really shy. Wouldn't make eye contact if she could avoid it. But she plucked up her courage and came to my office. I remember what she said, word for word. 'Excuse me, ma'am. Could you take a look at this, because I think there's something odd about these data.' Well, as you can imagine, it didn't exactly fill me with joy, but it was my job to play nursemaid so I got her to show me what she'd found."

Stella finished her brandy and clinked the glass down on the desk to her right.

"Let me guess. A pattern of people who'd escaped justice because of mistrials, jury nobbling or legal technicalities and had turned up dead within weeks of their acquittals?"

"In one. I told her to leave it with me. I took it to Gordon. He asked me to look into it. There were too many for it to be a coincidence and a surprising number killed by police firearms officers. Not all in London but all down south. A few different forces were involved. So I requested all the official bodycam video of the shootings. One in particular puzzled me."

"What happened? Which one?"

"Do you remember that aristocrat who chopped up his girlfriend? Off his face on crystal meth or crack or both."

"Yeah. What was his name, Nigel something?"

Callie nodded.

"The Right Honourable Nigel Golding, Seventeenth Earl of Broome and Gresham, to give him his full title. I watched that video about twenty times before I saw it. I was focusing on the police officers. But when I looked at him. I mean *really* looked, I spotted something. You could see him pulling the trigger on the pistol he'd taken from the armed escort, but there was no muzzle flash, no smoke, no recoil and no casings ejected as he pulled the trigger."

Stella nodded. Having become superbly well acquainted with the operation and maintenance of firearms in the past year or so, she knew what Callie was saying.

"The gun was empty."

"Exactly. He pulled the trigger a few times, then they gunned him down. Which would have been perfectly legal and in fact mandated by their training. But where were the bullets?"

"The escort had emptied the magazine before getting in with Golding."

"Uh-huh. And what clinched it was I went back and read the armoury report when the weapons were signed back in again. Each pistol and rifle was cleared and each magazine was dropped out and checked. The rifle magazines all had shots fired. Every pistol magazine was full."

Stella paused before speaking. Allowing her thoughts to assemble the blood-spattered jigsaw, not needing the dramatic picture on the box lid. *An SCO19 officer gets into a prisoner transport van with an empty Glock. Lets himself get overpowered. Surrenders the weapon. Prisoner stops van and exits. SCO19 already in position. Prisoner attempts to shoot firearms officers. Gun's empty. They return "fire." Prisoner dead. Empty pistol reloaded off camera. Classic PPM tactic.*

Callie continued speaking.

"After that, we realised something pretty bad was happening inside the Met and possibly further afield. While we were putting our investigative team together you went up to Ramage's place and then he died in the apparent house fire. Gordon told me to follow you. He thought, correctly as it turned out, that you were the key."

Stella shook her head. Trying to make sense of what Callie was telling her. Because as far as she could see, they had let her kill the other PPM members.

"Do you mean, you were on me when I—" She clamped her lips together. *Steady on, Stel. You were about to confess to murdering three lawyers and more or less admit to doing Ramage as well.*

251

"Killed Debra Fieldsend, Charlie Howarth and Hester Ragib? Yes."

"OK. No point in my denying those accusations, then?"

"Not really. But I wouldn't call them accusations. Not really."

Stella's brain lit up. If she'd been watching a cartoon called *Stella's Krazy Kills*, a giant lightbulb would just have popped into life above her head.

"You've been letting me do it. Haven't you? You couldn't have PPM exposed publicly. It would wreck the reputation of the British justice system around the world."

"They were so far beyond guilty there was no question that a jury would have convicted, but we couldn't be sure they'd ever let it get that far."

"You're like me. Vigilantes. Like PPM! This is beyond fucked up, isn't it?"

"Try to look at it rationally, Stella. If this had come out, it would have made institutional racism at the Met look like a minor breach of etiquette. We needed to have it kept quiet. And it wasn't just us. Gordon took it to the Department of Justice. The Secretary of State himself approved it. Then took it all the way to the top."

Stella ran a hand over her cropped hair, scratching at the skin beneath and wincing as her nails caught in the healed-over wound at the back, where Monica Zerafa's gold rings had laid her scalp open.

"I'm a government assassin, is that what you're telling me?"

"Better than being a government cleaning lady, believe me. I had to sort out Debra Fieldsend's freezer."

Stella experienced a brief flashback. An hour spent naked, using Debra Fieldsend's expensive kitchen knives, one of them mains-powered, to dismember the Crown Prosecution Service lawyer on her own kitchen floor after smashing her head in with a cast-iron skillet. *So much blood.*

"Sorry. I wasn't feeling myself that day."

Callie grimaced.

"It's fine. Let's just say it'll be a wee while before I buy frozen meat again."

Despite the grotesque subject matter, Stella was seized with an urge to laugh. She tried to hold it in but she felt she was being hijacked by her own brain. She slapped a hand over her mouth, eyes wide as she stared at Callie, but it was too late. As the hysterics rose, unbidden, she jumped up and grabbed a pillow off the nearer bed and smothered her face.

When the racking pain in her abdominal muscles outweighed the wild, cathartic joy of the laughter, she fell silent, and dropped the pillow.

Callie wasn't laughing. She wasn't giggling. Not so much as the ghost of a smile disturbed her features. Stella suddenly felt anxious.

"What is it?" she asked.

Callie reached into her inside pocket.

"I've got plans for you, Stella. Unfortunately, they involve your death."

42

DEATH NOTICE

JAKE Tanner turned to his neighbour, a pretty Indian detective constable whose skin he thought of as the golden-brown of autumn. He knew if any of his mates could hear his internal poet struggling to describe the precise shade, they'd take the piss for weeks. He'd been trying to pluck up the courage to ask Friya out since the first day she'd joined the command. Trying not to let himself be distracted by her almond-shaped eyes and flawless complexion, he asked the question he could hear being whispered all over the office.

"What's going on?"

"Search me."

Reflecting, ruefully, that although nothing would give him greater pleasure, the invitation was purely rhetorical, he shrugged.

"Guess we're about to find out."

They had been requested by email to gather in the CID office at 8.30 a.m. The email had come from Deputy Assistant Commissioner Rachel Fairhill, an officer so many rungs above them on the ladder that only her ankles were visible beneath the clouds.

As the thirty-odd detectives grew increasingly restive, the

whispers turned into murmurs, which turned into mumbles, then open conversation. Which was snuffed out like a candle by the *whuff* of the door opening.

In strode DAC Fairhill herself, followed by a new face. A slim, fortysomething woman in a sharp navy suit and medium-height heels. Auburn bob brushed back behind her ears. Deep-brown eyes that seemed to look right through each detective whose look she caught, lips accentuated by red lipstick, incongruous against the serious expression and sober outfit.

Fairhill spoke.

"Good morning ladies and gentlemen. I'm Deputy Assistant Commissioner Rachel Fairhill. And yes, before anyone says anything, it *was* a long climb down from my ivory tower, thanks very much for asking."

An appreciative ripple of laughter dispersed some of the tension in the room. Jake turned to Friya.

"Not bad for the brass."

She rewarded him with a smile that lifted his heart, and his hopes.

"I'd like to introduce Detective Superintendent Callie McDonald. As some of you may have noticed, Detective Chief Superintendent Collier hasn't been around for the last few days. That's because Adam has taken leave of absence. At this point in time, I can't tell you why," she paused as a second ripple passed through the room, of murmurs this time, rather than laughter, "but as soon as I can, and I very much hope it will be positive news, you will be the first to know. That's a promise. In Detective Chief Superintendent Collier's absence, Detective Superintendent McDonald will be assuming command of the MIC." She turned to Callie. "Over to you, Detective Superintendent."

Jake turned to Friya and whispered. "McDonald? They've parachuted in a bloody Jock!"

"Better than a bloody Paki, though," she deadpanned.

Jake felt the blood rushing to his cheeks.

"Oh, no, God, I mean, nothing wrong with the Scots, or the Pakistanis. I mean some of my best——"

"Relax. Joke. Plus, I'm Indian, remember?"

At the front of the room, Callie was speaking. Jake tuned back in.

"—of you may well be thinking, why the fuck have we got bloody Braveheart running things? And she's not even a chief super. Well, it was as big a surprise to me as it was to you. So, I hope to get to know you all personally over the next week or so. To get the ball rolling, and to make sure we all start off on the right foot, unlike a lot of bosses, I don't really care what you call me. Guv is fine. If clichéd." A subdued mumble of appreciation passed through the room. "Boss, ditto. Ma'am, if you must. Callie, at a pinch, if you're doing good work. Now—"

She paused, and Jake, being a keen student of body language, noticed a fleeting expression of sadness cross her face: indrawn brows, lips momentarily downturned, eyes scanning the far horizon. He turned to Friya.

"All overtime's cancelled."

She rolled her eyes. Callie resumed speaking.

"I'm afraid I have to begin my leadership of this command … this really, really, *fine* command, with some very sad news." She turned to the DAC, and a look passed between the two senior cops that Jake, despite all his enthusiasm for non-verbal communication, could not decipher. "It is with great sadness that I have to inform you of the death of Detective Inspector Stella Cole."

The room erupted. Shouted questions clashed in midair. Sobs were heard from more than one corner. Callie patted the air for silence.

"What happened, ma'am?" Jake called out.

"As you all know, DI Cole was, unfortunately, sectioned last week. We believe that the stress of returning to work after the deaths of her husband and baby daughter triggered some sort of psychotic break. While an in-patient at St Mary's Hospital, DI Cole was attacked by another patient. It wasn't serious, but after the attack she, well, she escaped, basically, in the middle of the night. She was hit by a car on Praed Street as she emerged from the hospital grounds. It was instantaneous. She didn't suffer."

The room erupted. Cries of anger, grief and bewilderment built in volume. Questions rained down on the newly installed boss of the MIC and she answered them, as best as she was able, until the DAC stepped in.

"I know this has been a massive shock to everyone here. You all knew DI Cole. She was an excellent example of what a detective working in the Met can achieve. There will be a memorial service the day after the funeral, which her family has requested be private. You will all be invited and can pay your respects then."

The briefing broke up. More than few of the assembled detectives, both male and female, were in tears. The new boss retreated to her office, having invited her new team to come and talk to her individually as they felt the need over the coming days.

43

AT LAST, SOME GOOD NEWS

STEAKS in America were bigger, juicier and more flavoursome than those in the UK. Collier liked steak so this was a decided plus. He'd shopped for meat in the extra time he found himself with after the early start. Now, on Saturday lunchtime, with a few of their neighbours invited round for lunch, he was salivating at the thought of eating one of the T-bones he was currently grilling on the gas barbecue. The gas barbecue in the yard. He'd adapted pretty quickly to the US, including the language. He talked about the yard instead of the back garden. About the sidewalk instead of the pavement. About elevators instead of lifts, closets instead of cupboards, vests instead of jackets, stores instead of shops, felonies and misdemeanours instead of crimes. Not everything had a new name, though.

In his preparatory reading for his induction week at the FBI's training academy at Quantico, Virginia, he'd learned that rape was still rape, murder was still murder, although homicide was the legal term, people trafficking was still people trafficking and terrorism was still terrorism. And, boy, weren't they keen on terrorism? Well, keen on eradicating it. His and Lynne's neighbours in their smart suburban neighbourhood would be discussing Russian human rights violations one minute, then nodding frantically the next as each in turn expressed the opinion that torturing terror suspects was not only rational but desirable.

When they'd discovered that he was "in law enforcement" as nearly everyone here referred to police work, it had cast an even brighter halo around him, with his "Briddish" accent and quaint "Olde Worlde" manners. That he was also good looking and always smartly dressed – no cargo shorts or saggy tees for Adam – had led to the racier neighbourhood women adopting him as a cross between a pet and a pool boy. At night, in bed, Lynne and he laughed at the lengths to which these "cougars" went to separate them at drinks parties, barbecues and picnics.

And now it was their turn, his and Lynne's, to have folk round to share a little hospitality, sink a few cold ones, run some gossip up the pole and see who enjoyed the flutter.

A bulky guy in his fifties came up on Adam's blind side and clapped him on the shoulder, making him jump.

"Whoa! Steady on, Jeeves," he said. His name was Gary Frewers and he fancied himself the mimic. His British accent was pretty good, Collier had to admit, if modelled on a class that had largely vanished sometime in the 1930s. His relentless use of it usually began to grate after the third or fourth beer.

"How are you, Gary?" Collier said. "And the lovely Greta?"

"Jim Dandy, old boy. Top hole, what? The missus is over by the pool bending your good lady wife's ear."

Collier picked up one of the steaks on a long-tined fork and slapped it back down on the hot, black bars, bloody side down. The gas flame flared briefly as hot fat spattered onto the elements, releasing a fragrant cloud of grey smoke, and the sizzle drowned out Gary's next sally into upper class Englishisms. Collier gestured with the fork at an ice-filled plastic bucket on the lawn.

"You couldn't grab me another beer, could you? The steaks are reaching a critical juncture and I don't want to desert my post."

Gary smiled.

"Leave it to Beaver, old boy. One Afterburner coming right up."

Collier sighed and turned back to the steaks. He heard a phone ringing. *His* phone. Looked around. He'd left it on a lawn chair down by the pool where Lynne appeared to be deep in conversation with Greta Frewers. He saw her turn her head towards the phone. He caught her eye and pointed at the chair. She nodded, said something to Greta then picked up and answered the phone. Her expression was hard to read as she walked towards him across the lawn, stopping a couple of times to receive hugs from newly arrived guests.

Reaching the barbecue she held out the phone.

"It's the station. In London." She frowned. "Someone in HR?"

Collier took the phone, poking at the steaks with the barbecue fork.

"Adam Collier."

"Adam, it's Linda. I have such good news for you. She's dead."

For one bizarre moment, Collier imagined that Linda Heath was talking about the Queen.

"Sorry, Linda. Who's dead?"

"Her! St …" the line dissolved into an underwater burble for a couple of seconds, " … out of danger."

Collier shook his head. Clamping the phone between ear and shoulder, he piled the steaks onto a platter and stuck it on the barbecue's warming shelf before ringing an old brass school bell Lynne had picked up in a bric-a-brac store the weekend they'd moved into the new house.

Men leading the way, the guests surged politely towards the meat. Collier smiled, gestured at the steaks with his fork then moved back inside, to a deserted living room. His heart was thumping, because he'd allowed himself to reconstruct the missing words in Linda's breathless speech.

"Say that again, please. You disappeared."

"I said, Stella Cole. She's dead."

"How? When?" Daring to allow himself to hope that it was all over. That he could actually start to enjoy himself.

"Three days ago. She was attacked in St Mary's and—"

Collier wanted to interrupt. He knew all about the attack didn't he? After all, he'd procured it. And he knew it had failed. Knew, thanks to his fuckup brother-in-law, that he'd failed. But Linda was in full spate.

"—she escaped. But guess what? She was run over. Oh God, that makes me sound like I'm nine years old. I'm just so excited. She was hit by a car. Apparently, the driver didn't have a chance. He said she just came sprinting out of the hospital dressed in pyjamas and basically ran out into the road in front of him. She died at the scene. Instantly. Isn't it marvellous?"

"Marvellous that a talented detective inspector has been killed after being illegally sectioned? I wouldn't go that far."

"Oh. No. Of course, I mean, no, not really I just meant that, you know, now you could stop worrying. You're out of danger."

"It's fine. Relax. Look, I have guests. I can't talk anymore. But thank you for calling."

"Wait, Adam! Wait." He detected a note almost of panic in her voice. "What about, you know, what about our work? Now she's gone, I mean? You can start again. Rebuild your team. I can help you. I am in HR, after all."

"I don't know. I need to think about this. I'm about to start a six-month stint with the FBI. Just, keep quiet for now, all right? Don't make contact again. Just—"

"Hurry up and wait? Isn't that what you say?"

"Exactly. Hurry up and wait."

Collier ended the call and pocketed the phone. Breathed deeply. Then let out a yelp of pure, unalloyed relief.

"Yes!"

He strode outside again and marched over to the barbecue. Selected the largest steak he could see, dolloped some of Lynne's coleslaw onto the plate beside it, grabbed a chunk of garlic bread and took the whole lot, plus another bottle of Afterburner, down the lawn to where Lynne was sitting with Greta Frewers and two other women. He put his plate down and, to stares of frank admiration from the other women, planted a long, lingering kiss on his startled wife's lips.

"Adam! What on earth brought that on?" she asked, turning a delicious shade of pink.

A dark-haired woman in a red-and-yellow sundress spoke. "Honey, when a man kisses you like that, don't ask dumb questions. Just say, 'thank you dear' and flutter your eyelashes."

This was Sarah Oliver, one of the cougars who clearly relished having this handsome Brit in their midst, even if he had brought the little woman along.

The others laughed and Adam played his role to the hilt.

"Sarah, I imagine you must spend your whole time saying 'thank you dear'!"

"I wish. Come on. Sit yourself down next to me, you gorgeous man and tell us about all those badass British crooks you put in jail."

Smiling outwardly, and laughing hysterically inwardly, Collier did as Sarah bid him, and sliced off a chunk of the beautiful, bloody meat. As he put it into his mouth, Sarah threw an arm round his shoulders and pulled him close, before snapping a selfie, pouting at the screen for all she was worth.

That evening, Eddie Baxter called Collier's mobile.

"Hey, Adam. You all set for your first day with the Bureau? I just got an email from our HR facilitator for the exchange program. Everything's ready on our end. Get yourself down to the Chicago field office at 8.30 a.m. on Monday. I'll meet you at the front desk and we can get you all processed, issue your credentials, all that, then I'll give you the grand tour."

"That's fantastic, thanks so much," Collier said. He realised just how much he was looking forward to the work, now Stella Cole was no longer a threat.

"Just don't get too comfortable in Chi-town. You're shipping out to Quantico for a couple weeks. They've got a kind of cut-down version of our full training program that they like to put our secondees through. It's tons of fun. Weapons training, interrogation techniques, which are all legal, by the way. Unlike our friends down there in Langley, we avoid waterboarding people."

"Remind me of the address?"

"2111 W Roosevelt Road. If you get lost, just look for a big glass cuboid. Like something IBM woulda had in the seventies."

On the Monday, Collier woke early, but not absurdly so. The decrease in his stress level following the call from Linda Heath had worked wonders on his sleep pattern. Lynne had gone out for a run, madness in Collier's opinion, given the heat and the humidity, but she enjoyed it, so who was he to complain? He scribbled a note on a Post-It, stuck it to the vast refrigerator and grabbed his car keys.

Their real estate agent, Yvonne Wallace, not only sorted them out with the house on W Webster Avenue, which as an added bonus faced a large wooded park, she'd also helped them buy a car. As Eddie had said, her brother-in-law ran the local Ford dealership, Fox Ford, and she'd driven the Colliers over there after their final viewing of the morning. On the way, Lynne had reminded him of their agreement to go for something sensible. A sedan, she said, smiling at him as she used the proper word. But then, as Yvonne pulled into the lot, Lynne pointed at a bright, fire-engine-red Mustang convertible.

"Changed my mind," she said. "I want that one."

Yvonne's brother-in-law – "Call me Stokie, everyone around here does. Only my Mom calls me John" – was only too happy for them to take the Mustang out for a test drive. With the roof down and the engine note making both Colliers smile, Stokie must have been chalking up the sale the moment they drove off the lot, Collier thought. And then he thought, *who cares?*

They signed the credit agreement as soon as they got back. Stokie assured them he'd happily buy the car back when – if –

they decided to return to England. He just didn't think they'd want to. "Kinda rainy over there's what I heard." They bought a second car without a test drive, a black Explorer SUV for Collier to drive to work.

Collier had dressed the part, in a new deep-blue suit, white shirt and sober, navy tie, despite Eddie's telling him that, "things have eased up on the dress-code front. Some of the guys even come to work in sport coats." He liked the match between his G-man look and the severe black SUV in which he navigated the morning traffic on N Halsted Street and N Ogden Avenue.

He found his way to the field office without incident and parked the Explorer between two virtually identical black SUVs. Eddie was right. The architecture screamed, "American corporate efficiency." A lot of right angles, glass, stone and steel. Five minutes later, he was giving his name to a smiling receptionist named Natalya, staring at a monitor-mounted webcam and having his visitor pass assembled.

Waiting for Eddie, he observed the people coming and going through the vast, brightly lit Atrium. *Made the right call on the clothes*, he thought. A voice made him spin round.

"Adam! Welcome to the FBI."

44

A BURIAL

THE funeral for Stella Evelyn Roberta Cole took place at Kensal Green Cemetery on a brilliantly sunny Thursday morning. No mourners attended the interment.

45

A SAD STORY

KIRSTY Noble, born out of wedlock to a fifteen-year-old, crack-addicted prostitute, had bounced around the British care system from the age of eighteen months until her sixteenth birthday. At which point, having been regularly molested by her latest foster father and his friends in the full knowledge, and with the connivance, of her foster mother, Kirsty had run away for the final time on March 17, 2011. Within hours, she had been swept off the street outside Victoria coach station by a well-dressed young Arab man who called himself Rick. Within a week, she had been repeatedly raped by Rick and his friends, introduced to heroin, installed in a flat in Pimlico with barred windows and three heavy-duty locks on the door, and put to work in the evenings. Within months, she had learned that her life had no value whatsoever, except as a source of income for Rick. She tried running away again. Was beaten for her troubles. When her jaw had healed, she was put back on the street, with a warning that further disobedience would lead to her mutilation, and then her death. Figuring, correctly, that she was out of options, she opted for the lesser of two evils and drowned herself in the Regent's

Canal, behind a supermarket carpark. Her body was spotted by a dog walker.

The lungs of the body, when examined, had been found to be full of water. Other than this feature, and evidence of multiple and frequent, violent sexual activity, plus intravenous drug use, no physical peculiarities were noted in the coroner's report. No long, brownish scar on the right shin, for example, where a person might have sustained an injury in a motorbike crash aged 23. And no tattoo on the right shoulder, of a mongoose that could easily have been named Mimi.

Once the coroner for Greater London, Inner West London District had released her body, the question arose of who would take responsibility for her. With no living relatives, and no-one to claim her mortal remains, she remained in the care of the state. In her particular case, the state meant the Metropolitan Police.

She was buried at Kensal Green Cemetery on a brilliantly sunny Thursday morning. No mourners attended the interment.

No mourners, but a single figure did watch the proceedings. Callie McDonald wasn't mourning Kirsty. She hadn't known her. She was, however, paying her respects. And offering a small prayer of thanks for her service, in death, to a greater cause.

46

MONEY LAUNDERER

AFTER a home-cooked dinner of Thai fish curry and coconut rice, Stella was loading the plates and cutlery into Vicky's dishwasher when the doorbell rang. Vicky looked at Stella, her eyes narrowed with tension. Stella picked up a carving knife from the still messy chopping board and gestured with it to the kitchen door.

"Check the spyhole. If it looks OK, answer it," she murmured. "I'll be just off to the side in the front room with the door open."

Saying this, she crouched, squat-walked her way along the hall, and hid just inside the front room, out of sight of anyone coming into the hall. Vicky approached the front door as if a monster lurked behind it, which, Stella reflected, had once been a very real possibility. She watched as Vicky put her right eye to the spyhole and, for a split-second, imagined a pointed steel weapon shooting through the brass tube and spearing Vicky through her skull. The image dissolved as Vicky pulled her face back and turned to her.

Stella's heart was racing.

Vicky spoke in a low voice.

"It's a woman. She looks OK. Slim, nice hair. I'm not getting 'murderer.'"

She smiled and opened the door.

Stella tensed and brought the red-pepper-smeared knife out in front of her.

"Can I help you?" Vicky asked, in the very English way that can mean, "How may I be of assistance to you?" but can also mean, "Who the fuck are you and what are you doing on my property?"

"Vicky Riley?" a soft Edinburgh voice asked.

Stella relaxed and dropped her knife hand.

"I'm sorry, you are?" Vicky asked, making it perfectly clear which of the two possible meanings she'd attached to her previous question.

"Callie McDonald," Callie and Stella chorused.

Stella came out of hiding.

"It's OK, she's a friend," she said to Vicky, then rounded the door to welcome Callie, who held a bulging supermarket carrier bag in one hand and a tissue-wrapped bottle in the other.

As usual, Callie had dressed for business. Today that meant an all-black outfit of tailored trousers and a sharply cut jacket that accentuated her lean physique.

"Come in, Callie. Sorry, we've both been a bit on edge the last few days, as you can imagine."

Callie smiled at Stella, then at Vicky and held out the bottle.

"I'm sorry if I frightened you. Here. Peace offering?"

With the Prosecco poured, and some tortilla chips and dips spread out on the table, the three women established who each one was and what role she was playing in the unfolding drama. Vicky was speaking.

"So, just to get this straight, Callie, you faked Stella's death using a Jane Doe then you told her whole team?"

"That would be the size of it, yes."

"So you're thinking, hoping, that whoever's working for him at Paddington Green will leak it and he'll drop his guard."

Stella interrupted.

"Which is brilliant. I know him. And I'm almost a hundred percent certain I know who'll have been on the phone minutes after you made the announcement."

Callie bent and lifted the carrier bag – from Tesco – onto the table.

"Do you still have the money you took from Freddie McTiernan's place?" she asked.

"Eight grand in used twenties. *Very* used twenties."

"I need you to go and get it. In exchange, I can offer you the contents of this handsome plastic carrier bag."

Whatever Stella had been expecting Callie to finally bring out from the bag, bundles of obviously used US currency weren't it. She watched, her surprise morphing into amusement then frank admiration, as Callie stacked the bundles of bills on the table, making a block almost three inches thick.

"I didn't realise Tesco's price promise extended to money laundering," Stella finally said.

"Aye, well, it's a special one-off promotion. Never to be repeated, you might say. There's twelve thousand, eight hundred US there. Finance used today's spot rate. One-point-five-nine. Technically that would have been twelve-seven-twenty but the kind wee souls rounded it up to the nearest hundred."

"And this is legal?" Vicky asked, gesturing at the bundles of dollars with the rim of her glass.

"Off the record?"

"Off the record."

"It's legal enough. Gordon has been meeting some extremely senior law officers and they have produced various documents and seals that cover our actions. Speaking of which—" She reached into the inside pocket of her blazer and withdrew a folded sheet of stiff paper, pre-printed in pink, white and green. She handed it to Stella as Vicky looked on.

"What's this?" Stella asked as she unfolded it.

"Travel insurance."

As she flattened out the document and saw the heading at the top, Stella smiled.

"Well?" Vicky said, impatiently. "What is it?"

"We call them cash cards. Basically, an Interpol customs waiver. It means although we don't *want* me to be stopped by customs, if they find the cash, I wave this and they waive the charges. So to speak."

"We use them for undercover work, normally," Callie said. "I mean, obviously it's not very clandestine to flash it in itself, but it allows undercover cops to play their roles to the hilt. Drug dealers, terrorists and people traffickers tend to avoid banks."

Stella refolded the cash card and stuck it in her own jacket pocket.

"How are you going to get into the States? Is Miss Stadden going to be making a reappearance?" Callie asked.

"I don't think so. Not unless I need her. Vicky and I have worked out a plan. I'm going in via Canada."

Stella spent the next twenty minutes answering Callie's questions about the proposed route. Then, together with Vicky, they worked through a set of contingencies, contact rules, codes and, the nuclear option, what Stella would do if her cover was blown at any point, or if Collier got wind of the plan and decided to run, or, worse, attack.

Two hours later, Callie's mobile buzzed. She glanced at the screen.

"My cab's here," she said.

She turned and stretched out a hand to cover Stella's. She opened her mouth to say something else, then shook her head, smiled and just squeezed. It was an eloquent gesture. Stella understood perfectly what it meant. *Be careful. Don't get hurt. Get him and then get out. I believe in you.* Who knew what else? Stella smiled back. Vicky showed Callie out, Stella following them down the narrow hall. At the front door, Callie turned, the still-bulky Tesco carrier bag dangling by her side.

"Don't get mugged," Stella whispered into her ear as they hugged each other goodbye.

"I don't intend to. But just in case, Gordon authorised me to carry this."

She lifted her jacket away from her left side to reveal a brown leather shoulder holster from which a black pistol butt emerged.

"Jesus! Are there any cops on the UK mainland not carrying?" Stella asked with a grin.

"Oh, there are. Just not the ones fighting off Pro Patria-fucking-Mori!"

And with that rejoinder floating in the air between them, Callie turned on her heel and left, walking down the path at a brisk clip back towards the cab waiting for her at the side of the road.

Back inside, Stella and Vicky sat at Vicky's laptop and found a travel website.

The morning after Callie's visit, Stella called her sister-in-law then drove over to the big house on Putney Heath. She told Elle she was taking a holiday in the States so not to worry if she didn't hear from Stella for a while. Under the pretext of using the upstairs toilet, Stella slipped into the guest bedroom and placed a package on top of the wardrobe, right at the back.

Back in Hammersmith, she and Vicky spent the morning slicing the guts out of a thick paperback and packing the cavity with bundles of twenty-dollar bills. Stella slid the book into the big rucksack she'd packed with her clothes for the trip.

"One more thing," Vicky said. "Maybe we should dull your hair down a bit. You stand out a bit too much for my liking."

An hour in Vicky's bathroom later, Stella's striking look had gone, obliterated by L'Oreal Casting Crème Gloss Chocolate, which had dyed her blonde hair a reddish brown.

"There," Vicky said, when she'd finished with the hair colouring and disposed of the thin disposable gloves. "Less Stella the blonde punk, more Stella the lesbian librarian."

Stella widened her eyes in mock outrage.

"How dare you! I need a safe space!"

They both laughed, although Stella found herself thinking that a safe space right now wouldn't be a bad idea at all. She reached round to the back of her head and felt for the shaved patch. The hair was beginning to grow back; it felt like fur. She shrugged, short of a weave, she couldn't do much to disguise it. *I'll just say it was brain surgery. That should get the pity vote.*

47

ILLEGAL IMMIGRANT

STELLA'S journey from Vicky's house to her destination in Canada took a full twenty-four hours. The first leg took her from Heathrow to Pearson International Airport in Toronto, an eight-hour flight.

After killing two and a half hours in Toronto, she boarded an Air Canada De Havilland DHC-8 400 twin-engine turboprop for the two-hour-eight-minute flight to Thunder Bay Airport in Ontario. There, she picked up a hire car and drove four hours to Lac La Croix, a town of 810 souls in a largely unpopulated area of the province, just north of the border with the US.

The rental contract called for her to return the car the following day. That wasn't going to happen. But they'd get it back in the end. She saw to that by leaving a note stuck to the windscreen under the wiper. And good luck chasing a dead woman for the late fee.

She checked her watch – 1.30 p.m. – and realised she was hungry. The town's main street boasted a single restaurant: a rundown-looking diner called Franklyn's. Stella pushed through the door, setting a brass bell jangling on its steel spring. A couple of the other patrons, burly guys in T-shirts, jeans and work boots, looked up from their mounded plates to see who'd disturbed their lunch. Obviously not finding the stranger sufficiently interesting to be worthy of note, they turned back to their meals.

Stella approached the stainless steel counter. To the rear of the serving space, a short-order cook wielded gleaming kitchen implements to fry eggs, burgers and onions, and rattled a basket full of French fries in an industrial fryer. His bald head gleamed under the lights set into the ceiling. Just as Stella was wondering whether she should try to attract his attention, a plump woman wearing white plimsolls and a pink-and-white, candy-striped work dress appeared from a side door. She bestowed a motherly smile on Stella.

"Yes, honey? What can I get you?"

Stella looked up at the menu, which was picked out in old-fashioned, white plastic lettering on a black pegboard above the counter.

"Er, can I have a Franklyn burger with everything on it, large French fries and a Coke, please? And a slice of coconut cream pie. And a coffee. With cream. And sugar."

The woman smiled.

"Take a seat, honey. I'll bring it over. Skinny thing like you, I got to wonder where you're gonna put it all."

"My mum said I had hollow legs," Stella said, returning the smile, and enjoying some human contact that clearly hadn't come from a company training manual.

"So did mine," the woman replied. "Only I guess I musta filled mine up."

Stella laughed. "Looks good on you."

She sat at an empty table by the window and stared through the glass at the town. Behind her, the woman called out her order to the cook, even though they were separated by no more than six feet of space and the restaurant was quiet.

"Burn one and drag it through the garden, double frog sticks."

While she waited for her food, Stella watched the comings and goings of the townspeople. Most were driving pickups. Here and there, she noticed darker-skinned people, who she realised must be

Indians or, what was the correct term round here? First Nations, that was it. One man, dressed much the same as the guys who'd checked her out, broke away from a small group who were smoking on a street corner and made his way across the road towards the diner.

Her observation was interrupted by the arrival of her food. It covered half the table. The motherly woman smiled down at her as she arranged the plates, glass and mug.

"There you go, honey. Enjoy!"

Stella set to, stuffing great mouthfuls of the excellent burger down and realising just how hungry she was. She quenched her thirst with half the Coke, smothered a belch, and returned to the food. As she ate, the Ojibway man pushed through the door as she had done not so many minutes earlier, setting the bell jangling again. He looked to be about fifty. In good shape physically, thick black hair tied back in a ponytail like the one she used to sport. He approached the counter, ordered a coffee and took it to an empty table at the far end of the restaurant.

Finishing her burger and fries, and starting on the pie, Stella let her thoughts centre on the plan to kill Collier. If he was on secondment to the FBI, the plus was he'd be easy to find. The minus was he'd be armed, she was sure. And during the day he'd be accompanied by a partner, also armed, probably given strict instructions to babysit the new boy. But to get within striking distance, she first had to get across the lake into the US. Find another rental car. Then make the long drive down through Minnesota and Wisconsin and into Illinois.

The plan she'd hatched out with Vicky had seemed wonderfully straightforward sitting in a cosy Victorian terrace house in Hammersmith. Out here in Lac La Croix, it had taken on rather more daunting aspects. Like, on her walk through the town after parking the rental car, she hadn't seen anywhere she could hire a boat. Not even a paddle-boarding concession, not that she was planning on crossing a one-mile stretch of open water on that mode of transport. She also needed to acquire a firearm.

Yes, Other Stella was quite capable of finishing off another human being with virtually anything that came to hand, from skillets to hair-dryers, but Stella was running a parallel plan in her mind to get rid of her malevolent alter ego once and for all. That meant she – the real Stella – needed a gun. Five minutes' research on the internet suggested that she could probably buy one from a private citizen. But the risk she might end up buying from a cop, or just a law-abiding individual with a suspicious mind, put her off the idea.

Stella didn't fancy her chances going down the illegal route. If she was arrested, she could kiss goodbye to her chances of getting Collier. Not to mention the chance that some gangbanger would try to take her money, then her life – or vice versa – and keep the gun for the next punter. So maybe buying one in Canada was the answer. Plenty of people owned rifles, for hunting she supposed. Where there were longs, there might be shorts. She knew she'd never get a Possession and Acquisition Licence, what the Canadians called a PAL. But maybe she could find a way to circumvent the law. Hell, it wasn't as if it would be a first.

When the diner lady came back to clear the table and offer her a refill, Stella asked the question she'd been rehearsing for the past ten minutes.

"Hi, er," she checked out the name badge pinned to the woman's matronly bosom, "Maureen. I was just wondering. If I wanted to try my hand at hunting, who would I talk to round here?"

"You mean bow hunting? A lot of folk do that round here."

Stella presumed that Maureen couldn't imagine a Brit wanting to use a firearm. She realised she'd seen a couple of people with what she'd taken to be archery equipment slung across their backs.

"Maybe. I was actually thinking, more of, you know, the rifle kind."

"Oh, well, a lot of people do that too, of course. There's not a range here or a tourist place or anything like that, but you could try seeing if someone with some land would let you hunt on their property, or—" she looked up and smiled. "Nope. Scratch that. I have a better idea." She turned and called over to the man drinking coffee on his own.

"Hey, Ken? Could you possibly come over here and talk to this British lady, please?"

The man nodded, though he didn't smile. He drained the last of his coffee, stood and ambled over.

"What is it, Maureen?" Then he looked down at Stella. "Hi."

"Hi. Please, have a seat. Can I get you another coffee?"

Maureen spoke.

"Free refills at Franklyn's. Here." She topped up both their mugs. "Ken, this lady, sorry honey, I didn't catch your name?"

"Stella."

"Stella was interested in going hunting. So, I will leave you two to get acquainted. Shout if you want anything else to eat, honey."

She bustled away to take more orders, collecting empty plates as she went.

Ken looked at Stella. He had striking eyes of the purest blue Stella had ever seen. The skin of his face was lined, and had the burnished look of old copper pans.

"My name is Ken White Crow." He offered his hand across the table. Stella shook it. His grip was dry, and hard but not the macho bone-crusher her male colleagues liked to affect. "Pleased to meet you."

To Stella's ears, the greeting sounded formal. Almost old-fashioned. Even though Maureen had already given him her first name, she followed his lead.

"My name is Stella Cole. Pleased to meet you, too."

"Tell me," he said, still unsmiling. "What is a *biiwide* doing all the way out here in Lac La Croix, wanting to go hunting?"

Stella's understanding snagged on the foreign-sounding word.

"Sorry, bi- what?"

He repeated it slowly, as if talking to a child, sounding it out as bi-wi-DEE.

"It means *stranger* in Ojibway. I'm Lac La Croix of the Salteaux First Nation. Part of the Ojibway tribe."

"OK. *Biiwide*. Sorry, I didn't mean to cause any offence."

"You didn't. We've suffered far worse, believe me. So tell me, why here? You're a long way from Toronto, let alone home. Where are you from?"

"London. That's England, not Ontario."

Her knowledge of local geography earned her a smile.

"Very good. And the hunting?"

She shrugged.

"I'm doing some travelling. I sold my house. I went straight from school to university then into work. I wanted to get out of the city and see some wilderness. The lakes looked pretty on the map."

"You ever fire a gun before?"

Like you wouldn't believe.

"I did some shooting in England. I can handle a rifle and a shotgun."

Ken didn't respond at once. He kept his eyes fixed on hers. It wasn't an aggressive stare. Stella had seen plenty of those, from drunks, football hooligans, terrorist suspects, rapists, the psychopath Collier had sent to kill her. They didn't faze her. She just stared back until they blinked or she got bored and started asking them her questions over again. Politeness, relentless, quiet politeness, eventually wore down even the most hardened criminals, she'd found. Ken's stare was more appraising. She waited. Letting him come to his judgement as to her character.

"We have land. Plenty of game. I can take you hunting."

Stella rejoiced inwardly, letting a fraction of her emotion out in the form of a wide smile.

"That's great, thank you. Of course, I'm willing to—"

"Pay? Sure. First you gotta show me you can shoot. I'm not having any gutshot animals running off to die in pain. Don't have the time to track 'em down and put them out of their misery."

"Fair enough. I can do that. And if I pass your test, how much would you want?"

"Why don't you tell me how much you think a day's hunting on authentic First Nation land is worth to a *biiwide*?"

Given her plans, Stella wasn't inclined to penny-pinch.

"A thousand dollars. US."

Ken smiled.

"For that, I'll even give you a tour round our town. Give you the full experience to take back home with you."

"It's a deal. Now, my next question. Where can a *biiwide* stay around here?"

"Talk to Maureen. She and Joe let rooms."

Later that evening, having arranged to meet Ken outside Franklyn's at 8.00 a.m. and booked one of Maureen's guest rooms for a few nights with the option to renew, Stella dozed off and dreamt of Lola again. For once, her baby wasn't burning.

48

TARGET PRACTICE

DRESSED appropriately, she hoped, for hunting, in jeans, a green sweatshirt and her bike boots, Stella arrived outside Franklyn's at 7.50 a.m. Twelve minutes later, a silver GMC Sierra pickup scabbed with rust and bandaged with silver duct tape stopped outside the diner. Checking Ken was the driver, Stella pulled open the door, which squawked in protest, climbed in and slammed it shut behind her. The cab smelled of smoke, and she realised she hadn't had a cigarette since arriving in Canada. Trouble was, now she really wanted one. She glanced at a crushed pack of Camels on the dashboard.

Ken must have caught the look because he offered her a smoke.

"Light for me, too, would you?" he asked.

She wound the window down and blew out a lungful of silvery-grey smoke into the still air.

"Oh, Jesus, that's good!" she said.

"They'll kill you in the end."

"I don't plan to live for ever."

He grunted.

"That's good. Live for now."

He pulled away from the kerb and accelerated down the long, wide main street towards the edge of town. Everyone coming the other way waved or gave a thumbs-up. The trucks were mainly older models, some even rustier than Ken's, although Stella's gaze was arrested by a shiny silver Mercedes. The driver, a brunette in large-framed sunglasses, stared straight ahead as the two vehicles passed and was the only one not to acknowledge Ken.

"Who's she?" Stella asked.

"Mayor."

"She didn't seem to like you much."

"Bad blood."

Stella smiled.

"Are you always this talkative, Ken? Or are you just putting on the chatty act for this dumb little *biiwide?*"

He laughed, and the action transformed his face. The creases at the corners of his eyes revealed themselves as laughter lines, and his mouth softened.

"You got me. It's not you. I'm kinda suffering for the sins of last night. Too many beers."

"Oh, right. No, I mean, don't worry. I've heard about, er, First Nations people having problems. I've had my own struggles with alcohol, so, you know, it's—"

"Wow, that's pretty racist. What, a guy has a hangover and you're seeing the poor alcoholic Indian already?"

Stella felt the heat rush to her cheeks. *Jesus, Stel. You've been in the guy's truck for five minutes and you've bummed a fag off him and played the white oppressor card. Way to go!*

"God, I'm, look, I'm sorry. That was unforgivable. I'm a guest in your country, in your car and now—"

Ken's laughter was even louder this time. Stella frowned. What had she done this time?

Wiping the corners of his eyes with the sleeve of his denim jacket, Ken finally found the wind to speak again.

"Oh, man, I'm the one who should be apologising. That was a

cheap shot. I was joking. I was playing backgammon with a few of the boys last night, that's all."

Relieved, Stella leaned her head towards the open window, letting the breeze cool her flaming cheek.

"And when you say 'backgammon', that's not a trap, right? You were actually playing it. Or were you dancing around in your underpants covered in war paint?" *OK, feeling confident, Stel.*

"Yeah, we were playing backie all right. We only do the war dance on alternate Wednesdays."

An easy, bantering relationship established between them, Stella relaxed. Ken drove at a steady forty-five along a two-lane blacktop through pine forest, which gave way from time to time to reveal a series of small lakes, their surfaces ruffled by the breeze.

Suddenly he leaned forward and stared up through the top edge of the windshield. He pointed.

"Look. Red-tailed hawk."

Stella followed his pointing finger.

Above and to the left, circling above the trees was a large bird of prey. Black-tipped flight feathers extending from the tips of its wings like fingers and a fan-shaped tail of tawny-red that seemed to extend directly out of the trailing edge of the wings.

"It's beautiful. Tell me its name in Ojibway."

"*Meskwananiisi.*"

Stella listened, processed and tried to repeat it faithfully.

"Mes-kwon-a-neesy?"

Ken offered one of his trademark grunts that Stella interpreted as grudging respect.

"Not bad."

"For a *biiwide.*"

"For a *biiwide*? No. Pretty good. We got some of the youngsters now who don't want to learn our language. They say we're living in the past. They want to leave, go to Toronto. Get white-collar jobs."

"Can you blame them? It's not just Ojibway teenagers who want to do that. Kids everywhere want to get away from their roots and see the world. Get jobs, houses, you know, they have a need to fit in."

"Huh. Maybe."

Ken lapsed into silence after that. They drove on for another couple of hours.

Stella fell into a trancelike state, hypnotised by the thrum of the engine and the unspooling landscape of wetlands, scattered stands of trees and the ever-present lakes.

Ken spoke, startling her into full alertness.

"We're here."

Stella looked ahead. A turning on the right was signposted, "Lac La Croix First Nation."

"Is this your—?"

"Reservation? Yeah, you can call it that. We just call it home."

He was smiling, so she smiled back. And punched him lightly on the right bicep.

"Teaser!" she said, and was rewarded with another crinkled smile.

Ken introduced Stella to everyone they met as they walked down the main street through the village. The women in particular struck Stella as attractive. Most wore their dark hair in long plaits.

"Come on, we'll go get a couple rifles," Ken said.

His house was a wooden, single-storey building, hung with silvered shingles and painted a bright kingfisher blue with white door and window frames. Inside, everything was immaculate, from the floral curtains to the highly-polished dining table. A flat-screen TV dominated the living area, but it was the room beyond that interested Stella. She could see a rack of long guns, fishing rods and other evidence of an outdoor lifestyle, from snow shoes to fur hats.

Ken led the way and stood back as she admired the kit.

"See anything you like?"

She leaned forwards and picked up a rifle with a highly-polished greyish-brown wooden stock and what looked like an old-time lever action behind the trigger.

"This one," she said. "It looks like something John Wayne would have used."

"Marlin 336XLR. Good choice. I'll take this one. She's my favourite."

Ken picked up a wooden rifle with a blued barrel and a telescopic sight.

"Nice. What make is that?" Stella asked.

"It's a Remington 798. It belonged to my father."

Half an hour later, Ken pulled the truck off the dirt road into a scraped-flat parking area surrounded by birch trees. Stella climbed out and, rifle slung across her back, followed Ken into the woods. The sun was warm on Stella's back and she found herself smiling. Birdsong filled the air along with a fine pollen dust that glinted in the sun arrowing down between the trees in light and dark stripes.

They emerged from the woods into a broad clearing, maybe two hundred yards by eighty. In the middle, a group of rabbits were nibbling the grass. Ken worked the Remington's bolt and fired into the air. The rabbits scattered as the report of the shell shattered the calm, running full tilt for the closest edge of the clearing and the protective cover of the scrub.

"Now we have the place to ourselves, let's see whether you can shoot," Ken said. "Can you hit that?" He pointed to a blue steel oil drum beside a wide-trunked tree. The distance was no more than fifty feet, Stella estimated. *OK, so you're not patronising me, but you want to be sure. That's fine, Ken, I can do th*at.

She unshouldered the rifle and worked the lever, which travelled down then up with a smooth, easy action. She pulled the butt hard against her shoulder and pressed her face against the stock's cheek-piece. The rifle wasn't fitted with a telescopic sight, just front and rear iron sights. The trigger fitted comfortably against her curled index finger, which she rested there while sighting on the drum.

On her first indrawn breath, she squeezed the trigger to what felt roughly like first pressure. As the breath left her lungs, she increased the pressure a little more. She waited for a beat of her heart, then squeezed off the shot.

The recoil jammed the gun butt back against her shoulder. Her tight grip meant it was a shove not a thump. So hopefully, no bruising.

With the noise of the shot echoing around the woods she peered at the oil drum. Thought she could discern a black hole left of centre surrounded by bright grey steel.

"Did I hit it?"

"Yeah. You hit it. That was the kindergarten shot. Let's move up a class."

Over the next twenty minutes, Ken led her to shooting stations progressively further away from the target. Each time she plugged the oil drum until its face was peppered with holes. His final request was for Stella to hit the drum from the far end of the clearing. A full two hundred yards distant. Before they set off away from the drum, he rotated it so Stella would be shooting at a clean face.

He said, "Your grouping is pretty bad, but you haven't missed it yet. Put a round into it from away over there and we'll go hunting tomorrow."

"Why not today?"

"I got stuff I need to do today. My truck's running rough, you mighta noticed on the drive over here."

Stella smiled. "OK. You're the boss."

And she thought about how pleasant it was not to be the boss. Not to be making decisions. Not to be responsible for anything more complicated than smacking holes in an old, blue oil drum with a rifle. Nor, she suddenly realised, to be taking orders from Other Stella, who had been absent for more than 24 hours.

When they reached the far end of the clearing, Stella turned to look back at the oil drum. Suddenly it looked very small indeed. She remembered shooting one of Ramage's bodyguards outside his house, Craigmackhan. She'd had a scope that day and a nice comfortable sniper's nest in the bracken.

She hoisted the Marlin up and settled it against the fleshy pad of muscle beside her shoulder. Then she repeated the sequence of movements she'd been using at each stage of her assessment. With the tip of her tongue between her teeth she looked down the Marlin's barrel, aligning the brass bead of the foresight with the raised rear sight. *This is it, Stel. Moment of truth. Ken thinks this is all about hunting. But we know different.*

49

HUNTING TRIP

IN a small, calm, silent space all of her own, Stella let the outside world drift away until she was nothing more than the rifle, aware only of the trajectory the bullet would take on its two-hundred-yard journey to the side of the blue oil drum.

She squeezed the trigger, leaning slightly forward into the stock to minimise the impact of the recoil. With a bang, the round sped away towards the target. She held the rifle up for a moment or two before lowering it.

Confident she'd hit the drum, she turned to Ken, who was staring downrange.

"What do you think?" she asked.

"I think, let's go and see. But I also think, you'd make a fine hunter."

Stella realised her heart was racing as they walked back to the oil drum. As they drew closer, she could see what she wanted to see: a hole with the characteristic irregular splash of grey where the impact of the bullet had blown the paint off the metal. She smiled to herself, but Ken caught the fleeting expression of joy.

"Yeah, you hit it. Plum centre. What did you shoot in England?"

Scotland, but let's not split hairs.

"You mean the rifle or the target?"

He shrugged.

"Both, I guess."

"The rifle was a Blaser. An R93 Luxus, if memory serves. And the target was," she hesitated, "big game."

"Didn't realise you had any in England. What was it? Buffalo? Some kind of deer?"

A fat thug in corduroys.

"Yes, a big deer. Red."

"Huh. OK, then. Listen, you want to help me with my truck? I could use a second pair of hands."

"Sure. I don't have anywhere to be. Just, you know, I'm more of a bike girl. But you tell me what to hand you or what to hit with a hammer, and I'm there."

With a smile he turned, and together they walked, in companionable silence, back through the woods, which had refilled with birdsong now the shooting was over.

Stella spent the rest of the day helping Ken work on the truck. He'd offered to take her to meet the shaman, but when they got to his house, the man was out. The windows were shuttered, giving the house a closed-for-the-season look. He gave her a lift back to Lac La Croix at 7.00 p.m., with a promise to collect her outside Franklyn's at six the following morning. To get an early start, as he said.

She was awake and dressed in what she now thought of as her hunting gear by 5.30 a.m., breakfasting on a sandwich and a flask of coffee she'd asked Maureen to prepare the previous evening.

The temperature outside was rising, but as she stood waiting for Ken, she was glad of the warmth the sweatshirt provided. The sun had just appeared over the horizon, throwing pink spears across the sky. She inhaled deeply. Mostly what she could smell was clean, crisp air, overlaid with the faint tang of pine needles.

The truck's familiar raucous engine note, smoothed off a little by the previous day's exertions, announced Ken's imminent arrival. Stella felt herself smiling at the prospect of a day outside, far from other people – especially the kind of other people who were out to kill her. Or, she supposed, the kind of other people she was out to kill herself. Having proved herself against the oil drum, she was looking forward to trying her hand at trickier targets. She remembered a girl she'd known at university in Bath. Sophie Abbott's well-to-do parents owned a successful farm, but she had turned her back on matters rural, from agriculture to hunting. From there it had been a short step to turning vegetarian.

"You shouldn't eat meat unless you're prepared to kill it yourself," had been one of her stock lines. And it worked against the city-bred kids who thought lamb chops came from Sainsbury's and not from baby sheep. Stella, always an argumentative girl, had risen to the bait – and the challenge.

"I'd be happy to kill my own food," she'd declared over coffee after a psychology lecture. "Why not? Our ancestors did."

A posh boy at the next table, Marcus something, who she always thought had a thing for her, had leaned over.

"Couldn't help overhearing, ladies," he said in that infuriatingly languorous upper-class accent so many of the students at Bath affected. "I'm going home on Friday after lectures. You could come along, Stella. My father likes to shoot for the pot most weekends."

She'd agreed there and then, more to provoke her friend than from any desire to relive the 1920s. And the weekend had been fun, more or less. Marcus's parents – the Belmonts, that was it! Marcus Belmont – were welcoming and, it seemed to Stella, genuinely friendly. Mrs Belmont had been a brilliant raconteuse and had kept their weekend guest enthralled with tales of her work as an analyst at MI6 during the Cold War. Mr Belmont loved his guns, his vintage Brough Superior motorbike, which he'd allowed Stella to ride down their half-mile-long drive and back, and his wine cellar.

On the Saturday, after a hearty breakfast of devilled kidneys, fried eggs and a pile of toast, Marcus and Stella had accompanied

Mr Belmont in his knackered old Land Rover out to a wooded corner of his estate where they proceeded to stalk and kill half a dozen rabbits and a couple of pheasants.

Stella returned to Bath with Marcus on the Sunday afternoon, happily anticipating her next encounter with the saintly Sophie.

Ken rolled up beside her, interrupting her reverie with a blip of the throttle. He wound the window down.

"Ready to go?" he asked.

Stella nodded, bent to pick up her daysack and walked round the front of the truck to climb in. She pulled open the door and was immediately met with a long, wet tongue.

"Hey, who are you?" she asked the over-eager mutt now slobbering all over her.

"His name's Chakabesh," Ken said, pronouncing it *chuh-kah-baish*. Then, to the dog, "Give the lady some room, Chaka." He dragged the dog back by its collar so Stella could get herself seated.

Ken pushed the stick shift into first and pulled away with a roar from the truck's high-mileage engine and a gust of stinking exhaust fumes. Chakabesh had obviously decided the *biiwide* was a friend and proceeded to lick her hand, her leg, basically any part of her he could reach. Which was fine by Stella. Uncomplicated, loyal and probably very clever: all qualities she could appreciate, in humans as well as dogs.

"Have you had him since he was a puppy?" she asked.

"Uh-huh. His mother belongs to my mother."

"What does his name mean? Is it Ojibway?"

"Yes. Chakabesh is from the folk stories of the Cree and Northern Ojibway peoples. Sometimes we call him the Man in the Moon. He could be foolish sometimes, rash, you know? His older sister was sensible, but Chakabesh ignored her advice. But he had courage and a faithful heart, and people always forgave him in the end."

"He sounds a little like The Trickster," Stella said.

"What?"

"Did you ever hear of Carl Jung?"

"Is he a folk hero of your people?"

"No, he was a—"

"Of course I've heard of Carl Jung! Do you think I'm some dumbass Indian who only knows the old stories? I took a minor in psychology at college before I came back to Lac La Croix."

Once more, Stella felt the blood heating her cheeks.

"Fuck! I put my foot in it again, Ken. I'm really sorry. It's just—"

Ken's loud laughter made Chakabesh pause in his fervent licking of Stella's left wrist and look up at his master. Clearly satisfied that nothing was amiss, he resumed his ministrations.

"No, *I'm* sorry," Ken said. "I'm just messing with you. Why *would* a backwoods Indian stuck out here in Western Ontario know about a Swiss psychiatrist?"

Stella sighed with relief. This slow-talking man was playing her like her professor at university had played the eager nineteen-year-old psychology undergraduate.

"Fine. So, having pulled my foot out of my mouth, I did psychology, too. I was going to say that Chakabesh sounds a lot like The Trickster archetype."

"Hmm. Maybe. Could be The Rebel, too. Or The Hero. Anyway, forget all that Jungian bullshit. Chaka's a great hunting dog."

Stella laughed as the dog tried to work his rough tongue up the inside of the sleeve of her sweatshirt.

"And if all else fails, he could always get a job as a physical therapist."

Two hours later, with Chakabesh happily asleep, his silky head on Stella's lap, Ken made a turn signal and pulled off the highway onto a dirt road. The dog woke up and looked straight ahead, as if to say, Hey! I recognise this. His tail began thumping rhythmically on the seat and his wide mouth dropped open in what Stella could only conceive of as a happy smile. He began whining softly, way back in his throat.

"Is he OK?" Stella asked.

"Oh, he's fine. He's just excited cause he knows we're almost there.

Chaka was right because after another ten minutes, Ken pulled the truck over and killed the engine. The two humans climbed out and eased off their muscles. Chaka, meanwhile, bounded away along a narrow track through the trees before running back, full tilt, then springing off in a new direction.

Ken handed Stella the Marlin she'd used the previous day and took his Remington off the gun rack at the back of the cab.

"Down there," he said, pointing at the first track Chaka had run off to investigate.

The track wound on for a couple of hundred yards through light, mixed woodland. Lots of birch, some oak, some pines and a lot of low-growing shrubs bearing thousands of pink and yellow flowers. The wood smelled of leaf mould, pine needles and sap – clean, green smells that made Stella smile. The rapid-fire knocking of a woodpecker directly above them made her stop and look up, but she couldn't see the bird. She felt Ken's hand on her arm.

"Wait," he murmured. "There." He extended his arm very slowly and pointed to a spot just in front of them and about thirty feet up.

"I see it," she said, barely able to keep her voice quiet with the glee she felt at being able to see the black, red and white woodpecker hammering away at the trunk of a sycamore tree.

They emerged onto a path that led around the perimeter of a clearing some twenty-five feet below their own level. The floor of the circular, sandy space was bare of bushes and scrub, and covered in a thin layer of moss and grass, punctuated here and there by bare stone scrapes. On the far side, where the ground sloped steeply upwards, Stella could see dozens of darker brown patches that, as she focused, resolved themselves into holes. A rabbit warren. She tried to see, not merely to look, as she felt sure Ken was doing at her right elbow. The ground between the holes was covered in rabbits. There must have been several hundred. Their colour was such a close match to the ground cover that until they moved, and their white scuts flashed, it was virtually impossible to see them.

"Dinner," Ken said quietly. She noticed that he never whispered, preferring to murmur. *Just like we used to*, she thought. *Harder to make out without the hissing sibilants.* And then she thought, *We? That feels like a different life.* Spending hours in converted transit vans on surveillance duty. Tailing drug dealers, or watching gangsters from a corner table in a rough pub. How had she come from that, to this?

You know the answer to that one, Stel, a soft voice whispered from somewhere in the deepest part of her brain. *Because those fuckers murdered your husband and left your baby to burn to death in her daddy's car.*

Stella shook her head, willing the voice, and its malevolent owner, to retreat. Ken was speaking again.

"You want to shoot one first?"

Stella nodded. She moved a couple of yards to her left where a slender birch leant at the perfect angle to make a shooting support. Turning away from the warren and shielding the rifle's action with her torso, she worked the lever down and up to chamber a round. The sound of the well-maintained action was minimal.

She faced forward again and rested the rifle against the birch tree, settling her cheek against the stock and preparing herself to shoot. The distance from her position to the warren was only half that of the previous day's marksmanship test. Even without the telescopic sight of Ken's Remington, she felt confident as she sighted along the barrel. She was shooting downwards, but over a relatively short distance she didn't think she'd need to compensate for the bullet's dropping much during flight.

She fired, and all but one of the rabbits scattered, darting towards their holes.

"Nice shot," Ken said. "Next time we shoot together, OK?"

Stella nodded.

Gradually at first, then with increasing confidence, the remaining rabbits re-emerged from the warren. Before long the ground was thick with them, despite the presence of the dead creature among them.

The two rifles sang out in unison, and two more rabbits died on the spot.

When they'd shot half a dozen, Ken held his hand up.

"That's enough for today. You shoot well for a city-dweller."

"Thank you. Shall we go and collect the bunnies?

Ken strung the rabbits together on a length of nylon cord, running it between the bones of the back leg and the Achilles tendon.

"I have coffee and sandwiches in the truck. You hungry?"

"Starving."

They walked back to the truck in silence. Ken wasn't a man to talk when he had nothing to say, and Stella liked him all the more for it. Her shoulder ached pleasantly. If it hadn't been for the question she'd framed in her head, she could almost fancy herself content. But Collier was out there, somewhere to the south. Enjoying life. Enjoying playing at being an FBI agent. And while he breathed, she couldn't. Not properly.

Back at the truck, Ken poured two tin cups of coffee and broke out ham sandwiches. Stella took a bite and washed it down with a swig of coffee. Then cleared her throat, preparing to ask her question.

50

AIRWEIGHT

KEN looked up from his sandwich.

"What is it?"

Stella took a deep breath and let it out in a huffing sigh.

"Can you help me get a handgun?"

Instead of answering, he took another bite of the sandwich, followed by a swig of coffee. He didn't take his eyes off her until he'd swallowed.

"Why do you need a handgun?"

"Self-defence. I'm planning to move on soon, and it's pretty isolated country out here. I need something to help me feel safe."

"It's against the law for you to buy a handgun in Canada, and that goes for me buying one for you. You know that, right?"

"Uh-huh. But, you know, I thought maybe you could sell me one you already own. I can pay. A lot."

Ken pursed his lips. Looked up at the sky, squinting against the sun. Then returned his gaze to hers.

"I need my guns."

"So could you get one for me? I noticed a gun shop in town."

"For self-defence?"

"Yes. Like I said, I——"

"You're lying."

"No. I just need——"

"Tell me the truth. Last chance. Tell me why a nice, pretty girl from England comes all the way out to Lac La Croix, pals up with a full-blood Ojibway, gets him to take her hunting, then asks him to buy her a gun. Lie to me again, and I'll take you back into town and we're done. Apart from what you owe me for the hunting trip."

Stella sighed. She'd already made the decision.

"I've come out here to find, and kill, the man who organised the murder of my family. He's in Chicago."

She added the names of the main PPM players and sketched in the group's activities in England. Having delivered herself of a cut-down version of the story, she watched Ken assimilate the information. His eyes never left hers. After a full minute of silence, he rubbed the sparse stubble on his cheeks.

"Show me your hands again."

Stella held out her hands, palms upwards.

He took her right hand and turned it over. Turned it back again. Told her to make a fist.

"You've got small hands," he finally said.

"I've shot a Glock 17," she blurted, afraid he was going to reject her request on the grounds of her anatomy.

"Yeah, I bet you have."

"Please, Ken. Don't say no."

"You want something small. Something you can keep in a pocket. You can't walk around Chicago carrying something that bulges out through your clothes."

Stella felt the black clouds of doubt dissipate in a second.

"So you're going to help me? Even though we've only just met?"

"Yes. Wanna know why?"

"Tell me."

Ken put the cup down on the truck's hood then turned back to face Stella.

"One, I trust you, and I believe you. Someone murdered my

family, I'd do what you're doing. Two, you're respectful, and you helped me with my truck yesterday." He paused.

"And three?"

"And three, you're going to pay me $6,000."

Stella had been expecting something in the high four figures. She was ready with a counter offer.

"Let's make it ten thousand. US. Including the hunting trip. This old heap of yours needs more than just the patch-up work we did on it yesterday. Maybe you can get yourself a new truck out of this. Plus, then you can throw in a boat trip across the lake to the US side."

"Ten? Why so much more than I just asked for?"

"You're taking a big risk with me. And I have enough to get by on once I reach the States. The money's under a loose floorboard back in my room at Maureen's."

Back at the Lac La Croix reservation, Ken drove the truck up to the side of his house. He invited Stella to come in with him. He led her through to the room with the rack of long guns and told her to sit on a battered leather sofa on the opposite side of the room. Kneeling in front of a tall bookcase, he reached under the lowest shelf and pulled out an olive-green metal trunk. The trunk bore faded stencilling on its side. Letters and numbers that Stella guessed were either a military service number or a serial number for whatever piece of kit the trunk had originally contained. Ken placed it on the coffee table in front of her then sat beside her on the sofa. She watched as Ken flipped open the catches and lifted the lid.

"This belonged to my dad," he said. "He served in Vietnam. Brought it back, along with a heroin habit and a two-ounce piece of NVA shrapnel in his leg."

He pulled out an olive-green hand grenade and set it on the table top.

"That's had the fuse taken out, right?" she asked, every fibre of her being telling her to move backwards at high speed.

He shook his head.

"Still live as far as I know. But the pin's in, so we're OK.""

The next item out of the trunk was a folded olive-drab shirt with a name – White Crow – stencilled in black on a strip of material stitched above the pocket.

A thought occurred to Stella as she watched Ken unload more military souvenirs.

"I thought Canada didn't fight in Vietnam. Isn't that why all the US draft-dodgers came up here?"

"You're kinda right. Canada stayed out of the war, at least officially. But thousands of Canadians went south to volunteer for combat with the US army. My dad was one of them. Mohawks volunteered, too. Fifty of 'em went down from Montreal."

He'd carried on unloading the trunk as he talked. Now, the top of the coffee table was covered by an assortment of khaki and olive-drab items of clothing, identity documents, fading colour photos, and to one side, a dagger, its steel blade pitted with rust. Ken reached over and picked up a cloth bundle about the size of his hand.

He put it on his lap and unwrapped the covering, one corner at a time. When the final corner was opened out, the contents of the bundle were revealed.

The revolver was small. Ken picked it up and placed it on his left palm. The gun didn't protrude over the edges of his hand in any direction. The grips were a shiny black material Stella thought must be plastic. The metal parts were a dull silver.

"Here," he said, "Take it."

Stella picked up the gun. It didn't weigh much, not even a pound. She curled her fingers around the grip and pointed it at a stuffed deer head mounted above the fireplace.

"What is it?"

"Smith & Wesson Bodyguard Airweight. AKA Model 38. My Dad took it off a dead VC. You ever see that photo from Vietnam? This South Vietnamese general is about to execute a guy."

Stella vaguely remembered seeing a black-and-white photo in

a documentary on the Vietnam War. The man holding the revolver looking almost bored as he prepared to blow his captive's brains out. The man about to die, flinching, his face a mask of terror and pain.

"Yes, I think so."

"He used a Model 38. The gun you're holding is the same age. It's clean, oiled and ready to go. You sure you can use it on another person? Taking a human life isn't as easy as shooting rabbits."

She thought back to her shooting of Leonard Ramage. Of the Albanians in Marbella who'd blinded Yiannis Terzi's daughter. Of Tamit Ferenczy's brother, bodyguards and, finally, the man himself.

"When the time comes, I'll do what needs to be done."

Ken nodded, seeming not to need to know any more than that.

"You've got a five-round capacity," he said, pointing to the cylinder. "It's single-action-double-action, which means you can cock the hammer back and pull the trigger to shoot, or you can just squeeze the trigger when the hammer's down and it'll cock then fire. One's slower but you got a lighter trigger pull. The other's faster, but you need more strength in your finger."

Stella turned the gun to look at the right-hand side. Read the engraved word: Airweight.

"I guess I'll have to find somewhere to practise and figure out which suits me. Have you got some ammunition for it?"

"Nope. But I can go into town and buy some. It takes Smith & Wesson .38 Special. How about I get you a couple hundred? You can do some practising on our land and save some for your friend in Chicago?"

Stella nodded.

"Sounds perfect."

Then a worrisome thought flitted across her mind.

"The gun. It can't be traced back to you can it?"

He smiled grimly and shook his head.

"Whoever that VC got it from's long dead. It was probably

military issue to the South Vietnamese Army. It's been sitting in that trunk since my Dad got back from the war in '73. You know, you never told me what you do for a living back in England. Or what you used to do before you decided to go travelling."

"No," Stella said, with a smile. "I didn't. It doesn't matter now, because I'm not going back to it."

He shrugged.

"Fair enough. Listen, let's take a run back into town. I'll pick up some ammunition and drop you at your hotel. You get the cash, I'll come find you and we can do the exchange. Then I reckon we ought to seal the deal with a beer or two. OK with you?"

"Sounds good."

Two and a half hours later, Ken swung the pickup off the highway and onto the town road that led into the centre of Lac La Croix. He pulled up outside the house where Stella was renting the room. Swivelling in his seat, he handed the cloth-wrapped revolver to Stella.

"See you in about twenty minutes," he said.

She nodded and climbed out, slammed the door and watched as Ken pulled away.

Inside, she stuck the revolver at the bottom of her daysack then repacked it with her waterproofs on top. She pulled back the worn, blue carpet in the corner behind the wardrobe and eased up a foot-long piece of floorboard. In the dusty space between the joists sat a plastic bag, wrapped into a neat rectangular package. She pulled it free and replaced the board and carpet. Sitting on the bed, she unwrapped the package and withdrew the paperback, a much-thumbed copy of a Michael Connelly novel, *The Brass Verdict*.

The book's title referred to criminal slang for a gangland execution. Now she was on the way to delivering her own, final brass verdict on Collier. Like a lot of cops she knew, Stella loved Connelly's Harry Bosch novels. He was one of the few fictional cops who thought, talked and acted like a real cop, warts and all. Plus, in a pleasing coincidence, Harry had been a "tunnel rat" in Vietnam. She let the book flop open to reveal the razored-out recess in which the $12,800 nestled. *Snug as a bug in a rug*, she thought, falling back on something her Mum had always said as she tucked her little daughter in for the night. Something Stella had said to her own daughter, during the all-too brief time she'd been able to share with her. *Soon, Lola. Soon he'll be dead. Then Mummy can come and join you and Daddy, and we'll all be together again.*

51

GOODBYE, STELLA

ANNIE'S Tavern was one of two bars in town. The other, La Croix Tap, was on the rough side, according to Ken, and they'd be better off meeting in the more salubrious surroundings of Annie's. After retrieving the cash, Stella walked down the main street and pushed through the black-painted door. It was just before six, and about half the tables were occupied. A row of early-evening drinkers lined the copper-topped bar, nursing beers in frosty mugs. All men, about half Ojibway, half white guys.

Weaving through the other tables and nodding hello or shaking hands with other drinkers, Ken found them a corner booth. He signalled one of the waitresses for a couple of beers. She brought two bottles of Moosehead Pale Ale a few minutes later and departed with a smile after leaving a till receipt under Ken's bottle.

Ken handed Stella a plastic carrier bag under the table. She took it from him noting its heft, and placed it by her left foot.

"You got two hundred rounds of Winchester .38 Special, Silvertip Hollow Point ammunition in there."

Stella handed Ken the copy of The Brass Verdict.

"You get much reading time?" she asked with a grin.

He flipped through the pages and grinned back.

"I guess I'll make time. Looks like a good book."

"Ten grand says you love it."

They clinked the necks of their bottles and drank.

"How am I going to get to Chicago, Ken?" Stella asked, signalling the waitress for another two beers.

"You mean, given what you're planning to do when you get there?"

"Exactly."

"This guy who killed your family – Collier. He knows you're after him, right?"

"No. He thinks I'm dead."

"How come?"

"Friends in England put the word out, and we're sure one of his foot soldiers got the word to him."

"And these *friends*, of yours." Ken said. "They in the same line of work as you?"

"Mm-hmm."

"Law enforcement?"

Stella hadn't wanted to reveal any more than she had to about her background. Not because she didn't trust Ken. Quite the reverse. But she felt it would be better for him if he knew the minimum. But now he'd asked a direct question and she owed him an honest answer.

"Yes. Law enforcement."

"OK. That's good: you got friends on the inside. And Collier's working for the FBI?"

"Yeah, and— Oh, thanks," Stella said to the waitress, who'd just placed another two bottles of beer on the table and snagged the long-necked empties between her knuckles. "And I guess that means he'll be armed."

"I guess it does. Plus his partner will be."

"So?"

"Even if he thinks you're dead, he'll still be vigilant. Watchful. I would be."

"But why? If he believes the threat's gone?"

"Did he see your dead body?"

Stella saw immediately where Ken was going. She played along, interested in how the interrogation would turn out and what she'd learn.

"No."

"Visit your grave?"

"No."

"See your death certificate?"

"No."

"He ran a death squad under the radar in the middle of London?"

"Yes."

"Guys like that, they don't survive long without being what you might call super-cautious. Let's say there's a rattlesnake in your cabin and you rush outside and call for your neighbour to kill it."

"OK."

"Your neighbour, who you never really trusted, goes in with a gun. You hear a shot. Then he comes out and says, 'Yeah, I killed it. You're all good.' He walks off whistling a happy tune. You gonna go in and take a bath or a nap or whatever?"

Stella smiled, and took a pull on her beer.

"Nope. Nuh-uh. I'm going to push the door open with a broom and stand well back. See what comes slithering out. I want to see a dead snake."

"So does your man, Collier."

"What do I do, then?"

"Like I said. Take your time getting there. No flying, no rental car, nothing that'd leave a trace."

"What then, walk?"

"You could. It's about six hundred miles. If you covered ten miles a day you'd be there in two months. You look pretty fit. You jog or whatever? Work out?"

"I run. When I can."

"So that's option one. Option two is you ride your thumb."

"No paper trail like there would be with a rental."

"No. And if the cops did pull you over, it'd be the driver whose papers they'd want to see."

Stella took a sip of her beer, weighing up the options. Walking six hundred miles didn't sound like a whole lot of fun. But then, as Ken said, if she took her time it would be manageable. Maybe take a couple of days off here and there if she needed to recharge her batteries. And he was right about hitch hiking. It was the only way to travel by car without risking appearing on Collier's radar. Who knew if he'd be exploiting his newfound access to FBI databases or police surveillance logs?

"What about trains?" she asked. "I could pay cash for my tickets."

"You could if there were any."

"Greyhound bus?"

"I guess so. You could go from Duluth. Probably do it in under a day."

"But then I'm arriving too soon. I need to let Collier unwind. Lower his guard."

"So, how about this? Mix it up a little. Plan on arriving mid-November. Walk the first part of the journey. Maybe take a break along the way. Then, when the weather gets colder, catch the bus or get a lift with someone driving to Chicago."

Stella picked up her beer and tilted the neck towards Ken. They clinked bottles.

"That," she said with a smile, "sounds like a plan."

The following day, Stella was back out on the reservation with Ken. He'd driven them to a patch of woodland a couple of miles from his house. Killing the engine, he turned to her.

"Ready for a little target practice?"

She nodded, feeling a buzz of excitement in the pit of her stomach. It was getting closer now. It was getting real.

Ken had brought a carrier bag full of empty soft drink cans. He arranged half a dozen along the trunk of a fallen tree. Thanks to its huge root ball and a couple of thick branches, the top side of the trunk was about five feet off the ground. He walked back to Stella, who was standing about ten feet back from the fallen tree.

"You want to load the revolver?" he asked, from a position just behind and to her right.

"Sure."

She thumbed the knurled release switch to drop out the cylinder. Five of the hollow point rounds slid home into the chambers. Then she snapped the cylinder back into the frame.

Stella adopted a classic shooter's stance. Feet apart, face-on to the target, both hands curled round the revolver. That was as far as she got before Ken intervened.

"You look great. Like you stepped straight out of a safe shooting manual. Maybe you better try something more true to life."

"What do you mean?" Stella asked, turning to him.

"I mean shoot one-handed. And don't aim, point. That's a close-up weapon. Effective range's only maybe fifteen yards. Guys in competitions can do pretty good out to fifty, but I'm thinking you're most likely to be up close and personal with your guy. Tell you what. Keep the gun down by your side. I'll shout 'go!' and you bring it up and fire two shots. Like I said, don't waste time on all that target acquisition crap they put on the forums. Just shoot it like you mean it. OK?"

Stella breathed in and let it out in a sigh.

"OK."

She looked at the centre can, which had once contained twelve fluid ounces of Coke. Tried to summon up Collier's face and superimpose it onto the red and white livery. Beyond the fallen tree, a few birches were swaying in the light breeze that had sprung up.

"Go!" Ken shouted, startling her momentarily.

Automatically, she brought the gun up, keeping her arm straight and pulled the trigger twice. The little revolver bucked in her hand but the recoil was mild compared to some of the other firearms she'd been wielding recently. She frowned. All six of the soft drinks cans were still standing in a row. The burnt propellant got up her nose and made her sneeze.

"Again," she said, not turning away from the cans.

"Go!"

Up went the arm.

Back went the trigger finger.

Bang-bang went the Model 38.

"Fuck!" went Stella.

She felt a hand on her shoulder and turned to see Ken smiling at her.

"Relax," he said. "Maybe try aiming after all. See if you can hit one of 'em with your next shot."

Stella rolled her shoulders, then shook herself like a dog after a swim.

"Fine. And if I can't, maybe you can drag a barn door out here with that truck of yours."

She brought the revolver up, slowly, deliberately, and extended her arm. She closed her left eye and sighted down the barrel, lining up the front and rear sights on the Coke can. She visualised the rest of Collier along with his face. With gently increasing pressure, she squeezed the trigger.

"Yes!" she yelled, with the noise of the shot still echoing away through the trees.

The Coke can had disappeared, flying backwards as the round hit it amidships.

Ken was laughing. He clapped a heavy hand on her shoulder.

"All right! Now reload, then we'll start again."

She reloaded. And they began again.

With Stella reliably hitting the target four times out of five, Ken told her it was time to go back to the point-don't-aim style of shooting.

Her right hand was aching, but she was enjoying the sensation of power each time the little gun jolted in her hand. And even though she could feel that somewhere not too far away, another version of herself was enjoying the shooting too, she didn't mind. Out here, with no enemies to kill, Other Stella surely wouldn't have enough to occupy her.

She looked up into the tree canopy, inhaling the smell of gunsmoke deep into her lungs. Sun was filtering through the blue-tinged air in narrow spears. A stronger gust of wind blustered its way through the woods, dispersing the smoke and driving a branch above her to one side before it snapped back. The unobstructed sunlight hit her full in the face, dazzling her and making her whip her head away.

And when she looks back, she is here, and she is gone.

— *No. I am Stella Cole. I am holding the gun.*

— *Oh, really, babe? Because from where I'm standing it looks like I'm the one holding this ridiculous little pea-shooter.*

— *No, please. Not now. Not yet.*

— *Fuck off. I need to get the feel of the gun and your aim is, frankly, shit.*

— *I hit four out of five!*

— *Yeah, if you count pissing about like you're at the fair. Do you really think he's just going to stand still while you plug away? Now leave me alone while I shoot.*

And Stella feels Other Stella shoving her hard, in the chest, and it's happening again. She's lost control. She's trapped in the trees like a wind-blown carrier bag, fluttering impotently as her Other smirks up at her.

— *Watch this, babe*, she hears in her head-not-head, because her head is down there, on her body.

— *Yes!* Stella tries to shout. *That's right. It's* my *body. Not yours*!

But Other Stella isn't listening. Other Stella is bored of listening. Bored of waiting. Bored of Stella's narrow concerns.

—*There's KILLING to be done, Stel.*

That's what Other Stella says now.

— *THERE'S KILLING TO BE DONE! LOTS OF KILLING!*

And her voice is so harsh, Stella feels it cutting through her … No! Cutting through the nerve fibres that connect them. Other Stella has finished being a passenger. And Stella? Where is she? Where is the detective with so much promise?

She feels her tattered soul shredding on the sharp branches of the tree, splitting along the fault lines, separating into narrow ribbons of self and then, one by one, as the breeze catches them, detaching themselves from the twigs on which they've snagged and flying up, twirling like ribbons on a little girl's plaits, spiralling up, away, into the far elsewhere until …

52

NO WITNESSES

OTHER Stella thumbs another five rounds home into the snug, smooth-walled chambers of the cylinder. She enjoys the feel of the cold brass on her printless fingertips. The rounds make quiet little *snicks* as they slot home. She seats the cylinder back into the frame and raises the snub-nose revolver to her nose. Inhales the delicious smell of burnt cordite deep into her lungs. *Her* lungs. Yes. It feels good thinking that. She decides she's had enough of Stella. Why should she have to skulk in the shadows, in the dark recesses of Stella's dumb, tortured little head until she's needed? Why shouldn't she be in charge? Permanently? A voice makes her turn her head.

"Sorry, Ken," she says with a smile. "Miles away."

"I said, it's a gun, not a bunch of flowers. Maybe you should shoot it instead of sniffing it."

She watches him closely as he speaks. Is that a fleeting frown she spies on that smooth, barely-lined forehead? Did those deep-brown eyes narrow, just for a fraction of a second?

"Of course. Silly me."

It would be better if she could speak more like Stella. But

somehow the words, the phrasing elude her. Unlike the targets she has planned out.

She whirls round, brings the revolver up in a single, flowing movement and looses off all five rounds without pausing.

Three of the cans Ken has reset on the fallen tree fly away as the hollow-points smash into them, tearing razor-sharp gashes through the whisper-thin aluminium skin.

"Oh, I loved that!" Other Stella purrs as she pops out the cylinder and reloads.

She is having to be careful with her voice because she nearly came as the last of the bullets exploded from the stubby barrel.

"Yeah. That was good shooting. Not so cautious as you were before," Ken says, scratching at his stubble.

"Before?" she asks, turning her gaze on him. *And while we're about it, why did they call you 'redskins'? Your skin isn't red. Blood is red. I'd call it cinnamon. Or maybe pale mahogany. I suppose "Kill all the pale-mahogany-skins!" sounds a bit limp if you're planning a massacre.*

"Yeah. The last set, you were kinda edgy. Now you seem more relaxed. And you enjoyed that. I could see it."

Other Stella pauses before speaking. Not because she's unsure what to say. She's calculating.

"What else could you see, Ken?"

"What do you mean?"

"Oh come on, don't be coy." She twirls the revolver around her index finger. "You saw me arriving, didn't you?"

Now it's his turn to pause. *Ha! I knew it.*

"In Lac La Croix? No. I arrived at Franklyn's after you, remember?"

"No. Not then. Just now."

He pulls his chin back and frowns. Spreads his broad-palmed hands wide.

"We got here together. In my truck. Of course I saw you arrive."

Not a bad act, she thinks. *But not good enough.*

"Oh, Ken. Kenny-boy. Kenneth White Crow of the Lac La

Croix of the Salteaux First Nation, part of the Ojibway tribe. You saw *me* arrive. And *her* leave. Didn't you?"

He steps back. Puts his hands out towards her.

"Yes, I did. Who are you?"

She points the gun at his midriff. Imagines the damage a .38 Special hollow-point will do to his insides at this range.

"Me? I'm Stella Cole. *She* used to call me 'Other Stella.' Which, to be honest, I found a little insulting. But she's gone now. So Stella's all we need."

Ken speaks. His voice is calm. Low.

"You need me, *biwiide*."

"No, babe. I really don't. Not now you've witnessed all …" she circles her free hand around her face, "… this."

She extends her arm and delights in the way his eyes widen. They flick left to a spot behind her as if he's trying to figure out an escape route. But better men than him have tried to do that and ended up decorating the walls of their clubs or the courtyards of their chambers.

She thumbs the hammer back.

Takes up the pressure on the trigger.

And squeezes.

The *bang* is as loud as the end of the world. A supernova ignites in her brain. Bright, white light then red and orange fire.

53

SHAMAN

LOOKING down at the crumpled body of the *biiwide* in front of him, the man known among his people as *Miskwaadesi*, and to the outside world as George Painted-Turtle, shook his head. The wooden club in his right hand was about a foot long and bound with a thong of caribou leather. It had split the *biiwide's* scalp, and scarlet blood was flowing freely into the grass.

Before him, Ken White Crow knelt at the woman's side, holding the back of his hand beneath her nostrils. He looked up at the shaman.

"She's alive."

Miskwaadesi nodded, running his left hand through his long, grey hair.

"I know how to hit for sleep or for death."

"Why did you follow us?"

"She has the look. She harbours an evil spirit. I saw it when you first brought her out here onto our land. When you took her hunting, when you sold her your daddy's gun from the American war, I knew she was going to try to kill you."

"We have to get her back. The one that arrived just now? The one you saw? She was not there before. You have to help save Stella from the *maji-manidoo*."

Together, the two men carried the inert form back to Ken's pickup truck and laid her in the loadspace. Miskwaadesi bandaged her scalp with a pad of soft fabric and secured it with a wider version of the thong around his club.

Back in the town, Ken parked outside Miskwaadesi's house, a large, two-storey, log-built building at the end of a long, tree-lined street. Together, they dragged and then carried the unconscious woman from the truck bed and inside.

"Bring her in back," Miskwaadesi said.

Ken picked her up and slung her over his shoulder. "In back" was a windowless room about twelve feet square. Hand-woven mats in shades of red ochre, mustard-yellow and pine-green covered the floor. At their centre stood a wide, flat, steel dish, its centre blackened by soot. A wooden rocking chair dominated one corner. The other three were occupied by a tall, fat-bellied drum, a wooden sculpture depicting a seal and hunter, and a woven grass basket of rattles, feathered sticks and arrows. The walls were draped with animal skins, and hung with grotesque masks with stretched mouths and elliptical eyes. The only light came from a hurricane lamp hanging from a bracket nailed to the wall.

Stooping to let Stella slide from his shoulder, Ken let her down gently onto the rugs, lying on her right side so as not to disturb the improvised dressing to the head wound. Her breathing was shallow, and she had not, as yet, opened her eyes.

"Now leave us, my son," Miskwaadesi said. "I need to speak to the *biwiide* myself."

* * *

The pain when she came round almost made Stella pass out again. She groaned and lifted her hand to her head, wincing and yelping as her probing fingers found the lump beneath the dressing.

"Oh, Jesus! What happened?" she asked. Then she caught

sight of the man sitting in the rocking chair. "Who are you? Where's Ken?"

"My name is George Painted-Turtle. I am the shaman of the Lac La Croix. Ken White Crow has gone. You are here because you tried to shoot him."

Stella wiped her forehead, which was slick with sweat. She felt sick. Not just the nausea caused by the throbbing pain in her head. She felt sick because she already knew what had happened.

"Did you hit me?"

"I hit somebody, yes. Did I hit you? I don't know. You tell me."

He leaned forward, placing his hands on his knees, and stared at her. His face was lined, deep craggy grooves on his cheeks and fanning out from the corners of his eyes. The look said, trust me. Trust me or else. Stella sighed. *I'm out of options.*

"I have a, I mean, sometimes there's another version of me. I call her Other Stella. She's violent and she hurts me. It was her who tried to shoot Ken. It was her you bashed on the head, not me. I like Ken. He's been good to me, really good. Please be careful. If she comes back I don't know what she'll do. I can't stop it happening. I can't stop *her* happening. It used to be stress that made her appear, but recently she's just, I don't know, taking over whenever she feels like it."

The shaman nodded. He stood and came to sit beside Stella. He took her hand in his, which was hard and dry, like polished wood.

"In Ojibway we have a word. *Maji-manidoowaadizi.* Say it."

Stella tried to wrap her tongue round the unfamiliar syllables.

"Ma-ji-mani-do-wad-izzi?"

"That is OK for a *biwiide.* You listen. That is also good."

"What does it mean?"

"Possessed by an evil spirit. By a *maji-manidoo.*"

"That sounds about right. Can you help me? You didn't kill me out there in the woods, even though you could have."

George Painted-Turtle nodded.

"Yes. I can remove the spirit. But you have to help me to help you. You must go inside your soul and fight it. Destroy it. But first you have to be ready. You will have to go into a trance. We say *inaabam*. It means to see things as if in a dream."

Stella had by now pushed herself into a sitting position, though the flashes of pain that kept jolting through her brain were making her dizzy.

"Tell me what to do. If I can, I'll do it."

"First, you must fast. Three days. I will bring you water. OK?"

"OK. Three days of fasting. Then what?"

"Then we will drink *ozhaawashko-aniibiish* together. It is a tea made with herbs and a special mushroom."

At the mention of mushrooms, Stella smiled.

"You mean *psilocybin?*"

George grunted acknowledgement.

"That is the *gichi-mookomaan* word, yes."

"White people?"

"Uh-huh. Or Americans. Sometimes we get kids travelling up here looking for the authentic First Nations experience. They want to take *ozhaawashko-aniibiish.*"

"What do you say to them?"

"I tell them to fuck off to Mexico and try ayahuasca instead."

Stella laughed, even though it set off a small grenade at the back of her skull. She groaned, but was happy she'd found something to laugh about, given her precarious mental state.

"Can you rescue my stuff from Maureen's?" she asked.

He shook his head.

"It's safe enough there. I'll call her and let her know you're staying here for a while. Now, give me your phone, your watch, and any jewellery."

Naturally slender, and a runner to boot, Stella had never dieted. Her trouble, if that's what you could call it, was mainly directed towards keeping her weight up, not down. After losing Richard and Lola, she'd lost virtually all her body fat, and had embarked on a dedicated programme of eating high-fat, processed foods to pile the pounds back on. Fasting, she discovered, was deeply unpleasant. Locked in the back room of George Painted-Turtle's house and only allowed out, under supervision, to use the toilet, she realised just how much of a struggle anyone on hunger-strike had on their hands. Or their guts. To begin with, she merely experienced the normal pangs of an empty stomach. Initially she'd even considered them pleasant, as though anticipating a good meal. When no food was forthcoming, her stomach had protested more vigorously, cramping, and crying out in a discordant symphony of growls, squeaks and grumbles for food to fill it. By the end of the first day, she craved something to eat, however small. A single peanut or crisp would have been enough, she felt. George brought her a glass of water instead.

With nothing to occupy her, not a book, not a magazine, and certainly no music, Stella wandered around the room, measuring its dimensions with carefully calibrated paces. Four by four if she took exaggeratedly long strides. Five by five if she paced more normally. She examined the designs of the rugs, which bore striking representations of antlered deer – elk, maybe, or caribou – wolves and rabbits, plus large birds she took to be eagles, judging from their white heads. Then the hunger pangs would come back, asserting their right to dominate her thoughts.

Curling up in a corner, she tried to sleep, and eventually dozed off, before waking in a sweat. With no natural light penetrating the gloomy interior, she had no way of knowing how long she'd been asleep. She hadn't dreamt, she knew that.

In this way, the days passed.

Periods of wakefulness were interspersed with light, dreamless sleep, then periods of vivid dreaming in which she imagined she was flying with the eagles from the rug. Every two hours, George would unlock the door and bring her a glass of water, always politely asking if she needed the toilet. Even that brought no clue as to the time of day as he had shrouded the bathroom's high window with thick curtains and she felt too weak to attempt to move them, feeling sure he'd also closed the external shutters.

The pangs of hunger had disappeared sometime during what she estimated was the second day. What appeared in their place was worse. A desperate craving for food that was more mental than physical. She felt light-headed all the time, dizzy if she tried to stand and woozy if she lay down. Worst of all, from time to time she could hear Other Stella's voice in the distance. The sound was too indistinct for Stella to discern individual words, but the tone was impossible to mistake. Sarcastic. Mocking. And something else. Something much worse. Other Stella sounded threatening.

She fell asleep curled into a foetal position on the rugs. She woke, her skin prickling and her eyes painful in their sockets. George was sitting cross-legged on the other side of the steel bowl from her.

The sounds that came from his mouth seemed out of sync with the movements of his lips, as if she were watching a badly dubbed foreign-language film.

"What did you say?" she croaked.

"It is time."

From a soft leather pouch at his waist, he pulled a bunch of dried herbs. He took a battered brass Zippo lighter from a pocket and flipped open the lid with a metallic click. The rasp as his thumb turned the wheel against the flint sounded deafening in the silence and the bright yellow flame that jumped up seemed to dance rhythmically before her tired eyes. He lit the dried leaves, which ignited with a crackle before he dabbed his palm against the flames to extinguish them. George passed the bunch of smouldering herbs under Stella's nose and she coughed as the sweet-smelling smoke entered her lungs. Then he laid them in the centre of the steel dish.

All this time, he chanted under his breath. Stella strained to pick out one of the Ojibway words she'd heard either from Ken, or George himself, but all she heard was the singsong intonation.

Though she hadn't noticed in the gloom, George had set a simple wooden tray on the rug beside him. It held a dark-green teapot, made of what she took to be bronze, and two brown-glazed clay cups. He poured a darkish liquid from the teapot, filling both cups to the brim.

He stopped singing, and Stella felt the absence of the chant almost as an echo inside her mind.

"This is the *ozhaawashko-aniibiish,*" he said. "After you drink, I will ask you to look straight at me while I tell you the story of the first shaman to journey into his own mind. You will not be aware of the moment you pass through, but I will, and I will be alongside you as you battle your *maji-manidoo,* the one you call Other Stella."

"But what if she takes over? She'll try to kill you."

George shook his head.

"In here? No. This is a sacred place. She has no power here." He leant forward and tapped Stella's forehead. "In there is the only place she has power. Now drink."

He offered her one of the cups and she took it from his hands with her own. Watching him for clues on the appropriate ritual way to drink, she was surprised to see that he just knocked it back. He shrugged.

"It tastes disgusting," he said.

Stella brought the cup to her lips and caught an acrid smell from the surface of the brown liquid. She wrinkled her nose. Then she tipped her head back and drank the cup down in one. She gagged as the foul-tasting, tepid tea hit the back of her throat. Held it down. And placed the cup back on the tray.

"I'm ready," she said, feeling dizzy and weighted down onto the floor at the same time. "Tell me about the first shaman."

As George began speaking in Ojibway, Stella tried to stay aware of her own state of mind. But she kept drifting off. Bringing her focus back to George's face, she noticed that he looked a lot younger – no, not younger, smoother – than he had a minute before. The crevasses that had criss-crossed his cheeks had gone. His eyes looked clearer, too. Then he spoke to her in English.

"It is time to face her. I will be with you."

54

OXFORD ROAD, PUTNEY, 6TH MARCH 2009

STELLA blinked in the sunlight. The day was unseasonably warm and Putney smelled as if spring were finally here. The London Plane trees were in bud and a few daffodils peeped out of window boxes or the postcard-sized patches of earth people in this part of southwest London called front gardens.

I know this road, she thought.

She turned to look up and down the street. More or less identical terrace houses of late Victorian vintage, brick-built with painted concrete window ledges and lintels. Front doors in bright yellows, blues, greens and blacks, ornamented with brass, chrome and brushed aluminium letter boxes, knobs, keyholes and knockers.

Halfway between where she stood and the northern end of the road stood a squat red cylinder. A pillar-box-red cylinder. A pillar box. With a domed top, scalloped around its edge like a pie-crust.

No. Not here. Please, not here.

The street was quiet, although here and there a lone pedestrian walked home, swinging a carrier bag from Marks & Spencer, or a smart leather briefcase. Plenty of professional people lived in Oxford Road. The only ones who could afford to these days. Doctors, accountants, executives.

Lawyers.

Human-rights lawyers.

Richard Drinkwater was a human-rights lawyer.

Or he had been until the side of his head met that pretty, red pie-crust doing thirty miles per hour.

After that, Richard Drinkwater wasn't anything except dead. Nor was his baby daughter, who burned to death strapped into the car seat her doting parents had bought to keep her safe.

Stella heard the screech of tyres and spun round. Nobody else seemed to have heard the noise. The roar of flames and the soft *whoomp* of an exploding petrol tank seemed not to bother the homeward-bound city workers.

The road was empty of traffic. No smashed and burning 1974 Fiat Mirafiori. No Bentley Mulsanne with a bruised flank, painted in *Viola Del Diavolo* and careening down the street before swinging wildly round the corner.

With a coordinated slam that echoed inside Stella's head, all the workers shut themselves in behind their gaily-painted front doors.

No. Not all the workers. One remained outside. She stood in the middle of the street, between the two pavements, just ten feet away. She spread her hand wide and grinned horribly at Stella.

"Miss me, did you, babe?" she called out. "This *is* what you wanted, isn't it? One final throw of the dice to decide who gets to go home with the body and who gets to FUCK OFF into the ether?"

Stella felt a rage banking up inside her. She clenched her fists and found that her right was curled around her little helper. The leather tube of pound coins had come in so useful in the past. Now it would again.

"Why here?" she yelled at Other Stella.

"Why do you think? This is where I was born."

Blinking back tears, Stella spoke in a low voice.

"No. This is where she died. Where my Lola died."

Other Stella laughed, then raised her bunched fists to her screwed up eyes and twisted them in a grotesque parody of grief, as a child would do.

"Oh, boo hoo. Get over it!" She adopted a weepy, actressy voice. "They killed my baby. Oh, my little baby is dead." Then she snarled. "Listen, you whiny bitch, we got them. Just Collier to go and then it's like I said. Open season on everyone who ever shared a meal, a car or a bed with them. The streets are going to run red by the time I'm through with them, but for fuck's sake, Stel, move on! OK, they shouldn't have killed Richard and Lola, but the more I think about it, PPM were doing a good job. Killing rapists, paedophiles, lawyered-up gangsters. You couldn't see justice done, so they did. You said it yourself a million times. 'The fucking jury got it wrong.' Maybe it's time we took justice back where it belongs. On the streets."

Stella stood there, open-mouthed, trying to process what she had just heard. The blood was roaring in her ears like a tide.

She marched out into the road and grabbed Other Stella by the throat with her left hand and smashed the little helper into her face.

And Other Stella laughed, wiping the blood from her broken nose. With a shake of her head, like a cat flicking milk from its whiskers, she undid the damage. The nose was straight again, the blood gone.

Other Stella bared her teeth, and Stella noticed she'd lost an incisor. She stretched her hands out, fingers curled like talons. Stella reached out and pulled them hard, so that the skin parted company with the muscles, tendons and bones beneath.

Seizing Stella by the left arm with one of the bloody claws, she pulled her close until their faces were just a couple of inches apart.

"This is the bit where you say, 'you win.'"

Then she pushed her right hand against Stella's chest, over the heart.

With a lurching sensation, Stella felt Other Stella's hand begin to move through her breast, and the muscle beneath, in towards her ribcage. Instinctively she knew she mustn't let Other Stella's questing fingers reach her heart. She tried to push away but Other Stella's grip was like a pair of Metropolitan Police handcuffs.

"No!" she grunted. Then she screamed it to with full force: "NO!"

And in her head, she heard George Painted-Turtle's voice.

— *Show her you have the power. Not her. The* maji-manidoo *has no power before a superior being. Imagine a totem pole. Old Stella is at the bottom. The* maji-manidoo *sits above her. But you. You are New Stella. You sit at the top, above them both. You are in charge. Act now. Banish her.*

Stella summoned up her dearest, sweetest memories of the brief months she shared with Richard and Lola: picnics, late-night nursery rhymes when Lola wouldn't go down, cuddles and tickling games, bedtime stories and splashy baths when everyone got soaked. With a scream, she reared back, knocking Other Stella's clutching hand aside. Then she punched hard, against her chest.

(the fist slid through the flesh)

"You," she screamed,

(and broke through the ribs)

"Aren't"

(and squeezed the pulsating heart)

"REAL!"

Feeling the stuttering pump twitching in her grip, she jerked her fist free in a welter of blood. In front of her, Other Stella rocked back on her heels. Stella held the quivering heart out and crushed it into a red mess between her fingers.

Other Stella's mouth opened wide in an *O*. Her skin lost its colour. Light from the far side of the street began showing through her features. The red hole in her chest widened and ribbons of blood streamed away into the air above her head. Her whole body was translucent, now, and if she was screaming, Stella couldn't hear it.

She stepped back and watched as Other Stella lost her edges, and the red hole expanded wider and wider until, with a tearing sound, she vanished.

Stella looked down at her right hand. It was still clenched. She willed herself to relax the cramping muscles and unfold her fingers. Her hand was empty. The blood was gone.

Around her, people were chatting with their neighbours as they returned from work, bending to stroke a neighbourhood cat, or stooping to smell flowers in a window box beside their shiny front door.

She heard George's voice again.

— *She is gone.*

— *What if she comes back?*

— *She will not come back. You confronted the* maji-manidoo *face to face. You did not do this before.*

Stella wondered how he could be so sure. She turned and walked back to the pavement. Wondered how she would get home to West Hampstead and her new house in Ulysses Road. *Oh, but Jason is selling it for me. I have nowhere to live. I have—*

55

ALONE AGAIN

— *TO wake up. I have to wake up!*

"I have to wake up," she gasped, scrambling to sit up.

The sudden change in altitude swamped her with nausea and vertigo and she leaned on both palms until the lurching in her guts settled down into a more manageable queasiness.

Beside her, George sat, cross-legged, as before. He took her chin softly between thumb and forefinger and tilted her face up to his. Staring into her eyes he muttered something to himself in Ojibway. Then he smiled.

"You are back among the living. Your *maji-manidoo* is gone. You did well."

Stella blinked back tears.

"How can you be sure? It felt real but how can a single magic mushroom, sorry, *ozha—?*"

"*Ozhaawashko-aniibiish.*"

"*Ozhaawashko-aniibiish,*" she stumbled over the Ojibway words, but persevered, "trip do away with, with," she tapped her temple, "all of that?"

George took her by the hand and pulled her to her feet then settled her into the rocking chair. He knelt in front of her.

"There are two answers. If you are a sceptic, you want the *gichi-mookomaan* answer. Which, before you ask, I know from talking to Ken. And Google. There is plenty of evidence that psychedelic drugs like mescaline and psilocybin can help treat PTSD and other mental health disorders. Also, when you have to share your mind with a second version of you, there is a line of thinking called perceptual control theory. Basically, for you, Other Stella was above you in a hierarchy of control systems."

"And so in my vision, when you talked about the totem pole, that was giving me a higher position still?"

"Exactly."

"But tell, me, how could you speak to me in my vision? You weren't, I mean, actually there in my head with me, were you?"

George shook his head.

"No. Not in the way you mean, anyway. But I took the drug with you and breathed the air of the burnt sage with you. I felt my way into your mind when I was telling you the story of the first shaman. I gave you suggestions then that would help you when you met her."

"You said that was the explanation for white people. Sceptics. What about the other explanation? For believers?"

George sat back and smiled.

"For that you would need to belong to the Lac La Croix. By birth. Or by marriage. So unless you are thinking of proposing to Ken, who is single, by the way, you will have to content yourself with the first explanation."

Stella smiled.

"In that case, can I ask another question?"

"Yes."

"Please can we go and get something to eat? I'm starving."

The following day, Stella woke at seven, feeling refreshed and so clear-headed it was as if she'd come off a month-long detox. George had returned her watch, phone and the ID documents she wore round her middle in a money belt. They sat, in a neat heap, at the foot of the bed. An hour later, after finding George at the town hall, and thanking him, again, for treating her, she was sitting next to Ken in his truck. They'd arranged to drive into Lac La Croix, where Stella would settle her bill for the room with Maureen, collect her rucksack and buy a pair of walking boots and a warmer jacket, then return with Ken to the reservation.

By 2.00 p.m., she was standing on a rough plank jetty that poked out into the lake like a long wooden tongue. Moored to one of the wooden poles was a clinker-built rowing boat with a black outboard motor bolted to its transom. Ken was sitting at the back. She handed her rucksack, which bulged with the extra clothes, down to Ken, then took his hand and stepped into the boat, sitting on one of the two highly polished thwarts. Once she was secure, she unshouldered her daysack, which contained a couple of bottles of water, some energy bars, the rest of the US dollars, the Model .38 and the remaining ammunition.

The trip across the lake took an hour. Ken was mostly silent, only speaking to point out natural phenomena. A trout, jumping free of the sparklingly clear lake water in a flash of silvery-pink, before splashing back. A sea eagle, soaring above them then swooping down in a power dive, talons outstretched, and regaining the air with a threshing silver fish clamped tight beneath it.

On the far side, the American side, he jumped out into water that reached mid-calf and pulled the boat into shore with the painter. He signalled for Stella to sit still while he tied the rope round a sapling then held his hand out for Stella. She shouldered her rucksack and grabbed her daysack with one hand before taking Ken's hand and stepping onto American soil.

"We have an hour's walk," Ken said. "My cousin will meet us in Voyageurs National Park. She'll take you on from there."

"Cousin?"

"Judith Fairbrother. She's a full-blood Chippewa of the Red Lake Band."

The forest floor was springy underfoot with leaf mould and pine needles. Around them, insects buzzed and chittered, and

Stella had to slap away mosquitos. After fifty-five minutes they emerged into a clearing fringed with birch and oak. On the far side, a dirt road curved away through thicker forest. Fresh-cut logs had been stacked in a long wall six feet high. As they walked past it, Stella caught the smell of sap from the cut ends of the logs, bright orange against the dull greenish-brown of the bark. A distant mechanical noise broke the silence. It sounded like a bike engine. It was getting closer. Ken turned to her.

"That will be Judith. I told her to meet us here at three."

Stella checked her watch: 2.55 p.m.

With a roar, a big quad-bike burst into the clearing. The racket startled a covey of pheasants, which clattered out of a birch tree cackling in alarm, their red eye patches like splotches of blood.

The rider brought the quad to a stop in front of them. She was smiling at Ken.

"Hey, cousin. How are you?" she asked, smoothing a long plait of dark-brown hair through her fingers.

"I'm good. Good. How are you?"

"Yeah, good, too. This your friend?"

"Stella, this is my cousin, Judith Fairbrother."

The woman dismounted, her long limbs graceful in comparison to the squat, mechanical look of the quad bike. She came to Stella, hand outstretched, the megawatt smile flashing white teeth against her reddish-brown skin.

"Hey, Stella. Pleased to meet you."

"You, too. Thanks for coming to help me out."

Judith shrugged.

"You're a friend of Ken's. That's all I need to know. Now, let's get your stuff stowed and we'll take off." She turned to Ken. "I'll see you soon. We need a proper catch-up."

He nodded.

Stella turned to him, arms wide.

"Hug," she said. A demand, not a question.

He complied and she held him tight for a few seconds before releasing him. She looked up into his eyes.

"Thank you. For everything."

He nodded. Emotions seemed to make him even more taciturn than normal.

"You have my cell number. Do what you have to do in Chicago, then call me. We'll get you out the same way we got you in."

She nodded and patted her pocket.

Five minutes later, Stella's bags were secure beneath a black nylon cargo net, and she was sitting behind Judith, hands gripping the grab handles by her thighs. She let go with her right to stretch out towards Ken. He took it briefly then let go and turned to walk back through the trees to his boat.

Judith twisted round.

"You all set?"

"Yup. Let's go."

Judith started the quad bike and motored round in a sedate circle before opening the throttle and powering away from the clearing, taking Stella a step closer to her target.

56

WELCOMING PARTY

NOT used to London's geography, still less that of its outer lying boroughs, Callie offered a silent prayer to whichever egghead had invented satnav. The final, well-modulated announcement signalled the end of her journey southwest out of central London towards Richmond this busy Saturday morning.

"You have reached your destination."

"Indeed I have, you toffee-nosed English cow," she said.

'Your destination' was an imposing Victorian red brick house, of which only the top floor was visible behind a tall laurel hedge. Access was barred by a pair of wooden gates. Callie climbed out and pressed the button on the intercom. She'd called ahead, so after she'd given her name, Jason Drinkwater's metallic voice squawked an 'OK' and the gates swung open on silent hinges.

The gravel crunched and popped beneath the tyres of Callie's pool car as she eased it through the gates and up the drive. She parked next to a black BMW M5 and a bright-yellow Audi TT convertible. *Nice to see southern estate agents make as much as their Scottish counterparts*, she thought to herself, then chided herself for displaying, even internally, that streak of enviousness her mother disapproved of. *If you want what other people have, Calpurnia,* she used to say, *then stop complaining, get up off your bottom and work for it.*

She walked up to the front door, which was painted a beautiful shade of pale blue, like a bird's egg, and rang the doorbell. Within seconds, the door opened. The man who'd answered was good looking, in a conventional sort of way, she thought, summing him up with a practised, detective's eye. He wore an expensive-looking sweater above his jeans and leather boat shoes.

"You must be Detective Superintendent McDonald," he said, holding out his hand. "Come in."

She shook his hand, warm, dry, as she'd expected.

"Please, call me Callie."

"OK, well you should call me Jason. Come on, I'll introduce you to Elle."

Elle Drinkwater was sitting in a carver chair at one end of a long, scrubbed-pine table in the kitchen, breastfeeding a tiny baby. She smiled at Callie and Callie thought she'd never seen anyone who looked more contented.

"Hello. I'm Elle. Sorry I can't get up but…" she gestured with her free hand at the baby, "Madam just decided she was hungry again."

Callie smiled back.

"Nice to meet you, Elle. I'm Callie. And who's this?"

"Georgina Stella Drinkwater. We call her Georgie."

"She looks happy enough. How old is she?"

"Seven weeks."

Jason made coffee for himself and Callie, and a camomile tea for Elle. When all three adults had their drinks, he asked the inevitable question.

"Is this about Stella?"

"It is, yes."

"She's all right, isn't she?" Elle asked, her brows drawn together, grooving two short vertical lines above the bridge of her nose. The baby snuffled and wriggled, and she resettled her.

"Yes. We don't know when she'll be back in the UK, but when

she does arrive, we need to speak to her immediately. You're her only family, is that right?"

"We're her closest family. I think she has a cousin or two somewhere, but I don't think she really sees them."

"So what I'd like to ask you to do is call me or email if she makes contact with you. In fact invite her to stay with you instead of going back to her place."

"She can't do that," Jason said. "I just sold it. Yesterday, in fact. I need to email her about it."

"So much the better. Look, this is me." Callie handed Jason a card. "Let me know as soon as you can if she makes contact. Then I can—"

Callie didn't get to finish her sentence. A little girl of five or so burst into the kitchen, swinging a Barbie doll by the hair and singing at the top of her voice.

"And we'll all go down to the seaside and we'll all—Oh. Hello," she said, looking at Callie with a frank, appraising stare. "Who are you?"

"This is Callie, darling," Elle said. "Callie, meet Polly."

Callie extended her hand, which Polly shook very seriously, three times, in a vigorous up-and-down motion.

"I am very, extremely pleased to meet you. What job do you do?"

Jason and Elle laughed. Elle spoke ahead of Callie's answer.

"Polly's going through a careers phase."

Callie nodded as if being interrogated by five-year-old girls was an everyday occurrence for senior officers in the Metropolitan Police Service.

"I am a police officer. A detective."

"Oh, that one again. Like Auntie Stella."

"Yes. Just like your auntie."

"Do you have a gun?"

"No. Only special police officers have guns."

"Then what would you do if a really, extremely bad man or lady tried to hit you or put a knife in you?"

"Well, I would probably have a special vest to protect me. And I would have colleagues with me so we could work together as a team to stop the bad person from hurting anyone."

Polly's eyes widened. Then she smirked.

"A vest?" She put her hands on her hips. "Well I don't think *that* would be any good. You should have armour."

Callie was about to explain that the type of vest she was talking about was made of Kevlar, not cotton. Then she realised a rabbit hole awaited. She changed tack.

"Do you know what, Polly. That is a very clever idea. Vests!" She rolled her eyes and tutted for good measure. "When I get back to my police station I am going to go straight to the chief of all the detectives and tell him we should have armour."

Polly seemed delighted by this turn of events. She smiled.

"I have lots of good ideas. About everything. If you want another one, talk to Daddy or Mummy, only she's a bit busy with Georgie, but anyway, tell them to ask me and I will send you another idea, you know, for uniforms, or police cars, or how to capture bank robbers or, or," she spread her hands wide, "anything!"

Over the adults' laughter, Polly made a gracious exit, curtseying and then skipping back out the way she'd come. Callie finished her coffee and stood up to leave, securing a promise from the Drinkwaters that they would get in touch with her should Stella turn up on their doorstep.

Back in her car, she reprogrammed the satnav for Vicky Riley's address in Hammersmith. It took her twenty-five minutes to reach the house. She'd phoned Vicky the previous day and arranged a short meeting. She went over the same ground with her as she had with the Drinkwaters. After discussing what Vicky should do if Stella were to appear, Callie broached a subject most coppers found distasteful at best and downright dangerous at worst. Media coverage.

"I know you have a job to do. And I respect that. But I have to ask you not to report on any of this." *And if you try to, your editors will find themselves served with a D-notice, so it won't do you any good.*

As if reading her mind, Vicky gave her an unexpected, but welcome answer.

"I expect you'd send anyone who agreed to run my story a D-notice wouldn't you? We call them 'Go To Jail' cards in the trade. Though I have to say, it strikes me as odd the way we still allow censorship of the media in the 21st Century."

Callie shrugged.

"Above my pay grade, as they say."

"Well you don't have to worry. As you know, I moved from being a passive observer to an active participant in Stella's crusade some time ago. I'm hardly in a position to turn whistle-blower."

Callie's last stop of the day involved a one-hour-five-minute drive right across London, from west to east. She pulled up outside a swish block of apartments in Docklands. Locked the car and pressed the intercom button.

"Hello?"

"Lucian, it's Callie McDonald."

"Come on up."

The latch clicked and Callie pushed through the door.

Though she didn't know it, her reaction on seeing the inside of Lucian Young's flat was identical to Stella's the first time she had called round.

"Goodness me! Are we paying our forensics officers more than our chief constables nowadays?"

Lucian smiled. He was a very attractive man, Callie thought. In a more interesting way than Jason Drinkwater. And a beautiful dresser.

"I made some money at university. A technology start-up. Stella gave me the third degree, too. I think she suspected I might be on the take."

"Compared to some of the people I've been looking into, a bit of low-level bribery and corruption would be a welcome change, believe me."

Accepting Lucian's offer of a tea, Callie sat down at his dining table and admired the view across the Thames from the picture window. When he joined her, handing over a mug and sipping from his own, she laid out the situation. As he worked for the Met, she went into fuller detail than she had with the Drinkwaters or Vicky Riley.

He spoke.

"So, basically, Stella's after Collier, in the US. Somehow, she's going to kill him and get out of the country without getting herself shot, or arrested, and when she makes landfall in the UK, you guys will scoop her up and, what, debrief her? Deprogramme her? Decorate her?"

Callie blew across the surface of her tea and took a cautious sip. The tea was very hot, but excellent. Nothing fancy, just English Breakfast.

"Much though I personally would like to give Stella a medal the size of a dinner plate, this whole thing is a whisker away from being the biggest shitstorm in the history of British jurisprudence. Though there's been precious little prudence since those shitty wee bastards started their little vigilante society."

At times of heightened emotion, Callie lapsed into a class of Edinburgh vernacular her mother, the Harper Lee-obsessed English teacher, would refer to as, "such a common way of speaking, Calpurnia."

"Who knows what's been going on?" Lucian asked.

"Well, let's see. Stella, for one. Obviously. Me. My boss, Gordon Wade. The Home Secretary. The Justice Secretary. The Prime Minster. Vicky Riley. You know her?" Lucian shook his head. "A journalist for God's sake, though I think we can count on her silence. And a slimy little band of PPM groupies that we're taking care of as we speak. So, as you can see, not a small group. But not a large one either. Everyone's either bound by the Official Secrets Act, their relationship to Stella, or their own desperate need to keep this secret. The consequences of going public would be, I think the best word is, severe. I'm sure we can keep a lid on it."

"How sure?"

Callie snorted.

"Let's just say between one of them blowing the whistle and me becoming the first president of an independent Scotland, I'd bet on me."

57

HITCHER, BEWARE

COVERING an average of twelve miles a day, and resting one day in three, it took Stella sixteen days to walk from Ericsburg to Duluth, Minnesota, hiking parallel to US Route 53. At a small town called Virginia in Minnesota, she briefly considered taking the scenic option of woodland trails, but just as quickly rejected it. The probable absence of accommodation would mean either buying and carrying a tent, or sleeping under the stars.

As Ken had recommended, she stayed in cheap, out-of-the-way motels and B&Bs. Without her unholy passenger, she felt clear-headed and completely focused on the final part of her mission to avenge Richard and Lola. She spent the time on the road working through possible scenarios for confronting and killing Collier. Yet the biggest challenge was far simpler. Where was he? Chicago. She knew that. But Chicago was a big place. The FBI headquarters was ridiculously easy to locate, and she'd already spent some time scooting round it on Google maps. But a full-frontal attack on Collier at his place of work would likely result in Stella's being shot to death way before she got close enough to use the Model 38.

She reached Duluth in early September, suffering from blisters.

Her plan was to take a few days off, then do some hitching until her blisters had healed. A few days turned into a week, as she realised she was physically, though not mentally, exhausted.

Ready to move on, Stella stood on the scrubby, glass-strewn shoulder of Route 53 on the southern edge of the city to pick up a ride. She'd been sticking out her thumb for over an hour without a single vehicle so much as slowing down to take a look at her.

"Oh, come ON!" she shouted, as yet another SUV containing precisely one occupant sailed past her. "I can't look that bad. I'm just an English cop on a walking holiday." *OK, a walking holiday followed by a hunting trip, but you're not the one who should be worrying.* It felt odd, hearing her thoughts expressed only in her own voice, but she was getting used to it.

Another half-hour passed and then, mercy of mercies, a pale-metallic-blue sedan slowed down as it approached her. The driver buzzed down the window on the passenger side as the car rolled to a stop beside her. He looked normal. Not an obvious psychopath, at any rate. Fortyish. Neatly cut sandy hair, gold-rimmed glasses and a cheap-looking but clean suit.

"Where're you headed" he asked with a smile. His voice was pleasant. Middle-class. Friendly.

She returned the smile, rejoicing inwardly and desperate not to put him off.

"Well, Chicago, eventually, but anywhere along the route would be great, so long as there's a motel or somewhere to stay."

His smile widened.

"You're English, right?"

"In one."

"Guess it's your lucky day. I'm going all the way to the Windy City. Job interview. You want to stow your gear in the trunk?"

Stella shook her head.

"That's OK. I'll keep it with me. Thanks."

She opened the door and settled into the deeply cushioned

seat, squashing her rucksack in between her legs and holding the daysack on her lap. The car smelled of aftershave. Strongly. But if that was the price for a free ride all the way to Chicago, Stella guessed she could live with it. He pulled away smoothly, not showing off, just piloting the big car back onto the highway. Keeping his gaze fixed straight ahead, he spoke.

"Name's Brent, by the way. Brent Coolidge. Like the president, you know?"

"I'm Jen. Nice to meet you Brent. I was beginning to think I'd be spending another night in Duluth."

"And I bet you were real sorry about that."

"Yup. I think I'd pretty much exhausted the city's delights after my third day."

"Third? Make it the second. Hell, make it the first."

"So, do you live there?"

"Uh-huh. Born and raised. But my Mom just died and left me some money so I figured, it was now or never. To get out, I mean."

"I'm sorry for your loss."

"Oh, don't be. She got meaner as she got older. Fatter, too. To be honest I'm glad the old bitch is dead."

For the first time since climbing into the car, Stella felt a twinge of unease. She squeezed the daysack, feeling for the reassuring lump of steel wrapped in cloth. Brent was smiling. He turned to her and spoke again.

"I guess that sounded kinda mean. Especially if you never met my Mom. Let's change the subject. You like movies Jen?"

"Yeah, I guess."

"What's your favourite? No, let me guess. One of them, whatdya call 'em?" He snapped his fingers. "Chick flicks! You like those? Where some lame-ass bimbo is all, like, Oh, I got cancer and I never found true love?"

Stella's antennae were twitching properly now. His voice had slipped down the social ladder a couple of rungs. She checked her door mirror. The road behind them was empty. She looked ahead.

A lone truck in the distance on their side of the road. A second coming towards them.

"Not really. I'm more into action films. Especially if they've got a female hero. *Kill Bill*. Films like that."

"Yeah? I saw that one. It had that blonde chick in it. What's her name? Uma something?" He pronounced the actress's name *Yuma*.

"Uma Thurman."

The oncoming truck roared past, making the car sway as the mass of air it was pushing ahead of its vast chrome grille buffeted the driver's side.

"Exactly right. So aren't you gonna ask me what kinda movies I like?"

"OK, Brent. Tell me. I'm guessing it's not chick flicks, right?"

"Ha! Good one. No. I'm into adult stuff. Lesbian, mainly, or barely legal. Those college girls?" He whistled. "They can really take it, if you know what I mean."

He turned to face her and she caught the look behind the eyes she'd seen many times before. Rapists had it. Child murderers. Paedophiles. Serial killers. Scumbags. It was the quiet, confident look of a natural-born predator.

Her pulse was bumping in her throat. She'd started loosening the clips on her daysack a few minutes earlier, sensing that Brent was about as far from a knight in shining armour as it was possible to get without actually being a dragon.

"You know what?" she said. "I've changed my mind. I think I'm going to walk back into Duluth and stay for a couple more nights. Just drop me anywhere here."

By way of response, Brent, if that was his real name, thumbed the central locking button on his side of the car.

"I have a better idea, Jen. Why don't we pull off the ol' 53 and find us a little privacy somewhere? I got a laptop back there," he jerked his thumb over his shoulder at the back seats. "'S got some real high-quality entertainment loaded up and ready to go. We could get comfortable and watch a little girl-on-girl action to get us in the mood."

Stella hardened her voice.

"Stop the car. Now. I'm getting out."

Her hand was inside the daysack now, unwrapping the cloth from the revolver. He didn't seem to have noticed. Maybe because he was now holding a butcher knife in his right hand. His grin had taken on a twisted quality. He glanced sideways.

"I don't think so, little lady, with your hoity-toity British accent. No. I think we'll do what I just suggested. Then maybe after that you can show me some proper gratitude, seeing as how I stopped to give you a ride and all."

And then, despite the absence of Other Stella, Stella felt an utter calm descend on her.

58

WHAT HAPPENS WHEN YOU FUCK WITH STELLA COLE

STELLA looked down at the butcher knife. It had been a long time since a man with a blade had frightened her.

She withdrew her right hand from the daysack. Smiling, she twisted round in her seat so she was facing Brent. She cocked the revolver. The click was nice and loud in the cabin. He looked across, and his eyes widened.

"Shit!" he said.

"You brought the wrong weapon to a gunfight, Brent," she said. "Now pull over."

He did what he was told. Like all of his kind, deep down, he was a coward. She really wanted to kill him. But that would have been Other Stella's way. She wasn't a vigilante. She was only there to exact revenge on her family's murderer.

When the car came to a halt, Stella unclipped her seatbelt and opened her door. Holding the Model 38 steady in his face, she wrestled her rucksack up from between her knees and dumped it out onto the shoulder. The daysack followed it.

Stella wanted to make a clean exit. She decided he needed a little warning.

"I'm leaving now. When I close the door, you're free to go."

He nodded frantically.

Keeping him in her sights, she put her right foot onto the tarmac.

He floored the throttle at the same moment, throwing her backwards and wrenching her left leg around as she was thrown backwards onto the shoulder.

As she rolled over and over, she heard his shriek over the engine noise.

"Bitch!"

She loosed off a shot, which shattered the rear window. The car swerved wildly for a couple of seconds then righted itself, and he was speeding away from her.

59

BAR JOB

"FUCK!" she yelled, in frustration, and pain.

She tried to stand but collapsed with a scream. Her ankle was twisted badly and wouldn't take her weight. She looked both ways along Route 53. The road was empty. Stuffing the gun back into her daysack, she bum-shuffled to the far edge of the shoulder where it met the verge, dragging the bigger bag by one shoulder-strap.

Leaving her bags on the grass, she rolled, painfully, onto her front then crawled over to the tree line. The woodland here was mostly pines and other conifers. The trees had been recently cut back and branches lay everywhere. Stella rummaged around, pulling lengths of branch towards her then rejecting them until she found a six-foot length she could use as a staff. She pulled herself upright, wobbling around as she fought to keep her balance, and her weight off her injured ankle. Then she hopped back to her bags.

"Great!" she shouted to the empty road. "Anyone fancy giving Gandalf's younger sister a lift back to Duluth?"

. . .

Stella's rescuer came in the form of a truck driver. She'd been leaning on the makeshift crutch for thirty minutes, waving her free hand desperately at every passing vehicle, however unlikely they might be to offer her a ride back to town. The big red truck with a barn-door-sized chrome grille honked its air horns as it slowed to a stop and pulled over onto the shoulder. The big man in the red-and-black plaid shirt jumped down, asked what the trouble was and, when she explained, simply pointed at the cab then helped her climb in. He hoisted her two bags after her as if they were stuffed with feathers, then crossed in front of the rig and swung himself up beside her. Fifteen minutes later, she was climbing out in Duluth, thanking her knight of the road and looking round for a hotel.

Realising that her sprained ankle and badly bruised ribs precluded any more hitching, let alone hiking, she decided to take a proper break. Within a day she'd found a friendly pharmacist who advised her on the best combination of painkillers to take. Within a week, the ankle, though painful, was able to bear her weight if she took it easy. She found a bar advertising for staff and walked in. The woman running the place loved her English accent, told her she'd probably double their daily takings if she just kept talking to the clientele, and hired her on the spot.

That night, Stella's phone buzzed on the night stand. A text from Jason telling her he'd just sold her house for £700,000.

And six weeks went by. Which suited Stella just fine. Kendra paid her cash-in-hand, she found the work a blessed relief after the previous few months, and she had time both to gather her strength and let her body repair itself. And she knew that Collier would be relaxing, little by little, every day and week that passed with no disruption to his newfound life as a Fed. *Ha! More fool you!* she thought as she poured a couple of her regulars fresh mugs of Hamm's Golden Draft.

By the middle of November, she was fighting fit. She'd even put on a few pounds, thanks to the free meals from the kitchen and the occasional after-work drinking session with the other staff.

Relaxing at the end of a boisterous Saturday night shift, which ended at 2.00 a.m., she clinked beer bottles with Kendra and told her she was leaving. Kendra was philosophical.

"Well, I guess a pretty English girl like you was never gonna hang around in a place like this for ever, honey. You worked hard, you were honest, and the clients loved you. I'll give you a bonus before you go tonight. Chin-chin!"

The next morning, Stella checked out of her hotel and headed for the Greyhound station at 228 W Michigan Street. She bought a single to Chicago and thirty minutes later was sitting by a window on one of the long petrol-blue-and-silver buses, her bags stowed below and an old Kate Bush album playing through her earbuds.

Stella slept most of the way, only waking as the bus slowed to enter downtown Chicago. The streets were slushy and whole corners of the sidewalk were roped off with signs warning pedestrians of the dangers of falling ice. Once again, she found herself checking into a cheap hotel, stowing her gear and wandering out for a pizza and a beer. Only this time, she was doing it in the same city where her final target was living and working. *Now all I have to do is kill you*, she thought, finishing her second beer and signalling a waitress for the bill. *But first, I have to find you.*

60

QUIS CUSTODIET IPSOS CUSTODES?

MISS Reid's voice echoed down the years from Stella's past.

"Quis custodiet ipsos custodes? Anyone?"

Stella had studied Latin at school. Unlike most of her classmates, she had enjoyed it. Her teacher, a stork-like woman, took apparent delight in beginning each lesson with a well-worn Latin phrase and asking her reluctant students to translate. Her grating voice came floating back down the years now.

"It's Juvenal, Miss. Who will guard the guards themselves?" fifteen-year-old Stella Cole had answered when pointed at by her teacher's long, bony finger.

Stella had always liked the Roman poet's quote, without really knowing why. Although the events of the last few years had given the phrase fresh relevance. And now, leaning on the retaining wall of a multi-storey parking garage three blocks west of the FBI headquarters building in Chicago, holding an expensive pair of binoculars to her eyes, Stella wondered what the Latin translation would be for, "Who spies on the spies themselves?" But then, were the FBI spies? Or was that the CIA? Didn't matter. Concentrate.

She'd been on duty at the northwest corner of the deserted top floor of the carpark for three hours every day from four until seven for the past week. Apart from the binoculars, her other main investment had been in some warmer clothes, Chicago in November being roughly on a par with the Antarctic, as far as she could judge. With the soft rubber eyecups pressed against her eye sockets, she watched the comings and goings from the main door and the exit from the FBI's parking lot.

At no point had she seen Collier. It didn't mean anything. A lot of the time, the glare of the sun on the departing vehicles' windshields obscured the drivers' faces. A back entrance clearly existed, as very few people left through the front door.

Surveillance had been the first step in her plan to identify and track Collier. Without realising it, over the past couple of years, she had gradually forgone her previous detection-based approach in favour of something altogether more paramilitary. Given the ruthless methods of her enemies, this was undoubtedly what had kept her alive.

Leaving the parking garage a little later than usual, at 8.00 p.m., she sighed with frustration as she recased the binoculars, slung them onto the back seat of her rental car and drove back to her hotel.

This isn't going to work, she thought, lying in bed. *I need to do it the old-fashioned way.*

The following morning, Stella bought herself a tall latte from a Starbucks and booked an hour's computer time in the public library on State Street.

Sitting in front of the screen, she flexed her fingers.

"OK, then. Where shall we start?" she asked herself under her breath. She typed her first query, more in hope than expectation:

Senior British Detective joins FBI

Nothing.

She shrugged. She hadn't been expecting to hit gold so easily. She worked steadily through a series of increasingly unlikely phrases, tapping them into the search box with growing impatience and frustration.

British police officer joins Bureau.

Nothing.

Top Brit Cop Now Fed.

Nix.

Fed gets its very own Sherlock Holmes.

Nada.

"Bollocks!" she said, louder than she meant to, so that a few heads popped up from their own screens like startled rabbits hearing an approaching fox.

"Sorry!" she added, in a more apologetic tone of voice, before bending to her keyboard again.

Maybe I'm looking in the wrong direction. What if the FBI doesn't issue press releases the way we do? Try the personal angle. Maybe the move made some local newspaper or website.

British couple set up home in Chicago.

Yes! She clicked the link. Then scowled.

.   .   .

Lakeview welcomed two news residents from "across the pond" last month, when Alison and Christopher Burley purchased a new home on W Wellington Avenue. Alison has just accepted a job with Wells Fargo and relocated from her old bank in London. Christopher, "Call me Chris," he told us, is a freelance graphic designer.

She finished her latte, which had gone cold, and decided on a third angle of attack. She logged into Facebook. *Why didn't I think of this before?* she chided herself. *Out of practice at old-fashioned detective-work, Stel.*

She typed "Adam Collier" into Facebook's own search box.

Under the People tab, she found plenty of men with the right name, but none with a profile picture matching the man she was after. *Maybe he deleted his account.* She clicked on the Posts tab and began scrolling down. At the bottom of the screen she hit the link marked, "Show all results." And smiled.

Cheek bulging with food, face flushed from sun or alcohol, Adam Collier was staring straight at her. The account belonged to a woman called Sarah Oliver. She had an arm draped round Collier's shoulder and was displaying a good five inches of well-tanned cleavage above the plunging neckline of her red-and-yellow dress. Lips plump, pink and pouting, she was looking, not at the lens, as Collier was, but at her own image in the screen, giving her the off-centre gaze of the narcissist. The caption had triggered the hit:

Who says the Brits are cold fish? Adam Collier looks pretty hot to me!!!

.   .   .

Stella clicked through to the woman's Facebook account. She'd left her privacy settings wide open, but annoyingly hadn't bothered populating any of her personal information beyond her gender, which was glaringly obvious, and her location, Chicago, which was equally useless.

Stella didn't mind. In fact, she was elated. This was still the key piece of intelligence she needed. Although Collier wouldn't appear on local property or tax databases, as he'd be renting his house, Sarah Oliver would. Correction, *probably* would. But as an unaccredited law enforcement officer, not to mention an illegal alien, Stella wouldn't be able to get anywhere near that kind of information. Or not personally, anyway.

Just to cover the bases, she googled Sarah Oliver Chicago. She scanned the first couple of pages of results, taking in the dozens of Sarah Olivers on LinkedIn, Facebook and all the other social media networks, and the lawyers, doctors and accountants, then puffed out her cheeks. With a decent team behind her, it would still take days to even call them all, assuming she could find their numbers. But on her own? No. She needed to move faster. Leaning forward, she searched again.

Private investigator Chicago.

This time, she was faced with an embarrassment of riches. The Windy City was home to thousands of PIs, all touting for business in matters matrimonial, commercial, personal and criminal. Feeling that even the most incompetent private detective could track down a woman as visible and unconcerned about privacy as Sarah Oliver, Stella clicked the first link and called the number displayed in vivid red text on the homepage. A man answered, his Midwestern accent roughened by smoking, drinking or both.

"Churchill Investigations, this is Ray. How can I help you?"

"Hi. I think my husband is cheating on me."

He sighed.

"I'm sorry to hear that, ma'am. Happens all too often, I'm afraid."

"I know her name, and I have a photo, but I want to know where she lives. It's in Chicago, that's all I know."

"OK, shouldn't be too hard. Can you come to my office? Better doing these sorts of sensitive conversations face to face."

The man sitting across the paper-strewn desk from Stella might have picked his look from a mail order catalogue called Clichéd Private Investigator. Scruffy brown suit, tie spotted with what looked like egg yolk, and a couple of days' growth of beard on his chin. Overweight, too, and the fingers of his right hand stained brown at the tips. *Yes, I was right about the smoking.* But he owned a friendly smile and seemed genuine enough. An aged PC whirred to his left, its bulky monitor plastered with yellow sticky notes and decorated along its top edge with small, multi-coloured plastic animals.

He caught Stella's glance.

"My daughter gives them to me. What can I do? She expects to see 'em when she comes into the office."

"They're cute. Maybe not quite the Sam Spade image you were cultivating."

He shrugged and plucked at a creased lapel.

"This? My wife says I look like a hobo. And I say, you wanna blend in, don't walk around in a Brooks Brothers suit and shiny shoes. Unless you're an undercover cop, of course."

Stella smiled out of genuine good humour. She remembered being deployed to a rock festival outside Birmingham as a part of a rotation with the Drugs Squad. She turned up for work in scuffed biker boots, ripped back tights, a Clash T-shirt and a black leather bike jacket. Hair scrunched up into a wild "do" with wax, and her face a joyously off-dress-code mixture of kohl-rimmed eyes, smudgy dark eyeshadow and a slash of crimson lippy. Her colleagues, all male, all clean shaven, were dressed alike: freshly laundered stonewashed jeans, some with actual ironed creases, dress shirts without ties, sports jackets or blazers and, yes, polished black shoes. She'd been secretly delighted as one after another, her colleagues were pointed out by the stoned and drunk music fans in the campground and subjected to catcalls, whistles and cries of, "Here come the Feds!" while she only had to contend with requests for "any gear" or, when she shook her head, "In that case, how about a shag?"

"You said you had some details about the third party?" Ray asked her.

"Yep."

Stella fished out her phone and turned it towards Ray. He picked a ballpoint pen from a wire mesh cylinder on the desk and jotted down a few notes.

"OK. Like I said on the phone, this is pretty basic stuff. I charge eighty an hour and I reckon on no more than an hour or two for her address and contact number. You want photos or audio? If you do, I offer a full surveillance package. You got your fixed, unmanned, mobile. Plus GPS trackers."

Stella shook her head.

"No thanks, for now just her address, please."

They agreed on a fixed fee of $160, and Stella strode away from the building walking a few inches taller, and with such energy that a panhandler proffering a battered Starbucks cup jingling with small change backed away as she drew level with him.

Ray called her that evening. After the pleasantries were out of the way, he told Stella what she wanted to hear.

"Sarah Oliver, 45, divorced, I know you didn't ask, but it was so quick I did some extra research for you. 1923 West Montana Street, Lincoln Park."

Stella asked the question she'd prepared on the walk back from Ray's office.

"Could you do another job for me, Ray? Still on this case?

Could you find out the address where she took the photo I showed you."

"The guy with her's your husband?"

"No, no, he's a mutual friend. He's——"

Ray cut across her.

"Hey, it's none of my business, and it doesn't matter anyway. It'll probably take me a day. So call it $600 including expenses, OK?"

"That's fine, thanks. Do you want me to drop round tomorrow with the money?"

"Nah. Let me do the job, then I'll give you a call. Maybe it'll be done by lunchtime anyway."

When Stella's phone rang again, it was three the following afternoon.

"Hi, Ray. Everything done?"

"Uh-huh. Your friend's address is 1927 on West Montana. Give me your email. I took a few photos for you. Two cars. I got both licence plates."

61

GET TO THE WIFE FIRST

STELLA waited until the following morning to pay her social call. The drive up to Lincoln Park only took twenty minutes. West Montana Street turned out to be a tree-lined avenue, more green than grey. From the makes and models of cars on the wide driveways—a few smallish SUVs, Toyotas, Hondas, Fords, Chevys —she knew she was in solidly middle-class territory. She parked a few houses down from Collier's, having first checked that one car remained on the driveway, a red Mustang. Good. So Lynne Collier was in. Or, possibly, out for a jog, in which case Stella reckoned she only had an hour to wait, tops.

She slumped in the driver's seat and settled down for the surveillance. Her plan, should a watchful resident ask her business, was to borrow Ray's trade. "Private investigator, sir/madam," was the line she'd rehearsed. Informative, yet terse, and shutting down any further inquiries. And, she supposed, true. Just not a licensed one.

While waiting for Lynne Collier to appear, she concentrated on forming a mental picture of the house. Not that she needed it, but it was one of the techniques she used to stay alert on surveillance. By the time she'd worked her way up from the porch and front door, the ground floor and the first, and was scrutinising the patterns formed by the roof tiles, her eyelids were drooping and she was craving coffee, or a cigarette. Worse luck, she'd decided to try quitting again while in Duluth. A movement saved her.

The front door was opening. Lynne Collier emerged, dressed not for running, but in jeans, what looked like walking boots and a thick, padded jacket in a metallic purple. The shade set off a painful memory, but Stella ignored it. The day, though bitterly cold, was sunny, and Lynne's face was half covered by enormous round-lensed sunglasses that Stella imagined the manufacturer probably labelled Jackie O. She had a cotton tote bag slung over her right shoulder. Empty, not full, so maybe she was going shopping. She pointed her right fist at the car. The indicators flashed. In she climbed, and Stella continued to wait.

Finally, the car moved, reversing off the drive, across the sidewalk and into the road. Stella slid right down in her seat and let Lynne Collier drive past before making a U-turn and following her. Traffic was light and Stella allowed the maximum distance between her and the red Mustang that would permit an effective pursuit without getting her noticed. Probably an unnecessary precaution, but who knew what Collier had told his wife.

Lynne eventually pulled in to the parking lot for a branch of Whole Foods Market. Stella followed her in and selected a spot a couple of rows further back from the front of the store. Keeping her own sunglasses on, she tailed Lynne into the store, where the heating was going full blast. She ran her fingers through her hair, approving of the way it had grown out of the ultra-short pixie cut.

Picking her moment carefully, Stella contrived to enter the fresh food market from one end just as Lynne arrived from the other. Keeping her basket in the crook of her left elbow so her right hand was free, she worked her way through the browsing shoppers, closer and closer to the woman she had begun to think of as her target.

When they were side by side, Lynne Collier examining

aubergines and Stella prodding at a package of lettuces, Stella turned and spoke.

"Excuse me, you couldn't pass me one of those aubergines, could you? They look so lovely."

Lynne Collier smiled as she passed Stella one of the glossy, dark-purple vegetables. Another unpleasant echo.

"You're English!" she said. Then coloured slightly. "Sorry. Of course you're English, duh! Me, too. In case you couldn't tell."

Stella returned the smile.

"It's OK. I've got used to it. Every time I ask for a coffee or speak to someone in a shop, sorry, *store*, it's 'Oh, I just luurve your accent!'"

Lynne laughed and suggested that once they'd finished shopping they have a coffee together in the store's cafe.

"We can see if you're right," she said, still smiling. She held out her hand. "Lynne."

Stella took it.

"Jen."

Cappuccinos and pastries ordered and sitting in front of them at a window table, Lynne asked Stella what she was doing in Chicago.

"Freezing my bum off! I had no idea it got so cold here."

"Me neither. Adam, he's my husband, told me I'd need to buy a new winter coat but I just laughed. I said my old one would be fine. Well, maybe for London, but here? I nearly got frostbite the first time I went outdoors in the winter. So when your bum is warm enough, what do you do?"

"I'm travelling. A career break. I was in Canada over the summer then hiked and bussed my way down here. I heard the people were really friendly."

"Oh, they certainly are. Not like New Yorkers. Or Parisians, for that matter. Here, they stop to chat. It's a bit disconcerting at first, but it's more like England." She took a sip of her coffee. "A career break, you said. That must be fun. What were you doing before?"

"I'm an actuary."

"Oh." Lynne's forehead puckered with thought. "That's insurance, isn't it? Or something?"

Stella nodded then took a sip of her cappuccino.

"You're right. Basically my job is, I mean was, to calculate the odds of bad things happening. It can be anything that insurers write a policy on, literally from pirates attacking a ship to someone nicking your Rolex. I specialised in life insurance. So, for example, I would work out the chances someone might die by falling down stairs, or being involved in a plane crash or even, oh, I don't know, getting killed by a burglar or shot in the street by a bank robber."

"Wow! That sounds kind of gruesome but interesting at the same time."

Stella nodded as she finished a mouthful of croissant.

"It is. Was. I was pretty good. I used to do a party trick where you'd tell me what job you did and I could give you the chances, the actual statistical chances, that you would die while at work."

Lynne's eyes widened and she smiled.

"Go on, then. Do me. I'm a teaching assistant in a primary school."

"Inner city or nice and leafy?"

"Er, if those are the choices, nice and leafy."

Stella paused for effect then quoted the last two digits of her warrant number.

"Two-point-seven percent. Probably a slip, trip or fall. Or a car accident on school grounds."

Lynne laughed loudly, drawing curious and then amused stares from a couple of their neighbouring tables.

"What are you, a human computer?"

"Nope. Just a very experienced actuary."

"Oh, you should do Adam. He'll probably come out way higher than me. He's a police officer."

"Uniformed?"

"Yes. But he's a detective. A chief superintendent. He's on a sabbatical." She leaned closer and adopted a stagey whisper. "With the FBI."

"Wow! That must be exciting. OK, let me have a little think."

Stella made a point of frowning and looking up at the ceiling. A vent directly above their table was blowing hot, dry air down at them, and she could feel sweat gathering in her armpits. She counted the number of slats directing the air. She returned her gaze to Lynne.

"One hundred percent," was what she wanted to say. As it was true.

"I would say, as he's very senior, probably no higher than ten percent. But almost certainly less. I mean, I don't want you to be worried."

Lynne shrugged.

"I stopped worrying about Adam a long time ago. Listen, why don't you come over one day? I'd love you to meet Adam."

Stella smiled brightly.

"That would be lovely. To be honest I am feeling a little homesick."

62

PARTY PEOPLE

BUYING drugs on the street is a dangerous business for the uninitiated. And sometimes for the initiated. Stella fell into the latter category, but despite the snub-nose revolver in her jacket pocket, she felt that heightened sense of awareness all good cops have when they're undercover. Hypervigilance was the proper term for it. When you seemed to possess 360-degree vision and hearing to go with it. You're constantly looking for things that should be present but aren't, and things that aren't present that should be.

Not knowing the territory made it harder to assess all possible threats, but she'd seen plenty of places like it back in London. She'd caught two buses and walked a block and a half to this vacant lot, identified after some more time on one of the public library's computers as a prime spot for meeting local drug dealers and their runners. At four in the afternoon, the day still had some light left to offer, but the sky was grey, pregnant with another big snowfall, and every vehicle on the street had its headlights on.

She'd unstrapped the flaps of her trapper hat and rebuckled them under her chin. The gap between down-filled jacket and hat she'd plugged with a woollen scarf, and her hands were encased in lined gloves. Her right hand was. Her left was bare, jammed deep into the jacket's pocket and clamped round the grip of the revolver. The steel frame was icy on her skin, which was fine. Never had freezing cold metal felt so comforting.

She scanned the snow-covered space. At its periphery, she spotted a likely looking character. In seconds she'd filed a mental ID. Black, male, 18-25. Tall, muscular inside his bulky jacket. Gleaming white hi-tops. He was leaning back against a wall, one foot up on the bricks behind him. In front of him, a fire blazed up out of an oil drum. Squaring her shoulders, she walked over to him, keeping her body relaxed, sending what she hoped were assertive but non-aggressive signals. Customer, not cop. Punter, not prey. As she drew near, she caught a movement to her right and half-turned her head. A second male had appeared from around a corner. *Keep going, Stel. You are Sparta!*

"What do you want, white bitch?"

She kept her eyes down, which would appear submissive, but allowed her to keep watch on his hands.

"Party drugs. Got anything?"

"Don't know what you're talking about."

"You think I'm a cop?"

"Are you?"

"Do I sound like a cop?"

"She's got a point."

This came from the other guy, who was now standing beside the first, stamping his feet in the trodden down snow.

"I'm not a cop, I swear," she said. "If you must know, I'm road manager for a British band playing over here at Buddy Guy's Legends. The lead guitarist is a total knob-end but he sent me out for party drugs so that's what I have to do."

The two black guys laughed.

"What did you call him? A knob-end? What the fuck's that?"

Stella flashed him a smile.

"It's a British insult."

He smiled back.

"I like it. I'm gonna use that. Knob-end. OK, so listen. You want party drugs? I got GHB. You know, roofies? That do you?"

Yes. As it happens I used it to help me murder a barrister back in England.

"Fine. Yes. How much?"

"Normally it's fifty a bottle, but since you gave me the dope insult, I'll let you have it for forty-five. K?"

"Fine. Thanks."

Leaving the revolver in her jacket pocket, Stella counted out the cash. She offered it to him but he shook his head.

"Not to me. To my man, here."

Stella handed second guy the cash, whereupon first guy unhooked a daysack and rootled around inside before handing over a small plastic bottle of colourless liquid.

The deal done, nods were exchanged and Stella hurried away, out of the lot and back to her car, cursing the cold as she walked.

63

STAR OF THE NORTH

AFTER kissing her husband goodbye and watching through the front window as he drove off, Lynne Collier took a leisurely shower before dressing. One of her new neighbours had invited her round for coffee later that morning, and she was looking forward to the company. At first, the move to Chicago had been exciting. And putting geographical distance between herself and her old life – and her old sadness – had worked. For a time. But when Adam had spent his two weeks at Quantico, she had moped around the house, run errands, attended the initial flurry of "welcome, neighbour" coffee mornings and jogged around the neighbourhood in an effort to distract herself. But without the routine demands of her job, she had begun to sink into depression. Theo was always in her thoughts. Why wouldn't he be? He was her only child. Her brave, beautiful boy.

Adam took pains to reassure her that she'd soon feel better and that, if he could swing it, he intended to apply for a permanent position with the FBI. And failing that, the Chicago Police Department. She'd agreed that the more space they could put between themselves and his former colleagues the better. Even if the detective with the vigilante complex was dead, it was still preferable to be thousands of miles away from the world of the Met and the possibility of his being investigated.

So when she'd bumped into another ex-pat, and a woman at that, in Whole Foods Market, it had seemed that here was a chance to do something about her own life, not just his.

At 8.23 a.m., her phone rang. Checking the caller ID she saw it was Jen. She smiled. Maybe things really were changing. She permitted herself a small flicker of happiness.

"Hi, Jen, how are you?"

The voice at the other end of the line was anything but happy. Jen either was, or had just been, crying.

"Oh, Lynne, I'm so sorry to do this to you, but I've just had such terrible news. It's my parents. They were killed in a car crash yesterday. A lorry on the M1. My sister texted me last night. I don't suppose I could come over, could I? Only I don't know anyone else in Chicago and I—"

"You poor thing. Come over now. Right now. Drive carefully."

Lynne put the kettle on. While it was boiling, she called her neighbour and cried off the coffee morning. She felt a thrill of anticipation. It wasn't that she was pleased her new friend had just lost her parents. It was just that, for once, she could help someone else cope with their grief instead of the other way round.

She'd just laid out some cakes and the tea things when the doorbell rang. Frowning, she checked her watch. Only ten minutes had passed. She went to the front door and opened it.

There stood Jen, red eyed, pale, hair standing up in damp spikes.

"I was already nearly here when I thought I'd better call you, in case you were busy or something. I'm sorry if I'm early."

Lynne pulled her across the threshold, kicked the door to behind her as a blast of freezing air forced its way into the hall, and drew her into a hug.

"It's fine. You're here. That's the important thing. Now, let's get your coat off and then we can sit down in the kitchen."

Jen looked a mess. Without makeup, she looked like a lost child, not a grown woman. Her eyes flicked here and there, hardly settling on anything for more than a few seconds. Lynne decided to take charge.

"Here," she said, pouring tea into two identical dove-grey mugs. "Drink some of this and then tell me what happened."

"Thanks, mate," Jen said with a sniff. She fiddled around inside the cuff of her cardigan and frowned. "Have you got a tissue please? I must have used up a whole box last night."

"Of course. Stay right there."

Lynne rose from her chair and hurried off to the downstairs bathroom. She returned with a peach-and-yellow box of tissues to find Jen sitting in exactly the same position as when she'd left the room. Her gaze hadn't shifted. She was still looking down at the surface of her tea.

"Do you want to tell me what happened?" she asked.

Jen looked up, her face impassive. Lynne recognised the symptoms. Her own grief had taken her so hard it had shocked her into immobility for hours at a time. She drank some of her tea while she waited for Jen to speak.

"They were driving to see an old friend of theirs in Derbyshire. The weather was lovely according to Frankie. She's my sister. Then according to the accident report, this huge purple lorry just swerved across three lanes and smashed into their car. Dad was driving and he lost control and they hit the crash barrier and the car turned over. It, it—" she sobbed. A loud, broken cry in the silence of the kitchen. "It caught fire. They were burned to death!"

Lynne reached across the table and gently placed her hand on Jen's shoulder.

"I am so, so sorry. How, just, how awful." She took another gulp of her tea. "When are you going back to England?"

"As soon as I can get a flight, I suppose. Frankie said she'll meet me at Heathrow."

Lynne watched her as she took a sip of her tea, then emptied her mug in one go. Lynne matched her, wanting to find a way to help but also needing something to do. She stood.

"Shall I make some more tea?"

"Yes, please. That would be lovely."

Lynne moved to the counter, bumping her hip on the corner of the table. While she refilled the kettle, she asked a question over her shoulder, just to keep Jen talking.

"How long had they been married, your, um … your parents?"

"Oh, you know, bloody ages! They had their golden wedding last year. We did this huge banner for the party. Marilyn and Ronnie. 50 Magic Years."

Lynne sat back down at the table while she waited for the kettle to boil. Her tongue felt thick in her mouth.

"Try to cling onto that happy memory, Jen. It's import— Oh."

A cold gust of nausea had flushed through her like the wind that blew off Lake Michigan.

"Are you all right?" Jen asked, from far away.

"Yes, fine. I just felt a little faint there for a, you know … That teapot must have boiled by now."

"I'll do it," Jen said. "You just stay where you are. You look a little pale."

"I'm five. Fine. I'm fine. I just need to —"

* * *

During the time she'd been in North America, Stella had grown accustomed to long-distance travel. So the five-and-a-half-hour drive from Chicago to Preston, Minnesota felt like a breeze. She'd checked out of her hotel early that same morning, made a few purchases at a hardware store, then used the ladies' room in a nearby branch of Starbucks to mess up her face and hair before driving up to Lincoln Park. Her only stop had been at a tyre place where she'd had winter rubber fitted.

Once the GHB had done its work on Lynne Collier, Stella had guided her into the rental car and driven straight out of the city on I-90. Finding a quiet spot to the rear of a retail park, she stopped the car and transferred Lynne's cable-tied form to the trunk. She'd taken care to fill it with a thick duvet and a spare down-filled jacket, so it made a comfy bed for her hostage. She wrapped her up and slid a knitted bobble hat way down over her ears then drove carefully through the northwestern suburbs: Avondale, Irving Park, Jefferson Park, Norwood Park, Rosemont. She watched the city disappear behind her and drove on, into the Illinois countryside.

The place she'd selected was so remote and so small, the mapmakers hadn't even bothered to name it. Minnesota might be a state of a million lakes for all she knew, but if they had names, they were too big. Too likely to have some eager beaver fisherman towing an ice hut onto the frozen surface. No. Stella wanted privacy.

She pulled into the courtyard of the Motel L'Etoile du Nord at 3.35 p.m. The sky was a uniform whitish-grey and looked to offer no more than an hour or so of daylight. Despite the cold, she chose the spot furthest from the office. If Lynne woke and started kicking out, the noise wouldn't carry far enough. She paid cash for a single night and returned to the car with the unit key. She popped the trunk to find that Lynne was snoring loudly, curled foetally under the down jacket.

After unlocking the unit and lugging her bags inside, Stella reached down into the trunk and brushed the back of her index finger along Lynne's cheek. The woman stirred and mumbled something.

"Hey," Stella said. "Lynne. Time to go. I can't leave you out here, you'll catch your death."

"What?" Lynne's eyes, gummy and red, opened. "Where are we?"

"Preston, Minnesota. Come on. Up you get."

Stella leaned over, grabbed Lynne under her armpits and hauled her into a sitting position. Then she worked her legs over the lip of the trunk and cut the cable ties around her ankles with a pair of scissors. With a bit more encouragement, both verbal and physical, Lynne tottered into the cabin, where she collapsed onto the double bed, face up.

Stella removed the cable ties from her wrists then fetched the revolver from her daysack. She made a cup of coffee then sat in the single armchair facing the bed and waited for Lynne to come round.

64

IN THE DARK OF THE NIGHT

AS a detective, Stella had worked a number of kidnapping cases. But as she sat guard over a gagged and retied Lynne Collier, she realised that in every case she and her colleagues had solved – and she was proud of the fact that they had solved them all – the kidnapper never worked alone. Two was a minimum, and depending on the victim it could be more. Yet here she was, trying to fly solo in an effort to lure Collier out of Chicago, away from his partner, far into the state whose motto the motel had borrowed. Star of the North. She pulled the curtain to one side.

Well they're certainly out tonight, she thought, swiping a clear circle on the pane and looking up at the pitch-black sky. She turned back to Lynne, who was lying on her side on the bed and watching her. Not struggling, not *mmff*-ing through the gag, which Stella had improvised using a strip cut from one of the towels. Just watching her. Time for the truth.

"My name isn't Jen. It's Stella. Adam might have mentioned me. Did he?"

Lynne nodded, her eyes wide now and staring. Breath whistling in and out through her nostrils.

"I'm not going to kill you, Lynne, if that's what you're worried about. But I'm afraid I am going to kill Adam. You know why, right?"

This time Lynne shook her head. She was trying to speak, huffing around the edges of the strip of towel. Stella decided to say her piece first.

"He and his cronies murdered my husband and my baby daughter. Then they covered it up. When I started getting too close to the truth, they sent a man to kill me. His name was Peter Moxey. He was a convicted rapist and murderer. When that didn't work, they sent a second man to kill me. Before he found me, he killed the godparents of a friend of mine. A journalist. I killed him instead. Then they had me sectioned. And while I was in the loony bin, your husband – because by then I had killed the rest – sent a Maltese woman built like a brick shithouse to do me in. She tried to throw me down a stairwell in the hospital. As you can see," she held her arms wide, "she also failed. Do you have any idea what it's like to lose a child, Lynne? Any idea of the pain? The incredible, disorienting grief? The funny thing was, it did drive me mad. Adam was perfectly within his rights to have me sectioned. He just didn't know it at the time."

Stella noticed that tears were rolling down Lynne's face. She went over to the bed and untied the gag, then stepped back and retrieved the revolver.

"Scream and I'll shoot you," she said. Not harshly, but simply to state a fact and keep Lynne docile.

Lynne coughed a couple of times and licked her lips, which the gag had dried.

"You just asked me if I knew what it's like to lose a child. Well, I do. Our son, Theo, was murdered when he was at university."

Stella was beyond being shocked by the misfortunes of others. So she asked a basic question.

"What happened?"

As Lynne retold the story of her son's stabbing, Stella listened intently. Old instincts were kicking in and she couldn't help starting to assess the way the investigation and subsequent court case had gone. When the story ended, "... he moved away, up to

Leeds, and started a new life for himself. An opportunity he forever took from Theo," Stella asked a question.

"I bet you wish Pro Patria Mori could have killed the little shit, don't you?"

Lynne's eyes flicked away from Stella's, up to the ceiling. Her lips tensed as if she was trying to stop words emerging.

"They did, didn't they?" Stella said. "They killed your son's murderer."

Lynne shook her head and spoke quietly.

"Not them. Just Adam. He did it last summer, just before we flew to Chicago. I wanted him to."

"How did it make you feel?"

"Good. Like we had avenged Theo."

Then her eyes grew wide. Her mouth fell open. Stella let the thought percolate for a while then spoke before Lynne could.

"You should get some sleep. Tomorrow will be a hard day, and you'll have a long drive back to Chicago."

Stella helped her decide by securing her wrists to the bed frame with more cable ties.

It was 2.00 a.m. Stella had switched Lynne's phone off after removing it from the kitchen counter back at the house in Lincoln Park. Now she turned it back on. While she waited for it to come to life, she looked across the darkened room at the hunched figure of Lynne Collier. Managing her in the cramped confines of the motel unit had been easier than she'd expected, as she could see the entire space, even the bathroom, from a single vantage point. She'd driven to a nearby pizza place and returned without incident, finding Lynne exactly where she'd left her. Police officers are at least as good as kidnappers at securing prisoners.

The phone buzzed in her hand. She looked down. A dozen texts and voicemails from 'Adam.' She scrolled through the messages, which began calmly enough but by the end of the string had escalated to a frenzied tone of despair. He was pleading with her to get in touch, wherever she was and whatever she had done. She didn't bother with the voicemails. Instead she called him.

"Lynne?"

"No. Stella."

"What have you done with my wife?"

"Nothing. She's sleeping."

"Where are you?"

"Minnesota. I'll send you the location in a minute or two."

"What do you want?" he said, in a low voice he presumably intended to be threatening.

"Me? I think you know full well what I want. I want you, Adam. You killed Frankie, didn't you? She had nothing to do with this, and you shot her anyway."

"She was putting the pieces together. I had no choice."

"That's not true. You always had a choice. You could have chosen not to murder a police officer. Forget Freddie McTiernan for a moment. He'd done enough bad things in his life that every day for him was a bonus. But Frankie? She was a good cop. A great cop. She looked up to you, and you rewarded her for her loyalty with a bullet."

"How do you know I won't turn up with a SWAT team?"

"I don't. Not really. But how do you know I won't be up a tree with a sniper rifle? I'd splatter your brains all over the snow before your buddies with the assault rifles got anywhere near me. And if they killed me afterwards, that's fine with me. I'm going to kill myself anyway when this is all over. That was always the plan."

"And if I don't come at all?"

"What? And leave the loving, loyal Lynne to be killed by an unknown assailant and dumped in a lake? I'd come back to Chicago and kill you anyway. At your desk if necessary. No. This is the deal. You come here. Alone. I let Lynne go, then you have a chance to kill me before I kill you. I know you'll be armed. How about that? We're the last two standing."

"Send me the location."

.   .   .

Stella finally fell asleep in the armchair around 4.00 a.m., wrapped in a spare duvet. She dreamt of Lola. A peaceful dream. No charred skin or crackling flames. No sardonic adult's voice emerging from her little girl's lips. No roaring car engines or smashing impacts. Just a mother and daughter, at peace in one another's company. She woke, smiling, at 6.15 a.m. and checked Lynne. She was still sleeping. She seemed peaceful, too. *That's good*, Stella thought. *Maybe when this whole business is over she can start afresh. Meet someone new. Move away from London and rebuild her life. God knows, someone has to come out of this alive and well.*

65

WRAP UP WARM

AMATEUR dramatics had never been Stella's thing. All those costumes turned her off. She'd never played dress-up as a child and didn't intend to start as an adult. However, something inside her mind had told her to make the final confrontation with Adam Collier as dramatic as possible. The colour red seemed important. Red for all the blood spilled. Red for the pillar box that had stolen Richard's life from him. Red mist … red sky at night … avenger's delight. So before taking Lynne from her comfortable middle-class home in one of Chicago's most desirable neighbourhoods, she'd bought herself a thick, lined, woollen coat in a shade of red the assistant in Macy's department store had described as "firetruck."

She was wearing the red coat as she drove out of the motel parking lot. Her movement was restricted thanks to the other garments beneath the coat, but at least she was warm, and the car's surprisingly efficient heater was on full blast, too. Lynne, without protest, had climbed back into her nest of bedding in the trunk, wearing the down jacket Stella had bought at the same time as her own coat.

Stella arrived at the unnamed lake at a little after 7.00 a.m., and was relieved to see that the entire area was deserted. The motel manager had said to her, in a broad Minnesotan accent, something that sounded like, "Uffda! We hadda big dumpa snow last week. Betcha never seen nothing like it in England. Bigger than they get up north, I think." Stella had agreed. He'd gone on to inform her that it hadn't snowed since, although, "It could easily reach the roofa ya house, dontcha know?"

The car slithered like a first-time ice skater, but she gently fed the wheel through her gloved hands and kept the nose pointing more or less forward until she reached the spot she'd chosen to confront Collier. A track led away from the road towards a sweep of birch trees that screened the complex of lakes. She eased the car onto the track, listening to the *crump* of the hard-packed snow beneath the winter tyres. She pulled up in a clear space between the edge of the birch trees and the lake. The surface was white, but she knew that beneath the covering of snow, thick ice would have formed. One ambitious fisherman had already towed a grey-and-blue wooden ice house into the centre. It stood like a sentry post in utter isolation among the white.

She checked her watch. She'd told Collier to be at the lake at 8.00 a.m. She wanted him to be tired from driving through the night. It was now 7.10 a.m. Leaving the engine running and the heater on, she got out, slammed the door behind her and released Lynne from the confines of the trunk.

"I need to pee," was the first thing Lynne said.

Stella swept her arm wide.

"Take your pick, but I'd be quick if I were you. You could literally freeze your arse off out here. Or worse. Don't think of running. We're miles from anywhere."

Lynne looked away from Stella and trudged off towards the nearest group of trees, her boots leaving crisp prints in the snow.

When she returned, she pointed at the front seats.

"Can we get in, please?"

Stella blipped the fob and Lynne climbed inside.

Shoulder to shoulder in their bulky coats, the women stared at each other. Both bereaved mothers. One a widow, one hoping not to be. One hoping for life. One for death.

"He'll kill you," Lynne said.

"He'll try," Stella answered.

"You said it yourself, he's already killed people."

"So have I. Including some very nasty individuals he sent to kill me."

"Can't you just walk away? Go back to England? Haven't you had enough vengeance?"

"I was asking myself that very question last night. Well, earlier this morning. For a while, the answer was definitely no. A side of me just wanted to wipe every trace of PPM from the face of the earth. Not just the members, but anyone, everyone, connected to them. You, for instance."

Lynne's eyes widened.

"Me? But I didn't know anything about it."

"I know that. And luckily for you, I'm not using the 'ignorance is no defence' line. I know you were innocent in all this, and that's why I'm going to send you home. You can take Adam's car. Alone or, if you're right and I'm wrong, together."

"You seem so calm. Can't you see that, rationally, this is madness? Why are you so hell bent on killing?"

"Why? I'll tell you why. And it's very, very simple. Because I have nothing left to live for. Literally nothing. They killed my family. And that nearly destroyed me. I'm still grieving for my husband and baby daughter. But they also took away my faith in the law. I joined the police because – and forgive me, I know this is such a cliché – but because I believed in the rule of law. I believed in justice. I used to belong to Amnesty International. I read about places where no such thing existed. Stalin's Russia, Hitler's Germany, Chile under Pinochet, Cuba under Castro, East Europe under the Communists ... all of them. They had no respect for the law and none for human lives, either. I wanted to work for the law in a country where it was a beacon for others. Jury trials, however often they got it wrong. Habeas corpus. Free speech. Parliamentary sovereignty. A free press. All of it, Lynne. It was my creed. And they shat all over it. Your husband and his cronies behaved as if they *were* the law. It broke something inside me."

Stella heaved a sigh before continuing.

"I am breaking the cycle of violence they started. I am returning Britain to a state of grace."

"Jesus! You sound like you have some kind of messiah complex. 'State of grace'? That's a bit high-flown for a serial killer isn't it?"

"And that's a bit self-righteous for the wife of one. Look, he's here."

Stella pointed out through the windscreen. Five hundred yards away, an SUV was approaching, slowly, across the snow. She pulled the Model 38 from her jacket pocket and thumbed the cylinder release switch. Five brass percussion caps faced her, their centres as yet un-dented. Though that would all change very, very soon. Following an impulse, she spun the cylinder with her fingers before snapping it back into place with a *clack*. She turned to Lynne.

"Get out."

By the time Lynne struggled out of the car, Stella was waiting for her, revolver held steady at her hip, pointing at Lynne's midriff. Lynne looked away, at her husband's car, which was now pulling to a halt a hundred yards away. She turned back to Stella, her forehead creased with anxiety.

"I'm begging you. Please, don't do this."

"I have to. I have no choice."

She grabbed the hood of Lynne's jacket, twisting it around in her gloved left fist. Then she stepped behind Lynne and pushed her forward, walking behind her and using her as a shield. Her own movements were awkward under the thickness and weight of her clothes. When they were halfway to the SUV, Stella tugged lightly on the hood. Lynne stumbled and stopped. Despite the bulk of her clothes, she was shaking. Stella could feel the trembling muscles as she held her hand down in the nape of Lynne's neck.

Collier climbed out of the SUV. He was wearing a heavy, brown leather jacket and a scarf wrapped round his neck. He pulled a black trapper hat on and smoothed the flaps down to cover his ears. Without coming closer, he shouted across the fifty yards that separated them.

"Let her go, Stella. She has nothing to do with this."

"Come closer, then I will."

To emphasise her point, Stella withdrew the muzzle of the little revolver from Lynne's back and held it to the side of her head.

Collier started walking. Stella watched him as he grew closer, saw the features that had earned him the nickname "The Model" gradually resolve themselves into clarity. The air was perfectly still and she could hear the creaks as his boot soles crushed the snow down. His hands were shoved deep into the pockets of his jacket. No way were they big enough to conceal a pistol, she thought. Or not the type he'd have been issued by the FBI, anyway.

When he was twenty feet away, he stopped. Pulled his hands out and held them wide.

"Let her go, Stella. Please. At least let one of us survive this."

His voice was only pitched at conversational volume but the cold, clean air relayed it to her as clearly as if he had been speaking right into her ear.

"That was always the plan," she said. Then she untwisted her hand from Lynne's hood.

"Go," she said, and gave her a little nudge in the back.

As Lynne slid forwards by half a step, Stella readied herself. Once Lynne was out of danger, she'd kill Collier. She'd use every bullet the little gun could spit at him. She thumbed the hammer back and curled her finger round the trigger. She looked down, checking the safety was off, then mentally kicked herself. *Fool! It's the stress. Revolvers don't have them. Remember what Ken told you.*

Stella looked up to see Lynne running, slipping, stumbling in a direct line between her and Collier, *obscuring the target,* she thought. She gripped the revolver tighter and prepared to fire.

66

TILL DEATH DO US PART

THE noise of the gunshot was immense. Lynne staggered to a stop. Stella gasped. She hadn't meant to kill Lynne. *Wait! I didn't shoot.* The gun hadn't bucked in her hand like it had when she was practising with Ken.

As Lynne fell face forward into the snow, blood flowing from her head wound to stain it scarlet, Stella stared at Collier. He had a black pistol in his bare hand, pointed at her. Instinctively, she pulled the trigger and dived to her left, rolling in the snow before scrambling to her feet.

He was firing now, groups of three shots. Stella fired twice then ran, zig-zagging erratically, for the cover of the birch trees that ringed the lake. No, no, no, no, this wasn't supposed to happen. She raced away, grateful for the months and years of running she'd done, the hundreds or was it thousands of miles – *oh, what does it matter, Stel?* – she'd racked up running in the night through the streets of north west London as she fought to shake off the crushing depression that had descended on her like a wet, charcoal-grey blanket after the hit and run and she heard the bullets singing past her to hit the birch trees, gouging pale-wheat coloured wounds beneath their silvery grey skin, and a searing pain in her left shoulder made her scream out, and she kept running but looked left to see blood darkening the red wool of the coat, where a rip had opened up over her deltoid muscle and she thought *flesh wound keep running adrenaline's your friend that's what the instructors at Hendon told us*. She had to be faster than Collier. Had to be. She was younger, fitter and more motivated. She dived behind a thicker tree trunk and swung round it before firing two more shots. He'd disappeared.

Panting, almost retching, she looked back the way she'd come. She could see her own footprints, but that was all. *Fuck! He's running.* She sprinted back the way she'd come and emerged into the clearing just in time to see Collier climbing back into the SUV. A trail of blood led all the way from the edge of the clearing, past Lynne Collier's body and towards the SUV. *I hit you, you bastard!*

The car engine started with a roar and Stella levelled her gun at the windscreen. The range was too great but she didn't have a choice. If she waited, he'd be gone and she'd have no chance to reload. Then she'd be alone out here with a corpse and an FBI agent making calls to the local sheriff. She pulled the trigger, aiming as best she could despite the ice clinging to her eyelashes.

The shot was hopeless. She didn't even hit the car. But Collier wasn't leaving. The wheels were spinning as they struggled to find traction, then he was slewing in a wide circle and coming round and straight towards her.

No time to reload! Fuck! Why couldn't I have more bullets?

She started running again, back toward the lake. She had one, final thought. *A last roll of the dice, Stel, and then we're done.*

With the car drifting left and right, sliding and slithering as it gathered speed, she threw the gun aside and reached into her pocket. *There you are! My friend. My little helper.* She grabbed the well-worn leather tube and pulled it free. Snapped off the retaining strap and tipped the thirty one-pound coins into her gloved palm. Waiting until the last possible moment, when she could see Collier's insanely grinning face through the windscreen, she hurled the coins at the glass with all her might, imagining them penetrating the toughened surface and smashing into Collier's head.

They spattered and cracked the windshield with dozens of white stars, rattling like distant firecrackers. She flung herself into the snow as Collier wrenched the wheel over and went into a slide. Side-on, the rear wheel hit a pile of sawn logs and the big car flipped over before landing on its wheels and sliding down a steep incline and out onto the ice. It spun round a couple of times before coming to rest thirty yards from the shore.

Gasping, Stella got to her feet and grabbed the revolver from the ground. She fumbled her glove off and fished out a handful of rounds from her pocket, but her fingers were shaking so much she couldn't insert them into the chambers. Finally, she pushed a single round home and rotated it to the top of the cylinder before snapping it shut.

A loud crack made her look up. Stretching out from the SUV, a deep-turquoise fissure had appeared in the ice beneath the front wheels. Another bang, as loud as a gunshot, sped away across the frozen surface of the lake. The front of the car jerked downwards. Then a volley of loud cracks rang out. The rear sank a couple of feet into the ice, as sharply as the front had done.

Stella ran to the edge of the lake. The ice looked thick. Certainly thick enough for some mad old fisherman to tow his ice house out there. But maybe there were thinner spots. Maybe the wooden house weighed less than a massive 4x4. She slithered out onto the ice, arms held out like a tightrope walker.

She reached the car as it sank up to its waist through the ice. Huge chunks had smashed and cracked and crept up the side of the car, crushing themselves against the doors and hemming the prisoner in. They were beautiful, she thought. Turquoise, sea-green, baby-blue. And inside, Collier was hammering on the glass. She reached the car just as he fired at the windscreen. The bullet had not been aimed at her. The already-damaged glass shattered and she saw his hands emerge, scrabbling for grip on the edge of the metal frame.

"No!" she shouted.

She flat-footed her way across the ice to the sinking car, which was now mostly below the surface. She clambered onto the hood, which was tilted up at a thirty-degree angle.

Collier's face was bloodless. She could see water swirling around his waist. He raised the pistol, but dropped it. His hands were flapping like fish. Eyes wide, he called out.

"Please! Get me out, Stella. I'm sorry!"

"I'm sorry, too," she shouted back, kneeling up on the sheet of freezing steel.

Then she leaned forward, stretched her right arm out just like she had back in Lac La Croix with Ken White Crow, aimed carefully, and shot Adam Collier straight between the eyes.

His head jerked back, fountaining blood onto the ceiling of the car. She retreated to the relative safety of the ice as the freezing waters of the unnamed lake outside Preston, Minnesota closed over the head of the final member of Pro Patria Mori, and murderer of her family. His face, fish-belly white beneath the water, sank out of sight, eyes staring, mouth open. Down into the dark.

67

HOME AGAIN, HOME AGAIN

SHE threw the revolver into the hole in the ice. Then turned and slithered back to the bank, avoiding the cracks radiating from the hole like a child's drawing of lightning bolts. Lynne Collier's body lay in the centre of a frozen red flower. Stella looked back at the hole in the lake. Bending, she took hold of Lynne's hands, which were as cold as the snow they lay on, and dragged her down to the shore and out onto the ice.

When she reached the hole, she looked down. The SUV had disappeared. Clearly the lake had a very steep drop-off here. She towed Lynne to the edge of the hole and then, kneeling, rolled her in to join her husband. The body sank slowly, leaving swirling strands of blood that coiled in the vortices created by the body's descent. She stood. Looked back at the drag marks. The snow looked as though an artist of non-human scale had stroked their brush, loaded with carmine, across the snow. For a brief moment, Stella contemplated obscuring the blood with more snow, but a thin, keening cry above her made her look up. Stark against the whitish-grey sky, a bird of prey was circling. Yes. Mother Nature would do a more effective job of cleaning up than Stella ever could.

Stella returned to her car, climbed gratefully into the still-warm interior and started the engine. She reached for her phone, intending to send a text to Ken White Crow. As she pulled her arm back to dig into her pocket, her injured shoulder made its presence felt with a sudden flare of pain.

"Fuck, that hurts," she hissed, remembering having read somewhere about the amazing anaesthetic effects of adrenaline and stress. With her own stress levels approaching normal, the nerve signals being fired into her brain from her shoulder were now being fully received and understood.

Leaving the engine running, and the heater on full blast, she wearily climbed out again and took her coat off, wincing with each movement. She dropped the coat onto the snow, another irregular red patch against the white. Twisting her head as far to the left as she could manage, she used the tips of her thumb and forefinger to spread the ripped woollen edges of her sweater and T-shirt. The skin beneath was torn away revealing a wet red stripe of flesh. It was bleeding freely, but not spurting. She went to the trunk and rummaged around under the duvet, hoping the rental company had seen fit to include a first-aid kit. No such luck. She lifted the carpet-covered boot floor by the steel D-ring. A mechanic or a valet at the rental company had left a half-used roll of duct tape inside the spare wheel. Sighing, she retrieved the tape, ripped off a length and strapped up her shoulder as best she could. Shivering violently, she bent to retrieve her coat.

Then she was back inside the cabin, pushing the selector lever into Drive. She pulled her phone out again and sent a short text to Ken White Crow.

Leaving now. Will be where we met Judith at 4.00 p.m.

Ken was waiting for her when she drove into the clearing. He nodded and held a single hand up in greeting.

"You, OK?" he asked, when she climbed stiffly out of the car.

"My shoulder's hurt. A bullet chewed a chunk of skin off."

Collecting her bags from the rental's trunk, he spoke over his own shoulder.

"We can get that seen to at the medical centre when we're back on the reservation."

Stella frowned.

"How are we getting back. The lakes down in Minnesota were frozen."

He smiled.

"Come and see."

Waiting at the edge of the lake was a two-person snowmobile with a small trailer hooked onto the back.

* * *

Half a world away, Callie had known all along, deep down, that she had to let Stella follow the trail all the way to its final, bloody ending. But she was far from content. She'd sat up half the night on the phone to Gordon, arguing back and forth over the pros and cons. In the end, he'd pulled rank.

"And believe me, it's not something I enjoy, Callie. But Christ, woman, ye leave me with no choice. Let Stella do what she has to do. Then you can grab her, knock her out, do whatever you have to. Understood?"

"Yes, boss. Understood. Just not happily."

"Aye, well, I can deal with an unhappy officer from time to time.

* * *

Stella stepped off the Air Canada Boeing 777 at Heathrow, two days later. No jetway being available, the passengers had to descend the stairs onto the concrete apron and walk to the terminal. The "cold snap" the pilot had advised them to protect against in his final message felt almost tropical in comparison to the bone-chilling cold of Chicago and Minnesota. Despite the sun's being out in a sapphire-blue sky, Stella felt the heaviness she'd been carrying all the way back from Lac La Croix intensify.

That's it, she thought, as she waited to go through passport control. *It's over. They're all dead. Even Other Stella is gone. Just me left.*

She'd called Jason from Toronto, and he'd said he'd pick her up from the airport. When she finally emerged into Arrivals, there he was, smiling and looking anxious at the same time.

Forty minutes later, he was carrying her bags into the house. Elle, with Georgie on her hip, and Polly greeted her, one warmly, the other effusively. Stella felt herself answering their questions robotically, as if Other Stella was still present, taking control and leaving her a mere passenger in her own body. Jason uncorked a bottle of white wine and poured the adults a glass each. He raised his own.

"We're glad you're back," he said. "Cheers."

"Cheers."

She took a mouthful of the chilled wine and felt something start to uncoil inside her as the alcohol hit her stomach. The tension of the past two years was finally, properly, beginning to leave her. She looked at Elle, who was smiling at Jason. She looked happy. Beautiful and happy. The baby had grown since Stella had last seen her. Her little fingers were curling and uncurling, like sea anemones, as she reached for her mother's glass.

"Looks like Georgie's got a taste for the good stuff," Stella said.

Elle laughed.

"Yup. But I think we'll keep *you*, Madam," she turned her eyes on Georgie and smiled, "on milk just for the moment."

"What about me, Mummy?" Polly asked with a petulant little curl to her mouth. "I don't drink your milk anymore so can I have some?"

"You won't like it, darling."

"Yes, I will. I will absolutely love it."

Elle rolled her eyes at Stella.

"Here you are then. But just a tiny sip, sweetie," Elle said.

She tilted the rim of her glass to her elder daughter's lips. Polly sucked at the wine then grimaced and spat it onto the floor.

"Yuk! That tastes like wee!"

Over the adults' laughter, she pulled a face then stomped off. Stella watched her go and felt the internal tussle of her emotions as an almost physical sensation. To leave this living family behind to join her own. Was that really her only option? But every day without Lola and Richard had been a struggle to get through. Resuming drinking had helped, although this time round she'd been careful never to retrace her steps down the booze-soaked path that had opened up before her after their funerals. The pursuit and destruction of the members of Pro Patria Mori had given her a sense of purpose that had sustained her over the previous two years. But now, having drenched herself in the blood of her victims and seen friends and allies caught in the crossfire, she realised she didn't want to go on any longer. *I'm tired. Tired of it all. I just want to rest. And tomorrow I will.*

"You all right?" Jason asked, pulling her attention away from her inner world.

"Yeah, I'm fine. You know, just a little tired, Jet lag."

"Is that all? You look sad," Elle added, reaching across the table to take Stella's hand.

Stella sighed.

"I was just thinking of Lola. She'd be two-and-a-bit by now."

"Oh, Stella. You poor thing. Has seeing Georgie brought it all back?"

Stella shook her head.

"Not really. It's never gone away. I told you I thought she was still alive, didn't I? And all the time it was only Mr Jenkins."

"You did. Look, what can we do to help? You'll stay here with us for a bit, won't you?"

"I'd love to, thanks."

"That's great. And there's really no hurry. Take your time. Go back to work. Get yourself sorted and whenever you're ready to start looking at houses, Jason will help, won't you darling?"

Jason took Stella's other hand, so that for a moment she felt as if she was under arrest. He smiled and it was an expression so full of compassion that Stella felt the tears pushing and squeezing their way out.

"Of course I will."

She smiled at him. The Drinkwater brothers were beautiful souls, both of them. It was just so unfair that hers was dead.

After a meal of spaghetti and homemade meatballs with garlic bread and red wine, Stella pleaded exhaustion and headed upstairs. In the guest bedroom, she sat on the bed and pulled her boots and socks off. The feel of the carpet under her toes reminded her of the dreadful night when she'd first seen Other Stella. Her alter ego had stepped out of the wardrobe mirror to explain that her baby was dead and what she was clutching to her breast, what she had been checking on every evening before going out running, was Lola's teddy bear.

She pulled the chair over to the wardrobe and climbed up. She reached over the decorative cornice, fingers outstretched, and swept her hand right to left. Her stomach lurched. The Glock had gone. No! It was further back than she remembered placing it. Her fingers closed round the grip and she drew the gun towards her before lifting it down.

After the little snub-nose revolver she'd used to kill Collier, the Glock felt unnaturally clumsy in her hand. She turned it this way and that, examining the various controls. The slide release catch. The magazine release switch. The trigger safety. Using muscle memory, she closed her eyes and dropped out the magazine, catching it in her left palm. She thumbed out the remaining rounds and tossed them up and down in her hand so that they clinked and jingled against each other. Then, with a practised, efficient movement, she thumbed them all back again.

Tomorrow, she thought. *I'll do it tomorrow. I'll walk to the cemetery. Go to their graves. Rest my back against the cold stone. It won't hurt. Not if I do it properly. Then we'll all be together again.*

Stella stuffed the Glock deep into her rucksack. Closing the bedroom door behind her, she walked down the hallway, the carpet soft under her bare feet. As she reached the midpoint of the stairs, she heard Jason's voice. He was speaking to someone. *Elle*, she thought at first. But then, *no, not Elle. He's on the phone.*

"Yes," Jason was saying. "I picked her up from Heathrow this afternoon." Pause. "No, she seemed fine." Pause. "OK, we'll see you about nine."

"Who were you calling, darling?" Elle asked.

"Callie. She's coming tomorrow to pick Stella up."

"Do you think she's all right?"

"Who, Callie?" Yes, she's—"

"No, Stella. She won't say what she was doing in the States all that time. She can't just have been travelling. She's not a student."

"That's why they want her back again. Callie needs to interview her."

Coughing loudly on the stairs, Stella made her way down and entered the kitchen. Jason put on a smile, which, Stella thought, was the worst attempt at playing "an innocent man" she'd ever seen.

"Hey, you. How's your room?" he asked.

"It's fine," she answered. "Snug as a bug in a rug."

The following morning, Stella got up at five. She pulled the curtain back. The garden was dark. She dressed quickly, retrieved the Glock from her rucksack and went downstairs.

68

COP KILLER

WEARING the red coat she'd bought in Chicago, Stella walked on silent feet through the kitchen and unlocked the back door. She looked up. No stars. Clouds had blanketed southwest London overnight, and the temperature was cold but still balmy compared to the wilds of the northern USA. She walked to the far end of the garden, where an old oak tree rose majestically out of the lawn, its gnarled trunk swollen at its base.

Stella sat with her back against the tree.

She closed her eyes and tilted her face upwards, imagining, despite the dark, and the cold, that she was facing a warm summer sun, feeling its kindly rays heating her skin.

The gun was heavy in her hand, but that was fine. She still had strength to lift it, and place the hard steel of its muzzle against her chest, right over her heart.

She pressed hard. To make sure. She didn't want anything to go wrong. Ending up a quadriplegic was not part of the plan.

Then, from far away, she heard a voice. A little girl's voice.

"Mummy!"

She opened her eyes. The cold had gone, to be replaced with summer's warmth. And so had the garden. She found herself in a park, bright with cherry blossom from an avenue of trees. The tree she was leaning on had been planted near a hedge. From the other side of the hedge she could hear the excited screams of children playing on the swings and clambering up the brightly coloured climbing frame to wave to their delighted parents.

Through a dazzling white mist that made her squint, she could see a man walking towards her, his right hand loosely clasping that of a little girl, of maybe three years old.

The man was waving. And she recognised him. Richard. She smiled with gratitude.

She tightened her right thumb on the trigger, sensing the internal mechanism blocking the firing pin start to disengage.

The little girl broke free of her father's grasp and started running towards her mother.

Stella was weeping now, but it didn't matter. It was good. Soon they'd be together again. The three of them.

Stella held her thumb quite still as the little girl came closer.

She launched herself towards Stella, arms outflung, mouth wide in a smile of pure joy. Stella watched as her progress through the air slowed, then stopped. She hung there, suspended. Waiting.

Inside the pistol, metal parts began sliding past each other again, clearing the passage that the firing pin would take on its short, purposeful journey towards the primer at the base of the cartridge.

Stella smiled back. Then she spoke. Just a single word.

"Lola."

The thump against her side drove the breath from her lungs in an explosive gasp. The pistol fell from her hand and she toppled sideways.

69

GETTING BETTER ALL THE TIME

STELLA opened her eyes.

Polly Drinkwater had dived onto her aunt's lap and thrown her arms around her. The impact of the little girl's three stone nine pounds caused Stella to cry out. Pain flared in her old bruises from her encounter with the blacktop on the road outside Duluth.

"Auntie Stella! Do you have in-some-near as well? Oh, what's that? Is that your police gun?"

She was reaching for the Glock, which had tumbled from Stella's grasp and now lay beside her pointing into the woods at the back of the garden. Stella shoved it behind her and then wrapped her arms around Polly.

"Yes, it is, Polly Wolly Doodle. But what are you doing out here so early?"

"What I said, silly! I wake up early. Mummy says I have that thing I said. In-some-near. Do you have it too?"

Instead of answering, Stella clutched Polly to her breast. Felt the tears coming and let them flow – hot on her chilled cheeks. And she realised that nothing would ever bring Lola back. But something else as well.

Nothing would take her closer to Lola either. Certainly not

putting a bullet through her heart. What had she been thinking? Leaving a bloody corpse in the back garden for poor little Polly to find.

You must be mad, Stel. Oh, wait. You're not. Not anymore. They're all dead. Including her. But here is another little girl who loves you. Who you love.

It was as if the world had righted on its axis, having been spinning off kilter for millennia. Stella saw, as clearly she'd once seen the inevitable need to put a 9mm bullet through her own heart, that she'd been wrong all along. The brittle emotional carapace she'd grown around herself to protect her from ever feeling anything, for anyone, ever again, burst apart.

"Auntie Stella! You're hurting me."

"Oh, Jesus! I'm sorry little one."

Stella relaxed her grip on her niece, turning it into a cuddle. The little girl was warm and her brushed-cotton pyjamas were soft under Stella's hands. She snuggled closer. Pulled Stella's head down so her lips were touching Stella's right ear. She whispered.

"You said, 'Oh, Jesus.' That's naughty. Mrs Lemon said so."

"Is Mrs Lemon your teacher?"

"Yes. Can we go in now? I'm cold."

Stella wiped her face dry with her sleeve and accepted Polly's help, clambering to her feet.

"Come on then. Let's make some hot chocolate."

Polly's eyes darted downwards.

"Don't forget your police gun."

They kept Stella lightly sedated and under observation during the two-hour drive to the private psychiatric hospital for her evaluation, treatment and rehabilitation. A month of intense, inpatient psychotherapy followed, though not at St Mary's in

Paddington, from which the head of the psychiatric unit had recently taken an unexplained leave of absence.

Stella endured multiple electroencephalograms, MRI and CAT scans, Rorschach ink-blot tests, psychiatric assessments and sessions of one-to-one and group therapy. Her doctors even administered the Hare Psychopathy Checklist. Stella took the test twice, yielding two scores, one for her answering as herself, and one answering how she imagined Other Stella would have responded. Stella scored zero out of thirty. Other Stella scored a rather more worrying twenty, although this still placed her inside the bounds of "normal" behaviour. So, neither version of Stella was a psychopath. Which was good news. Especially for Callie, who'd asked to be kept informed of Stella's progress on a daily basis.

Finally, in early March, Stella was released from the kind and compassionate care of the staff at The Sanamente Centre in rural Hertfordshire. Among her possessions, she could now claim a piece of paper proclaiming her to be "of capacity." At no point during her stay had she experienced so much as a whisper from any other version of herself, malevolent or otherwise.

No intrusive thoughts. No hallucinations. No out-of-body experiences. No sarcastic or biting remarks. No self-harming.

Stella Cole was whole again.

70

NEW LEAF

CALLIE McDonald wasn't used to meeting civil servants. Not those serving the Scottish Parliament at Holyrood and certainly not those doing a similar job in Whitehall. The Home Office conference room in which she now found herself reinforced her opinion that too much money was sloshing around in Westminster, and the sooner the Scots managed to vote themselves into independence the better. The ceiling alone gave her indigestion. Some fourteen feet above her head, it sported ornate plaster mouldings around the edge – ivy leaves, bunches of grapes, cherubs – and an intricate ceiling rose from which an actual, crystal chandelier hung as if waiting for Regency toffs to dance and play cards beneath it.

Sitting on her left, Gordon Wade looked relaxed. As well he might, she reflected, having brought the hideous, bloody perversion of justice called Pro Patria Mori to an end without a single whisper reaching the media. To her right, Stella seemed equally at home in the grand surroundings of the conference room. She was popping the catch on a sweat-stained leather tube and refastening it. She looked up, following Callie's gaze.

"My wedding cake wasn't as pretty as that ceiling rose," she said.

"Tax payers' money paid for that, you know," Callie retorted, feeling cross with herself for not being able to rein in what she realised was chippiness.

"Compared to what they were paying for until a few weeks ago, I'd say a poncy chandelier is a pretty good deal."

"Stella has a point, Callie," Gordon said. "Given a choice, I think most of us would opt for a few baubles over bloody death squads, eh?"

Unable to lay her hands on a suitable riposte, Callie fell silent. All that remained was to meet the mysterious man working for some unspecified organ of state security who, they had been assured by the minister for justice, would make the remnants of PPM "disappear like morning mist over the Serpentine."

"Keeping us waiting. That's a bit old, isn't it?" she said. She wanted to sound bored but realised she sounded nervous. Which was, annoyingly, true.

"Relax, Callie," Gordon said. "We just say our hellos, hand over Collier's notebook and bugger off for a decent lunch and a couple of decent single malts in a pub somewhere."

The door opened, startling Callie. Inwardly cursing her jumpiness, she stood, then sat as she realised neither Gordon nor Stella had budged from their chairs.

Two men entered. One older, late sixties, perhaps. Iron-grey hair, twinkling eyes set in a lined face. Grey suit, highly polished shoes. One younger, midthirties. Short dark hair. Scar on his left cheek. Not bad looking at all in his jeans, white shirt and navy linen jacket.

They all shook hands and introduced themselves.

The older man spoke.

"I understand you have a notebook for us."

Callie pulled the notebook from her bag and slid it across the polished rosewood table. The older man didn't open it. Instead he passed it to his number two.

"There you are, Old Sport. That should keep you and your team busy for a few weeks, don't you think?"

The younger man opened the notebook and flipped through the pages. Then he closed it again and nodded. He looked at Callie. *Nice eyes*, she thought. *But you've seen sadness, haven't you? You have what my Granny would've called "a dowie look" about you.*

"There are a few firearms officers on this list," he said. "Will they have weapons?"

She shook her head.

"They've all been placed on administrative leave. Told the jig's up. They've been led to believe that now they've signed the Official Secrets Act and promised to keep quiet, they'll be allowed to retire quietly and draw their pensions."

"Just not for very long."

"No."

The older man cleared his throat. Callie looked at him. He was frowning.

"Forgive me, but I'd like to ask Stella a couple of questions. If that's all right with you, Stella?"

"Shoot. No pun intended."

"Just wondering what your plans are? I gather you're on leave just now."

"That's right. I've had what you might call a traumatic couple of years."

"Oh, of course, of course. Hmm, mm-hmm," he said, humming quietly through his nose. "Any thoughts about what you might do when you rejoin the workforce?"

Stella shrugged.

"I've been talking to Callie about a new team she's setting up. What did you call it?"

Callie answered.

"Special investigations unit."

"Interesting word, 'special.' You know, special birthday, special child, special event." He paused for a beat. "Special Forces. We used to work in that general arena, didn't we, Old Sport?"

The younger man smiled. Exchanged a glance with his neighbour that Callie couldn't read before answering.

"Yes, Boss. Yes we did."

"Going after the really bad guys, Callie?" the older man asked.

"Something like that."

He smiled.

"An admirable ambition. Which we share." He pulled out his wallet and extracted a white business card, held it out across the table to Stella. "Here's my card. Why don't you give me a call when you're back in harness?"

"Speaking of harnesses," Callie said, "hold your horses. No poaching, OK?"

"My dear Callie, on my honour as a soldier – well, an ex-soldier – no poaching. But I assume you wouldn't be averse to the occasional chat about intelligence sharing, or joint operations? After all, we're all on the same side. Now, if we're finished with the business part of our meeting, I wonder whether you'd let me take you all to lunch?"

In the pub, after an excellent lunch of steak and kidney pie and chips, washed down with pints of London Pride bitter and topped off with a round of single malts, Stella leaned closer to the younger guy.

"He all right, your boss?"

He nodded.

"The best."

Stella nodded.

"So's mine."

Later, after she'd written in her journal, a suggestion of the counsellor she was seeing twice a week, Stella curled up on the sofa. She poured herself a glass of wine and pulled a photo album towards her from the other end of the sofa. She opened the album, whose first page bore a single Polaroid photo of a very sweaty but happy Stella Cole holding a newborn baby.

On the wide, white margin below the image, Richard had written, in blue biro, "Mummy and Lola, 6.14 a.m. Monday 7 December, 2008."

She touched the photo with her fingertip, smiled, then turned the page.

The End

Read on for the opening of book four, Let The Bones be Charred ...

LET THE BONES BE CHARRED

THEN

Malachi awoke and knew immediately that trouble lay ahead.

The sheet beneath him was wet and he could smell the tang of urine. Before he could even think how to escape his punishment, Mother appeared by his bedside. She grabbed him by his skinny bicep and dragged him from the narrow bed.

'You dirty little boy!' she shouted. 'Lying in your own filth. Not even trying to be good. As God is my witness, I will teach you to behave yourself like a decent human being. You are five years old. You should have stopped this disgusting behaviour years ago.'

She dragged him down the hallway. He stumbled and cried out in pain as his arm twisted in its socket.

'Don't, Mother!' he screamed.

She clouted him on the side of the head.

'How dare you shout at me! Remember the fifth commandment. What is it?'

'Honour thy mother and thy father.'

'Well do it, then.'

She pushed open the door to the spare bedroom. The room was devoid of furniture. Not even a carpet softened the hard-edged cube, although thick, plum-red velvet curtains kept the outside world where it belonged. Outside.

In the centre of the bare boards stood a six-foot-tall wooden post, eight inches in diameter. It had been mounted on a sturdy platform which was screwed down through the floorboards and into the joists. To stabilise the post, a braided steel wire ran through a neat hole drilled through it, three inches from the top. The wire was secured to eyebolts in opposite walls and strung to a humming tension with heavy-duty galvanised turnbuckles.

The boy struggled half-heartedly. He knew it was pointless. Mother was so much stronger than him. For now. And the punishments weren't usually painful. More uncomfortable, he supposed. Though he hated the feeling of powerlessness they imposed upon him.

'Put your hands behind you,' his mother said.

He complied, interlacing his fingers around the pole. He felt her rough hands tying the knots that bound his wrists. Swore to himself, once again, that there would come a reckoning. A Judgement Day.

When she'd finished, she came round to stand in front of him. Bent closer so he could smell the alcohol on her breath, see the fine hairs on her cheeks where the grains of powder had caught.

'The Christian saints endured so much suffering for their faith. Yet you cannot even live like a civilised human being amongst all this luxury we provide for you.'

She turned and left him there, although she didn't close the door.

When she returned, she was carrying a kitchen knife. And she had the strange twist to her lips that he'd christened 'the danger smile'.

There were other times after that. Mother was determined to instil in the boy the correct attitude to faith. Obedience. Self-discipline. Chastity.

422

The first time she touched him while he was lashed to the post he recoiled, earning himself an extra three hours in the room on his own. He passed the time by going into his head, an increasingly troubled place but one where he could escape Mother's endless sermons, strictures and alcohol-fuelled fits of weeping self-pity.

Once, he walked into the bathroom to wash his hands before tea and stumbled on his mother, naked, one foot up on the edge of the bath. Her breasts were white and flabby. She was looking down at herself. Holding something in her right hand and sort of scraping it against the hair on her – *fanny!* He said the word in his head. The other boys said it out loud at school, down the field, far from the buildings, where the teachers wouldn't hear. And worse words, too.

She looked up at him and her eyes blazed so it looked as if they would burst from her face. She snatched a towel from the rail and covered herself up.

Red in the face, she didn't scream as he'd expected her to. She just pointed to the door across the hall.

'Go and wait for me,' she said, in a voice all the more terrifying for being so quiet.

She tied his hands behind the post, then fetched the kitchen shears she used to cut up chickens. She dragged his trousers and underpants all the way down round his ankles, then pulled his penis out with her thumb and forefinger, so hard he thought it might actually come away. He didn't cry out. He knew better. Mother opened the jaws of the shears and placed them around the pathetically stretched length of tissue.

She looked him in the eye.

'You are filth. Don't you know it is a sin to do what you just did? Would you lie with your own mother? Fornicate with her?'

He tried to answer in a way that would placate her, but it was so hard to know which words and phrases would achieve the desired effect and which would only enrage her. Her eyes were glistening and her cheeks flushed.

'No, Mother,' he said, finally, in a whisper, feeling sick with the anxiety of losing his 'thing'.

'No, Mother,' she repeated.

She drew the tip of her tongue over her top lip, then straightened suddenly and withdrew the shears.

'What you saw, you must unsee. What you thought, you must unthink. Lust is a deadly sin, as well you know.'

Then she left, towel clumsily wrapped around her.

A little while later, just as he was wondering whether he'd be able to control his bladder any longer, and fearing what would happen if he couldn't, the door opened. She was standing there. Slowly, she came towards him, her eyes full of pity. She moved behind him and began untying the knots.

NOW

MONDAY 13TH AUGUST 12.05 P.M.

Detective Chief Inspector Stella Cole watched, frowning, as bloody foetuses were shoved into the women's clenched faces. The TV news showed them pushing the horribly realistic dolls aside and hurrying into the clinic.

A female reporter's voice spoke over the footage.

'LoveLife's pickets have been on duty at The Sackville Centre for the past week. The centre claims on its website that it offers advice on sexual health and contraception, but the protesters I spoke to earlier have a different take on it.'

The picture cut to a woman wearing a cream blouse and an angry expression on an unmade-up face, helmeted by coarse-looking iron-grey hair.

'We are sure in our hearts of one thing. That place,' she jerked a thumb over her shoulder, 'is an abortion clinic. Pure and simple. A murder factory!'

The director cut back to the unfolding events.

'Look at it closely,' Niamh Connolly, the charity's glamorous chief executive said, speaking through a megaphone. 'Beyond those walls, unborn babies are being slaughtered. It is nothing more than a whited sepulchre. But no amount of modern design or pristine paint can mask the stench of death within.'

Stella had seen Niamh Connolly on TV before. It seemed to her that the CEO knew her swept-back blonde hair and well-maintained good looks made her a magnet for the TV cameras.

'Mrs Connolly, aren't you actually restricting these women's rights to have what is, after all, a perfectly legal procedure?' the TV reporter asked.

Niamh smiled as if to say, *it's OK that you're stupid*. She waved her left hand at the protesters who at the time were offering leaflets to a hunched young woman walking up the path to the clinic's solid-looking front door.

'Nobody's restricting anyone's rights, Janine, except the doctors and nurses inside that building, who are denying unborn children their right to life. Because let's remind ourselves of something. The overarching document that enshrines people's rights is called the Universal Declaration of Human Rights.

"Now the two words that really matter in that title are 'Universal' and 'Human'. Its drafters didn't call it the *Partial* Declaration of Human Rights. Nor did they call it the Universal Declaration of *Women's* Rights.

"So unless you are going to deny that a foetus is human, in which case I would invite you to tell your viewers which species you believe a foetus belongs to. Or you're going to say that although a human foetus is *indeed* human, it is not part of the universality of the human race. Then I think you have to agree with me that a child, even an unborn child, has the same rights as every other human being. And first of all of these is the right to life.'

The young reporter sounded flustered. Stella felt a degree of sympathy. She was just doing her job, after all.

'But your people are—'

'I'm sorry, I must interrupt you there, Janine. Those people are not "my people",' – she made air quotes – 'they have volunteered their time and their prayers to speak up for those who have no voice of their own. I do not employ them.'

'But you organise them. You encourage them.'

'No. I offer them my help, my support, my prayers, and the resources of LoveLife. They have chosen to exercise their right to free speech. As have those misguided souls.' Niamh pointed at a crowd of about thirty counter-protesters who were waving placards asserting a woman's right to choose. 'I take it, as a journalist, you're not in favour of restricting freedom of expression?'

'Of course not. But they are harassing women who may not even be thinking of having an abortion.'

'And good for those women if that's true. Good for them! But as everybody who lives in Mitcham knows, The Sackville Centre is one of the biggest abortion clinics in South London. Legally, since you are fond of quoting the law, a baby has been defined in case law as a gift from God. As a devout Christian who draws her inspiration from God, I believe it is not just wrong but evil to take that gift and treat it as a tumour. Something to be cut out of a woman's body and dropped into a bloody bucket to die.'

At that point, and presumably fearing a tongue-lashing from her producer, as she was reporting for a lunchtime show, Janine Everly ended the interview with a hurried thank-you.

Stella switched the TV off and changed into her running gear. She'd worked the last ten days straight and was enjoying the prospect of two days off.

As she entered that blissful, flowing state of mind that arrived when her heart and lungs had adjusted to the new demands she placed on them, she thought back to the news item. She wasn't opposed to abortion. Not exactly. She knew plenty of women who'd had them. But she also carried around with her the grief of losing her own baby daughter. For her, 'getting rid' of unwanted babies carried a devastating emotional charge.

Even though Stella had killed the people responsible for Lola's murder, and that of her daddy, the pain still lodged in her heart like a thorn. She'd grown a strong, protective sheath around it, but it was still there. Once she had thought it would kill her. Her colleagues thought it had.

* * *

Stella would never forget the day she came back from the dead. On March 5th 2012, her boss, Callie McDonald, had convened the Murder Investigation Command on the fifth floor of Paddington Green Police Station at 8.00 a.m. with a promise of 'some very good news indeed'.

The whole team, upwards of fifty detectives, crime analysts, forensics officers and civilian employees, were gathered in the CID office. Most were sitting on tables or standing. A few of the older detectives leaned back in their chairs as if to say, 'go on, then, show me something I haven't seen before'.

Callie had told Stella to come in at 8.05 precisely: they'd synchronised their watches. She'd followed orders, walking quickly but not fast, through the civilian-staffed reception area, before swiping her Metropolitan Police ID at the access-controlled doors leading to the rest of the station. The goggle-eyed stares and dropped jaws her passage through the ground floor occasioned made her stomach flip.

But it was the reaction from her former colleagues that was the real concern. Would they go into shock? Cry? Shout at her? Laugh? Scream? She had to admit to herself, she had absolutely no idea. After all, it wasn't every day you got to meet a colleague the new boss had told you had been run over and killed while escaping from a secure psychiatric unit.

She elected to take the stairs rather than the lift, reasoning that she'd be less likely to meet someone on her way up to the fifth floor and, even if she did, it would be orders of magnitude less uncomfortable – *Uncomfortable, Stel? How about unbelievable?* – than being trapped in a toilet-cubicle-sized stainless-steel box.

She arrived on the fifth-floor landing breathing easily: in the previous few months she'd walked almost six hundred miles from the US-Canadian border to Duluth, Minnesota.

Wishing she'd not had anything to eat for breakfast, she walked along the corridor towards the double doors at the far end. Stella peered in through the left-hand square of wire-reinforced glass positioned at head-height in the plain wooden door. Everyone bar Callie had their backs to her. Callie was speaking, making expressive gestures with her hands. Stella felt a sharp pang of grief as she saw that a new detective was sitting at her old DS's desk. Frankie O'Meara and Stella had been a team. Then their boss, the now-dead Detective Chief Superintendent Adam Collier, had murdered her. He'd shot her with a police-issue Glock 17 at the house of a former gangster, then staged the scene to look like an arrest gone wrong.

She leaned closer to the crack between the two doors and heard Callie clear her throat.

'Now, in setting up the Special Investigations Unit, I realised I would need to call on the very best detectives I could find. And… and there is one officer in particular whom I just couldn't do without. She'll be my right-hand woman as well as heading a team of her own as DCI.'

Stella looked around the room and saw, with a sinking feeling, that a few of the detectives were looking round at DI Roisin Griffin, who was struggling to keep a smile off her face. Stella's heart was bumping in her chest and she suddenly realised Callie would have to change her plan. *There's no way she'll be able to keep order once I go in.*

Callie resumed her speech.

'Now, some of you attended the memorial service for Stella last year.'

Eyes that had been on her a moment earlier were now downcast.

'And I know you thought you were doing right by her.'

People looked up and frowned at her.

Stella caught her eye again and thought, *This isn't going well at all. Abandon ship! Women and children first.*

'Oh, shit!' Callie said with a sigh. 'Look, there's no easy way to say this. I, we – no – *I* lied to you. About Stella, I mean. She's not dead.'

The room erupted. People were shouting, launching questions at Callie. The cynics had pulled their feet off the desks and were leaning forwards, mouths open. Callie simply looked over at Stella and beckoned her in. Stella inhaled deeply, plastered on a smile she wasn't feeling and stepped back into her old life.

The noise hit her like a wave. A collective gasp immediately segued into laughs, shrieks and, from one or two of the younger women in the room, sobs. Everyone leaped out of their chairs, pushed away from walls or jumped down from desks and rushed towards her. Feeling she might be trampled to death before saying as much as 'did you miss me?', she did the only thing she could think of and held her hands out in front of her, palms outstretched like Moses parting the Red Sea.

The noise decreased a little, but everyone was still talking at once. She was relieved to see that they were smiling or, in a couple of cases, laughing. Suddenly tongue-tied, despite having been awake half the night rehearsing possible openers, she said the first thing that came into her head.

'If anyone's been using my coffee mug, I'll kill them!'

Stella accepted hugs and kisses from every member of the MIC. They were firing questions at her and she gave them the answers she and Callie had cooked up between them the previous night.

'Where were you, then, if you weren't dead?'

'It was a joint operation with Lothian and Borders Police. I couldn't tell anyone for operational reasons.'

– I was in the US, killing your and my former boss for his part in the murder of my husband and baby daughter.

'When did you get back?'

'Only last week.'

— Three months ago, but I was undergoing intensive psychiatric care and psychotherapy to make sure I was sane.

'Do you know what happened to The Model?'

'Adam enjoyed his sabbatical with the FBI so much he asked them to make it permanent.'

— He was trapped in his SUV as it sank beneath the freezing waters of a lake in Minnesota and I made sure he was dead by shooting him between the eyes.

Shaking her head to free it of the vision of Collier with that obscene crater in the centre of his forehead, Stella ran on.

MONDAY 13TH AUGUST 12.05 P.M.

After answering questions from a few more reporters, Niamh drove herself back to her house on Wimbledon Parkside. She arrived at 'Valencia' at five past twelve and parked her white convertible Mini on the gravel drive beside her husband Jerry's dark-green Jaguar XJ saloon. He ran an insurance brokerage in the City of London and cycled down to the station every morning to catch the 7.38 to Waterloo.

They'd bought the house in the nineties with the proceeds of a spectacular insurance deal Jerry had closed as a new partner in the firm. A tall yew hedge shielded the occupants from passing traffic, wide entrance and exit gates the only clue that a substantial house lurked behind the evergreen foliage. While she waited for the cloth roof to lock into place with its satisfyingly muted clicks, she checked her makeup in the rear-view mirror. *Not bad for fifty-two, Niamh. Not bad at all.*

She ran LoveLife from a converted stable block that abutted the house. No secretary, no assistant, no marketing executive. She had people to organise her schedule, coordinate her social media campaigns, book meeting rooms or negotiate speaking fees, but they all worked from home, as did she. 'Just as long as I have my iPhone, I'm fine,' she liked to say to people who questioned her lack of in-house staff.

She checked it now. One meeting scheduled for 1.00 p.m. with

MJ Fox, CEO, GodsGyft. Then nothing until dinner with Father Reid from The Sacred Heart at 7.30 p.m. Plenty of time for a shower and a change of clothes, then a light lunch before her visitor arrived at the house.

Even in the few steps it took her to reach the ornate oak front door from the car, the heat boiling off the pea shingle drive brought a light sheen of sweat to her top lip. Cream hydrangeas in rust-red glazed pots each side of the door were watered automatically by a computerised system Jerry controlled from an app on his phone, but even so, the flowers looked unhappy. Brown edges scarred a couple of the blossoms, and as she pulled a few dead leaves free they crackled between her fingers.

She pressed her thumb to the pad to the right of the door and waited for it to open automatically on its silent, German-engineered mechanism.

'Come on, come on, you stupid thing,' she muttered, cursing Jerry and his obsession with automating everything in the house, 'I'm getting heatstroke out here.'

As soon as the door had swung open far enough to admit her, she stepped through into the deliciously air-conditioned interior of the house and practically ran up the thickly carpeted stairs, so eager was she to cool down under the stinging jets of her wet room shower.

In her dressing room she stepped out of her skirt and hung it and the matching jacket on a hanger on the airing rail. The cream silk blouse went into the laundry hamper. Bra, knickers and tights she laid out on a second airer. The 'Niamh Connolly look' as she thought of it, and as one or two social media commentators had noticed, was part of her brand image, but in a summer like this one, extraordinarily uncomfortable. Freed from 'the look', she pirouetted clumsily in front of the full-length mirror, her arms stretched overhead to lift her breasts, before walking out of the room and into the en suite bathroom.

A noise from downstairs stopped her in mid-stride. But as the house was empty, and Niamh Connolly was not an easily scared woman, she put it down to the air-conditioning system and turned on the shower. As she paddled around on the slate floor tiles, letting the temperature-controlled water jets sluice the heat of the day from her skin, she missed a second sound, this time from the stairs. A riser creaking as the summer heat dried the wood, perhaps.

* * *

Twenty-five minutes later, she applied fresh daytime makeup, rather more subtle than her 'TV slap' as she called the matte foundation, eye-catching red lipstick and full-go eyes. She dressed in a pale-green linen blouse, a white skirt and soft loafers that matched her blouse, and misted her wrists, throat and cleavage with perfume. With the light fragrance of orange blossom coiling its way into her nose, she slipped on a pair of discreet emerald earrings and her beloved rose-gold Patek Philippe watch, a wedding present from her parents, and went downstairs.

She sat at the kitchen table, a glass of sauvignon blanc to her left, scrolling through her messages as she forked tuna salad into her mouth, careful to avoid catching even a morsel of the food on her lips. Mostly they were emails asking her to speak, agree to an interview, or contribute to other pro-life charities. A death threat from some loony-left, women's rights type that she moved to a folder headed 'Crazies'. And a note from her lawyer about the charity's funds.

Yes, well, that little problem should all be sorted once I've met the lovely MJ Fox, she thought, finishing the salad.

A soft click from the hall made her turn round in her chair. It sounded like the latch on the front door engaging. But that wasn't possible. She'd heard it close behind her on the way in, hadn't she?

She rose from her chair, dabbing her lips on the white napkin by her plate.

'Jerry?' she called, turning towards the kitchen door. 'Is that you, darling?'

She left the kitchen, feeling ridiculous as her eyes fell on a white marble rolling pin on the countertop and she briefly considered picking it up.

The front door was closed. Of course it was. *Silly fool, Niamh. You're getting menopausal. Now, relax. You've ten minutes before MJ gets here.*

Someone tapped her shoulder.

Order your copy of Let The Bones Be Charred

COPYRIGHT

ACKNOWLEDGMENTS

I want to thank the following kind, knowledgeable, patient and talented people for helping me make this novel as good as it could be.

Sandy Wallace, for her insightful first reading; Martin Cook, Melissa Davies and Arvind Nagra, for their medical expertise; Claire Snook for helping me navigate the provisions of Section Two of the Mental Health Act 1983; Lynnea Linquist, for her photographs and help with the dialect of Minnesota – Uffda! Couldn't have done it withoutcha; and Ross Coombs and Sean Memory for their help with police matters.

Michelle Lowery for her usual skill and deft touch with editing. John Lowery for his superb proofreading. Ann Finn, Simon Alphonso, Yvonne Henderson, Vanessa Knowles, OJ "Yard Boy" Audet, Nina Rip and Bill Wilson for being my "sniper spotters."

Darren Bennett for yet another fantastic cover design.

And, as always, my family, for their patience, advice and love.

Andy Maslen
Salisbury, 2018

Write Copy, Make Money

Persuasive Copywriting

ABOUT THE AUTHOR

Andy Maslen was born in Nottingham, in the UK, home of legendary bowman Robin Hood. Andy once won a medal for archery, although he has never been locked up by the sheriff.

He has worked in a record shop, as a barman, as a door-to-door DIY products salesman and a cook in an Italian restaurant. He eventually landed a job in marketing, writing mailshots to sell business management reports. He spent ten years in the corporate world before launching a business-writing agency, Sunfish, where he writes for clients including *The Economist*, Christie's and World Vision.

As well as the Stella Cole and Gabriel Wolfe thrillers, Andy has published five works of non-fiction on copywriting and freelancing with Marshall Cavendish and Kogan Page. They are all available online and in bookshops.

He lives in Wiltshire with his wife, two sons and a whippet named Merlin.

AFTERWORD

Want to know more?

To get two free books, and exclusive news and offers, join Andy Maslen's Readers' Group at www.andymaslen.com.

Email Andy at andy@andymaslen.com.

Follow and tweet him at @Andy_Maslen

Like his page "Andy Maslen Author" on Facebook.

Printed in Great Britain
by Amazon

81239321R00261